TALES OF THE
SHADOWMEN

Volume 2: Gentlemen of the Night

TALES OF THE
SHADOWMEN

Volume 2: Gentlemen of the Night

edited by
Jean-Marc & Randy Lofficier

stories by
**Matthew Baugh, Bill Cunningham,
Win Scott Eckert, G.L. Gick,
Rick Lai, Serge Lehman,
Jean-Marc Lofficier, Xavier Mauméjean,
Sylvie Miller & Philippe Ward, Jess Nevins,
Kim Newman, John Peel, Chris Roberson,
Brian Stableford** and **Jean-Louis Trudel**

illustrations by
Fernando Calvi

A Black Coat Press Book

Acknowledgements: I am indebted to David McDonnell for proofreading the typescript.

Visit our website at www.blackcoatpress.com

ISBN 1-932983-60-0. First Printing. January 2006. Published by Black Coat Press, an imprint of Hollywood Comics.com, LLC, P.O. Box 17270, Encino, CA 91416.

Table of Contents

Fernando Calvi's cover rough

Introduction

Wishing Upon All Stars...

They say that a journey of a thousand miles begins with a single small step. It seems to apply as well to the long road that has led to the *Tales of the Shadowmen* anthologies.

In the introduction to Volume 1, I wrote about the French paperbacks of my youth. This is about more recent events, starting with my collaboration on Roy Thomas' *The Young All-Stars*, a wonderfully literate comic that was published by DC Comics in the late 1980s. Roy and I had been collaborating in multiple forms (exchanging ideas, sometimes dialoguing, other times helping with the plots) so, by 1988, we were already used to my lending an occasional helping hand to the creative process.

The previous year, I had helped cement the history of the late and lamented Global Guardians in *Infinity, Inc.* No. 34, drawn by Todd McFarlane, who went on to create *Spawn*. Just a few months earlier, Roy had developed an idea I had given him about incorporating Project M into *The Young All-Stars*–that became issue No. 12, "M is for Monster." But that was minor compared to what was to follow.

Both Roy and I share a deep interest in popular literature–we are talking here about the man who brought *Conan* and *Unknown Worlds of Science-Fiction* and *War of the Worlds* to Marvel Comics. And long before Alan Moore and Kevin O'Neill's deservedly popular *League of Extraordinary Gentlemen*, Roy had already embarked upon the idea of making the newly-created *Young All-Stars* a proto-League of literary characters. Roy connected Iron Munro (a name itself borrowed from pulp) to Philip Wylie's seminal novel *Gladiator*; later, the All-Stars visited Professor Challenger's Lost World and met Mary Shelley's Frankenstein. Suffice it to say that this was a penchant that I encouraged from the start, offering helpful advice and research assistance whenever possible.

One of the collaborations on which Roy and I had worked previously, one that had fallen by the wayside as a direct result of the rearranging of DC's continuity in *Crisis on Infinite Earths*, was a "secret origins" of Aquaman–but not the well-known Arthur Curry Aquaman of what was then Earth-1, but the Golden Age Aquaman of Earth-2, who had made a few cameos in *All-Star Squadron*, and whose past was a reasonably unencumbered slate that we could use to our liking.

With Roy's full approval and support, I had plotted a very detailed origin that explained how hapless sailor Arthur Gordon Pym from Edgar Allan Poe's eponymous *Narrative of...* had fallen upon the remains of a Lost City of the Dzyan, an Elder Race from Madame Blavatsky's *Secret Doctrine*, in the Antarctic. Mastering their vril-based science–a form of psychic energy from Edward Bulwer-Lytton's *The Coming Race*–Pym had built the *Nautilus* and become the science pirate known as Captain Nemo (do I really need to source that one?) and even sunk the *Titanic*. Eventually, Pym's grandson, for reasons too complex to recount here, had become Aquaman.

We were just waiting for an artist to be assigned to draw the story, when the word came from above that the Aquaman of Earth-2 no longer existed. That was it for the "secret origins" of that Aquaman, unjustly relegated to the dustbin of history. But a good story is like kudzu: get rid of it here, it'll pop up elsewhere.

A year or so later, with *The Young All-Stars* firmly established, Roy decided to resurrect the story but use it as the "secret origins" of Neptune Perkins instead. This became the basis of "The Dzyan Inheritance" which appeared in *The Young All-Stars* Nos. 16-18, drawn by Michael Blair. In it, we learned that Neptune Perkins was indeed the grandson of Pym/Nemo, and that the Nazis of the Black Order of Thule were hell-bent on seizing control of his latest, vril-powered super-*Nautilus* dubbed *Leviathan*. Needless to say, thanks to the All-Stars, they failed miserably.

This could have stopped there, but remember the kudzu analogy...

We had killed Pym/Nemo in *The Young All-Stars*, but I, for one, felt I wasn't done with the character. I knew there was more to him than had been revealed in the few pages allocated to his amazing journey in the comic.

Twelve years later (writers are nothing if not patient), in 2001, when French artist Gil Formosa suggested that Randy and I create and collaborate on a "steampunk" science fiction series for French publisher Albin Michel, I immediately suggested–*Robur*.

Robur is, of course, Jules Verne's other science pirate, whose superpowered flying machine terrorizes the world in the novels *Robur the Conqueror* and (coining a term since then applied to so many villains) *Master of the World*–the latter adapted into a 1961 movie starring Vincent Price and Charles Bronson.

But our Robur was not merely another avatar of Nemo and Arthur Gordon Pym! Before that, he was also the notorious alchemist known as Joseph Balsamo, a.k.a. Cagliostro, whose prodigious life was recounted by Alexandre Dumas in several novels.

In that world, obviously Neptune Perkins and the Young All-Stars did not exist, but other literary characters did: Gurn, a.k.a. Fantômas, Dale Ardan, the granddaughter of Michel Ardan who circumnavigated the Moon in Verne's *From the Earth to the Moon*, Josephine Balsamo, Countess of Cagliostro, Arsène Lupin's arch-nemesis, Larry O'Keefe from Abraham Merritt's *The*

Moon Pool, a young, hawk-nosed aviator named "Kent Ballard" and many, many others...

Tales of the Shadowmen continues the journey, from one medium to another, happily bringing together the best of Pulp Literature from all around the world. In this book, you will find Irene Adler and Christine Daae, Harry Dickson and the Sâr Dubnotal, Arsène Lupin and Kogoro Akechi, Zenith the Albino and Zigomar and many more.

The array of international talent, both experienced and new, gathered between these pages is equally worthy of the limelight: Fernando Calvi from Argentina, Jean-Louis Trudel from Canada, Kim Newman and Brian Stableford from England, Xavier Mauméjean, Sylvie Miller and Philippe Ward from France and, of course, many of our regular contributors from America: Chris Roberson, Bill Cunningham and our friends from the New Wold Newton Meteoritic Society: Matthew Baugh, Win Eckert, Greg Gick, Rick Lai, etc.

So, from a humble contribution that began as the origins of a hero who did not exist, grew a trilogy of graphic novels and, now, a series of anthologies about many heroes who refuse to die.

Let's have a round of applause for the new All-Stars!

Jean-Marc Lofficier

Thanks to the alphabet, Matthew Baugh again opens our anthology, this time with an "East Meets West" tale, expanding the playing field to include characters created by the wonderful Japanese writer Hirai Taro, better known as Edogawa Rampo, a pseudonym he reportedly coined to resemble the rendition of Edgar Allan Poe's name in his own language. Once more, we find ourselves back in that Modern Babylon that is Paris, but this time towards the end of the Années Folles–the "Crazy Years"–about which Marc Chagall wrote: "The sun of Art then shone only on Paris..."

Matthew Baugh: *Ex Calce Liberatus*

Paris, 1931

Letter to Charles Folenfant, Paris, 12 June 1931:
My Dear Folenfant,
First, allow me to congratulate you on your promotion to Inspector. It is (in my estimation) something long overdue. I know that I am three years tardy in my felicitations, but our paths have not crossed since that time.
I am delighted to learn that you have been assigned to the case of the missing swords. I would wish you success in your investigation, but your success would mean my failure and I am afraid I cannot permit that. I am seeking the greatest of all British treasures and I am determined to succeed. *Ex calce liberatus!*
With warmest regards,

Arsène Lupin

Letter to Justin Ganimard, Picardy, 13 June 1931:
My Dear Chief Inspector,
I hope that you and Madame Ganimard are enjoying your retirement. I am somewhat envious of you. The country is lovely this time of year. I am sorry to disturb you, but I remember your promise to advise me if he should ever return. I received a note from him yesterday afternoon in which he boasted that he was behind the "mystery of the missing swords."
You may not be familiar with this case, which has not yet found its way into the newspapers. It concerns a series of mysterious occurrences at the Musée Veronica. In case you are not familiar with it, this is a wax museum that sits on the Grands Boulevards, not far from the famous Musée Grévin. The Veronica is not nearly as opulent as its rival but keeps a healthy business through unique exhibits and very high quality wax figures.

Their latest exhibit, which is set to open next Friday, is of the world's great swordsmen. It is unique because the figures will be wielding the actual swords the swordsmen used in life. The weapons are from the collection of the recently deceased Baron de Villefort, who spent his life collecting them. The museum is sparing no pains to publicize this, and has attracted several local celebrities, M. Philippe Guerande and M. Oscar Mazamette, to lend their names to the project.

Three nights ago, one of the swords disappeared. It was a splendid rapier, which once belonged to Cyrano de Bergerac. The management reported the matter to the Police and I assigned a man to look into it. He found nothing, but the next morning the rapier was back in Cyrano's grasp and another sword, belonging to Bussy d'Amboise, was missing.

Realizing that this was no ordinary robbery, I took over the case myself. I posted myself in the gallery with two men to wait for the thief. Around midnight, we were roused by a noise from one of the other galleries. We went to investigate, taking no more than five minutes. When we returned, Bussy d'Amboise's had his sword once again, but that of D'Artagnan that was missing. When we looked further, we found that a folded piece of paper was tucked in the famous Musketeer's belt. It was from note from him, and I have attached a copy for you to see.

What could he be up to, sir? I confess that I find the whole thing baffling. More importantly, how can I catch him?

Very respectfully yours,

Charles Folenfant

Letter to Justin Ganimard, Picardy, 14 April 1931:

My Dear Chief Inspector,

I have contacted the Baroness de Villefort by telephone. She claims to know nothing of any secret concealed in the swords but has agreed to my visiting her this afternoon. She says she will ask a priest named Dulac to be there as well. He was an old friend of the Baron's and a fellow antiquarian. The Baroness says the two of them spent many hours studying the collection.

You had asked about the people involved. I suppose I should begin with M. Arthur Moreau. He is an Englishman of French descent who was recently hired as sculptor for the museum. He seems a fine old gentleman whose zest for life belies his white hair and beard. Before coming to Paris, he worked for many years at Madame Tussaud's in London, and has an excellent reputation. Unfortunately, he recently suffered a stroke, which has left his hands unsteady. He says his doctors expect him to recover most of his ability. Until then, he is forced to rely heavily on his assistant, Emile Deschamps.

Emile is a great brute of a man. He stands over six feet and has enormous hands and shoulders. He is polite and soft-spoken, but I find him disquieting despite this. This is not helped by his condition. Emile suffers from acromegaly, which has distended his face and thickened his features. He also has a twisted spine, all of which combines to make him seem a perfect brute.

M. Moreau has made the most of this. He used Emile as the model for one of his wax figures, that of Lagardère in his disguise as the "Hunchback." It is most effective.

The model Moreau is using right now is a lovely young woman named Nora Fuset. This may surprise you, but several of the swordsmen in the display are actually swordswomen. Nora was the model for Agnes de Chastillon, and for Lady Jirel of Joiry.

Mlle. Fuset is a remarkable creature. When I first saw her, she was posing in the nude for another figure. She had her hair arranged in the Japanese style and held a sword concealed in the handle of a parasol.

She is an enticing thing and seemed justly unashamed of displaying her splendid figure. The one imperfection I saw was what appeared to be a black lizard perched on her shoulder. On closer examination, I saw that this was a tattoo. It is so cleverly designed that her movements make it seem to crawl.

This lizard is an appropriate emblem for Mlle. Fuset. She is something of a chameleon herself. When I first met her, she seemed the model of Oriental beauty. Later, when she had dressed, she seemed perfectly European. M. Moreau explained that her father was an Asiatic but that her mother was French. She has learned to blend seamlessly into either culture.

In any case, I found her as charming as she is lovely, but that does little to further the investigation so I shall spare you any further reflections.

As I mentioned before, the two investors were brought in as much for their names as for their money. The affair of the Vampire Gang may be nearly 20 years past, but the heroes of that matter are still remembered.

There is nothing to report of Philippe Guerande. He is traveling in England at the moment, though he will be back for the grand opening this Friday. Oscar Mazamette is a different matter. He is constantly in and out of the museum with all manners of questions and suggestions for M. Moreau. He will even drop in at odd hours to look at the figures. He is quite friendly and energetic, but I find his behavior most eccentric.

One more note, sir. There is a private detective who I have invited to consult on the case. He is a young fellow named Kogoro Akechi who is visiting from Japan. He has crossed paths with our nefarious friend before and, apparently, got the better of him. As fate would have it, he had business of his own with M. Moreau and seems excited to be involved in the mystery.

I look forward to your thoughts with great interest, Chief Inspector.

Your servant,

Charles Folenfant

Letter to District Attorney Kasamori, Tokyo, 14 April 1931:

My Dear Kasamori,

I'm certain that you remember the famous Arsène Lupin who we encountered late last year in the Gold Mask case. It seems I have a chance to cross swords with him again. I'm here in Paris as the request of Count Mishima. The Count has loaned a valuable sword-cane out of his collection to his friend, M. Guerande, and asked me to accompany the weapon to guard against theft. It seemed the ideal opportunity to combine business with pleasure by bringing Fumiyo along on a delayed honeymoon trip.

The sword is the famous zantetsuken (iron-cutting sword) and it was placed on display with a remarkable wax likeness of our blind swordsman. I was pleased to see that the sculptor Moreau gave him the shaved head and simple kimono of a low-caste masseur. The "Orientalist" Van Roon's assertion that Ichi was a "blind samurai" has always annoyed me.

Since Lupin is involved in some mischief concerning the wax museum, I feel I owe it to the Count to safeguard his sword. My poor Fumiyo will be disappointed with me for this. Perhaps the shops of Paris will keep her happy until I can resolve this matter.

I will write again when I have appraised the situation.

Your friend,

Kogoro

Letter to Justin Ganimard, Picardy, 15 April 1931:

My Dear Chief Inspector,

I'm afraid the trip to see Baroness de Villefort was simply a waste of a full day. The Baroness detested her husband's obsession with ancient weapons and made it a point to know as little about the collection as possible.

The Priest wasn't much more help. He was at least able to translate the phrase ex calce liberatus which is Latin "set free from the stone." He says he has been out of touch with the Baroness since her husband's death and was saddened, though not surprised, to learn that she had loaned out the collection. In any case, he has offered to come to Paris and examine the swords to see if he can help glean their secret.

Père Dulac is younger than I had expected, about 40 I should say, and in good shape for a priest, but is otherwise unremarkable. I'm afraid I don't see this line bearing many results.

Your servant,

Charles Folenfant

Letter to District Attorney Kasamori, Tokyo, 15 April 1931:

My Dear Kasamori,

Inspector Folenfant allowed me to come along with him today to the Chateau de Villefort. It proved a very interesting trip, mostly for the person of the

Priest we met. Père Dulac has the quiet bearing and humble manner one would expect of a priest, but his bearing is military and he has the distinctive gait of a cavalryman. His hands boast a small collection of the sort of scars a fencer or a knife-fighter is likely to acquire and the small finger of his left hand is missing.

I believe that this man's knowledge of swords is far removed from academic curiosity.

He told us the meaning of Lupin's mysterious Latin phrase, "set free from the stone." When I pressed him, he told me that it is probably a reference to the British King Arthur and his Sword in the Stone. Indeed, he admitted that some scholars think the name "Excalibur" is a corruption of the phrase ex calce liberatus.

This is especially interesting for I noticed that one of the swords on display was set in stone. There is a figure of a valiant prince, Hugrakkur of Thule. He is the hero of an Arthurian fragment by the 12th century poet Chrétien de Troyes. The Prince's "singing sword" was encased in a scabbard of carved marble. Could this blade be the legendary sword of King Arthur? I suspect there is more to it than that or Lupin would have already stolen it, but I feel the key to the mystery is connected somehow to the sword, the stone scabbard and our mysterious priest.

Your friend,

Kogoro

Excerpt from an article in Le Mondial, *Paris, 16 April 1931:*
"...Police are investigating the strange death of Oscar Mazamette last night at the Musée Veronica, Boulevard des Italiens. Policemen were on duty guarding the display, which has been plagued by pranksters for several nights. At approximately 12:30 a.m., M. Mazamette arrived and asked to be let in. He was in the habit of touring the building after hours and the guards saw nothing wrong with letting him in.

"At approximately 1:15 a.m., the Policemen heard a loud cry and entered the building to find M. Mazamette dead in a pool of his own blood, his head some distance from his body. He had been decapitated with one of the display swords, a blade known as the Demoiselle Grise. This is an ancient weapon said to be the first sword forged of iron. Tradition claims the blade carries a curse on it. It will make its wielder supreme in combat, but will also bring about the death of any unworthy soul who tries to use it..."

Letter to Justin Ganimard, Picardy, 16 April 1931:
My Dear Chief Inspector,

You cannot imagine what this morning has been like. I was awakened just past 2 a.m. this morning with the news of M. Mazamette's death. The scene was ghastly, with all of the wax figures standing over his lifeless body.

We searched the building thoroughly on my arrival and there was no one. My men were on guard at all entrances, and no one could have left. If the method of death did not preclude it, I should be forced to conclude that this was a suicide.

As the papers suggest, there is a strange history surrounding the sword known as the Demoiselle Grise. It is a long, slender weapon with markings on the blade in different languages. There is an Egyptian glyph, which I am told is the mark of its forger. There is also writing in Greek, Latin and English. The last, Moreau translated for me. It reads:

"Gray Maide men hail Mee
Death doth Notte fail Mee."

Of all the swords in the room, this one was kept in a display case rather than placed with a wax figure. Moreau says he knew of the blade's grim reputation and was loath to offer it the disrespect of placing it in wax fingers.

He also pointed out something my men had missed in all of the confusion. D'Artagnan's sword was back in place and another was missing. This time it was the sword of one of the sculptor's own ancestors, André-Louis Moreau, who was known as the "Paladin of the Third Estate" back in the days of the Revolution.

This makes me wonder if M. Mazamette did not accidentally walk in on him in the midst of a crime. Could he then have been forced to take up the sword and do Mazamette in?

It is all very perplexing.

Your Servant

Charles Folenfant

Letter to District Attorney Kasamori, Tokyo, 16 April 1931:

My Dear Kasamori,

The case has taken quite an interesting turn. There has been a murder and I am afraid Inspector Folenfant is out of his depth. I honestly don't know whether he is incompetent or whether he is being deliberately obtuse.

One of the investors, M. Mazamette, was beheaded with a sword last night. Folenfant has taken the absurd position that Arsène Lupin committed the deed. When I pointed out that Lupin does not have a history of cold-blooded murder, he simply shrugged and said "the man is a criminal," and it was "only a matter of time" before he did something like this.

On investigation, it was perfectly clear that it was not Lupin. There were crumbs of flesh-colored wax on the victim's clothes. I believe these were from a person wearing a waxy makeup to resemble one of the figures in the display.

I examined the figures and found that the clothing that had been spattered most heavily with blood was that on the figures of Lagardère and Lady Jirel. This leads me to believe we are dealing with two assailants, a man and a woman. I believe that the man seized Mazamette and held him fast while the woman struck the fatal blow.

My first thought was of Emile and Nora, the models for those figures. I checked and could find no records of either person going back more than a few months. I checked on M. Mazamette and learned that he had helped break up a criminal gang 15 years ago. They were called the Vampires, and they first came to public notice when they committed the murder by decapitation of a Police Inspector named Durand.

A little more checking turned up the fact that one of the leaders of the Vampire Gang was named Irma Vep, a name that is an anagram of "vampire." From there, it was a simple step to seeing that the name Nora Fuset is also an anagram. The letters unscramble to form the word "nosferatu." Irma Vep was reported dead years ago, but Nora could easily be her daughter.

I wish I could bring this to Folenfant but I cannot without more convincing evidence. I know his type. He will cling to his theory with pig-headed obstinacy. I plan to watch the gallery tonight in an attempt to gain more compelling evidence. Possibly I can even figure Lupin's role in this.

Your friend,

Kogoro

P.S. As to the matter of the sword in the stone scabbard, I examined it and found it to be nothing more than a modern replica. That mystery will have to wait awhile.

Letter to Justin Ganimard, Picardy, 17 April 1931:

My Dear Chief Inspector,

Things have taken an unusual turn this morning. I received a phone call from M. Akechi who asked for me to come to the gallery at once and to have MM. Moreau, Dulac, Deschamps and Mlle. Fuset summoned as well. I arrived there not half-an-hour later to find that Père Dulac had arrived but the others were late.

Akechi said that he had great revelations for us, but that they must wait until all the *dramatis personae* were assembled. (Sir, in your experience, do all amateur detectives have this tedious obsession with the dramatic?)

We had been there only a short time when one of my men came in with a note addressed to M. Akechi. Once the detective read it, his whole attitude changed. He told us that he was sorry to have bothered us with his foolish theories, and admitted that he really hadn't a clue about the thefts or the murder. He had simply hoped to gather all the players together and hoped to bluff one of them into a confession. Having realized how foolish this was, he was withdrawing from the case.

I demanded to know what had been in the note that had changed the man's mind. Akechi said that was from his wife Fumiyo. She was very angry with him for leaving her alone to work on a case in the middle of what was supposed to be a romantic vacation. He apologized but said that he was not willing to face the prospect of divorce to solve a mystery.

Père Dulac thought this sounded suspicious and demanded to see the note. Akechi spread it out for us, but it was written in Japanese.

With no reason to hold him, I let him go. I am focusing my efforts on the opening this evening. I plan to have so many men there that we can trap him, or the Vampires, if either have the nerve to show up.

Some time after Akechi left, Philipe Guerande showed up. He was shaken by his friend's death but is determined to go ahead with the grand opening of the exhibit this evening.

Your servant,

Charles Folenfant

Note to Kogoro Akechi, 17 April 1931 (translated from the Japanese):
Detective Akechi,

Your wife, Fumiyo, is with us. You will say nothing to the Police. You will excuse yourself immediately and come to the bench nearest the west entrance to the Garden of Luxembourg. You will not allow the Police to follow you. You will sit there reading a newspaper until we contact you. You will keep both hands in sight at all times. If you do these things faithfully, we will bring Mme. Akechi to you, alive and unharmed. If you fail, we will begin to send one of her body parts to you each day, starting with her feet. Either way, you will eventually have her back.

The Vampires

Letter to District Attorney Kasamori, Tokyo, 17 April 1931:
My Dear Kasamori,

I can't tell you how helpless I felt when I received that note. I rushed back to the hotel (stopping only to pilfer something I needed from the museum) and confirmed that my wife had not been seen since that morning. I then proceeded to area designated in the letter.

I went through an impressive number of newspapers as I sat there. *La Capitale* ran a story about M. Mazamette's death and discussed the "cursed sword" at some length. *Le Mondial* ran a story which (correctly) speculated that this was an act of revenge by the Vampire gang. I was disappointed to find that *L'Echo de France* said next to nothing about the matter. I had hoped to be able to gauge Arsène Lupin's thoughts, and *L'Echo* is often the vehicle by which those thoughts are revealed.

Sometime after full dark, a large automobile pulled us near and a woman emerged. She wore a one-piece dancer's costume that covered her body, arms and legs, a short black cape, a tight black hood, and there was a domino mask, all in black. Two men also stepped out holding my wife between them.

I told the woman that I knew she was Nora Fuset. She was shocked but recovered with admirable self-possession. She seemed politely impressed as I explained my deductions, and gratified when I told her there was something I hadn't figured out. To stand rigid enough to pass for a wax figure would be incredibly difficult. I asked her how she and M. Deschamps had managed it.

She laughed and told me that I had been correct about her mother's identity. Her father had also been a criminal, she said. He was called Y'uan Hee See and he was an associate of the brilliant scientist, Dr. Natas, who had invented a drug which induced an artificial *rigor mortis*. A large dose would temporarily turn a person into a living statue. A smaller dose would allow a person to remain motionless voluntarily for long periods of time.

As Nora said this, she noticed the barrel of a pistol poking across the top of my newspaper. I had a trick of my own. I had borrowed a wax arm from the museum. One of my arms holding the paper was a wax dummy while my real arm covered her with the pistol.

Nora pointed out that we were at an impasse. If either of us did anything, both she and Fumiyo would die. I admit I could not see a good way out of the situation until fate intervened. A dark figure came out of the night and launched itself into the two men. It was Père Dulac, and he fought with a frightening efficiency. Within a few minutes, we had subdued the two Vampires, but Nora had managed to slip away in the darkness.

Dulac explained that he had lived in Nagasaki for a time and was able to read Japanese. He had read the kidnap note and had followed to help me.

We hailed a cab and headed back towards the museum. It seemed increasingly clear to me that Nora had wanted to keep me away from the grand opening for some reason of her own. I told Dulac of my deductions, speaking in Japanese so not to be overheard. When he answered, I noticed that he used an archaic dialect, like someone transported from the days of Nobunaga.

I know this must sound insane, but it occurred to me that there had been a Jesuit settlement in Nagasaki from 1570-1587 AD, before the expulsion of westerners. I wondered if he could possibly be that old. It also occurred to me that I had read of a knight with a missing finger while I was researching the swords. In the romance, the knight had lost the digit while ripping loose the bars from the window of his lady's cell.

I mentioned this to Dulac and wondered aloud how a man could be alive after so many years.

"The same knight you are speaking of was a traitor." He said, "The woman he loved was the wife of another. Many suffered and died for their love. As an act of penance, he took up holy orders. Perhaps his penance is not yet done."

I told him it seemed a long time to atone for any misdeed.

He smiled sadly and said, "Perhaps he is not truly penitent. Perhaps he loves the woman so that he would sin for her again given the chance."

I let that end our strange conversation. We arrived at the museum moments later, though too late to prevent a near-tragedy.

Your friend,

Kogoro

Excerpt from an article in La Capitale, *Paris, 18 April 1931:*

"Last night's gala was interrupted at 10:10 p.m. when all of the gallery lights went out. There was a great deal of confusion.

"When the lights were restored, no more than half a dozen seconds later, the Demoiselle Grise had disappeared from its display case and had impaled M. Philipe Guerande through the left shoulder. M. Guerande's life was apparently saved when M. Arthur Moreau accidentally stumbled against him in the dark, causing the blade to miss his heart.

"The Police have taken M. Guerande into protective custody and are tending his wounds at an undisclosed location. Inspector Folenfant assures us that an arrest is imminent.

"When asked about the participation of Japanese detective Kogoro Akechi in the case, Inspector Folenfant had this to say: 'We are grateful for the advice M. Akechi has given us on this matter and are saddened by his decision to return to his country immediately. This was necessitated by concerns for Mme. Akechi's health and has nothing to do with the ongoing investigation.' "

Letter to Justin Ganimard, Picardy, 18 April 1931:

My Dear Chief Inspector,

Akechi is gone, returned to Japan with his wife. I can hardly blame them. He didn't give me all the details, but he let me know of his wife's kidnapping and near murder. It's a shame, but probably for the best. He didn't ever contribute anything of use to the investigation.

I am still no closer to uncovering this murderous plot of his, though there has been an unexpected development. I am forwarding you a copy of a note I have just received from M. Guerande. Rest assured, this time no malefactors will slip through my security.

Your servant,

Charles Folenfant

Note to Inspector Charles Folenfant, Paris, 18 April 1931:

Inspector Folenfant,

I have the solution to several mysteries and am ready to reveal them. I know all about the method used in the attempt on my life and the culprit. I also know all about Arsène Lupin and the mysterious treasure he seeks.

I will not reveal anything until I have met with all of the interested parties in the display room.

Please gather together M. Moreau, Mlle. Fuset, Père Dulac and M. Deschamps at 8 p.m. tomorrow evening.

Sincerely yours,

Philipe Guerande

Letter to District Attorney Kasamori, Tokyo – Sunday, April 19

My Dear Kasamori,

There have been some very interesting developments today.

At M. Guerande's request, Inspector Folenfant gathered all of the parties involved in the case, with the exception of M. Moreau who could not be located.

I had spoken to Guerande before this gathering and had told him all about Nora Fuset and the Vampires and now he revealed all of this to the assembly. Of course, Folenfant immediately had his men seize Nora and Emile and placed them under arrest.

As to the means by which the Demoiselle Grise had vanished from her case to strike Guerande down, that was simplicity itself. He explained that it had been a replica of the sword in the display case. When the lights had gone out, one of the Vampires had pressed a secret release. The replica had dropped into a hidden compartment in the base of the display. As the false sword "vanished," Emile, in his guise as the figure of Lagardère, took the real Demoiselle from its hiding place and hurled it at Guerande with all of his brutish strength.

As for Lupin, he had been under everyone's noses all along, disguised as Moreau. That, of course, was the reason the sculptor had not attended the evening's gathering. The real Moreau was currently living well at Lupin's expense, working on a commission in Prague. He was quite in the dark about the whole affair.

Lupin had learned that the secret of the treasure, reputed to be the burial place of King Arthur himself, was hidden in one of the swords in the collection and had used his position to examine the swords minutely, one-by-one.

The Baron de Villefort was a member of an ancient secret order, devoted to keeping the location of Arthur's treasure a secret. Père Dulac was also a member and Guerande called on him to reveal the secret.

Dulac took the marble scabbard from the figure of Prince Hugrakkur. "The secret rests here, but I will never reveal what it is," he said. "I will take this and hide it somewhere that even Arsène Lupin will never find it."

Folenfant nodded to his men at that point. They released Nora and Emile and seized Guerande and Dulac while the Inspector covered them with his revolver.

I am sorry to say it, my dear Kasamori, but Nora Fuset had seduced poor Folenfant with her beauty and the promises of wealth and power. He was her pet and his "Policemen" were actually disguised members of the Vampire gang.

"The secret of the treasure is ours," Nora purred, "and tomorrow the papers shall tell of two more deaths by the cursed sword."

Emile took up the Demoiselle Grise and moved towards the captives.

Suddenly, a pistol shot rang out. Folenfant dropped his pistol and clutched his wounded arm.

As you may have guessed, I was in the room all along and I had fired the shot. I stepped off the podium where I had been posing as blind Ichi and covered the group. As I had mentioned to Nora, it would take tremendous discipline to pose as a motionless wax figure. Fortunately, I have such discipline, thanks to a ninja trick I have mastered.

As I stepped down, Guerande threw off his captors and produced his own pistol from his sling.

"Excellent, detective!" he cried gaily, "Our plan has worked beautifully."

Nora looked shocked and poor Folenfant was dumbfounded as they recognized the voice of Arsène Lupin coming from the journalist's mouth.

I explained that the gentleman burglar and I had come to an arrangement. Tomorrow, he would go back to theft and I to trying to capture him, but first we resolved to put an end to the Vampires.

Unfortunately, both Lupin and I had forgotten the hidden switch that the gang had used to plunge the room into darkness once before. Nora pressed the switch and, in the sudden darkness, the Vampires attacked.

My eyes took only a moment to adjust. Lupin and Dulac were struggling with the Vampires and I have never seen anyone fight as fiercely and well as those two. Nora was fleeing with the scabbard.

I started to chase her but was distracted by Emile who was harrying Lupin with the cursed sword he still carried. I fired a shot that drew a grunt of pain, but failed to stop him.

"A sword!" Lupin cried, "I can deal with him."

I tossed the zantetsuken to him and turned to race after Nora.

She had a good lead on me. As I ran, I saw the front door open and Nora's form silhouetted there. I fired a shot, hoping to wound her leg. Instead, I hit the scabbard, shattering it. She cried out in rage and slipped into the night air.

I tried to catch her but she ran like a deer. After five minutes of pursuit, she had lost me in the streets of Paris. I returned to the Musée Veronica to find the Vampires subdued and a wounded Dulac standing guard over them. Lupin was gone. So were the fragments of the stone scabbard.

Emile was dead. In trying to run Lupin through, he had sunk the blade into the wall where it hit an electrical line. Perhaps there is something to the sword's legend after all. She seems to have saved him from Lupin's blade, only to kill him herself through a bizarre accident.

I will remain in Paris a little longer, and perhaps I shall catch Lupin yet. I must admit, a part of me has lost interest in the chase. I owe him a debt, after all. Besides, I promised my wife a honeymoon and should keep that promise.

Your friend,

Kogoro

Letter to Justin Ganimard, Picardy, 12 December 1931:

My Most Excellent Ganimard,

I understand you followed the recent case the papers are calling the "Mystery of the Cursed Sword." As you have no doubt deduced, I left the museum when there was no longer any need for me to remain. I kept the zantetsuken in the hope that I might find a worthy soul to pass it onto someday.

I understand Detective Akechi was given the honors due him for the capture of the Vampires and returned to Japan with his lovely wife. Several months later, he foiled the plans of a female master criminal called the Black Lizard. I suspect that this was none other than our Mlle. Fuset.

I wonder if the detective ever made the connection? Perhaps not, he only ever saw Nora in her European guise and I don't think he ever knew of her tattoo.

You will note that our friend Folenfant recently escaped from prison. Please do not be alarmed by this. Though he stumbled once, I believe there is hope for him yet. I have arranged his early departure from confinement and promise to take a personal hand in his rehabilitation.

As for the mysterious Père Dulac, I saw him again. As I left the museum that night I took the fragments of the stone scabbard with me. I noticed a most remarkable thing about those fragments. There were letters carved into the stone in the inside of the scabbard. It was only when the scabbard was broken that the message was "set free from the stone."

I had been carrying that phrase around for months not knowing how it fit with the mystery, but now it was clear.

Following the directions I found my way to a barrow in the English countryside. (Please forgive me if I am vague about the location.) Inside I found a treasure indeed. Would you think I was mad if I said it was a noble body laid out on a bier and so perfectly preserved that it seemed to be asleep?

As I gazed on the treasure, I became aware of another entering the barrow. It was Dulac with a sword in his hand. We spoke for a time and he asked my intentions. I told him I would sooner desecrate a cathedral than loot this sacred place. He thought for a moment then raised his sword. I made no move to resist as the blade came down, once, twice, three times.

And that is all I shall say of that matter ever again. I rose and left that place its newly made guardian, and not even Sir Lancelot du Lac shall be more zealous in that duty than I.

Your humble servant,

Arsène Lupin

Bill Cunningham took a break from his Hollywood duties to sneak in a diaboli-cally clever short-short (more about that type of story later) about a certain child and the trauma he experienced when he witnessed a bloody murder. No, this is not about the Bat-Man, but the consequences are nevertheless similarly far reaching. And we are also left to reflect upon two very different father-son relationships...

Bill Cunningham: *Trauma*

Paris, 1916

The boy's lower lip trembled in fear.

"Just tell the Policeman here everything you saw, son, like a good re-porter," whispered the boy's father standing over his shaking son.

Maigret smiled an inviting smile and opened his notebook as the boy's ac-count poured forth.

"I didn't see him at first, I was too busy looking at all the books," stam-mered the boy. "Dad had stepped out, and Prince Vladimir was talking to me, and then suddenly he wasn't. I turned around and it, excuse me, *he* was wearing this black mask and coat. He must have come in through the window."

"Did you recognize the Prince's killer?" asked Maigret. "The color of his hair? How tall was the man?"

"All I could see was his eyes. He was all darkness surrounding these wild eyes. Then, he raised the knife," blurted the boy. "I couldn't move. All I could do was look. I wanted to scream but it wouldn't have stopped him. He just kept stabbing him. Like the green hornets we saw in Africa last year. Remember, Dad? Just stinging and stinging him, over and over..." The boy curled into a ball and fell silent. Maigret followed the boy's gaze across the room.

In the corner of the study, the Prince's body lay draped in a blood-soaked sheet. Maigret recognized the tell-tale marks of a dozen or more stab wounds.

His father hugged him, gave the boy strength. The father, a reporter, looked at the Policeman. "Prince Vladimir contacted my paper with something he said was of great importance. My son and I changed our travel plans immedi-ately and came to Paris because His Highness said there was no one here he could trust. He was so afraid he committed nothing to paper." The boy's father let the words hang in the air. "I hope this has been of help to your investigation, but you'll understand if we take our leave. I should get my son back home to Detroit." The newspaperman clutched his son tightly. "We're not used to this sort of... *activity*, even there."

Maigret nodded, understanding. He then leaned down to the boy–another in a long list of those tainted by Fantômas' evil. He met the ten-year-old's shocked stare.

"It's going to be all right, Master Reid. One day you'll forget all about this night..."

But even as he said it, Maigret knew it was a lie...

For the uninitiated, the character of "Shrinking" Violet Holmes, who stars in this tale, was created by Matthew Baugh and Win Scott Eckert in order to explain Clive Reston's genealogy. Reston was featured in Marvel Comics' The Hands of Shang Chi: Master of Kung Fu *series. Violet helps connect the Sherlock Holmes and Fu Manchu novels. Baugh established her as Mycroft's daughter, while Eckert provided her name. Violet's aunt is Sherlock Holmes' wife, Mary Russell, from the novels by Laurie King. Philip José Farmer's* Tarzan Alive *identified Sir Denis Nayland Smith as a nephew of both Sherlock and Mycroft Holmes, thus making him Violet's cousin.*

Win Eckert: *The Eye of Oran*

Oran, Algeria, 1946

No one will ever be free so long as there are pestilences.
The Plague, Albert Camus

FROM: A.L.
TO: Lieutenant Aristide, Section Afrique du Nord, Service National d'Information Fonctionnelle, Paris.
DATE: June 16, 1946
SUBJECT: Oran situation.

Object, Eye of Oran, reputed to have arcane power. True or false, the gem still has great pecuniary value. Secured object from Natas and have secured it in a temporary but protected location. Am at large in Oran. Natas seeks to recover Eye and utilize as means to control masses who believe in its occult properties.

British agent Reston missing in mêlée while procuring object; presumed dead, but arranged for delivery of object to me before going missing.

Oran under strict quarantine due to outbreak of bubonic plague. Plague bacillus has unusual features, according to medical personnel on scene (Doctors Rieux) and is proving difficult to treat with standard serum. Escape from Oran more problematic than anticipated.

Will report again at designated weekly interval.

FROM: SNIF.
TO: Lieutenant Aristide, Section Afrique du Nord, Service National d'Information Fonctionnelle, Paris.
DATE: June 17, 1946
SUBJECT: Your report re: Oran.

Frankly am concerned that you have chosen to engage services of known criminal A.L. in this affair. A.L.'s skills as a thief and ability to escape from precarious situations are as well known as dedication to own self-interests. Furthermore, is not A. L. rather elderly for involvement in this business?

Against better judgment will grant slight latitude in this matter. If no positive results forthcoming, will be forced to ask SDECE to send FX-18 to Oran.

The city was yellow and dry. The heavy rains at the end of June had given way to the oppressive and unstinting heat. The sand and dirt whipped through the streets, and the people of Oran, already quarantined by the plague–*la peste*–secluded themselves even further in the ostensible safety of their homes and cafés.

In the *Kasbah* was one such haven, the *Café Diable*. Behind the Café, a series of tunnels and warrens led underground to a set of interconnected chambers. The Asian opulence of the lair, accented in jade and gold, would have surprised the listless patrons. They would have been even more surprised to learn that the Café and its hidden lair were built over a temple of uncountable age.

Thousands of years earlier, before recorded history, this had been the site of a Temple of Dagon. When the god's right eye–the Silver Eye of Dagon–had been stolen, a great warrior princess named Bêlit had ventured into the dark realm of the mound-dwellers to retrieve it. She had succeeded where all others failed and became a queen. In the intervening centuries, it was passed down that only a great woman would be capable of ultimately liberating the silver gem from its homeland.

As the years passed, the exact location of the temple faded into obscurity. But the legends of the Silver Eye of Oran, as it came to be known, persisted.

And Doctor Natas knew that there was more to the Eye than its mere financial value. The legend that only a woman could remove the gem from the vicinity of Oran was preposterous, of course. But the other tales of the Eye... To one who had already accomplished impossible wonders, such as the transmutation of base matter to gold, the other stories were a lure impossible to ignore.

Hordes of monstrous fish-men rising out of the sea, bulging eyes and webbed feet, implacable and inexorable, would be his to command. Others had come close to controlling this power. The ancient *Méne* cult. The more recent Esoteric Order of Dagon. With the Eye in his possession, Natas would create and control whole armies of the unstoppable amphibians and succeed where the others had failed.

"Huan Tsung Chao," he called from the shadows. Only cat-green eyes glittered out of the darkness, the rest of his figure draped in black silks.

"I am here, Master," his chief of staff replied.

"Lupin is still in Oran. I can feel it."

"Yes, Master. I agree he cannot have escaped. The city walls are too well-guarded, even for him."

27

"We have spent too much time and effort here, recovering the Silver Eye. I cannot allow Lupin to make away with it."

"The only way he could escape is with help, and he has had none from the criminal element in this city. If he had, we would know. Smuggling operations in Oran are controlled by Signor Ferrari's gang and we are paying him quite well to keep us informed."

"Summon Pao Tcheou."

"Yes, Master."

When the new arrival entered, he bowed deeply. "I come to serve you, O Li Chang Yen, my cousin."

"I will have the Silver Eye back, Pao Tcheou. Since we cannot locate Monsieur Lupin, find the English spy's wife. If she does not know where the Eye is, then at least Lupin will come for her. He will not ignore a 'damsel in distress.' "

"As you wish."

"Once she is located, bring her here. Send the Korean."

"It will be done."

"Fen-Chu," Natas called next.

Another shape emerged from the dank shadows and asked: "Hanoi Shan?"

"Notify the Council that we shall be arriving soon. And alert Doctor Ariosto to accelerate his timetable. With the Eye at my command, spawning the armies of Dagon will take considerably less time than previously thought."

"By your leave." Fen-Chu bowed and left.

Adélaïde Johnston jumped up as Doctor Rieux came out of the back bedroom of his small apartment.

"Doctor, how is Violet? It's not... *la peste*, is it?"

"No, no. Mademoiselle Holmes shows none of the tell-tale signs, no buboes at the joints. She is, however, suffering from grief and exhaustion. She needs rest."

"May I go in to see her?"

"Of course, but please do not tax her."

Adélaïde went in to the nondescript bedroom and closed the door. Violet, sprawled on the small bed, looked up without energy at her friend. "Hullo, Adélaïde," she said with affection.

"Vi, are you all right?"

"Yes, just a touch of... exhaustion, the doctor says." Violet smiled wanly. "I'll be fine."

"Vi, I have to tell you, you're looking a little green around the gills, so to say. Are you sure it isn't that... thing?

"The gem?" Violet laughed, sharply. "Don't be silly, dear. You can't tell me you actually believe those stories."

"Well, Charles put some stock in them."

"It was Charles' job to believe. That doesn't mean I do." This was true. Her late husband, Charles Reston, had been an agent for the Diogenes Club, the least known and most eccentric instrument of the British Government, which dealt with matters more unfathomable and *outré*. Reston was a protégé of Beauregard, who had stepped down as the head of the Club's Ruling Cabal several years previous. That the current Cabal had loaned him to S.N.I.F. indicated a state of affairs that touched on both the political and the unknowable. Violet, on the other hand, had been known to refer to the Club and the cases they dealt with as "a bunch of superstitious rot," which had caused some friction between the young couple, but there it was.

"But Vi," Adélaïde continued, "you have to admit, it is awfully odd that you've become sick since Charles died and you started carrying the Eye around with you. You could let me hold it for you for a while."

"It is not awfully odd that I'm all done in. And it has everything to do with my husband being killed by some madman, and us being stuck in this god-forsaken city surrounded by the sick and dying, with a very good chance of becoming sick and dying ourselves," Violet retorted with the trademark Holmes acerbity. "Now, stop mother-henning me and let's get down to cases. This Eye was the responsibility of my husband and his French partner. They're both gone now—not that I ever did lay eyes on the mysterious 'A.L.'—so it's up to us. Those devils must know that Charles arranged to have the Eye delivered to me following his death, and that we now have it. I'll hold on to it, but we've got to figure a way to get the hell out of here with it, and we can't wait for this damnable plague to end. They'll find us long before it runs its course and the city re-opens."

Adélaïde wasn't offended by her friend's tone. In fact, she was long accustomed to it. The two women had first met years ago in finishing school and had become fast friends. When Reston had been loaned to S.N.I.F. and assigned to Algiers, Violet had been left at loose ends in a strange city with no friends. He had suggested that she ask Adélaïde down for an extended visit and all had agreed. After all, when Adélaïde wasn't around, Violet had a tendency to get herself into trouble.

Not that Adélaïde's presence had saved them this time. She was here, having accompanied Violet back to Oran from her recent sojourn in London, and now they were in the deepest trouble of their lives. Through the kindness of Doctor Rieux, they had a place to hide, but it couldn't last long.

"All right," Adélaïde agreed. "There's a man who comes around sometimes to visit Doctor Rieux. It's the reporter, Rambert. He's a journalist for my favorite Parisian paper, *L'Echo de France*. He's trapped here like we are and is desperate to get back to his wife. I'll see if he can help."

Raymond Rambert had readily agreed to include the two young women in his escape plans, and now the three sat together at the Spanish restaurant near the docks waiting for their contact. They had waited the better part of a week for the meet, during which time Violet's condition neither bettered nor worsened.

"The man we're waiting for is called Gonzales," Rambert explained. "It took me weeks to get to him, first through the smuggler Cottard, then through what seemed like an endless series of middlemen. The plan is to hook me up with two of the city guards. When they have sentry duty together and none of the regular soldiers are on duty, that's the time, we'll sail through the gates as if no one was there at all."

"And this man Gonzales won't be upset that you've added the two of us into the mix?" Violet asked.

"Maybe, but he's too close to getting paid. This is to be our final meeting, where he'll introduce us to the two sentries, go over the schedule, and agree on the exact date we go. It's costing me 10,000 francs. I don't think they'll be too upset at the prospect of an extra 20."

Adélaïde nodded, a Red Apple cigarette dangling elegantly from her full red lips. "Ten thousand each is a lot, but we're good for it."

"Yes, especially when the alternative is a hail of bullets," Rambert agreed. Escape attempts and the resounding echoes of gunfire from the city walls had been a nightly occurrence.

Their food arrived; Rambert and Adélaïde dug in, while Violet picked at her own fare.

"Monsieur Rambert," Adélaïde said, "my mother was also a journalist and I find it fascinating. I simply must know—what brought you to Oran? It seems a bit off the beaten path for a Parisian reporter."

"A combination of professional and personal interest, Mademoiselle. I read the reports at the start of the plague, how it spread so quickly throughout the city. I asked to cover the case and arrived a few weeks ago, just before the quarantine was imposed. The accounts intrigued me. They bear certain similarities to a horrendous plague my father witnessed and reported on years ago in Paris."

"Your father? Surely you don't mean—ah, but I see you do! Your father is Charles Rambert, the noted journalist who wrote for *La Capitale* under the by-line 'Jerôme Fandor!' "

"Yes, that is so. My father crusaded against a terrorist called Fantômas, who once released plague-infested rats on an ocean liner. If Fantômas has returned..." Rambert paused to light his own cigarette, a Morley. "Well, as I said, there are certain similarities."

"Monsieur, forgive me if I overstep, but didn't I hear once that your father might have actually been related to Fantômas?"

"Yes," Rambert responded quietly. "Some believed he was his son... No one has heard from Fantômas in years, but if he is behind this plague as well... I'm convinced it is unnatural but the information is too dangerous for telephone or telegraph. I must personally bring my report back to Paris and contact the authorities there. In fact–" He broke off as three men approached. "Ah, if it isn't Magistrate Othon! What brings you here this fine day, Monsieur?"

"Won't you introduce us to these two lovely ladies, Rambert?"

"Of course, where are my manners?" Rambert stood up. "May I present Mesdemoiselles Johnston and Holmes, acquaintances of Doctor Rieux. But I am sorry, I have not had the pleasure?" Rambert inquired.

"Indeed," Othon said, "these are my colleagues, Inspectors Fabre and Fauchet of the Sûreté."

The three newcomers seated themselves, and Fauchet, a squat Corsican, spoke first. "Mesdemoiselles, Monsieur, let us come straight to the point. We have reason to believe that you intend to leave Oran by less than legal means."

"I'm sorry, Inspector, I may have been misinformed," said Violet innocently. "Are there legal means of leaving Oran?"

"Ah, well, Mademoiselle, this is the crux of it, is it not? You see, no one is free to leave Oran right now–Fabre. Fabre! Stop staring, it is impolite!"

Without a doubt, Inspector Fabre was unabashedly staring at Adélaïde, at her dark eyes and even darker hair bound up in its French roll. "I'm sorry Fauchet, but… Mademoiselle Johnston, you seem very familiar to me. Perhaps we have met somewhere before?"

Adélaïde laughed, a soft tinkling sound. "No, I'm sorry, it is quite impossible–Violet, dear, are you quite all right?"

The blood seemed to have drained from Violet's face. Her eyes bulged. She looked a little green. Cupping her hands over her mouth, she made a beeline for the back of the restaurant. Dammit, this was no time to be sick, like some weak-kneed ninny! But autonomic reflexes took over and she retched violently as she reached the bathroom. She turned on the water full-blast. The sounds of her sickness and the gushing of the water pulsated in her eardrums, as she heaved and heaved.

What seemed like hours passed, but it must have been only minutes. Nevertheless, when she emerged from the washroom, the scene had changed dramatically. All the other patrons had departed. Many of the wooden tables and chairs were destroyed, caved in and splintered as if they had been chopped in two. Wooden pillars which formerly supported the ramshackle roof lay on the floor, broken in half. Adélaïde and Rambert lay on the floor, unconscious. Fauchet, Fabre and Othon were in no better condition.

And in the middle of the room stood an enormous Korean clad in a black three-piece suit as if he was off for a day at the track. He was almost as wide as he was tall. He removed his black bowler hat and the next thing Violet knew, its steel brim was embedded in the wood pillar next to her, almost severing it in half. He slammed the side of his right hand into the last remaining pillar. His hands must have been as hard as teak wood.

The roof started to come down. The Korean advanced on her. She never had a chance.

31

"Miss Holmes?"

Her eyes opened and vision blurred, then cleared.

She was lying on a settee of Chinese design, comfortably propped upon pillows of the finest yellow and red silks. She tried to sit up, but a new discharge of pain in her skull effectively dissuaded any further movement.

"Please, Miss Holmes," the voice continued solicitously, "do not make any further sudden movements and I assure you that you shall feel better in short order."

Violet looked in the direction of the voice; as her vision continued to clear, a tall, lean Asian man came into focus. He was dressed in black silk robes and a black cap was settled upon his skull. He sat, surrounded by flickering candles, upon a dais across the room, which she now saw to be some sort of underground cave decorated with silks and tapestries. Water came down various sections of the cavern walls in tiny rivulets. She didn't know enough about the local geography to know whether the moisture was unusual or not. Certainly it contrasted sharply with the current dry dustiness above ground in Oran. At least, she assumed she was still near, or under, Oran.

She refocused on the man who was leaning toward her, an expression of concern written across his high brow. His hands, clasped together in front of him in a pyramid–a gesture that evoked memories of her uncle–were adorned with long, sharp nails which seemed to be lacquered in black varnish. His eyes were green. Just like the cavern walls.

"Where am I?"

"You are my guest." The man gestured at the cavern. "I must apologize for the accommodations. One makes do with what one has at hand."

Once more, ignoring the blinding pain, Violet moved to sit up. As she did so, her hands moved down her sides and what she felt was discomfiting. The familiar lump that the Eye made in her pocket was gone. In fact, her clothing–khakis and jodhpurs–was gone, replaced by a calf-length, formfitting silk gown in the style of the Chinese. And nothing else. Her eyes widened, and she snapped a glare at the man on the dais.

"Yes, yes. I do have much to apologize for. It was necessary to search you. Your clothing was also searched. There is an object I seek, Miss Holmes. I did not think that you had it. In fact, I was almost positive that you did not. But why take chances?" He leaned back and sighed, somewhat dramatically, she thought. "But I was right, you did not have it, which means that damnable Frenchman still does."

Now her mind raced. She *did* have the Eye. Or at least, she had had it the last time she had checked for its reassuring lump in her pocket. That had been back at the Spanish restaurant.

Where the hell was it? her mind screamed, but she kept her composure. Which was all the more remarkable, given what else she had just realized. Or perhaps it was not that remarkable; she was a Holmes, after all.

"You killed my husband," she said calmly.

"Yes, as I said, I have much to apologize for. To you, dear lady, if not to him." His eyes narrowed, taking on a cruel cast. "Fortunes of war, and all that, as you British would say."

"May I at least know the name of my husband's murderer?"

"Murderer? It was a battle. We were opponents. He lost. I won." He drew himself up regally. "You may call me Doctor Natas."

"I see."

"You do not appear to be surprised."

"I suppose I'm not, at that. This is all too surreal for anything else. And it all fits. Of course, I've heard tales of 'Fu Manchu' before... Your jousts with my uncle, your ongoing battle of wits with my cousin..."

"I would hardly call it a 'battle of wits,' my dear."

"Ah yes, and the fabled charm, too... Is that how you populate your harems, Doctor, on charm alone? Or do you resort to kidnapping the women you desire, drugging them, dressing them as you wish"–she looked pointedly down at her gown-clad form which provocatively revealed every contour and curve–"and keeping them captive for years on end?"

Natas' eyes burned a brighter green, as he replied, "I assure you, Miss Holmes, that I wish you no harm. If you had had the Silver Eye of Dagon, you would be free by now. As it is, you are merely a lure. Once the damnable Frenchman knows you are here, he will return for you and your companions. He will give me the Eye, you will all go free and the matter will be concluded."

Dammit, Violet thought, *we're never getting out of here. The Frenchman doesn't have the Eye, I do. Or did,* she amended.

"Furthermore," Natas continued, "I have too much respect for your vaunted family to treat you with anything other than the utmost deference which you deserve. Neither you, nor your companions, shall come to harm while in my care."

"Adélaïde and Rambert, where are they? And what do you want with this Eye anyway? Surely no mere gem, no matter how exquisite, can be worth all this."

"Your friends are being held safely close by. They have also been searched, as a precaution. Of course, neither of them had the Eye either. As for it, it is merely a key–a key to a deep and unfathomable power. With it, uncounted masses will bend to my will, or else be swept away in the current of history."

Violet was beginning to suspect that Natas was a tiny bit mad, although neither her uncle nor her cousin had ever hinted at that. She decided it would be prudent to get off the subject. "All right, then. If you had already searched us all and didn't find what you wanted, why bring me here for this elaborate audience? Why not just let us go?"

"I can't, Miss Holmes... Not until Lupin comes."

"Lupin? *He's* the mysterious Frenchman? You *are* insane! He'd be, what, in his seventies by now? Besides, I doubt the great Arsène Lupin would ever work as mere agent of French Intelligence. It wouldn't be his style."

"You are mistaken. I know for a fact that Lupin was your husband's partner. And now, he has the Eye."

"Fine then, whatever you say. But how the hell do you know he's coming at all? He could be thousands of miles away!"

"No, Miss Holmes, he is still trapped here, in Oran. He is not free. My little plague has ensured that."

"Your... little... plague? My God, you monster!"

"I created this particular strain in payment for a service the admirable Fantômas rendered me some years ago. I always pay my debts. I held some in reserve for my own use at the appropriate moment. I would say the present situation qualifies, wouldn't you agree?"

"No."

"Ah, of course not. But, Miss Holmes, are you quite all right? It may be the peculiar phosphorescence in these caverns, but you're looking a little green."

Doctor Natas rose, walked over and crouched down to examine her. Was it really the grotto's phosphorescence, or... No. Natas lost consciousness, hitting the cavern floor with a rather ignominious *thud*.

Violet quickly rose, thinking to take advantage of this amazing stroke of luck. Her thoughts of escape, however, were short-lived. She felt a faint odor of mushrooms. Then the cavern spun and swirled and she, too, passed out, falling back on the settee.

FROM: A.L.
TO: Lieutenant Aristide, Section Afrique du Nord, Service National d'Information Fonctionnelle, Paris.
DATE: July 10, 1946
SUBJECT:Oran situation.

Conditions here deteriorating. Tell Champignac his sleeping gas works perfectly, but bag of tricks running out. Plague initiated by Natas in order to prevent escape from Oran and delivery of object. Doctor Rieux highly dedicated but overwhelmed. Plague same as strain used in 1911 by Fantômas aboard British Queen *en route from Southampton to Durban. Suggest American medical expert, if available.*

Object is still safe. Request extraction support. Route response through Parisian reporter Raymond Rambert. If necessary, will report again at designated weekly interval.

It had been almost a week since Violet, Adélaïde and Rambert had been mysteriously rescued from Natas' clutches. They had come to outside of Doctor Rieux's laboratory near the Place d'Armes, and now were in hiding there. It was very kind of him to provide them shelter, without asking too many questions, and he wasn't there much anyway, spending upward of 18 hours a day tending to plague victims.

What was more, the Eye of Dagon was back in Violet's possession, safe and sound, at least for the time being. It was all very strange, but apparently the "damnable Frenchman," Lupin, *had* come for them, just as Natas had predicted. In fact, he must have been in Natas' lair before they even arrived, although that seemed impossible on its face. But how else to explain the mystifying transference of the Eye from Violet's pocket to where it was ultimately found when they awoke outside Rieux's? For it had been found in Adélaïde's generous, raven-colored hair, tucked in her French roll.

Adélaïde had laughed it off with her natural good humor. "After all, Vi," she said, "Monsieur Lupin chose the perfect hiding place. Not even those terrible men thought to look there. And you must admit, dear, that while your hair is quite lovely, it is not quite as abundant as mine, yes?"

Violet had been forced to admit that this was true.

Now, with little else to do but wonder if Natas and his minions would find them again, the days passed slowly, until finally there was a break in the monotony. Since the quarantine, various airlines–TWA, Pan Am, Oceanic, Air France and so on–had generously donated planes. Now, relief cargo flights made regular passes over the city, dropping the usual cartons of supplies and foodstuffs for the trapped citizens. This time, among the usual containers, Rieux received a new drop of plague serum, as well as extensive notes on this strain of the plague.

The new serum came from an unnamed American doctor who had set up an encampment outside Oran to consult on the crisis. Along with it was an unsigned message addressed to Rambert:

M. Rambert:

Tell Lupin to follow the Boulevard du Front de Mer to where it meets the city walls at midnight tomorrow night. There he will find escape.

Rambert, not understanding why he had been identified as a contact for Lupin, or how to contact him, naturally shared the note with Violet and Adélaïde. Though they commiserated about it–after all, Lupin had rescued them from Natas, and what kind of gratitude was it showing to just strand him here?– the three finally agreed that, in the absence of any way of contacting him, they may as well exploit this new escape plan themselves.

As they arrived at the appointed place and time, an airplane flew over the city. The craft's engines must have been muffled, because only Adélaïde's extremely sensitive hearing picked up the noise. Even after she pointed it out to the others, they couldn't see the plane, which was flying without running lights.

Shortly afterwards, a black spot appeared above them, blotting out the stars as it became larger and larger. Eventually the dark spot resolved itself into a black-painted crate, approximately a cubic meter, which was attached to a parachute and a small, absolutely silent engine, both of which were also pitch black to blend in with the night. The engine guided the gently falling crate to a perfect and silent landing next to the three astonished watchers.

The crate had apparently been designed to open upon landing, for the top flopped open and then the four sides of the box separated at the corners and fell to the ground. Violet, Adélaïde and Rambert approached cautiously.

"What is that?" Rambert asked.

As they came closer, they realized that the shapeless object within was encased in packing material, which came away easily and quickly. What lay revealed within took their breath away, at least momentarily.

It was cylindrical and made of metal, glinting in the sparse moonlight. It stood on four fins which were attached to the bottom of the cylinder at 90-degree angles. The cylinder came to a conical point, which was topped by three horizontal rings. In between each fin was a nozzle which pointed at the ground. It looked like nothing so much as a miniature-sized rocket ship from a Saturday-matinee movie serial. Six straps of leather, with buckles at the ends, were attached to the assembly at various points.

Next to the cylinder sat a helmet.

"Um. A rocket pack." Violet paused. "I think I've seen one like it before."

"Well?" asked Rambert.

"You see, this leather belt buckles around the waist, and the other ones go about the shoulders, like so."

"You can't be serious!" Adélaïde said.

"I am." Violet looked at Adélaïde. "I'm getting out of here. Are you coming?"

"Mesdemoiselles, this thing. That thing might carry two, but surely not three," Rambert said. "Your need is greater than mine."

"Are you sure, Raymond?" Violet asked.

"Yes, now that we know that Fantômas is not behind this plague, and that matters will be resolved when you and Mademoiselle Johnston escape with the Eye, I am content to stay and help Doctor Rieux fight this plague in whatever small way I can. Now quickly–you must go!"

"Thank you for all your help." Violet took his hand and held it for a moment, warmly. Then she continued to heft the cylinder onto her back and secure it with the leather bindings.

"Well?" she asked Adélaïde, expectantly.

Adélaïde just shook her head unenthusiastically, as if to say, what madness! She slipped her arms around Violet's waist and tightly through the leather straps, clasping her hands firmly.

"Go," she murmured, "before I change my mind."

Violet nodded and before anyone could say another word, she hit the ignition button.

Flames erupted from the four nozzles, and without further adieu, the two women soared into the air. The flames backlight their airborne figures. Violet, in her jodhpurs and boots, looked the perfect picture of a daring aviatrix test-flying an innovative new device. Adélaïde presented a different picture, holding on to Violet for dear life, her dress fluttering about in the wind, exposing her thighs above black stockings and garters. Rambert didn't even have time to chide himself for impure thoughts, as gunfire from the sentries erupted a second later.

The rocket pack discharged even more flames and noise, and the two women accelerated over the sea. Although the rifle fire continued, the bright dot of the rocket quickly became smaller and smaller, and eventually winked out.

Rambert wished both women a silent *bonne chance* and turned to make his way back to Rieux's laboratory before the guards came to investigate.

Doctor Francis Ardan, as he was known to the French, continued to listen, his bronzed face immobile as he patiently took in the remainder of the fantastic tale. A young, dark-haired man with a thin, white vertical scar down his right cheek sat in the background, representing the British Secret Service. They were aboard a schooner, the *Orion II*, now headed for France. Violet and Adélaïde were wrapped in warm blankets, nursing mugs of strong, black coffee. However, they continued to shiver as much from fatigue as from the dunking in the cold water.

"We were out over the water, still flying. We didn't know how to land the thing. You didn't exactly include an instruction manual, Doc," Violet said, a note of accusation in her voice.

The scientist shrugged. "The rocket pack was meant for Lupin. He knows how to fly it."

"Hmm. Well. We were flying, Adélaïde was barely hanging on, we didn't know how much fuel was left–"

"More than enough," Ardan said.

Violet glared at him and continued, "–and since it was pitch black and we couldn't tell where we were, or what direction we were going, we decided it was better to try to descend. Next thing we knew, we hit the water. Of course, your rocket pack made us sink like a stone, and I didn't think we would make it, but thank God you found us and fished us out in time."

"I followed the tracking signal," the scientist said. "We were following you the whole way and you could have come down at any time."

"Yes, well, no way of knowing that, right?"

"As I said, the pack was intended for Lupin. He would have understood." Violet suspected that Ardan was beginning to become irritated, although he didn't show it. "Do you know what became of him?"

Violet stood up and slammed down her mug. "No, I don't bloody know what happened to Lupin! I never saw the man once the whole time I was there. Now excuse me, I've had quite enough of this."

She stomped off and down the narrow gangway. Stopping, she turned back. "I am grateful, Francis. But this has just all been a bit much."

Ardan nodded, and she continued down the gangway, the young man from British Intelligence following her.

"Violet," he called, and she turned around.

"What is it, James?" she asked, as he moved to take her in his arms.

"Thank God, you're safe now."

"Safe," Violet said.

"Yes, safe. Look, I'm sorry about Charles."

"Yes, well, so am I. I treated him pretty shabbily. Obviously, we wouldn't have lasted. At least now he'll never know."

"Yes. I *am* sorry." He paused. "But you've escaped that devilish place. I'm here to take you back to London, get you well again. You're free now."

"Free? *Free?*" She slapped him hard, once, across the cheek. "I'm *pregnant*, you bastard. I'm not feeling terribly free right now." She stalked off, slamming the cabin door behind her.

Upstairs on deck, Doctor Ardan approached Adélaïde. Remarkably, now that she had cleaned up and dried off, he could see that she was quite beautiful. Remarkable, not because he was immune to feminine beauty (he wasn't), but because he rarely allowed himself to take note of it. She was tall, six feet, and her dress clung to her perfectly proportioned curves in all the right places. Dark, lustrous hair fell about her shoulders. She was, in a word, stunning.

Ardan got ahold of himself and held out a bronzed, cabled hand. "Mademoiselle? We weren't really properly introduced. I'm Doctor Francis Ardan."

Adélaïde sized him up, rather boldly. "Yes, Doctor, it is a pleasure to meet you. I've heard so much about you. The newspapers paint you as an adventurer. How do you say it... a wild man?" she asked provocatively.

"I see." Ardan cleared his throat, choosing to ignore her question. "Yes, well. Mademoiselle, I still have some more questions, and Miss Holmes doesn't seem up to it right now."

"Of course," she said. "What about?"

"About the Silver Eye of Dagon."

"The Eye? We gave it to you."

"Yes, thank you. But how did you come to have it?"

"I don't understand?" Adélaïde looked at him quizzically. "We've given it to you. Isn't that enough?"

"Yes, but, no... I...." Ardan felt out of his element. He was never very at ease with women, but for some reason was even more out of his depth with Adélaïde Johnston.

He took a deep breath and started over. "I am not a representative of the French government, but I have agreed to work with them in this case."

"Yes?"

The scientist started to gain momentum. "They very much appreciate the recovery of this object. But we–they–wish to know. How did it come into your possession? They sent a man here, Lupin, who was supposed to help recover the Eye for them. I expected to find Lupin. Instead, I find you and Miss Holmes, and you have the Eye in your possession. I still don't understand how that happened."

"Well, it was all very strange." Adélaïde made eye contact and held Ardan's gold-flecked eyes. "Violet and I were hiding at Doctor Rieux's laboratory near the Place d'Armes after we escaped from Natas, when Rambert came to us with a message." She wandered over near the rocket pack and sat down heavily on the deck.

"Go on, please."

"He had received that message in the last medical drop of plague serum. I assume that serum came from you?"

Ardan nodded. "Yes, after Lupin sent his information, I obtained samples of the plague strain Fantômas used over 30 years ago, and was able to develop a serum to combat it. The *peste* in Oran should start to abate shortly."

Adélaïde continued. "The note was anonymous, but it instructed that this Lupin go to a place near the city walls at midnight last night. There he would find a way out of the city."

"Mademoiselle Johnston, that note was supposed to go to Lupin. I arranged to remote-parachute the rocket pack and I don't blame you for using it, but what happened to Lupin then?"

"I don't know, I tell you!" Adélaïde started to sob, slumping further down on the deck next to the rocket pack.

"Mademoiselle Johnston–" Ardan crouched down, close to her.

"Please, Doctor, no more, I am spent!" She hugged herself closer to the pack. "Just hold me, please, a little, and then I'll try to be strong, and answer all your questions."

This was mostly uncharted territory for Ardan. If there were women involved in his adventures (and often there were), he usually left it to the wolves among his five aides to deal with them. *No such luck, this time*, he thought uncomfortably. He leaned down further to console her, and held her as she cried it all out.

Finally, her sobs dwindled, and she nestled further into his arms.

"Mademoiselle–Adélaïde, please," Doc began tentatively. "I need to know."

"Yes?" she murmured, distantly.

"What about Lupin? Do you know anything about him, or what happened to him?"

"Lupin, Lupin, Lupin! Always this man Lupin!" She pushed him away, sharply. "All right, I'll tell you!"

That was when Ardan noticed. Her right arm was now tightly looped through the two leather straps of the rocket pack. Her left hand was also near the pack, fingers poised above the ignition button.

"What—?"

"So you want to know about Lupin, do you? All right, I'll tell you!" The fingers of her right hand flicked, and as if by magic, the Silver Eye of Dagon appeared, held tightly between them.

If Doc Ardan was at all capable of shock, this was certainly the time for it. She had actually managed to lift it from his inner vest pocket without him noticing, quite a feat.

Adélaïde leapt up, left hand descending toward the ignition button, propelling herself toward Ardan. Her lips brushed his cheek at the same time she hit the button. As she launched into the air, accelerating away, she yelled down at him over the blast of the rockets. "You dear, silly man! You want to know where Lupin is? She is right here! You think *my father* is the only one capable of pulling this off? *I* am Lupin!"

She waved at Ardan as she flew higher and higher. "*Au revoir, mon cher Francis, au revoir!* We shall meet again! Thank you for the Eye, it's lovely!"

Ardan stared up at her as she receded into the distance, her dress billowing about her shapely stockinged legs. Some of the same impure thoughts that Rambert had had also crossed his mind, and he also chided himself, not for his lack of purity, but for his lack of focus on the matters at hand. A lack of focus directly attributable to Adélaïde Lupin. A.L.

And then she was gone.

She was right. They *would* meet again. He'd make sure of it.

FROM: SNIF.
TO: Sous-Lieutenant Aristide, Service National d'Information Fonctionnelle, Paris.
DATE: July 19, 1946
SUBJECT: Your report re: A.L.

Am more than disappointed with your performance, to wit:

Poor decision-making: You either engaged A.L.'s services sight-unseen, or else knew A.L. was actually Lupin's daughter and failed to inform me. Either alternative is unacceptable. Dealing with Lupin (or a member of his family, obviously), is always a risky business. You should have foreseen that she would double-cross us and keep the Eye. Her acquisition of Doctor Ardan's rocket pack only compounds your missteps.

Using S.N.I.F. funds and resources unwisely: You paid A.L. in advance for services not fully rendered. S.N.I.F. must now dedicate further resources to recovering the Eye from A.L.

You are hereby demoted to the rank of Sous-Lieutenant. Had ultimate objective of securing Eye from Natas not been met, you would be facing immediate termination. Report directly to Montferrand for reassignment

In the first installment of The Werewolf of Rutherford Grange, *a young Harry Dickson was dispatched by Sexton Blake at Sir Henry Westenra's request to work protection duty for a diplomatic conference to be held at Sir Henry's country estate. In the train, Dickson met Lord John Roxton, his niece Christina Rutherford and the beautiful Gianetti Annunciata, assistant to the mysterious Sâr Dubnotal, invited to the neighboring Rutherford Grange by Mrs. Rutherford, a Spiritualist, for a séance. At Westenra House, Dickson is assigned to share rooms with a young Indian, Darshan Kritchna. In the library, he comes across the journal of Christopher Westenra that mentions a mysterious tragedy that occurred two centuries earlier. Dickson's first night is far from uneventful when he and Darshan come across the gruesomely slaughtered corpse of the house cat. And now, the conclusion of...*

G.L. Gick: *The Werewolf of Rutherford Grange*

Surrey, 1911

Shards of falling glass had rained on our hair, skin and clothing, or bit painfully into our feet as we stepped blindly about in the darkness. But our discomfort was as nothing compared to the still, small form lying grotesquely upon the pillow before us: the body of Colleen, the kitchen cat, sprawled lifelessly upon the bed, a small, intensely crimson geyser of lifeblood pouring out of the maw of her neck.

Where her head might be, neither of us could say.

"Damn," I heard Darshan mutter blackly, unable to tear his eyes from the horrible sight. "Is that Colleen? What could have done this? An owl?"

I refrained from replying. I was too busy snatching the candle from my reluctant roommate, leaning forward for a closer examination of the body. My mentor had made a point once of showing me how various animals killed, and owls had been among them. It was true owls often preyed upon cats; I had seen one do it myself back in the States, but this looked like no injury from a bird of prey I had ever seen. The one I had witnessed had struck the back of the creature's neck with its beak, instantly snapping it, but it did not shear the head clear off. For a moment, I debated whether a shard of glass might have severed it, but no; I would've expected the wound to be more jagged. This was very neat and even. It was hell running my fingers through the bloody fur, trying to peer through the gusher of life, but after a moment, I found tiny marks about what remained of the neck, bearing no sign of having been made by beak or glass. They were deep and even, and could possibly have been made by talons, but

42

somehow I found myself doubting it. In fact, if I didn't know any better, I could swear these were…

…teeth marks.

Scthwump, schtwump wump wump wump

Kritchna and I shot looks at each other. There it was again–the wet, sucking, peculiarly incomplete sound we had heard just before the cat had come crashing down upon our heads. It pattered with its strange sloshing swiftly along the edge of the eave outside–and then, what small sliver of the moon Kritchna's tiny, blocked window allowed inside was suddenly darkened and we heard a great whuffing sound and the struggling of branches. Whatever it was had either leaped or fallen out off the roof, down to the bushes some three stories below!

Hastily, I scrambled to my feet on top of the bed, ignoring the glass and slippery pools of blood soaking into the mattress. If I could just get my head out the window, see what it was–no good. Not all the pane had shattered, but what was left had turned into transparent jagged knives: I'd behead myself like Colleen if I dared try stick my head out the opening. I fumbled with the lock but was again frustrated. It was too still from disuse. Below I could hear something struggling in the foliage. Leaping to the floor, and nearly knocking Kritchna over in the process, I yelled: "Come on!" and threw open the door. If we hurried, we might just make it in time–

–Slamming into Mr. Appleby, the butler, was, I assure you, entirely unintentional.

"Great God Almighty!" the butler, clad in robe and slippers, exclaimed–and for such a devout Christian, to do so meant he was very, very annoyed indeed. "What is the meaning of this ruckus? Do you wish to wake the masters? Explain yourselves at once!"

"See for yourself," I snapped back, jerking my thumb back toward the bed. I felt a bit bad about it; I rather liked the man and had no wish to be rude, but time was of the essence. I pushed past the butler, dashed down the small flight of stairs, through the hall, down the main stairway and out the huge front door to find–

–Nothing, save for the chirruping of insects and the occasional call of night birds. The gardens surrounding the House were silent. Nothing stirred, nothing appeared. The full Moon beamed down benevolently, bathing threes and bushes in an ethereal halo. You'd never imagine something slinking about it had just slaughtered an animal.

But the shrubs I wanted were along the west side of the House, and whatever it was might not have been able to have extricated itself yet. Still clad in nightshirt and bare feet, the dew cold on my still-bleeding soles, I made my way along the length of the House as swiftly and silently as possible, my ears pricked to catch the slightest disturbance. The window to Kritchna's garret would be right around this corner. I paused to listen; I could hear no rustling; no *schtwhumping*, nothing unusual to speak of. Taking a deep breath, I whipped around the corner, prepared for anything, only to find–

–Nothing again. Absolutely nothing. Just a clump of flattened rosebushes, the stems bent and broken as if a great weight had crashed upon them. My prey, whatever it had been, had escaped.

I scanned the ground for footprints, indentations, anything that might tell me the direction my fugitive went. But even in the soft, dewy grass, I found no sign of anything. Yet something was shining on the flowers in the moonlight, something thick and sparkling, like dew only much more viscous.

"Find anything?"

I nearly jumped as I found Kritchna waiting beside me. So intent had I been on my examination, I hadn't even heard him approach. I also noted he had had the presence of mind to pull on a pair of pants and shoes before joining me. As well as having brought an electric torch. I felt rather like kicking myself.

"Appleby's upstairs trying to find a hatbox or something for Colleen," he said. "What have you discovered?"

"Nothing yet," I admitted reluctantly. "But, here, shine that torch here a moment. I want to see something."

Kritchna complied. As the beam flashed over the broken flowers, his face screwed up in distaste. "What on Earth is that mess?"

That mess was a concoction the like of which I had never seen in any chemistry laboratory; a clear, sticky, pus-like substance dribbling slowly down the stalks and petals like slow, cold treacle. The bushes were saturated with it, like those I tossed my water-filled paper bags upon out the windows of my brownstone as a boy in New York. It pooled slowly at the base of the plants, steadily soaking down into the ground. Wait–no, it wasn't! It was drawing into itself, shriveling into smaller blobs, evaporating into the air.

"Hmph. What does this thing do, melt?" Kritchna snorted. "I've never seen anything so disgusting."

"Says the fellow who sits through *Little Neddy* pictures," I grunted, kneeling to carefully swab a bit up, rubbing it between my fingers. Cool to the touch. Odorless, as well. I found myself wishing I had brought a specimen jar. Peculiarly, I could find no trace of the same substance on the grass itself. Just upon the crushed rosebushes and directly beneath.

"Funny, though," Kritchna was continuing absently, having also taken up a bit to examine. "I could almost swear I have seen something like this before. If only I could remember where..."

With a sigh, I stood and wiped my hand on my shirt. "Well, whatever it is, it evaporates quickly. Look, it's almost all gone already. I don't know what it is, but it's clear we're not going to learn anything else tonight. We might as well go back inside."

We must have made a sorry sight as we tramped back upstairs, half-dressed, disheveled, scratched in several places on our arms and legs. Appleby

44

certainly wasn't impressed. "Darshan, your blankets and sheets are simply soaked with blood. They're completely ruined!"

"Better them than us, Mr. Appleby," Kritchna stated wryly.

"Well...yes," the butler sighed, looking down at the bed. Resting on what remained of the mattress was a plain brown hatbox, lid closed. It didn't take a detective to guess what was inside. "Mrs. Mulligan shall not be pleased. Did you find out what it was?" I shook my head. "Well, perhaps it was an owl, then." Somehow I sincerely doubted that, but as I had no better theory, I did not contradict him. Gently he made a little "cross" over the box with his fingers, then picked it up.

"Well, I'd best get this somewhere for the night." He ran his gaze over us. "And get you some iodine and bandages. You're cut all over. Probably bleeding all over the carpets, too, like as not. Heaven knows where I'm going to put you, Darshan, but you can't sleep here tonight. You might as well take my room. I'll sleep on a divan in the hall." Pleased and more than a little surprised at this generosity, we thanked him gratefully. He coughed. "Yes–well. I'd best be getting that iodine. Wait here." He quickly darted downstairs.

"Told you he was all right. Just comes on strong," Darshan said.

"You were right."

We moved to sit side-by-side on the steps, shaking the glass from our clothing. "Do you think it was an owl?" Darshan asked at last, shuffling over to give me more room.

I shook my head. "I can't think of what else it could have been. Although I've never seen an owl do anything like that before. The only other creature it could be is a dog or a fox, and neither of those could've gotten up to the roof. Could they?"

Now it was Kritchna's turn to shake. "No. Colleen could climb just about anywhere she wanted, but nothing else. Still, that had to be the most disgusting thing I've ever seen."

I smiled, wryly. "Says the man who watches *Little Neddy* pictures."

"Hm?" Kritchna glanced at me puzzled. "What are you talking about? I hate *Little Neddy*."

That's strange, I thought. I had very definitely heard him tell Appleby he had slipped away from his duties to see a motion picture in Wolfsbridge, only now to hear him say he couldn't stand the very star of the same. So why would he have bothered to go to it in the first place? And if he hadn't been at the cinema, where had he been? The questions must have been plainly visible on my face, for no sooner had they crossed my mind than Kritchna quickly changed the subject: "So. How did you get into detective work, may I ask? Did you always want to be one?"

The sudden switch did nothing to ease my suspicions, but I was willing to go along with it for now. "Pretty much. I'd always admired great American detectives like Nick Carter and King Brady, and my father knew this old actor who

45

used to be a Secret Service agent. He'd tell me and my sister all these old stories; I think he made half of them up, but I didn't care. So I decided to become one myself. When Father sent me here for my education, I made a point of seeking other detectives out. That way I met my mentor, and the rest, as the saying goes, is history. Runs in the blood, I suppose. My father helped on a few cases himself, with a master thief, of all things, and my sister even married a very influential detective, back in the States. Let's see, little Franklin should be going on two by now. And you? Your family?"

"Ah." Darshan shifted uneasily in his seat and for a moment it looked as if he'd almost rather talk about *Little Neddy*. "Well, my family's a bit difficult to talk about."

"Oh? You're not an Untouchable or anything like that, are you?"

"No!" Kritchna shook his head violently. "No. No, no, no. Nothing like that. We're Brahmins."

"Brahmins?" My astonishment only grew. "Then why on Earth are you in..."

"Service? For my own reasons, Dickson. But, back to my family—as I said, it's a bit difficult to explain them. We're not just of the Brahmin caste, you see— at least, so my family claims. What we are, what we've always traditionally been, is—well, I guess you would have to call us wizards."

I raised my eyebrows. "Wizards?"

"You know—Indian wizards. Fakirs and yogis and all that rot. We're supposed to come from a long line of them; Protectors of the Ancient Secrets and so on. It's all rubbish, of course. What we are is a bunch of street magicians—you can find thousands of them in any Indian city. Snake charmers, fire-walkers, things like that. We're just higher-caste than most."

I nodded, smiling, beginning to understand. "Yes, I know. My father's a magician; he taught me half those tricks himself."

"I'm sure. But to listen to my family, it was all real, at least once. We've just fallen on hard times, according to them. Once, we were supposed to be court magicians to Chandragupta himself, or so the stories go. The power's still in our blood, my great-uncle Nadir used to say—it's just waiting to be rediscovered. But my father was having none of it. He'd seen the signs—the English ruled India now, and it was their ways, not ours, that was going to shape the future. So he turned his back on it. My great-uncle was none too happy about his decision, for he wanted my sister and I to be his apprentices, but Father refused and that was that. My uncle's in the Philippines now, trying to re-find the magic, or so I've heard."

"You have a sister, then?"

"Had. She's gone now." The young Indian fell silent. Part of me wanted to ask more, but Kritchna's face had gone cold and stony. So I decided to refrain. Besides, Appleby was just coming back up with the iodine. Neither of us felt like playing Ishmael and Queequeeg now, so after retiring to Appleby's room, I slumped into a chair while Darshan collapsed into the bed. As I was just about to drop off, I heard Kritchna murmur something softly that should have shot me straight up if I wasn't so exhausted. I forgot about it almost immediately.

"Y'know, I do remember where I've seen that stuff before. My great-uncle showed me some once."

"Really?" I yawned, not able to stay awake a moment longer. "What was it?"

"Oh, just something he said was used in his work. Ectoplasm, I think he called it."

Mrs. Mulligan was indeed not pleased upon learning the fate of her beloved Colleen the next morning, and spent most of breakfast sobbing inconsolably.

Mr. Appleby tried to comfort her the best he could, but to little avail. As for Kritchna and myself, we blinked, and yawned, and looked guiltily into our eggs, but said nothing. I could tell both of us were feeling we should have done more, but really, what else could we have done? The poor thing had been dead even before she had landed on our bed. Things only became worse when Appleby admitted Sir Henry had told him to just toss the body into the incinerator. He was such an unempathic individual.

But like him or not, it was still my duty to assist with the conference, so I dismissed Colleen and turned my mind to the matter at hand. The rest of the security should be arriving that afternoon, and Sir Henry would no doubt have a completely incompetent plan about what to do and when. I'd have to see if I could rearrange that without his knowledge. And then there was–

I almost didn't notice Old Jack slipping a paper next to my plate. "This just came for ye," he said in the longest sentence I had heard from him yet and turned away. Curiously, I tore it open. It was the response to the telegram I had sent to Joseph, answering the query I had about Miss Annunciata's mysterious employer the Sâr Dubnotal. It was short and sweet and simply read:

Harry: Trust him. Joseph.

I sat looking bemusedly at the words. Trust him? Trust an obvious fraud, a man who preyed on the lonely and gullible, who espoused occult nonsense for a quick *sou*? I wondered what was wrong with Joseph. He was usually much more reliable.

"What's that, Dickson?"

"Oh," I crumpled the telegram in my hand. "Nothing, Kritchna. Just an answer to a query I had about the Rutherfords. I had the pleasure of meeting them yesterday."

"The Rutherfords," Mrs. Mulligan paused from her tears long enough to sigh. "Poor people. They're such dears. It's a shame, all the tragedy in their life."

"That reminds me. There's something Old Jack said to me yesterday I didn't understand. I mentioned Miss Christina and he asked 'Did she howl?' What does that mean?"

Mrs. Mulligan and Appleby exchanged glances. "I'll talk to him," the butler rumbled and rose from the table. Mrs. Mulligan rubbed her forehead and sighed again. "Well, we're really not supposed to discuss it. The Rutherfords are fine Christian people–now. It's just that… well… once they weren't."

"Eh?"

"Old stories, Dickson," Kritchna put in. "Nobody really believes them anymore."

"No, go on."

"Oh… well, just this once." Mrs. Mulligan looked very much like she didn't want to be there. "You need to understand that, in the old days, the Rutherfords were just as important around here as the Master's family. They weren't as rich as the Westenras, but old family, you know? In fact, this area used to called Rutherford's Green. But that got changed about the 17th century or so."

"How?"

Mrs. Mulligan took a deep breath. "The Rutherfords were rather... eccentric. They were friendly with a lot of people most folk would rather not associate with back then. Like Jews. And Catholics. And Gypsies. Especially Gypsies. There was a small clan of them that would come around every few years, and old Roger Rutherford would always go out and stay with them a few days. He just said he liked them, but rumor got around that he was learning things from them. Things like black magic and spells. He denied it, but there it was. And then, the sheep started being killed. Everyone thought it was just some dog at first. But then one of the farmers actually got to see the thing. It was big, bigger than any dog had a right to be, and it looked right at him. And then, it laughed."

"It *laughed*?"

"Yes. Laughed. Like 'ha, ha.' It stood there and it laughed at him, and then it ran away. No one had ever seen anything like it. So Christopher Westenra, he was the one who owned the House then, got a bunch of men together to go and hunt the thing. One night, they finally found it, and shot at it–but it got away. But not before Mr. Westenra had wounded it in the leg. And the story goes, they followed it, they followed the trail of blood it left, through the woods and over the fields–until it led right to Rutherford Grange. And inside, they found Roger Rutherford, with his wife and the Gypsy chief, with a wound to the leg

"I suppose you can guess what happened after that. Real dogs don't laugh at people, and how could they shoot it in the leg and find a man right after with a wound in the same leg? Roger Rutherford claimed that he had been out looking for the beast, too; that it was something brought by the Gypsies that had gotten away. He said it had attacked him and bit him in the leg. Nobody believed him. They accused him of being a werewolf; that the Gypsies had taught him how to change his shape, and dragged him and his wife and the old Gypsy chief out of

48

the building and down to the town. They hauled them right to the bridge and without a trial or anything, they…"

"Hung them," I finished for her. "Hence the name Wolfsbridge"

"Yes," she nodded, "And the killings stopped right after that. Of course, the story is that Roger Rutherford swore one day he'd be back for revenge; that his ghost would return and haunt those responsible. But nothing ever happened. And it got to be a joke around town that whenever you said something about a Rutherford, you had to say 'And did he howl?' I think it's awful. Anyway, after that, the Rutherfords–Roger's son was away at school–kind of fell on bad times. But they're good people, now. I hate to think that story's still following them after all these years."

I nodded. Something had come to my mind. "Would you excuse me?" I quickly left the table.

In a moment, I found myself back in the library. Glancing quickly about to see if anyone was present, I swiftly ran my eyes along the shelf, searching for the volume I had snuck a look at the afternoon before. Ah, there it was. Yes: *The Journal of Christopher Westenra.* Flipping quickly through the pages, I located the paragraph I had left off and hurriedly scanned the rest. This is what I read:

"I have buried the body under the bridge where no one will think to look for it. As soon as we have a good flood, the grave will be smoothed out. I dare not let anyone know what I have discovered. If it should be learned, I would be the one hanging off the edge of the bridge, not the Rutherfords. Damn them and their wretched Gypsies! If they had just remembered their place, this never would have happened. Not that I'm sorry Rutherford is dead, but I will forevermore be looking over my shoulder. And damn the beast for not dying when first I shot it. It probably did attack Rutherford, just like he said. But the chance was too good to pass up. Now I am rid of an enemy. But the cost!

"Still, at least the beast is truly dead now. I blew its head apart myself. I still have no idea what it is–it certainly is neither dog nor wolf–but I am well rid of it. But if anyone should learn the truth, my life would be forfeit. May that never be. As for Rutherford's curse before he went over; well–I should be king if I had a penny for the times anyone has damned me. Still, the look on his face– but no. Once again my fears run away with me–"

"Reading something interesting?" came a mild voice.

I whipped around, terrified I was going to find Sir Henry or Alexander about to pounce upon me for reading their private histories. But instead, it proved to be a slight, fair-haired, sallow figure, good-looking in a weak way, who smiled gently at me and said, "Don't worry. I won't tell." He stuck out his hand. "You're the detective, aren't you? Harry Dickson? I'm Peter Westenra."

So this was the son I had not yet met, but had heard so much about. Peter Westenra. I had to admit he looked bloody awful. He had obviously been on the town the night before and had yet to recover. His eyes were red and bleary and his breath still smelled like a keg. And from what I had gleaned of his prefer-

49

ences, I was a bit leery of shaking his hand. But the grip was firm enough and he smiled self-depreciatingly as he said:

"I know it doesn't look it, but I really do hate gin. It's just that when it calls, I must answer." He laughed shortly. "I was just going along to the kitchen to get a glass of tomato juice. Care to come along?"

I must have mumbled something affirmative, trying to turn his attention from the fact I had just violated his family's privacy, but he seemed to take no offense at it. He kept up a patter to small talk as we returned to the kitchen and said:

"Ah, Mrs. Mulligan. I heard what happened last night. I'm so sorry. Where are you going to bury the body? What, the incinerator? That won't do; that won't do at all. Look, there's a little corner of my garden that's rather secluded, why don't you bury her there? What Father doesn't know... no, no, that's all right, Mrs. Mulligan. I had a dog once as a boy, myself." Taking his glass of tomato juice, he sat across from Darshan and I. "So, Dickson, what do you think of Westenra House so far?"

I harrumphed. "It's, well, certainly unique," I began.

"It's the bloody ugliest house in the county," Peter smiled. "Not that I'd ever tell Father that, of course." Despite myself, I smiled back. No, Peter certainly was not like the other Westenras. Beside me, I was aware of Kritchna seeming to relax more. He may have despised the rest of his employers, but he didn't seem to mind Peter. "To be perfectly frank," the young man continued, "I'm not looking forward to this conference at all. It's just another meeting to see what we can get from the Far East without putting anything back. Not that we should just let the Russians have it, of course, but there it is. And I was never good at this diplomacy thing, anyway. Wanted to be a writer, but Father wouldn't hear of it."

He seemed almost pathetically glad to have someone to talk to. I suppose I couldn't blame him. With a family like his, it was probably difficult to have the slightest of meaningful conversations. This was proven just a few seconds later when the door flew open and Alexander burst in.

"Appleby! We're going to have to redo the entire seating arrangements! Nayland Smith just cancelled and–what, are you finally up, Peter? Another bender last night? I suppose I shouldn't be surprised." He shook his head in contempt. For his part, Peter merely shut his eyes and sighed. Alexander continued, totally ignoring the rest of the staff. "It's not like I haven't tried to help, Heaven knows. All the women I introduced you to in India. I even dragged you to a couple of whorehouses, and you know how easy Woggie women are. But no. Still, try at least not to embarrass us at the conference tomorrow, hm? Act like a man for just one night?"

"I'll try, Alexander," Peter said at last, voice low.

"I should hope so. You know how important this is for my–Father's career. Oh, Dickson–" He turned, putting the lowered head and red face of his brother

50

completely out of his mind. "The rest of your crew should be arriving sometime around two. Give them the lay of the place and tell them to meet Sir Henry in the drawing room at four. He'll give you the rest of your orders then. You can handle that, can't you?" He swiveled back as if to go back into the main rooms, only to find his way blocked. For some reason Kritchna had risen and quietly placed himself directly in front of the door.

"Well? Out of the way, boy." There was a pregnant pause, then without a word the young Indian stepped aside.

As soon as Alexander had gone, he said, "Excuse me," and left via the servants' hall

"I should go, too," murmured Peter.

I was left alone in the kitchen, save for Mrs. Mulligan who made a great show of concentrating on the dishes. I tried to absorb all I had just learned.

Why had Kritchna so obviously placed himself in Alexander's way? I knew he hated the man, but that was grounds for dismissal. Was he trying to lose his job? And why was he condescending to work here anyway? He was too intelligent for Service, and it was clear his employers despised his race. Something was going on here And what had killed poor Colleen? What was it Darshan had called the stuff? Ectoplasm? I knew what that was–chemical mixtures used by fraudulent Spiritualists to make suckers think something came from "Beyond." I thought of the upcoming séance at Rutherford Grange. Did that have something to do with it? Had Miss Annunciata been trying to play some sort of prank on us? I smiled grimly. She was a beautiful woman, but was no more a psychic than Roger Rutherford was a real werewolf, no matter what the superstitious peasants of the 17th century had believed. Spiritualism was all rubbish! Rubbish!

The rest of the day passed uneventfully as I made a concerted effort to keep my mind on my official duties. What had happened 300 years ago was none of my business, what was going on at Rutherford Grange was none of my business, and the relationships between the Westenras and their staff was none of my business. I did not see Kritchna for the rest of the day. I was concerned, but decided that, whatever was happening, he should handle it. He was an adult and did not have to let me into his personal affairs if he wished. I had more pressing matters.

As Alexander had stated, the rest of the conference's security force arrived at about two. We gathered for a brief discussion, and I found them much as Mr. Blake had predicted. Good-hearted. Eager to please. Bovine. Most had been expecting Blake himself, and when they found I was merely his apprentice, they smiled, patted me on the head–not literally but the metaphor was annoying enough–and told me how lucky I was. Clearly, I would get nowhere with them. If anything truly bad were to happen, I would be on my own.

Kritchna reappeared at dinner, making no comment on his odd behavior, and I did not pry. Once again, we bunked together in his garret (now clean with fresh linen) but made only small talk.

The night passed without incident, and bright and early the next morning I rose, put on the fine suit Sir Henry had lent me, and went downstairs to watch the official guests arrive.

For all his haranguing, Sir Henry's rules for our behavior had been quite simple. Keep quiet, do not speak to anyone of the least importance, keep out of the way, and, above all, do not touch the food. The others smiled and nodded like eager puppies, caring only for the wages at the end of the weekend. I simply said I would endeavor to satisfy. Sir Henry stated that remained to be seen.

As per my instruction, I hung back in a little alcove off the Great Hall as the officials arrived, mentally checking each one off as they came. There was Hale, usually connected with China but brought in from previous experiences in India. D'Athys, well-known explorer of Indochina. Ingles, the writer. A dozen others, all their hordes of faceless assistants. They milled about, smiling, joking, renewing old acquaintances though the formal introductions would not come until dinner. And then, at the end, the most important and famous of all. The Duc d'Origny.

He must have been an astoundingly handsome man in his youth; now age had faded that somewhat but even so, he carried himself with an air of poise and dignity that many of his much younger compatriots lacked. But it was neither cold nor self-important; his was the confidence of a man comfortable with both his strengths and flaws, a man who knew what he was capable of but who was not afraid to laugh at himself. The Duc d'Origny neither wanted nor needed any prestige, and it was that, more than anything, that made him such a natural leader. He accepted Sir Henry's gushing welcome and posturing with good grace, clearly realizing here was a weak man with little to offer, but willing to suffer him for a while for the greater good. Still, it was a surprise when he caught a glimpse of me out of the corner of his eye and instantly diverted his steps to come and shake my hand.

"The Duc d'Origny, young fellow. And you are?"

If my eyes were raised, Sir Henry's were practically bulging. Any more and his optic nerves would rip themselves out. Still, my mother had raised me to be honest. "Harry Dickson, Your Grace. I'm afraid I'm not a guest, just a security officer."

"There's nothing 'just' about it, young man," the Duc replied in his perfect English. "Every position is an important one in some way or other, and nothing to be in the least shamed over. Remember that. And now, Sir Henry, you were saying something about my quarters?" He smiled again, turned and rejoined his host, who by this time was suffering from massive eyestrain. I couldn't help but grin. This was going to be an interesting conference after all.

I had no idea.

The dinner was finished, the brandy and cigars broken out, and the guests shuffled slowly out of the dining room into the main hall. The hired musicians started up their instruments as Appleby and the other servants, dressed in their best, moved in unobtrusive grace among the crowd, refilling glasses and ready to answer every need. About them the guests mingled, sipping their brandies, chatting blandly about general politics, the weather and other such mundanities. The real discussions would not begin until the morrow. This was merely an after-dinner party, not the conference proper.

I hung back a reasonable distance from the main crowd, keeping a sharp eye on the proceedings. So far, all had gone well, if you discounted the fact most of the rest of the "security" had been surreptitiously helping themselves to the liqueurs for quite some time now. A few were just teetering out now to go on "patrol." I sighed. It was so hard to find good help these days.

Among the crowd, I noticed Darshan; the handsome Indian cutting a striking figure in his finery. Not that anyone was paying much attention to him. He was merely a servant, and a Hindu at that. The fact that they were there to discuss the future of his own homeland mattered not one jot. Still, I couldn't help but wonder why some young maid back in Bombay hadn't snapped him up yet. Ah, well. It was none of my business, really. If Kritchna wanted to tell me his secrets, he'd do so on his own time. Still, I was supremely grateful when he sidled up to me, casually handed me a brandy and said, "You look as bored as I feel."

"Worse," I replied, sipping the drink. "I need a smoke. But Sir Henry made it clear we mere detectives were to keep out of the way and not have any fun at all. Not that it's stopped any of the others."

"True," Kritchna grinned. "Two of them have been taking turns kneeling on the floor of the loo since the brandy came out. God, what help. But if you insist on doing things on the cheap, you get what you pay for. Present company excepted, of course."

"Of course," I smiled. "Have you seen the Duc yet, by the way?"

"As a matter of fact, he actually spoke to me for a moment. I was giving him a drink and he insisted on asking me what part of India I was from, what I thought of the Russian threat and so on. Charming man. If only half the rest of these were like him rather than the host. And look, there's the Great Man now, lording over his court." He nodded toward the center of the room, and, sure enough, there stood Sir Henry, pontificating to anyone within earshot of the sorry state of Empire and how the Lower Classes didn't know their places anymore. At his right hand waited Alexander, nodding at whatever his father had to say, while a few paces back stood Peter, shuffling his feet and looking like he very much didn't want to be there.

"Well, I'd better get back to the guests," Kritchna said. "But, gad, this is tedious. I'd almost rather be at that séance they're holding at the Grange. At least, it would have to be more interesting than this."

"Please," I rolled my eyes.

"Not interested?"

"Several years ago, my father was approached by a man who showed him a frog. He said this frog had the ability to put on a little top hat and sing ragtime. Needless to say, all that frog did was sit there and croak. And that's all the dead can do. Sit there and croak."

Kritchna snickered. "All right, Dickson, all right. You sound just like my father–eh?" His head swiveled toward the front door. Nor was his the only one. A sudden hush had fallen over the entire crowd and everyone was turning to stare at the new arrival who had just stepped majestically into the foyer, closing the door behind him. A tall, erect figure, radiating self-importance, who gazed out calmly at the crowd with the slightest glint of amusement in his eyes. A figure who had definitely not been invited.

I knew, for I had made a point of going over photographs of every one of the official guests. None even approached the appearance of this man. Tall, as I said, with a patrician, hawk-like face that held an air of dignity and intelligence I had seen in few others. His features were definitely European in origin, but with his darkly tanned skin, as bronzed as Roxton's, his neat, immaculately groomed beard and spotless white turban resting comfortably upon his dark hair, he would've passed easily for an Arab or Sikh. Nor was this his only concession to the East. While his suit was European in fashion, and of the finest cut, around his waist rested a long, multicolored kilt-like garment I would later learn was called a *lungi*, a decoration from India. The combination of attires was jarring enough in this sea of cummerbunds and tuxedos, but there was something else, an aura of knowledge and dominance about the man that was unnerving. At his feet rested a large, perfectly ordinary carpetbag.

"I truly apologize for disturbing your soirée," he stated in a pleasant voice, "but no one answered the door so I was obliged to let myself in. Tell me, does anyone know if the Duc d'Origny is present? I just endured a most tedious train ride to get here and would like to see him."

Darshan leaned close to me, frowning. "So who thinks he's Doctor Mystery, then?"

"I don't know," I grunted, "but he's about to leave." I began roughly pushing my way through the throng. Sir Henry was going to roll someone's head over this, and I was determined it was not going to be mine. Murmurings were already shooting up and down the gathering: "Who is that? Some damned native lover, it looks like," but none dared confront him.

It was Appleby who reached him first, taking a card the stranger produced smilingly. The butler peered at it curiously a moment, then, in an uncertain voice, announced, "The, ah, Sâr Dubnotal. The Great Psychagogue, Napoleon of the Intangible and Conqueror of the Invisible!"

The Sâr Dubnotal? Good Lord! What was that pretender doing here? Shouldn't he be at Grange, if anywhere? I had to get him out of here, and quickly. "All right, sir," I started as I reached him, "kindly explain yourself and why you have just intruded into a private conference..." I stopped in my tracks. For as I spoke, the patrician features had turned to me and I had to take a step back. His eyes. They were the deepest I have ever seen, glinting like sunlight on water, yet dark, boring, hypnotic, locking onto yours as drawing you in until you feared you would be lost in them forever.

"I never explain myself, young man," he said to me calmly. "It's entirely unnecessary. Suffice to say that I am the Sâr Dubnotal and that I am here." His smile grew broader. He didn't seem angry, just that his very presence should answer everything. It didn't, of course, and I was about to tell him so when I was interrupted:

"Doctor! Doctor, is that you?"

Immediately, the Sâr had turned his back to us, throwing out his arms in welcome. "Michel! My dear dear friend!" And he was embracing none other than the Duc d'Origny as if he were a long-lost brother!

"Doctor!" the Duc exclaimed, hugging the new arrival with the greatest of enthusiasm. "How long has it been?"

"Six years, ever since our adventure at the Devil's Gate, old friend! Far too long! How are you?"

"Fine! Whatever are you doing here? Were you invited?"

"No, no–I was in London visiting a friend on Cheyne Walk. We were interviewing an archaeologist about some very interesting occurrences on the Siberian Express a few years ago. But when Gianetti called and told me you'd be here, I just had to drop everything and come and see you!"

"Well, I'm glad you did! You're right, it has been far too long! Oh, by the way, may I present M. Dickson? He has the honor of heading security for the conference." He gestured kindly toward me.

"Yes," the Sâr beamed, giving a slight bow. "My assistant told me I might have the pleasure of meeting you. The Rational Skeptic." He made an amused little clucking sound in his throat. Clearly he had met "Rational Skeptics" before.

This more than a little irritated me, so despite the presence of the Duc, I flushed and responded hotly, "I am, sir. And proud of it. It is the Rational Skeptics that made the advances that pulled the world out of the Dark Ages, not those who claimed to follow the guidance of so-called 'spirits' and ended up dragging themselves and everyone who would listen into the black pit of superstition and occultic nonsense."

"Like me, of course," the Sâr's smile didn't fade.

"Yes." Every eye in the Hall was upon me, but I ignored them, turning instead to the Duc. "I apologize, Your Grace, if this man is indeed an old friend of yours. But I will not have myself and the teachings of my mentor spoken down to by anyone who fancies himself the 'Conqueror of the Invisible.' " I wheeled back toward the Sâr, daring him to reply.

He did. He burst out laughing. "Excellent, Dickson, excellent!" he clapped his hands. "Well-spoken, indeed! Shake hands, sir; I'm glad to know you!" Before I could protest, he was pumping my right hand vigorously. "I see Gianetti did not lie when she spoke so highly of your spirit! And I'm certain Michel takes no offense, do you, Michel? Indeed, I find it an absolute pleasure to meet such a determined unbeliever in the Ab-Normal. As, I can plainly see, you are as well, sir." He glanced toward Appleby.

"I?" The butler frowned. "I am a follower of the Lord Jesus Christ, sir. I refuse to have any truck with such satanic claptrap as the raising of spirits."

"And very wise, too, for the raising of spirits is far more dangerous that the popularity of Spiritualism would have to believe. But the fact you are a Christian nevertheless means you believe in something supernatural, does it not? No? Yes? Well, no matter. I am by no means a Christian myself, but better to have faith in something beyond yourself than faith in nothing at all." His eyes flicked pointedly toward me "Nevertheless, you are correct for the most part, Dickson. Most of so-called 'occult phenomena' is merely delusions or frauds specializing in smoke and mirrors. Ninety-nine percent, at least. But it is the remaining one percent that make all the difference."

"Perhaps," I started, "But I—"

"Mr. Dickson," the Duc suddenly said. "I can guess how odd my friend's methods must seem to you. But believe me when I say they work. With this man I have seen... wonders. And terrors. He does not boast when he says there is more out there than Man can fathom."

I sighed. This was getting out of hand. "Be that as it may, Your Grace. But the fact remains I have a duty and this man is a trespasser at a sensitive Government Conference. If you do vouch for him, something may be done, but if not, I am afraid I must ask him to leave before—"

"*Dickson!!!!*"

"That happens." But it was already too late. The rotund form of Sir Henry Westenra loomed over us like a just-awakened bear while everyone else in the area quickly turned their heads and started making their way to the far sides of the hall. Alexander, ubiquitous as ever, hovered at his father's side as he roared, "Who is this man, Dickson? What kind of security do you call this? How did he get in, and why hasn't he been removed?"

He made as if to physically grab at the Sâr but the tall, regal man turned his deep, intense eyes right upon him. Sir Henry froze instantly.

"I realize that I arrived here without an invitation, Sir Henry," the Sâr began in a cool, quiet voice. "But I was certain my dear friend the Duc here would speak up for me. My actions were admittedly rude and I fully intended to apologize for them, but I have not met my friend here in so long I simply could not pass up the opportunity to see him again."

Sir Henry's eyes flashed from the Sâr to the Duc, from the Duc to me, and back again

"I concur, Sir Henry," the Duc put in. "My friend the Doctor here has never been known for his tact, but I would stake my life on him. I give you my word he intends no harm toward this conference. So, you can do one of two things. You can welcome him as my personal guest, at my responsibility, or you can continue to look like a complete and total jackanapes in front of your guests." He folded his arms defiantly.

The Duc's words seemed not only to break the spell over Sir Henry, but deflate him as well. He vented a huge amount of air out his mouth as he tried to regain his composure and color. "I...see, Your Grace," he stated at last. "Please, forgive me. Certainly, if you recommend him I would be... glad to have this gentleman here for the evening. In fact, why don't you go out into the gardens and talk there? It's lovely and quite private. Alexander can show you where it is." He nodded toward his son, and, as if by a prearranged signal, the younger put his arm around the Duc, guiding him away. "Right this way, Your Grace."

"But I think—"

"Oh, it's no trouble at all, Your Grace." And they were out of earshot.

Very, very slowly, Sir Henry turned back to us, glaring evilly. "We. Will. Speak Of. This. Later." And he stalked away, pulling Appleby with him.

"Well," said the Sâr, "it seems my presence has gotten you in a bit of a mess, Dickson."

"You think so?"

"Now don't go losing your temper, young man. As it happens, I've had occasion to meet your mentor a time or two. We don't really get on, but I'm sure that if something should happen, I can cover things for you. But who is this?" He glanced behind me.

Kritchna was waiting there, regarding the proceedings with a wry eye. "So you haven't thrown Prince Zaleski out yet?"

"That's the Sâr Dubnotal, young man, although I prefer 'Doctor' or 'El Tebib' if you know Arabic," the Sâr snapped sharply. "I take it you're one of the servants here." Then he frowned, peering intently as the young Indian. "Tell me, sir, are you at all psychic?"

"Me?" Kritchna's eyes rose at the unexpected question. "No. Why?"

"Are you certain? You should be." The Doctor's eyes probed the servant up and down intensely. "Your aura is one of the strongest I've ever seen. It practically screams of psychic potential. Dickson doesn't have it; my friend Michel doesn't have it, and as for our host—well, he's practically sterile. But you—the only ones I've seen nearly so powerful are those of my assistant, some old enemies of mine, and my fellow countryman, M. Solange. And the Figalillys, but they're so fey."

"I–I'm afraid I have no idea what you're talking about."

"No? Well, never mind. As I said, I'm merely here to see my friend. Nothing more."

"Nothing?" I asked. "So you're not here for the séance at Rutherford Grange?"

"Not in the least. Why should I? It smacks of pure fakery anyway, and my assistant is more than capable of exposing that. Grigori Yeltsin? Never heard of him. Probably a false name. No, I am simply here to–"

But what he was about to say, we would never learn. For, suddenly, the air was rent with the most horrified scream of shock and pain I have ever heard. It screeched through the room like a sharp, tentacly knife, sending shudders down the spine of everyone who heard. Then it was gone–cut off as quickly as it had come.

The crowed stood frozen in stunned silence. The scream had come from the gardens. And now came another sound–a long, loud, mournful howl, as if from the throats of a dozen dogs. It hung like a dirge over us and ended in a crescendo of snarls. I have never heard the like before.

"Michel!" the Sâr cried.

That was all I needed to hear. I tore through the crowd toward the garden doors, shoving my way past servants and diplomats alike. A mere half-pace behind me dashed the Sâr, gripping his carpetbag. For him, the crowd parted like the Red Sea. But no sooner had he passed than they immediately fell in behind him, trooping for the garden.

I pulled the glass-enclosed doors open with a mighty yank, my shoes clattering over the cobblestones of the walk. The Doctor was but a step behind. He very nearly collided with me as I stopped short, unable to believe what I was seeing.

"My God!" I heard a voice exclaim in a quaver–and was astonished to realize it was my own. For was what waiting before me was a scene of sheer impossibility

Alexander Westenra lay flat on his back, head bloody from a gash in his forehead, desperately trying to crawl backwards from the horror looming over him. Half a yard away upon the grass the body of the Duc d'Origny lay, eyes staring, a mass of red flesh and bone jutting out from where his throat had been. And standing over them like a nightmare, bent over Alexander in a bent parody of human posture, claws and teeth dripping with crimson, was a wolf. A wolf fully seven feet high at the shoulder, black-furred, eyes glowing redly, shimmering with power and muscle. A wolf looming upright–upright!–on its hind legs, legs that ended in long, splayed feet like that of a distorted kangaroo's, reaching out its forelimbs toward the elder Westenra scion greedily. The paws on those forelimbs were too large, too thick for real paws. They looked more like the three-fingered hand of a giant. It stepped forward, clumsily, as if uncertain of its balance, but unhesitatingly toward its prey.

It was laughing.

Laughing, a deep, rumbling, from the center of the torso laughter. "Hree ree ree." And with each step there was a peculiar sucking sound, like water sloshing in a paper bag.

Instantly, I knew what had killed Colleen two nights before.

"Lord save us!" screamed a voice I recognized as Appleby's. "It's the Werewolf! The Werewolf of Rutherford Grange!"

Impossible, I thought automatically. What was standing before us, salivating blood and foam from its jaws, could not possibly be the legendary Werewolf of Rutherford Grange. Why? Because werewolves did not exist, that's why! Werewolves did not exist!

If so, someone should have told the terror bending over Alexander Westenra. It threw back its head and howled, a bellow filled with hate and malice. With a little hop, it advanced before the cringing man. Then with a ravenous snarl, it sprang–

–And something rushed past me with the velocity of an exploding volcano, literally launching itself into the air to pound itself right in the center of the creature's chest, knocking it off its already precarious balance and causing both of them to fly backwards, skidding across the hard cobble.

For a moment, the Beast actually looked surprised. But it had no time to digest what had happened for now its attacker was furiously beating it across the face and snout with a fireplace poker it had seized, slamming the black bar against it again and again

"*No!*" Darshan Kritchna roared. "That bastard's *mine!*"

"Darshan!" I cried, the shock of what I was seeing freeing me from my temporary immobility. I dashed forward, not thinking of the danger, just knowing I had to do something, when the Beast–for I can call it nothing else– screeched and with a mighty heave of a powerful arm, swatted the man away like a gnat. Kritchna flew back, colliding with a set of patio chairs. He rolled over, groaning, and lay still.

The Beast was already back upon its feet, snarling, and shot a hand-paw out toward me. I felt myself hoisted off my feet and then everything turned on its head as I found myself hurtling through the air to land almost right upon a panicked Alexander Westenra. I was only able to extricate myself when a hand grabbed me by the collar and pulled; Peter Westenra had seized his brother and myself and was desperately trying to haul us to safety.

Everywhere else, pandemonium was ensuing, as diplomats, servants, aides, musicians and everyone else screamed and headed for the doors, shoving, cursing, trying to push their ways inside before the monster could charge them.

"Alexander!" screamed Sir Henry and shoved his other son away to grab at his eldest boy. A thick foot landed on my chest as he pulled Alexander to safety. Unseen, Peter quickly joined them. But the Sâr was moving forward; at the first sight of the creature, he had dropped to his knee, grabbing his carpetbag, and tore it open to pull out what looked like–Good Heavens! Some sort of semi-large, vaguely star-shaped stone. What did he plan to do with that, bean the creature?

Apparently not, for he thrust out the hand gripping the stone like a crucifix, showing a side that had some sort of drab, rune-like figure painted on it. From his mouth flowed a torrent of strange words, in a tongue I could not identify.

The Beast stopped dead in its tracks. In the Sâr's hand, the Stone almost seemed to glow–but it had to have been a trick of my blurry vision and the moonlight. "*Isha Thar Ch'tanid!*" the man seemed to be saying, and the Beast pulled back. But then it struck out, arm moving like lightning, sending the stone from the Sâr's hand skittering over the cobbles and the Sâr himself into the lawn. Shaking as if in pain, it whipped around to find any other threats.

It was something I would never have imagined of him, but somewhere in the portly frame of Mr. Appleby was a wellspring of courage previously unseen. He darted between the Beast and his masters, making the Sign of the Cross in the air and screaming, "In the name of God, *begone!*"

At the words, the Beast flinched, as if having been struck, lightly. It paused for only a moment, then the massive jaws split into a skeletal grin and it lunged its teeth for the servant's throat. Appleby fell over, tripped by his own feet, just in time. "Lord Jesus help me!"

Once again the Beast dropped back a bit, as if in some pain. Struggling to rise, still smarting from my blow, I tried to clear my head enough to think. Why was the Beast pausing? At Appleby's pleas? But those were merely words–weren't they? And what had the Sâr been thinking of?

Whatever it was, Appleby's delay gave the Doctor enough time to roll for the odd star-shaped stone again. Sweeping it up, he shot to his feet in a fluid movement, thrust it out once again and cried: "*Ch'nan vykos Nodens ka!*" Whatever that meant. And, in almost the same breath, "Do it again, man! The prayers! Say the prayers!"

For a dazed moment, I wondered whom he was yelling to, but then Appleby started again with the pleas to his God: "Our Father, Who Art in Heaven, Hallow'd Be Thy Name..."

Simultaneously, the Sâr advanced quickly upon the Beast, shouting out in his unintelligible tongue.

The Beast stopped, roared, and began to tremble violently. Caught between the two "chanters," it trembled like a cord strung between batteries–at least, that's the thought that came to my mind. It staggered, swaying drunkenly upon its legs, and for a moment, it seemed as if the fur and muscle of the creature was actually shimmering. Then, it twisted, falling down upon all fours, and darted away across the lawn for the wall separating the estate from the outside world.

With one spring, it shot into the air, clearing the top with inches to spare, and vanished down the other side–and the wall was a good ten feet in height. Then there came one long, last howl–and it was gone.

It seemed an eternity before anyone moved. Then like a wave it hit, voices everywhere at once going: "God, what was that thing?" "A monster!" "The Duc! The poor Duc!" "What if it comes back? We've got to get out of here!"

In the midst of the crowd, Alexander was mopping his brow. "We had just came out to the garden when that thing leaped over the wall! Before either of us could move, it grabbed the Duc and tore his throat out right in front of me! Then it came for me! Me! I just thank God I'm alive!"

Sir Henry patted his shoulder. "There, son, you're safe now. I saved you."

Darshan and myself slowly picked ourselves up, heads aching. We looked at each other, daring the other to speak first. "Why?" I said at last.

"Because I want to kill him," Kritchna said quietly.

The Sâr had risen and carefully picked up his star-stone, looking out in the direction the creature had gone. "Where does that lead?" he asked quietly.

"Toward Rutherford Grange," replied Kritchna.

The Sâr said nothing. He pocketed the stone and went to the prone body of the Duc. Gently he knelt, cradling the staring head a moment. "My dear, dear friend." Then he gently closed the corpse's eyes.

"You!" The Doctor found Appleby standing over him. "What are you? A witch of some kind? A magician? Are you responsible for that–that thing?"

"Neither and no," the Sâr snapped back. "What that Beast was and why it was here, I haven't the slightest. Yet. As for myself, I am merely a student of the Ancient Mysteries."

"A student of the Devil, more like! I saw you use that talisman!"

"I'll admit the Star-Stones have no particular link to Christianity," the Sâr snapped, "they represent other Powers. But *not* the Powers of Darkness–they were created to ward off evil, not strengthen it You have nothing to fear from me, Christian. The Powers I serve may not be exactly yours, but they are on the same side."

"That's impossible! There's only one God! I don't know who you are, but I know deviltry when I see it!"

"So do I," the Sâr gestured angrily. "And it just went over that wall. It's killed one of my dearest friends, it almost killed one of your masters, and if I don't get after it now, it will certainly kill again! If you cannot help me, Appleby, then kindly get out of my way! I must–here! Release me, sir!"

These last words were not said to Appleby but to Sir Henry, who had come up from behind him and seized the Sâr by the arm.

"You!" the master of Westenra House roared. "I don't know how you did it, but you've ruined everything! This didn't happen until you arrived! Alexander! Peter! Hold this man until I figure out what to do! Everyone else, stop! Come back! No–no Police! My career–I mean, we can't let this get out! Everything here is too sensitive! Wait! And you–" With his other hand he grabbed me. "You were supposed to be running security here! What kind do you call this? Now a guest is dead from some animal and my son was nearly killed! How dare you? How dare you?" He was shaking me violently and I was in no further mood for it.

"Let go of me now, Sir Henry."

"Why? What you are going to do, boy, tell your employer? Your former employer when I get through with him?"

Something poked the fat man in the neck. The tip of a fireplace poker. "He said to let go of him, Westenra," Darshan said dangerously. "Now."

"Kritchna, stop!" Appleby cried.

"Not this time," Kritchna said coolly. "I've been wanting to do something like this to you for a long time, Westenra, after what your son did to my family. And I will if you don't let Dickson go. Right now." He pressed a bit upon the skin for emphasis.

"What are you talking about?"

"Oh, don't tell me you don't know. You and Alexander–Appleby! Let go!" He tried to wrench the poker from the butler's grasp but the elder man held firm. "Stop this, Darshan, before it's too late!"

"It *is* too late," came a voice and Alexander grabbed the Indian about the waist, pulling him away from his father. Arrogantly, he tossed him to the ground. "What do you mean, you damnable woggie?"

"My sister!" snarled Kritchna staring up at the man. Blazing hatred shone in his eyes. "Ashanti!"

"Ashanti?" Alexander blinked. "Ashanti? Who–what, you mean that little whore from Bombay? She was your sister?"

"She was," spat the Indian, "And she was no whore. Ever. You seduced her. Like you did dozens of other girls. Then when you got her pregnant you threw her aside!"

Alexander snorted. "Please. Not my fault. If the girl couldn't control herself around white men, it's no affair of mine. And I'm certainly not going to take responsibility for some little mulatto. Anyway, last I heard, she lost the brat, anyway."

"She did."

Alexander shook his head, glancing in bewildered amusement at his father, his brother and the crowd who stood listening. "What, you're blaming me?" he asked the latter. "Please. It's not like I didn't do what any of you've not done in India. Besides, think about this ridiculous idiot here. He decides to come to England and infiltrate my family's staff, just so he can get revenge on me for a woggie stillborn!"

"For more than that," growled Kritchna. "Oh, don't look so innocent. You know what else you did. The very day your family leaves to go back here, my sister disappears from Bombay! You killed her! I know you did! I've been looking for proof ever since I got here! What did you do to the body, drop it in the river?"

Now Alexander actually looked surprised. "What are you talking about? I never saw the bitch after I told her to get out. I suppose I should thank you for saving my life from that–that creature, but knowing why you did it, I won't. In fact, I think I'm going to throw you out like I did her!"

He lunged for the younger man. Automatically, I broke away from Sir Henry, thrusting myself into Alexander, but suddenly a dozen hands from everywhere had seized me and were dragging me away, through the House and out the front door, through the gardens toward the gate. I was vaguely aware of voices, apparently Peter's and Appleby's, crying out in protest, but it was no good. The gate was flung open and the hands shoved me forward, and both Darshan and I landed undignified onto the road. The gate slammed shut behind us.

For a few minutes, we just lay there, panting as the voices faded. Then, slowly, we rose

"Well," Kritchna said ironically, dusting himself off. "That could've gone better."

I hit him.

"What did you do that for?"

"Just what did you think you were up to, you imbecile? Were you just going to up and murder Alexander in his sleep? Is that it? For what, because you think he murdered your sister? Where's your proof?"

"I was looking for it!"

"So that's why you lied about going to the cinema. Let me guess, questioning the villagers to see if any of them knew anything? I thought so. Damn it, why didn't you just tell me your suspicions? I'm a detective! I could've helped!"

"Vengeance belongs to my family," Kritchna said without remorse.

"Well, you know what's going to happen now, don't you? Eventually Sir Henry is going to think *you* sent that–that whatever-it-was to kill his son!"

"Oh. I hadn't thought of that."

"Did you?"

"Send that thing? No. I don't even know what it was, and that's the truth. Appleby said something about it being a werewolf. A werewolf? Do you really think so?"

I finally paused, out of breath and my imagination and emotions exhausted. "I don't know," I said at last. "But I do know I've got to get you out of here. I honestly believe you were as surprised as I was about the appearance of that Beast, but it won't be long before they're coming after you for it. Now the only way to prove your innocence is to catch it."

"I'm so glad to hear you say that." From out of the bushes along the road, the Sâr emerged, carting his carpetbag as always. "I have a friend to avenge, and could certainly use your help."

I glared at him suspiciously. "How'd you get out here?"

"Climbed over the wall during the melee."

"And how do we know *you* didn't have anything to do with this?"

The Doctor's eyes turned cold. "You don't. But if you don't want your friend there to end up in jail or worse, you have no choice but to trust me. Now, quickly, into the bushes! I hear cars coming!" Without preamble, he was shoving us into the rushes, and for some reason we let him. Just as we did so, the gates to Westenra House swung open and a parade of cars sailed out, as fast as their wheels would carry them. We were close enough to see some of the drivers' faces; they were the aides of many of the diplomats attending.

"Looks like the conference is over," whispered Kritchna. "Do you think they're getting the Police?"

I shook my head. "I doubt it. Try explaining what happened to a country constable. No, if I know Westenra, he's going to do his damnedest to keep this whole thing quiet. If this got out, it would mean the end of his career. Not that it will work. The guests are bound to tell their superiors. Then, God knows what will happen."

"But it gives us an edge, nonetheless," replied the Doctor. "A few hours, at any rate. Dickson–you mentioned the Werewolf of Rutherford Grange. Tell me about it, quickly." Without knowing why, I did so. At the end, the Sâr frowned. "I have never heard this legend. And while I am no expert on therianthropology, I know enough. We must get to this Grange at once. Kritchna, do you know the way?"

"Certainly."

"Then let us go. My assistant is there already–and I have a very ugly feeling about this."

Hastily but cautiously, we slipped along the rest of the wall through the shrubbery, pricking ourselves several times but not daring to speak. Once on the far side, the foliage ended into long, grassy fields along the road–and no cover. We would have to be extremely careful, and not just to avoid being found by the Westenras. This was the direction the Beast had gone.

"Do you think it's still out there?"

The Sâr smiled grimly. "I'm sure we'll find out."

We moved quickly down the road, keeping our senses peeled for any signs of pursuit. There was nothing. Apparently the Westenras were too busy simply trying to save their conference to waste time chasing us. The Moon was out, giving us an excellent view of our surroundings. So it was that, about a half-mile down, we first saw the burly figure draped limply across the middle of the path.

The Beast lay still, its sides slowly rising and falling, but otherwise it did not move. It appeared to be dying. Cautiously, the Doctor removed another Star-

Stone from his voluminous bag. He held it out toward the creature, murmuring words I could not clearly hear, but the Beast made no attempt to rise. It stared at us with its red eyes, panting, the face bruised where Darshan had struck it.

"How could this be?" I found myself whispering. "It's impossible."

"Many things in this world are 'impossible,' Dickson," the Sâr said quietly, "But they happen anyway."

"Should we kill it? Or run?" asked Kritchna nervously.

"Neither, I think. If it could've attacked us, it would've by now. It's hurt. The trouble is, I don't know why. This is most peculiar. The Star-Stone and the Incantations of Nodens should be drawing the curse out of this poor man, not physically harming him. He should've become human again by now." He paused. "In fact, it should have worked the first time back at the House. Why didn't it? They were clearly affecting it, but not as they should have. The only time this poor creature actually seemed truly struck was when both Appleby and I worked together."

"That reminds me," I said, "just how was all this supposed to work? Appleby was praying. Does that mean there's really a–"

"Not necessarily, Dickson," the Sâr said. "But what Appleby has is faith. That is great power in and of itself. Faith really does move mountains, you know. Sometimes it doesn't even really matter if the thing you believe in exists or not."

"He certainly didn't take to you afterwards," Darshan pointed out.

"He was frightened and disturbed by what he could not understand. I don't blame him for that. But this is getting off the subject. We need to find out why this creature exists, and who it really is. Look! Something's happening."

The Beast raised its head and whimpered. All about it, from the tip of its toes to the tips of its ears, the entire mass of fur and skin somehow seemed to be shifting. Flowing downward off the body like water.

Fangs dripped away into nothingness, skeletal structure and musculature ran off into pools of liquid upon the ground. It was incredible. This was not blood or any other bodily fluid, this was the body itself, turning into a thick, gooey substance that poured off itself, the form growing smaller and smaller as it did. With a shock, I realized I knew what the stuff was. It was the very goo I had found on the bushes beneath Darshan's garret two nights before.

"Ectoplasm," I heard the Sâr mutter. "This is unheard of."

For both of us, I thought. The head and snout had almost entirely melted away by now, slowly coming to reveal a wet mass of blond hair beneath the fur. Claws fell away, showing the long pink fingers of a woman. Chest and back fur slipped away into the remains of a crumbled blue dress. At last the full features of the person under the Beast became clear and I gasped in astonishment.

"Christina! Christina Rutherford!" I cried disbelievingly. "Christina Rutherford is a werewolf?"

65

The prone figure of Miss Christina Rutherford lay across the road before our stunned eyes; beautiful features marred by streaks of goo and thick bruises. Hair, skin and dress were sopping wet from the pouring away of the glop that had surrounded her–ectoplasm the Doctor called it–and her eyes, while open, stared blankly at us. Then it seemed as if recognition and memory all flowed back at once. Her mouth opened and she let out a howl, not of wolf-like malice and hatred, but one of terror, a long, drawn-out wail of horror and misery. She tried to rise but fell back, screaming: "Mama! Mama!"

Curiously, it was Darshan who first knelt and gathered her up, pulling her close. "It's all right, Miss, it's all right. You're safe now"

"My God! Mother! Mama!"

"Miss Rutherford!" The Sâr gently took her from Kritchna. "My assistant, Gianetti. Where is she? Is she safe? What do you remember?"

"Gianetti?" She paused, not recognizing this man and unable to find the words to answer him. "I–I remember sitting at the table. Mama was there, and Uncle John, and Gianetti–and we were calling on Papa–and then–and then…"

"Go on," the Sâr said softly.

"And then…. and then, I felt hate. The most vicious hate. Coming over me."

"Hate? From within? Like something was invading your soul?"

"No…" Christina shook her head. "Like… like something from outside was covering me up, cocooning me. And I saw Uncle John jump and Mama screamed… and then I reached out for her but my hands weren't my hands any-more–and I–and I–" She burst into tears. "Mama!"

"Enough," Darshan demanded. "Leave her alone."

"Someone's coming," I interjected.

The beams of headlights were flashing through the night toward us, but not from the direction of Westenra House–from the opposite, the direction of the Grange. In an instant, a car which I recognized as the Rutherfords' own swerved toward us, screeching to a halt by the side of the road, nearly banking into the ditch.

Lord John Roxton was out of the driver's seat before it was even fully braked. A rifle was slung over his shoulder. "Christina! Thank God you've found her!" Without preambles, he shoved the Sâr away to take his niece in his arms. He looked haggard. "Christina, Christina, it's Uncle John. It's all right."

"Doctor!" cried another, and an equally-haggard Gianetti Annunciata climbed out of the passenger side, racing toward her mentor. "Doctor, what are you doing here?" She seized his hands. He smiled down at her, in evident relief, but if she would have liked more, he made no move toward it.

"Gianetti, what has happened? Tell me everything!"

"Doctor, it's horrible! Mrs. Rutherford is dead! Killed by that creature!"

"It's worse than that, my dear. It was here too. It killed Michel."

"The Duc? He was killed too? Oh, sweet Mary."

"Doctor?" Roxton said. "Your employer's here? My God! It's you!"

"Ah." The Doctor smiled, briefly. "Hello, Roxton."

"You're this 'Sâr Dubnotal' character? You? Back when I knew you in India, you called yourself–"

"No names, please." The Sâr held up a warning hand. "I left that identity behind a long time ago. For good reason. But the past isn't the issue right now. This young lady here is."

"You're right," Roxton replied. "In the car. We'll talk as we go. Christina, do you think you can walk? Let me help." Gently he placed his arm around the girl and assisted her to the vehicle. Gianetti took her other side. Gently, they set Christina into the passenger side, and Gianetti slid in beside her. Roxton looked at us, particularly the Sâr.

"Well, if you're coming, get in. This sounds like something you'd be involved in. Damn that séance!"

"Right," said the Sâr. "In!" Almost without thinking, Kritchna and I obediently piled into the back. The Sâr followed and the automobile revved into life, turning around and heading back the way it came.

"Uncle... Uncle John. Is Mama–"

"Shush, my dear. She's beyond any pain now."

Christina burst into fresh tears. Tenderly, Gianetti set her head upon her shoulder. "Don't hold it in. Just let it out!"

"Gianetti, I don't remember anything! Just–just that awful sense of hate. And then I felt myself change..."

"Enough!" The Doctor's voice was firm. "Explanations. Now."

"All right," Roxton said. "I take it you knew about the séance this evening? Damn it, I warned Althea not to have it! Not that I honestly thought anything like this would happen–I was afraid she'd be defrauded! You know as well as I how many of these so-called Spiritualists are fake."

"And I daresay you thought Gianetti was, too."

"Well, I didn't know she worked for you. Anyway, the other two–Grigori Yeltsin and Rosemary Underwood–arrived right on schedule. We had dinner and then Althea wanted to set the séance right up."

"Wait. Describe these other two mediums."

Now Gianetti spoke up. "I knew something was wrong as soon as I met them, Doctor. Yeltsin–a very fat, obnoxious man–claimed to be Russian, so I wondered why I had never heard of him, being as you take such precautions to know what psychics are from there. But I could see at a glance he was nothing but a fraud. His aura was nil. Russian, yes, psychic, no. But Miss Underwood... she was different Her aura sang of power. Sang! I've never seen the like, except–well, except in this young man here." She gestured toward Darshan. The Indian blinked, shifting uncomfortably. "His is almost as strong as hers. Very odd, too, considering how drab she looks physically. Very plain, very colorless. But there was something else about her I simply couldn't put my finger on. Still, she seemed eager enough to help Mrs. Rutherford, and I thought with my guidance, we might be able to brush Yeltsin aside and actually summon Christina's father."

Finally, I found the words to speak. "But something happened?"

Gianetti nodded, miserably. "The séance started according to plan. We had gathered around the table, linking hands, and started the summons of Mr. Rutherford. I was at the foot, Mrs. Rutherford was at the head, with Christina next to her. Then, there was Yeltsin, and then Lord John, and myself. We recruited two maids to help, and then Miss Underwood was seated. I was keeping my best eye on Yeltsin. I expected him to try something. But then I felt the power."

The beautiful woman shook her head. "It was overwhelming, Doctor! But it wasn't like any other summoning I've ever done before! I–I can't describe it."

"Like the presence of an Outer Monstrosity?" the Sâr asked.

"No. Nothing so... alien. But hateful. Yes, something filled with hate. It swirled over us, like a great wind, and then..."

Lord John interrupted. "I would never have believed it. Even with all the two of us encountered back in India. But I was feeling it, too–something was actually coming. But it wasn't Althea's husband. I knew that, from the core of my being. It seemed to hover above us, like... I'm not certain, like it was trying to decide who to take. And then it fell. Fell right upon Christina. And then she changed."

"Changed. Changed into the lycanthrope?"

"Changed into something. Christina trembled and tried to cry out–and then suddenly it was like a shimmering halo had surrounded her, and she turned into that... that thing. Althea screamed. Christina was up, knocking over the table, and then she threw back her head and howled at us. Then, before any of us could move, she was reaching for her mother. Althea collapsed. The shock killed her instantly."

"That makes sense," the Sâr murmured softly. "The first impulse of the werewolf is to kill that which it loves best."

Gianetti cleared her throat. "Mrs. Rutherford wasn't the only victim," she said quietly. "We all panicked. Yeltsin especially. Of course, the last thing he would ever expect would be something like this. He actually tried to run past the Beast. But the Beast... was quicker. Then it burst through the window to the outside, and from there... well, you already know what happened."

"And Miss Underwood?"

"Fainted, but unharmed. As are the two maids. They're terrified, but we persuaded them to stay and look after Miss Underwood until we got back. They're keeping themselves securely locked in the cellar."

"Doctor," Roxton said. "I know the story of the Werewolf. Everyone in these parts does. But I never believed it until now. Did we do it? Did we call up the spirit of Roger Rutherford by accident?"

"I don't know yet, John. A moment." He produced his Star-Stone mineral. "Miss Christina, please. I need you to hold this a moment. Yes, that's it. Now: do you feel anything strange? No shocks? Not even a tingle? Thank you. John, as soon as we get to the Grange, I need to do a complete examination of the scene. There's something very peculiar about this entire affair, and I want to find out what it is."

I feel so lost, I thought to myself, turning my head away to try and collect myself. In the past 20 minutes, my world had been stood on end. All my knowledge, all my training–right now, every bit of it seemed in vain. Psychics? Werewolves? Ghost werewolves? Murderers and kidnappers I could handle, but this!

"We're here," Lord John spoke, pulling the car to a halt. Peering over his shoulder, I got my first look at the infamous Rutherford Grange.

It was everything Westenra House wasn't.

Rutherford Grange hung back a little off the road, non-walled, non-gated, far more welcoming to strangers than Sir Henry's domicile. Much smaller, of course, with only two stories instead of three, and far less imposing, but nonetheless I could tell that it had been a grand farm in its day. The Rutherfords no longer planted, the fields being overrun by long grass and wildflowers, but the outbuildings were still there, worn but well-maintained, and I could hear a sheep bleat in the distance. The Rutherfords maintained a small flock and a couple of horses, but these were pets, not working beasts. Surrounding the house on all sides was a sea of colors: peonies and violets and a hundred and one other types of flowers everywhere, along the wall, in great clutches in the yard, around the great elms surrounding the house like welcoming parents; none planted to add to the aesthetic and proprietary value of the house but simply because they were lovely. Something stiff and proper martinet like Sir Henry would never think of.

The house itself was brick and Georgian–apparently the original building had burnt down years ago–and, like the surroundings, looked a bit shabby compared to its grander neighbor–some of the bricks were cracked and worn; the great green wisteria growing up to the roof was droopy, but all the same there was a sense of comfort here, a sense of belovedness. This was a home, not just a place someone lived in; a place where children played and laughter would not be hushed up lest the neighbors hear, a place where nobody cared too much if the cat scratched the furniture; a place where an old couple married for years still would sneak a kiss under the full Moon. The Rutherfords had influence and money, but refused to let it rule them. They preferred instead the better things; home, family, caring. The place practically rang of love.

And of tragedy.

A servant girl, haggard and frightened, opened the door. "Miss Christina!"

We gently moved our way inside and, despite the tragedy we knew was within, I found myself more and more impressed. The interior was by no means as fine as the House, or as fresh, being old and worn-down. But that was the wonderful part–this home looked used rather than simply existing; like people actually lived and loved and laughed here. Books weren't just set solemnly on the shelf, they were piled everywhere. Two or three cats moved among the furniture, mewing when they saw us. A large portrait of Mr. and Mrs. Rutherford hung over the mantel–but unlike the solitary Sir Henry, who stood alone, Mr. Rutherford had his arm about his wife as his other hand gently rested in both of hers. I liked this place. So it saddened me far more than perhaps it might when I found the two figures lying on divans, sheets drawn over both.

"Mother!" Christina made to draw the linen back from the smallest figure, but Roxton caught her hand. "Don't, my dear. It isn't pleasant." Christina sank to her knees and cried. Gianetti joined her there, placing her arms fully around the younger girl.

"Dickson," the Sâr said quietly, beckoning. I joined him as he carefully lifted the corner of the other sheet. I winced as I saw what had happened to Mr. Yeltsin.

"I don't recognize him," El Tebib muttered. "Not a Russian spy, then. Probably an Englishman using the name to make himself sound more exotic." He dropped the sheet. "Lord John, can you take me to where the séance was held?"

The Dining Room was shattered. What had been comfortable if worn chairs had been dashed against the walls, jarred to pieces. China dishes, which had been previously lining the walls, were cracked or broken entirely, tinkling down to the floor with dull clinks Something had lifted the main table and hurled it aside, bringing it down upon its flat. And what looked as if it had used to be a tablecloth was tossed ripped and crumpled in a corner. The edges were wet and crimson.

Two maids were there, trying to clean the place up as best they could, but there was someone else as well. This one was being watched over by what I assumed to be the butler, who gathered the maids and left when Lord John motioned for them to go. She sat on a chair silently, hands folded, looking very small and plain in an ordinary grey dress, brown hair dull and lifeless as her eyes. Her nose seemed rather long for an Englishwoman's. She gazed up listlessly as we came in.

"Miss Underwood?"

The medium called Rosemary Underwood nodded. "Yes, that is I," she said in a dull, rather monotonous tone.

"I apologize for holding you here," Roxton said, "but I needed everyone to stay until we found Christina."

"Is she all right?"

"For now. The… Beast is gone from her."

"Only for a while," Miss Underwood spoke softly. "It will be back. She has been possessed by an evil spirit, and we are all doomed while she walks."

"I don't think so," the Sâr said, and the girl looked up in surprise. "Do you know me, Madam? I should think my name would be famous in your circle. I am the Sâr Dubnotal, Conqueror of the Invisible!"

"I... think I may have heard of you," the girl said at last, after a long pause. "What do you want to me?"

"Tell me. Tell me everything that happened here."

"Well, it began when Mrs. Rutherford contacted me about attempting to summon the spirit of her late husband..." Miss Underwood told her story. Apparently, the drab young woman made her living from using her gifts as a medium, after having discovered them a few years back. She had established herself in a town not far from Wolfsbridge and spent most of her time doing much the same as she had this night. It seemed odd to me—most of the Spiritualists I had met over the years were far more colorful and confident than this shy, unassuming woman. They had to be—they were all confidence tricksters at heart.

"...But this time, something was different. I felt it. I thought it was because that Mr. Yeltsin was so obviously a nonbeliever. He was just in it for the money. But I felt Hate coming... vicious, enraged Hate. And then Miss Rutherford turned into that thing. The rest, you know." She shrugged. "Take my advice, Doctor. Leave here. Let us all leave here. There is no help for her now. She has become the Werewolf of Rutherford Grange, and her soul is lost."

"I doubt that," the Sâr replied. "I'm no expert, but I know a bit about lycanthropy and other manifestations of it. The werewolf sightings in New England in 1799, the infamous wolf and man-cat of Paris, the Serbian feline shape shifters... even the Ring of the Borgias. I'm sure with a bit of investigation, I can find the solution to this. In fact, I'd appreciate it if a talented psychic like you might care to assist me."

For the first time, a bit of color appeared in the girl's cheeks. "I'm afraid I can't," she started. "I must go at once I don't want to deal with demons. It's safer—"

"It's safer if you stay here where we can see you," Roxton declared firmly. "That way, we can watch over you. Trust me, Miss Underwood, I know this man. Oftentimes I don't believe him, but he knows what he is doing."

"Lord John." Darshan Kritchna stuck his face through the door. "Miss Christina is asking for you."

Automatically, we had turned to follow the sound of his voice. And that's when Miss Underwood chose to make her move. Darting up faster than any of us would have expected, she shot past me and made for the back door, which I could see through the kitchen

"Stop! Come back here!" Roxton cried, and dashed after her. The last I saw was of a brown cloud of skirts being held up as the girl ran across the fields as fast as her legs could carry her.

"Damn," I said. "I'll get the car; I should be able to catch up—"

"Let John do it," the Sâr said suddenly. "He'll either catch her or he won't."

I gazed at him, amazed. "But–"

Roxton came panting back in. "She's gone. I wouldn't think a woman that small could move so quickly, but–"

"Let her go, Lord John. She can be no further help to us. We can find her if we need her again." Roxton looked dubious but the Sâr turned to Christina. "My dear, I know how horrid you must be feeling, but I need your help for a moment. I need you to make a telephone call for me."

"Wh–who are we going to call?" The girl looked up as bravely as she could. For that, she had my deepest admiration.

"Someone we need very much."

Ten minutes later, the doorbell rang. Christina, still sniffling, opened it.

"Miss Rutherford!" Appleby cried in concern. "Whatever is the matter? Why did you ask me to come?"

"We–we need your help, Mr. Appleby."

"With all due respect, I cannot possibly see what I can do for you what your own servants could not. Sir Henry will be furious–"

The Sâr gripped him by the arm and yanked him inside. Before the butler could protest, he had clamped one hand over his mouth and was peering intently into his eyes.

"Appleby, listen to me. I know your beliefs. I'm not asking you to change them. I know how frightened you are of all this. And you should be–working with the Spirits is always the most dangerous of propositions, no matter how experienced you are. But you know as well as I–there's a monster out there, Appleby. One that I believe is a threat to your masters. And if we're going to save them, I'm going to need your help. You may not like me. You may not like my methods. But believe me when I say our objectives are the same–to prevent a great evil from occurring here. When I take my hand from your mouth, if you still do not wish to help, I will not stop you. But I need you, Appleby. I need what you can give to us. So I ask–will you assist us? The answer is totally up to you."

The two stared into each others' eyes for a long time. Then, slowly, Appleby motioned for the Sâr to remove his hand. "Sir," he said quietly, "you are right that I believe your... views are not the correct ones. But I know what I saw tonight, and it was total Evil. Evil that must be fought. I will not use your methods for myself. But... if somehow I can call upon God to help you, I shall."

"That's all I wished to know, Appleby. Thank you. Now, quickly–what is happening at the House?"

"Sir Henry is in a frightful state. Mr. Alexander and Mr. Peter are too. All the guests have fled. No one even stayed to help with the body–I had to do that. We're keeping him in a side room, properly covered until Sir Henry can decide what to do."

"You mean he hasn't summoned the authorities?"

"No, sir–he is adamant about that. He wants no one from outside to know what happened. I'm not certain he has even informed the Government yet–I asked if he wished me to call the Office and he refused. But they must find out, and soon. The other diplomats are certain to inform their superiors."

"What about the rest of the security?" I demanded. "Where are they?"

"Gone, as well, sir–as are the rest of the servants. They're all too terrified to remain. I can't blame them.. But Sir Henry cannot possibly intend to keep this whole thing a secret."

"He probably does," said the Sâr. "He's the type who would, just to salvage his career. But we have little time. The normal authorities cannot possibly handle something like this, even if they would believe it. If the spirit of the Werewolf of Rutherford Grange is truly about, we have to deal with it ourselves."

I folded my arms skeptically. "And just how do we find out if this is the real Werewolf?" I scoffed.

'Simple," the Sâr said calmly. "We're going to have to talk to the source of the legend himself."

"We're going to what?" My voice must have cracked with my incredulity. "Please, please, please tell me that you're joking."

"I never joke, young man," the Sâr replied flatly. He carried a chair to the far side of the room and set it down. "Not about this, at any rate. Here, Kritchna, help me with this table."

"But–but another séance!"

El Tebib glanced at me sardonically from beneath his turban. "Does the Prince of Rationality have a better idea?"

All about the destroyed dining room the Sâr and Miss Gianetti were rummaging about, moving chairs, picking up bric-a-brac, and sweeping debris from the center of the room to form a clearing in the rough shape of a circle, large enough for the six of us to stand around it, or sit if we scrunched. In the center of this clear area, the Sâr had been careful to remove the slightest bit of dust or dirt. He then opened his carpetbag and pulled out a gangly, shapeless mass of metal and wires. This he set within the circle and started to rearrange it, clicking together two bars here, untangling strands of wire there, until the whole thing came together and I realized that it was some sort of collapsible pentacle of some sort, but one which did not quite match the geometry of a perfect pentagram. The points seemed too curvy for one thing, and it was placed in such a way that the angles were not exactly compass-straight. The Doctor straightened up, looked at it, didn't seem satisfied, and shifted it slightly to the left. Then, apparently content, he unraveled of all things an ordinary extension cord and asked if anyone saw an outlet.

"One of Thomas's electric pentacles?" asked Gianetti.

"A variation of my own devising," the Sâr replied. "You have to sit inside one of Thomas's. With this, we stay outside and it stays inside."

"A pentagram!" cried Appleby in something of a strained voice. "But you said—"

The Sâr held up a hand. "Be at peace, Appleby. Yes, it's a pentagram. I know the associations with Black Magic it holds. But there are reasons for that—it works. This shape applies to both White and Black Magic, and none of us who do battle with the more sinister aspects of the Ab-natural can do without it." Continuing to gaze upon the butler, he smiled gently and sympathetically placed a hand on his shoulder. "I know all too well what you're feeling, Appleby," he said, "I told you that I have never called upon the Infernal Powers for assistance, and I'm not about to start now. In my own way, I serve the same Powers as you. In fact, that's why I asked specifically for your assistance. You bring something very valuable to our project."

"And what might that be?"

The Sâr raised his eyebrow. "The power of faith," he said simply. "Faith is a far more powerful force than most realize. Especially faith in something greater and more good than ourselves. That grants much protection against the forces of evil. They cannot face the idea of Faith."

"Oh, that makes no sense whatsoever!" I snapped. "If that is the case, then you could ward a vampire off with enough faith that the sky is blue!"

"You think so?" the Doctor asked. "I'll remember that the next time I en-counter a vampire. But, seriously, Appleby, your presence is more necessary than you might think."

"Please, Mr. Appleby." Gianetti took his arm. "El Tebib is right. He would never ask you to do something so against your beliefs if it wasn't absolutely necessary. At one time, I didn't trust any of this, myself. Did you know I was actually going to become a nun? Oh, yes. I'm a very devout Catholic." Tenderly she fingered a rosary hung about her neck. "But I have a gift that, for whatever reason, I firmly believe God gave me. When it first manifested, I thought I was going insane or was possessed. And I nearly was. An evil woman named Ma-dame Sara was trying to use me to call up—well, I don't want to talk about that. But if the Sâr hadn't found me and taught me how to use my ability properly, taught me how to use my own faith to channel my powers, let's just say some-thing—bad—would have happened."

"Indeed," the Sâr exclaimed firmly. "The great difficulty here is that this place has already been used for evil, and that attracts more evil. It's only be-cause Miss Annunciata's abilities are inborn to her, along with my own learning and devised defenses, that we have even a chance in succeeding in our mission. But succeed we must, if we are to stop even more deaths from occurring. Add-ing your own faith, as well as"—he nodded toward Darshan—"this gentleman's innate psychic gifts, whether he wants to acknowledge them or not, I believe

74

that, with caution, we stand a great chance of summoning the spirit of Roger Rutherford."

Appleby still looked skeptical, but I could tell the pleading face and gentle persuasion of the beautiful Miss Annunciata was winning him over. I shot a glance at Roxton, practically begging him to interfere. But the great adventurer simply shrugged in defeat. This had come too far and the Sâr had reminded him of too much he had seen over the years to back out now.

"Still," the Doctor said, "I will not force anyone to participate in this if they truly do not wish to. So, if you want to back out, now is the time. Gianetti?"

She shook her head. "You know I won't."

"Roxton?"

Lord John took a deep breath and sighed. "I'm still not certain about all this," he said at last, "but if it will find out the truth behind that monster and avenge Althea I'm with you. But must Christina—"

"Hush, Uncle," the young woman said, stepping forward, face tear-stained and bruised, but very determined. "This... thing forced me to kill my own mother. Of course I'm in." She squeezed Gianetti's hand for strength. The elder woman was more than willing to give it.

The Doctor turned. "Mr. Appleby?" After a moment, the butler nodded. "I feel like Saul approaching the Witch of Endor," he said quietly. "But there is something evil here that must be stopped. And while I will not call upon your powers over my Savior, I will pray that He somehow chooses to reveal the truth here."

"You don't have to," the Sâr proclaimed. "Just ask for the Hand of Ria-thamus to be upon us as we embark upon this journey. Kritchna?"

The Indian simply nodded.

"And you, Dickson?"

Everyone's head turned toward me. I paused, unable to believe what I was doing here. No, I thought, No. This went against the grain of everything I was ever taught, everything I had ever trusted. There were always rational explanations for everything that happened. Everything. The supernatural simply did not exist.

But what if I were wrong?

If I was wrong–and I wasn't yet certain that I was–then, that Beast would still be out there, ready to kill at a moment's notice. And this might be the only way to stop it. So, in spite of myself, in spite of my mentor, in spite of everything I ever knew about the world, I found my mouth opening and these words issuing out: "I'll do it."

The Sâr nodded. For a second, I thought I saw a glimpse of admiration in his eye. "Good. Then everyone gather here at the edge of the circle. Join hands. Appleby, if you wish to pray, start now."

Quickly, he plugged in his contraption, which began to glow softly with a gentle blue electricity. Then he switched off the lights and squeezed between

Darshan and myself. "Gianetti will do the actual summoning. All the rest of us have to do is be still and think 'Roger Rutherford.' "

In the dark of the room, the pentacle's glow grew brighter. Out of the corner of my eye, I could see Roxton gently grasp his niece's hand more tightly. Gianetti began to mutter words under her breath. Her eyes had drawn back into themselves and she seemed to take no notice of where she was or whom she was with. Next to Darshan, I could hear Appleby gently chant: "Our Father, Who Art in Heaven, Hallow'd be Thy Name…"

I swallowed silently. In the midst of the circle, the blue of the pentacle sparked and crackled in tiny pops. I tried to catch Kritchna's eye but he was staring intently into the middle of the circle. I did as well, but could make out nothing. Then, suddenly, Gianetti threw back her head and cried out at the top of her voice: "Roger Rutherford! Roger Rutherford! We ask you to come beyond the Winds of the Shadow to us to stop a great evil! Roger Rutherford! Are you there?"

And now, I paid more attention than ever. I knew all the tricks of the Spiritualist trade; every one of them. Trumpets used to throw voices. Special wires to lift tables. Everything. If the Sâr or Gianetti or anyone was up to trickery here, I would know of it. Swiftly, I glanced across the circle; everyone was still gripping each other's hands. Everyone's eyes were open and they were all looking into the clearing. Neither the Sâr nor Gianetti made any move.

Then, very slowly, there was another sputter of the pentacle and it seemed to throw off a blue spark. The spark flew upward, just over the top of the clearing, and paused, seeming to hang in the air itself. Then it expanded–expanded up and out, still hovering over the floor, but fleshing out to become a small, floating illumination that flickered and licked upwards like a tiny fire. I felt no heat from it, nor cold. It was simply there. I probed for any sign of a wick, a torch, an electric light, anything that might tell me where it was coming from. But I could see nothing. And then the voice came.

"*I… am… here.*"

"Roger Rutherford?"

"*Yes. I have… been allowed… to come.*"

("Allowed?" I heard Appleby whisper. "Allowed by who?")

Quickly, I checked the Sâr. There was no movement of his lips, no pulsing of the throat that might indicate ventriloquism. But I had met professionals before. I kept my eye on him as Gianetti continued to speak:

"Do you know why we have summoned you?"

"*Yes. The Beast.*"

"Are you the Beast? Is it your ghost or the ghost of one of those hung with you?"

"*Difficult…to speak beyond the veil. Very… dangerous. But no… it is not. It is… something different. Something not… of this side.*"

"Then what is it?"

"*I cannot explain. It is not... of this side. That is... all I know.*"

"Were you ever the Werewolf of Rutherford Grange?"

"*No. I was... only a man. I did not... practice the occult. That is why I was allowed to come... to tell you.*"

"Then what was it?"

"*A gypsy beast... that escaped. Spotted and laughing. Fierce. It... hurt me. and I was taken for it. But only... a beast.*"

That matches what I read in the diary, I thought. Spotted and laughing–that sounded much like a hyena. Could the gypsies have brought a hyena with them and it escaped? That would certainly fit the description–a creature bigger than any dog anyone in the area had seen, very ferocious, and which would've "laughed" when they saw it! Almost certainly no one in Wolfsbridge would have ever seen one before–they were not stupid people, but with their lack of education, it certainly would've seemed like something supernatural! But then the thing I saw looked no more like a hyena than it did a real wolf.

Very quietly, the Sâr spoke. "Do you know who is responsible for this?"

"*You... already know.*"

"Indeed I do." The Sâr nodded sagely. "I thank you."

"*I... must go. Already the... dark dwellers approach. And the voice... calls me home. I... must go. But Christina... Christina Rutherford...*"

"Y–Yes?" the girl asked uncertainly as tears streaked down her face.

"*Your family told me... They love you. They love you... Christina.*"

She swallowed. "Tell them... Tell them I love them, too."

"*They know. The dwellers come. Good-bye. Good-bye...*"

"Wait!" Darshan cried out, almost breaking his hold on the Sâr's hand and reaching out to the light. "I must know! My sister! My sister, Ashanti! Is she there? Is she there with you?"

There was a pause. Then:

"*She is not... On this side of the veil. That is all I know. The dwellers... Must go... Must go now...*"

The voice faded and the blue glow began to shrink. But in its place something else began to form. It began as a pinprick, just a sliver of blackness at the bottom of the blue, somehow seeming darker than the room itself. But it was growing swiftly, growing wider and stronger, seeming to absorb all light, even the light of the pentacle, and at the very core of my eardrums I heard a strange sound... a sound that seemed like the inane chattering of evil apes...

"*Pull out!*" cried the Sâr, tearing his hands from ours and extending them toward the pentacle. "Gianetti, pull out *now!*"

With one heave, he yanked the cord from the wall. The light of the pentacle instantly went out and the blackness vanished like the reverse snuffing of a candle. Gianetti fell backwards, and it was just barely that Lord John managed to catch her. I found sweat beading down my face. I was feeling most uneasy. Throughout the entire sequence, I had looked and looked, and had found nothing

77

my father had taught me to look for when dealing with a hoax. And that noise at the end... somehow that reached deep into my soul and made it tremble. I dared to take a look at Appleby. He was on his knees, thanking God. The Sâr clapped a hand on his shoulder.

"You sensed them, didn't you?" he asked. "If it were not for you, the Dwellers in the Dark would certainly have interfered that much sooner. We were fortunate."

The butler shook his head. "Don't thank me, sir. Thank God."

The corner of the Doctor's lips twitched. "Perhaps you're right," he said and went to attend to his assistant. Gianetti was gently being helped up by a worried Christina and Lord John.

Kritchna came over to me. "What do you think?"

"I don't know what to think," I had to admit. "I'm just... I'm just very confused."

"So am I. But somehow–somehow, I think that was real. Don't ask me how I know, I just feel it. In my bones. That's why I asked about my sister. At least now I know... she isn't dead."

"But if Alexander didn't kill her, where could she be?"

"I don't know."

The older men were carefully helping the girls into chairs and bringing them water. The tears were flowing freely down Christina's cheeks. "They're all right," she whispered. "They're really all right."

"Well, Doctor?" Roxton stood before the Sâr. "Did that little contretemps really solve anything?"

"Indeed it did, Lord John," the Sâr replied seriously. "I know precisely what we're dealing with now."

"And that would be?"

A grim smile played across the Sâr Dubnotal's lips. "Let me make one more telephone call. And then, you might wish to load your rifle."

For the next half-hour, we made our plans. The Sun was now up, spreading its light into the gloom of the Grange. Under normal circumstances, the dawn was the most welcome of visitors to this house, but now it appeared a intrusive stranger. I found myself making a vow that this would be the only time that would ever be. The Sâr had sent the servants away, with strict instructions not to speak to anyone, and assured them that Miss Christina was now free from any possession and that the Beast would be conquered. Not even my mentor could sound so convincing.

We managed a quick breakfast, then the Sâr took Appleby into the kitchen to make a call. When they returned, the butler looked very uncomfortable. The Doctor just looked determined and spoke in low tones with Roxton and Gianetti. Then we all settled down to wait. Roxton waited by the door, rifle by his side, while the girls huddled together, speaking lowly. Darshan noted the Electric

Pentacle was still assembled and asked if the Doctor wished the power turned off. The Sâr told him to leave it as it was.

Ten minutes later, a car pulled up outside. There was a furious knocking upon the door.

"Open it, Appleby," the Sâr Dubnotal said.

Nervously, the butler complied. Sir Henry and Alexander Westenra pounded in, red-faced and looking extremely tired, with Sir Henry barking: "Damn it all, Appleby, you'd better have an explanation of what you're doing here instead of at the House!" His eyes widened as he took in me, Kritchna, and above all, the Sâr. "What are you doing here? What is the meaning of this?"

"Sit down, Sir Henry." The Sâr gestured to a couple of empty chairs near the Pentacle.

"I most certainly will not!"

"I think you will," said Roxton, shutting the door behind him. He fingered his rifle, now lifted, pointedly.

They sat, looking from one to the other of us in confusion and irritation.

The Sâr regarded them solemnly, fingers steepled to his chin. "I can see you're quite exhausted, gentlemen, so I will keep this as short as possible. You are, of course, perfectly aware of what happened to my old friend the Duc d'Origny at your estate last night. What you may not know is that this Beast was also here, where it killed Mrs. Althea Rutherford and one of the Spiritualists she was hosting."

"So it's true?" Alexander asked "They really did call up the spirit of the Werewolf Grange?"

"Nonsense," snapped Sir Henry. "It was just some creature this man bought to disrupt the conference. I know it!"

The Sâr paid him no mind. "Oh, they certainly called up something during the séance, there's no doubt about that. But if my theory is correct–and they are never wrong–it was by no means a ghost."

Now it was my turn to be surprised. "What? Then what was it?"

The Sâr frowned at me, making it clear he disapproved of my interruption. He turned back to his unwelcome guests. "May I ask you a question, Mr. Alexander? During your time in India, you frequented many places, did you not?"

"I don't know what you mean."

"That is, places where an Englishman of your standing would rather not be seen if he wanted to keep his reputation. I don't mean brothels. I mean your other associations–such as those with certain Russian agents you met. And temples of certain cults the British authorities consider dangerous and illegal. Oh, don't look so shocked. I've heard of your exploits, as has Lord John here. You were a wild and reckless youth back then, weren't you? Always looking for fun. You even made the acquaintances of several native women, or so I've heard." He glanced toward Darshan, who was looking at the Westenras as a cobra does his prey.

"So? That proves nothing! I'm no traitor!"

"I didn't say you were. And then, your father was always there to pull you out before things got too bad, wasn't he? Good for him. But, you may have heard of a few things when you were associating with the darker magicians and occult masters you enjoyed so much. So I was wondering, have you ever heard of a *tulpa*?"

"A what?"

"A *tulpa*. It's very special."

"No."

"Ah. Then listen carefully. A *tulpa* is something very difficult to create. Very. Indeed, only the most learned or powerful of yogis can even try. But if you can... then, you have created yourself a very powerful weapon. If you can control it. And that's the hardest part. You see, a *tulpa* is a form of being created from the mind itself."

"What?" I was incredulous. "Now this is going too far!"

"Quiet, Dickson." Lord John said quietly. "The Sâr is right. I've seen these things in Tibet."

"Right enough," the Sâr replied. "We saw them together, didn't we? But to get back to what I was saying, the *tulpa* is neither a ghost nor a natural spirit. It is pseudo-life: an animated creature, often in the form of a natural beast or person, created from ectoplasm by the imagination of the yogi. As I said, only a few people can make them. And even fewer can control them for any length of time. They're very fierce–for they know that they are not real and you are, and they resent it. You should have years of study and meditation before even attempting such a feat–but a *tulpa* can be created, if you're powerful enough. Not very well, but you can."

By now Alexander was beginning to look bored. "All right, yes; I've heard of them. But what does this have to do with anything?"

"The Werewolf who killed Mrs. Rutherford and my friend last night was no ghost. It was a *tulpa*."

Sir Henry took the cigar out of his mouth. "For God's sake–" but the Sâr continued.

"I first began to suspect when my Star-Stone didn't draw any curse out of poor Christina here–yes, gentlemen, she was the 'werewolf.' Not of her own accord–someone used her. When we found her in the road, surrounded by ectoplasm, I knew we weren't dealing with a true lycanthrope. The Werewolf was a shell around her, not a physical transformation. One that temporarily controlled her, but not strong enough to last permanently. That made me think it must not be a very experienced psychic who created it; otherwise, it could exist in and of itself, and whoever did it needed a base to form around it. A 'skeleton,' as it were, so the Beast could move and walk and do what its creator wanted it to."

The audience sat spellbound by the Doctor's words. So intent, in fact, that even Roxton had turned his attention away from his surroundings, leaning forward to catch every word. So he did not notice as I did when the drawing room door slowly and silently began to creak open.

"Look out!"

To his credit, Roxton was instantly alert and turning, bringing up his rifle to face whomever it may be, but the door burst open and the cold barrel of a pistol pointed directly toward his heart.

"Hold up there, Lord John, if you please," Peter Westenra said mildly. "Now, kindly lower the rifle to the floor... That's it. Thank you. Now, please, move over there with the others. Everyone else, kindly stand with your hands in the air. That means you as well, Doctor."

"Ah," the Sâr said calmly. "I must admit I wasn't expecting you to follow your elders, young man. Careless of me."

"Oh, I doubt that, Doctor. In fact, I think that's exactly what you wanted." He gestured with the pistol. "All of you, in one group, over there. But please do not think of rushing me, for I would hate to have to shoot one of the ladies. And I shall, if you try anything."

All of us, Appleby included, obeyed. Sir Henry heaved in relief. Even Alexander was impressed.

"Thank God, Peter!" he ejaculated. "Finally you ended up doing something right! Here, kick that rifle toward me, and we can–"

"Alexander," Peter stated calmly, pointing the pistol straight at him, "shut up." And he sent a bullet through his brother's head.

Christina screamed. Alexander Westenra, blood streaming from the hole in his forehead, teetered a moment, as if unable to quite process what had happened. Then he fell over, spreading crimson upon the carpet.

"Son!" cried Sir Henry and made to go to the body, but the pistol had swerved to cover him while its holder never took his eye off us.

"Get over there with the rest of them, Father. Now!"

"Peter Westenra, what the Hell are you–"

"Do it!!!" screamed Peter, finger tightening on the trigger. The look on his face was the antithesis of the sallow, sad expression I had known before "Get over there!" After a moment, unable to tear his eyes from the body on the floor, Sir Henry obeyed.

"I have to admit you surprised me on this one, young man," the Sâr said. "I honestly did believe it was your brother."

Peter smiled, bitterly. "The more fool you, then. Isn't it always the one who seems the meekest? Actually, I'm bloody surprised you didn't figure it out, Dickson–you're supposed to be the great detective, after all. Ah, well–the truth never matches up to the fiction."

"Son!" Sir Henry cried, "What are you doing? "

"Oh, it's 'son,' now, Father? Please. You never paid any attention to me before, why start now? After all, I've only ever been an embarrassment to you. Because I was sickly and weak, and never came up to your standards of manliness. Kindness and compassion were always detriments to you." The pistol held steadily at us. "Well, congratulations! Years ago you finally burned all the compassion right out of me. Including whatever I may have felt for you. Oh, I hid it well. I decided to. There were too many advantages. That way, you left me alone. And you never stopped to consider what I might really be getting into while in India."

"Of course," I said. "When Alexander took you around, trying to make a 'man' out of you. You must have met fakirs among the rest of the riff-raff he made you associate with. They taught you about *tulpas*."

Peter nodded. "They taught me quite a bit, actually. The only problem was, I didn't have the innate talent to use it. None of us Westenras have. So I had to find someone who did. And, lo and behold, she came to me. Would you like to meet her?" He dared a quick look toward the door. "Come on in, darling."

From the doorway, there was the sound of light footsteps, and a woman walked in. No one was surprised to see Rosemary Underwood, also holding a pistol. But we were when she reached up and yanked the drab brown wig off, revealing a long mass of luxurious dark hair and rubbed her cheeks with her hand, brushing away the greasepaint that gave her a Caucasian appearance. Beneath that makeup, her skin was a light brown, smooth with young womanhood, and as a false nose came off, the green eyes took a more lustrous tone. The classical features of a most beautiful Indian maid appeared before us. And Darshan, eyes boggling, cried:

"Ashanti! Ashanti!"

"Hello, brother," the former Miss Underwood said, pointing her pistol at him.

Darshan's sister! Still alive! Darshan obviously couldn't accept it, either.

"By the gods, Ashanti! We thought you were dead! Mother was heartbroken! I searched and searched, but–" He seemed to become aware there was a gun in her hand. "What are you doing?"

The girl almost seemed sad. "What I must, Darshan. For you, I'm sorry, I truly am. But I'm not sorry he's gone..."–she gestured to the body on the floor– "or that he's going to go." She motioned to Sir Henry. "Or about the rest of these."

"That's why you ran away," I pointed out. "You weren't afraid the Sâr would recognize you. You were afraid Darshan would."

"For God's sake, why?"

She looked pointedly toward her brother. "Two reasons. First, revenge. You know what that bastard did to me. It wasn't enough he seduced me, he had to throw me out when I got pregnant. And he felt nothing when I lost the child. But Peter–Peter came to me." She smiled at her companion. "Unlike everyone else, he treated me kindly. He gave me money when I needed it. And we fell in love."

"But–but that's impossible!" Sir Henry interposed. "Peter, you're–"

82

"No, Father. I'm not. You assumed I was. Because I wouldn't sleep with the whores you and Alexander brought, even while you were married to Mother. It simply became easier to let you believe it. Even when you tried to marry me off to poor, foolish Christina here. Yes, my dear, I regret to say I had another lover while we were 'courting.' She had something I wanted; I had something she wanted. Love was just an added bonus to our relationship."

A cold smile crossed Ashanti's beautiful lips. "Which brings me to my second reason. You know how Father denied us our birthright, Darshan–the powers that were supposed to be ours. You didn't care. But I did. I wanted to learn. And Father wasn't going to let me. But then Peter came up with the per-fect solution."

"Might I guess?" asked the Sâr. "Young Westenra wanted revenge on his family for years of neglect. You wanted revenge on the same. So you made a deal. Peter would arrange for you to meet other fakirs who would teach you the use of your psychic abilities. In return, when the time was right, you would use those to kill his family. He must have paid to send you here alongside him, where you set yourself up as Spiritualist Rosemary Underwood. When news of the conference arose, the two of you saw your perfect opportunity."

"Not quite," Peter said. "When the séance arose, we did. Destroying the conference was just a bit of opportunistic coincidence. We were simply going to kill Alexander and let Father destroy himself mourning–but why not remove his reputation and career while we were at it? The legend of the Rutherford Were-wolf was perfect to use. Of course, Ashanti had never tried to form a *tulpa* be-fore. It needed testing. So two nights before the conference, we tried to summon one up as a test."

"The footsteps on the roof," I said. "The thing that killed Colleen."

"Yes. Killing the cat wasn't intentional, by the way. She simply got in the way. But we found that, despite her power, Ashanti still didn't have the exper-tise to create a *tulpa* out of whole cloth. The first fell apart very quickly, as you found out, Dickson. The ectoplasm–the remains of our first tulpa melting away."

"But we needed a solution, and quickly," Ashanti continued. "So we came up with the idea–we couldn't create a full *tulpa*, but we could create the shell of one. And if we put it over a living being–"

"You could temporarily control that being through your personified rage at the Westenras," the Sâr finished. "The person–Christina–would have no con-scious control over her actions. The *tulpa*'s rage would be her driving force. A rage bent right toward the Westenras."

"But my mother–!" screamed Christina.

"Ah, yes. Poor Althea. We underestimated the bloodlust of the *tulpa* shell. But then, according to legend, the werewolf always kills first what it most loves Still, for what it's worth, neither your mother nor the Duc were our intended tar-gets. Only Alexander, and, if possible, Father. The other two–simply got in the way. It happens." Peter shrugged.

Roxton cursed them, deeply and bitterly.

During this time, Sir Henry was sinking further and further to the floor, mopping his brow, unable to comprehend everything he was hearing. "This is not possible My own son–!"

"Believe it, Father. It's the last thing you'll ever do."

The Doctor raised an eyebrow. "So I suppose you intend to kill us all now? I wonder how–if you shoot us, the Police will certainly look to the only surviving Westenra"

"Naturally," Peter said, lowering the pistol. "But we don't need bullets to kill you." He smiled, a long, wide thing that seemed to split his face in two. As he spoke, Ashanti had closed her eyes. My first instinct was to charge them, but I knew they could raise and shoot within a second's notice.

"We're going to bury the body of poor old Alexander where no one will ever find it," Peter was continuing, and, somehow, he seemed to be becoming larger as he spoke. The hair on his arms was thickening, and a peculiar shimmering filled the air about him. His nose and lips seemed to be extending, pushing themselves out into one snout-like appendage. But no–it wasn't. Something from the air itself was surrounding the man, shaping itself like clay about the form of Peter Westenra, taking on fleshly color and solidity, then rippling as a thick mass of fur ran over it. The voice became deeper and harsher, the words more difficult to enunciate or understand. "But, you–what remains of you will be found." The hands seemed to extend out, fingers merging into a thick thumb and two digits. Claws appeared on the ends of them. "They'll never be able to put any of you back together, of course." The body slouched over as the knees of his legs seemingly reversed themselves, bending in the back like the hind legs of most canines. "And don't think your precious prayers or magic stone will work this time–it didn't work the first!"

Peter Westenra, now covered in the form of a Werewolf, threw back his head and howled.

Ashanti laughed and stepped aside, gazing admiringly at her handiwork. Unable to reach his rifle, Roxton placed himself before the women and poised himself. He knew he had no chance against this monster, but he was prepared to defend his niece till his last breath. The rest of us, consciously or not, did the same. Save Sir Henry, who, terrified, shrank back, making little noises and an awful smell coming from his pants. Our carefully-prepared plan was in shambles. Peter was nowhere near the Electric Pentacle and was obviously going to make no attempt to do so!

Grinning and laughing its terrible laugh, the Beast slowly rotated its neck across us, trying to decide whom it should kill first. Moving to the side, Ashanti's foot brushed against the outer rods of the Electric Pentacle. It made a dull clinking sound as she did, and the Beast's attention pricked, turned to see what had caused it. The red eyes fell upon the girl, who was stepping away from the contraption with a frown.

The werewolf always kills first what it most loves.

That must have been the reason. Whatever true feeling Peter Westenra may have had for Ashanti Kritchna, whatever humanity hadn't been dried up by years of being raised by Sir Henry, had been buried under the rage of the *tulpa*.

Ashanti clearly hadn't expected it. She looked up, surprised as the Beast turned fully toward her. "Peter?" Then she screamed as it leaped toward her.

"Kritchna! Dickson!" the Doctor yelled and all three of us dashed forward.

Roxton lunged for his rifle on the floor. Our only thoughts were to get this monster away from the girl and into the borders of the Pentacle. But it was too late for Ashanti. The great claws had reached out and ripped the flesh from her face, and she joined Alexander on the floor, dead instantly.

Darshan roared and shoved the Beast forward. Startled, it tottered backward, stepping over the metal rods until it was in the center of the Pentacle.

"Appleby! Pray!" cried the Sâr and he began to dash about the Pentacle's edges, chanting in a loud voice. From various pockets, he brought forth Star-Stones, dropping them in what seemed to be random places (but weren't) and never pausing for a breath.

The *tulpa* paused, snarled, tried to step out of the Pentacle–but couldn't. Something seemed to be keeping it inside. It drew back, glaring at us evilly with its little red eyes

The Sâr paused long enough to cry, "Peter! Let it go! Let the *tulpa* dissolve! Otherwise, it will burn!"

He only got a howl in response and the Beast threw itself at the edge again and again. But it still failed to step beyond.

"Appleby! Keep praying!"

The butler did. As did the Sâr, continuing his monologue. And now the Beast was stepping back, wincing, just like I had seen in the garden of Westenra House. But now something new was happening.

All over the *tulpa*'s body, arms and legs and face, the fur and skin were bubbling

Tiny bursts of ectoplasm, like miniature geysers, were erupting from all parts of its torso and up and down its limbs, expending themselves in obscene, squishy pop-pop-pop noises that made me think of great boils somehow lancing themselves.

It turned to face us, painfully. It tottered uneasily on the bent, twisted appendages that served it for legs, as the true, human limbs of Peter Westenra beneath trembled uncontrollably. The look of pain on the monster's face was horrific. I could only guess what was happening to the man beneath. Peter Westenra was now controlled by the rage and hatred of his own creation, and lunged again and again at us. But for some reason it could not go beyond the last rod of the Electric Pentacle.

Behind me, I could hear Appleby increase the determination of his prayers; I could see before me the creature flinch with every word. For his part, the Sâr was practically dancing about the Pentacle, dropping Star-Stones and chanting his deep, unintelligible syllables. I sensed Gianetti and Christina clutching each other, I heard Lord John bravely but fumblingly load more bullets. But the *tulpa* would not relent.

It advanced, menacingly, but was forced to stop at the edge of the Pentacle. Placing its hand-paw against the air, it seemed to push against it, like an invisible wall was holding it back. The bubbling was continuing, and the top half of the Beast's head had almost melted away. I could see the beginnings of Peter's forehead show from beneath the ectoplasm. It was smoking—turning red and blistered as the power of the Pentacle and the incantations worked upon it, the fur on his arms peeling away to show black and burned human flesh, white bone beginning to show beneath the skin.

The fair hair had been burned away, leaving scorched scalp. Our nostrils were assailed with the stench of cooking meat. I myself could only stand there, watching in helpless fascination as everything I'd never believed in stood there and melted like it was made of hot treacle.

Craning its percolating neck, the *tulpa*'s eyes bored on the figure of the Doctor. It breathed heavily, as if gathering up its strength for one last attack. The latter had stopped both his dancing and chanting now, gazing evenly but with pity at the snarling Beast in the Pentacle. "It's over, Westenra. Surrender. You'll die if you don't. I don't want that."

The creature that had been Peter Westenra snarled. And then, it leaped at the edge of the Pentacle with all its remaining might, shoving against the invisible "wall."

For a moment, I almost imagined the air bending outward like a bubble beneath its power. Then the bubble burst and the *tulpa* was outside the Pentacle and its power. It seized the Sâr and knocked him to the carpet.

By now, the werewolf form was almost entirely gone, leaving a charred, burning, but still-alive Peter Westenra behind. But whatever humanity he had, if he indeed had ever truly had any, had been burned away as well. Only the animal remained. Teeth gleamed between the charcoal-black lips, reaching down for the Sâr's unprotected neck...

Instinctively, I lunged for the Beast. I heard something explode and then nothing but red pain was before my eyes as something tore into my side. Lord John had reacted automatically as well, shooting toward the Beast. But I had gotten in the way. I fell as the bullets tore into my hip.

Someone—Christina or Gianetti—screamed, and I was only vaguely aware of Kritchna pulling me away. Lord John, unable to reload, was still attacking the *tulpa*, using the rifle as a club, striking it again and again with the butt. Given the briefest of escapes, the Sâr tried to reach out for a star-stone. But Peter stepped upon his hand. In one arm, with the strength of a madman, he held back Roxton, pushing the rifle away with the other. Then, with a heave he sent the aristocrat to the ground. Before he could rise, the *tulpa*, now almost totally Peter

Westenra, threw himself upon the Sâr, pushing back the Doctor's head to bare the tender flesh of the throat.

Peter threw back his head and howled.

Then screamed.

For he had forgotten the others.

On either side, two Star-Stones were suddenly and firmly pressed into his cheeks. Smoke poured from the indentations. But Darshan Kritchna and Christina Rutherford stood firm, pushing the stones further and further into his face.

Free, the Sâr began his chanting again–as did Appleby, who was now going through the only thing he could remember, the *Ave Maria*. I could hear the voice of Gianetti call out, a Latin prayer I could not immediately identify. And, lastly, despite my pain, I heard another voice ring out again and again, and could not believe it was my own:

"When the impossible has been eliminated, whatever remains, however improbable, must be the truth. When the impossible has been eliminated, whatever remains, however improbable, must be the truth."

Peter Westenra, black and bleeding, trembled.

"Get back!" There was the click of a gun being primed, and then explosion. What remained of Peter's head went up in a ball of crimson fluid. The body twitched just one last, brief moment and became still.

Lord John staggered back, dropping his rifle.

There was only the sound of Sir Henry, sobbing in the background.

Somehow, in the midst of it all, I managed to roll over onto my back.

"You know, I was going to call in my mentor to see what he could make of all this," I said weakly. "But now, I believe I shall refrain."

"You're a very lucky young man, Dickson," the Sâr said as he finally finished wrapping the bandages around my waist. "You were in just the right position for the bullets to miss any organs. I wouldn't try anything strenuous for some time, but you should recover." He smiled broadly. "Certainly you shouldn't go hunting any more werewolves."

"Werewolves," I sighed, shaking my head wearily. "*Tulpas*. The occult."

"You still do not believe, do you, Dickson? Not really."

I was quite for a long time. Then: "It goes against everything I was ever taught, by my mentor or otherwise. Even now, I wonder if it could not have been some form of mass hypnosis, something we saw because we were supposed to see it."

The Doctor turned on the sink to wash his hands. "I cannot make you believe, Dickson," he said. "Only point you in the direction. Ultimately, it's up to you. If you choose to feel there's a rational explanation for all that has happened, I'm certain you'll come up with one. Until then, make your own decision." He tossed the towel aside. "Or perhaps you could try Appleby's way, and just have a little faith."

The door opened and Lord John strolled in. "Well, I just got off the telephone with the Government. M's sending a contingent to wrap things up. You know M, don't you, Dickson?"

"We've met," I smiled.

"Well, he's asked that we all remain until his men get here. Debriefing, I suppose. God knows how they'll square all this with France, being as one of their most influential diplomats is dead. He also said he'll take care of things with your employer, Dickson."

"Oh. Goody." I could just see that. As well as the red ears I would get when I returned.

"By the way, I poured through Roger's old journals. Found a picture of the original 'werewolf.' Look." He held up a book, opening to a certain page. On it was a rough drawing, that of a spotted, sloped creature vaguely like a dog, but much bigger and ratty. "A spotted hyena. Found in Africa. Just as we suspected. There was no real werewolf of Rutherford Grange after all."

"That's good," the Sâr declared as he picked up his omnipresent carpetbag. "But I'm afraid you'll have to give our regards to M. Gianetti and I are leaving for Paris."

"What? But you can't leave! Not when M wants to speak with you!"

"Certainly I can. I despise debriefings. I'm sure you'll do fine without us." He paused at the door, turned back, and smiled. "Besides, knowing you, Dickson–you'll come up with some rational explanation for our departure."

Thus ended the Adventure of the Werewolf of Rutherford Grange. A cover story was set up about a huge and feral dog on the loose, killing people, but most seemed to accept it. It was better than the truth. Only a few more things remain to be said

Two days later, the funeral for Althea Rutherford was held. Sir Henry Westenra did not attend. He was a broken man: deprived of one son, betrayed by another, forever lost to both, his career was in ruins and no amount of favors owed could help him now. Eight months later, the town Constable found him with a broken neck and eyes rolled back to his forehead–he had taken a rope and hung himself from the very bridge his ancestor had hung three innocent people almost 300 years earlier. I wish I could say I felt sorry for him. I presume the family of the Duc d'Origny had their own ceremony, but I was not invited to that. If the Sâr Dubnotal attended, I am not aware of it.

Although I had sworn never to return, I did visit Wolfsbridge again almost a year to the day later, when Lord John Roxton gave Christina Rutherford away to a young Indian named Darshan Kritchna. I served as best man. I think more people were perturbed about Christina marrying out of her race than the fact her mother had been horribly killed, but I was thrilled. The two had suffered much and in looking for comfort, found each other.

Darshan never told me what he did with his sister's body, and I did not ask. The vengeance he had wasted years trying to gain had been ripped from him and it was painful for him to face it. They moved back to India, where I understand Roxton used his contacts to gain for him a comfortable job as some sort of go-between between the Government and various factions in Bombay. I wish them both the best.

Appleby left Service. He returned to school, even at his age, to finally fulfill his dream of becoming a preacher. He did well and eventually made quite a success for himself as a speaker–against Spiritualism and the occult. I had occasion to meet him on a London street one day and ask him about it. He clearly still respected the memory of the Sâr but said, "A fake séance raised a *tulpa*, Mr. Dickson. Have you any idea what a real one might call up?"

I had no answer to that.

As for myself, I returned to my apprenticeship with Mr. Blake, where my ears were promptly blistered for not calling him immediately. Then he listened in fascination while I told him what happened. I returned to school and eventually did realize my dream of opening my own agency–although it took the Great War and much Intelligence work to finally work a callow youth into a mature, thinking adult. You may have read some exaggerated versions of my adventures in the popular magazines. To this day, I still don't know what to think about it all, so wisely I don't. A mind so powerful it can call entities into being right out of the aether? A mixture of science and the supernatural to call up the ghosts of the dead? It still goes against my grain.

What's that, you say? And whatever happened to Gianetti and the Sâr Dubnotal?

Well, that's hard to say… for I have no intention of ever writing down about our second encounter…

In the story he wrote for our first volume, Rick Lai cleverly brought together the worlds of Kung Fu movies and spaghetti Western with that of pulp literature; in this tale, he continues in the same vein by importing characters from B movies. Here, he draws on a little known, yet wonderful, Spanish horror film, La Residencia, *a.k.a.* The House That Screamed, *and brings its story and characters into the mythos of the Shadowmen.*

Rick Lai: *Dr. Cerral's Patient*

Paris and Avignon, 1890

In his personal laboratory at the Countess Yalta Memorial Hospital, Dr. Anatole Cerral filled a syringe with curare. An injection of this South American poison would bring quick death to the recipient and leave the outward symptoms of heart failure. Dr. Cerral had never before contemplated murder, but a man would soon be arriving who might threaten to jeopardize the surgeon's marriage and career. That individual was Victor Chupin, a private detective from Paris.

The Countess Yalta Memorial Hospital was located in Avignon. The institution was named after a wealthy Russian aristocrat who had been a celebrity in Parisian society. Nine years earlier, the Countess had suffered an accident that resulted in the loss of one of her hands. She had died shortly after that misfortune, and her considerable wealth had been bequeathed to one of her male admirers. Rather than spend the money on selfish pleasures, the heir of the Countess had sought to honor her memory by financing the construction of a hospital. The principal function of this institution was to treat laborers who had lost limbs in industrial accidents.

In a private room at the hospital, a young female patient awoke screaming. Dr. Cerral was summoned from his private laboratory by an orderly. He spent the night calming the distraught girl.

"I dreamed that I was disciplining another student in the boarding school, Papa," murmured the girl. "God then punished me by destroying my hands. "

The next afternoon, the disturbed girl was playing the piano in a room in the hospital. Her soft delicate hands swept deftly over the keyboard. As she played, a middle-aged woman with dark hair sang a cabaret song. When the song was concluded, the older woman motioned her accompanist to sit besides her on a nearby table. On its surface laid *Isis Unveiled* and *The Secret Doctrine*, two books by the occultist Helen Petrovna Blavatsky.

"Your father told me you again had a difficult night, but you have nothing to fear. You now have a new life… a new existence," asserted the middle-aged singer. "Let me show you your destiny."

90

The older woman took a pack of Tarot cards from her handbag. She proceeded to remove cards from the deck and place them on the table.

It was in June 1890 that Victor Chupin received a telegraph from his sister, Victoire. He had just returned to Paris after a difficult investigation that had forced him to spend over three months in London. The message indicated that there was an urgency to discuss the status of her daughter. Chupin immediately settled his affairs in Paris and departed for Normandy.

Chupin was nearly 41 years old. He was a lean, short man with blonde hair. When he arrived at his sister's residence, he was greeted at the door by a slim athletic 16-year old boy.

"Victoire is in the kitchen making dinner," intoned Raoul d'Andresy.

The investigator critically scrutinized his young host. Chupin had always felt a tinge of resentment towards Raoul because of the critical role that the boy had played in his sister's life. Victoire was five years older than Victor. They were the only children of Polyte Chupin, a pickpocket and a drunkard. Their father's intoxicated rages had caused her to flee the Chupin household when she was 14.

Like his father, young Victor had drifted into a life of crime. At the age of 18, Victor had become a member of the notorious Mascarot blackmail ring. When the gang was smashed by the famous M. Lecoq of the Sûreté in 1867, Victor had surrendered to the Police. Rather then prosecute him, Lecoq had arranged for the young miscreant to become a *protégé* of the wealthy Champdoce family. They sponsored Chupin to become an apprentice to a private inquiry agent. As a reward for his assistance in solving the mystery of the Chalusse heirs in 1868, Chupin received sufficient capital to start his own detective agency.

After 12 years, Victor Chupin was running a sound and profitable business. Nevertheless, he was deeply dissatisfied with his life. He had lofty ambitions of expanding his agency into a nationwide venture that would become the French equivalent of the American Pinkertons. He just needed to solve a case that would give him the enormous publicity needed for his dreams to reach fruition.

Raoul d'Andresy had almost provided the means to achieve Chupin's hopes.

In 1880, Paris had been stunned by the theft of the Queen's Necklace, the property of the Duc of Dreux-Soubise. This article of stolen property had enormous significance in French history. It had been purloined in 1785 as part of a complex swindle that severely damaged the reputation of Queen Marie-Antoinette. The original thieves had removed all the diamonds, but the intricate setting of the necklace had survived. The Dreux-Soubise family had arranged for new diamonds to be placed in the setting.

At the time of the robbery, Henriette d'Andresy had been living as a servant at the Dreux-Soubise residence with her six-year old son, Raoul. Due to the loss of the Queen's Necklace, the Dreux-Soubise family had fallen on financial hardship and had to discharge Henriette. A Police investigation proved that Henriette d'Andresy was incapable of having committed the theft.

In the manner of C. Auguste Dupin in the Marie Roget case, Chupin had devoured the details of the investigation in the newspapers. And like his illustrious predecessor, he had come to a correct solution of the crime: the thief must have been young Raoul.

The question in Chupin's mind was whether the boy had perpetrated the crime as some sort of prank or as the accomplice of an adult. Chupin had located Henriette and interviewed her. It became apparent to the astute sleuth that she was an honest woman in poor health. She clearly had no suspicion that her son was indeed the architect of this audacious crime. Chupin had thought it wise not to enlighten her about Raoul's thievery.

Chupin had also talked to Raoul, whom he had pegged as a rude and obnoxious child. After leaving the apartment, he had continued to watch their dwelling. When Raoul had left the building, Chupin had followed him for a few blocks. The boy had met a woman, whose age was in the mid-thirties. She looked vaguely familiar to Chupin. Raoul had handed her an envelope. Once Chupin overheard her first name, he began to surmise her true identity. Raoul had called her Victoire. She was Chupin's long-lost older sister.

Chupin's subsequent queries had revealed his sister's sordid past. She had once been arrested for transporting stolen goods and had served a year in prison. Victoire had never married, but that did not prevent her from giving birth to a daughter, Irene, in 1870. Four years later, she had been hired as nurse for the infant son of Théophraste Lupin and his wife, Henriette.

Chupin had wondered if his niece was the daughter of Théophraste Lupin. After an intense quarrel, rumored to concern an extra-marital affair, Théophraste and Henriette had separated. Henriette had resumed her maiden name of d'Andresy and kept the custody of their young son. Victoire was dismissed as Raoul's nurse. Chupin had concluded that Henriette had learned of a love affair between her husband and Victoire.

Chupin had a difficult choice to make. It became clear that Raoul had stolen the diamonds from the Queen's Necklace and was now passing them to Victoire. There could also be no doubt that Victoire was using her criminal contacts to convert the stones into hard currency. Chupin had a chance to gain national acclaim by solving the celebrated theft. But the only way to achieve this end would be to send his sister to prison.

In order to understand the consequences of his decision, Chupin had concluded that it was time to become reacquainted with his sister. One day, pretending that family ties were his sole motivation, he had knocked on his sister's door. Victoire gave him a cold reception. The investigator had no qualms about sacrificing his sister for his own personal glory, but an unexpected factor stayed his hand.

Chupin had developed a rapport with Irene.

His niece had bridged the gulf between Chupin and Victoire. Consequently, the detective had relinquished the opportunity to secure enormous publicity. Victoire had never realized that her brother knew of her role in the Queen's Necklace affair.

Through observing his sister, Chupin had deduced the true motive behind the robbery. The proceeds from the fencing of the diamonds were anonymously mailed to Raoul's mother. The naïve Henriette had concluded that these funds were donations from a philanthropic source and had used the money to secure better lodging for herself.

Her new prosperity had softened Henriette's heart towards Victoire and she soon had re-hired her. Both Victoire and Irene had come to live with Henriette and Raoul.

As the years passed, Chupin frequently visited Irene at Henriette's residence. He played the role of an indulgent uncle and often purchased gifts for his niece. She proved to be an excellent student during her elementary education. Irene possessed a love of literature and a gift for foreign languages. At the age of 13, she was already fluent in English. This achievement prompted Chupin to buy her several books by Charles Dickens. By the time she was 15, she was studying Spanish and Italian. She also had some skill as an artist. On the wall of his office, Chupin had framed a sketch that Irene had made when she was only 14. It was a portrait of himself. Her firm strong hands had captured his likeness perfectly.

Chupin's business often took him outside of Paris. One evening, in 1885, he had arrived at the d'Andresy residence and discovered, to his dismay, that Irene had left for the College for Young Women, a boarding school in Provence. Victoire had explained that the school would give her daughter a better opportunity to pursue her interest in the foreign languages.

The following year, Henriette had died from natural causes. Victoire had taken charge of her employer's orphaned son, and the pair of them had moved to Normandy.

Irene had spent five years at the College for Young Women, until a monstrous series of events turned her into a patient at the Countess Yalta Memorial School.

Entering the kitchen, Chupin discovered his sister making a salad. She ceased her labors once Victor entered the room.

"I just returned from Avignon. Dr. Cerral refused to let me see Irene," said Victoire.

"Did he give any reason for this prohibition?"

"He simply stated that she had no wish to see me. He gave no further explanation."

"Cerral cannot forbid your visit. Irene is sill a minor. In fact, she won't even reach her 20th birthday until the autumn. You remain her legal guardian, Victoire."

"I tried to make that argument, but he would not listen."

"Did you threaten him to go to the authorities?"

"Such a threat would have been useless, Victor. The Avignon Police will do nothing to disturb Dr. Cerral. They feel indebted to him for his help with the College Girl Murders. I made a far worse threat."

"Which was?"

"I warned Cerral that you would be forced to pay him a visit."

At the *Tivoli* cabaret in Avignon, singer Mathilde Grévin entered the office of the nightclub's manager to discuss her status.

"I'm sorry, Mathilde, but you can longer be a star attraction at the show. We need to give top billing to a younger star. All that notoriety surrounding Teresa's enrollment in that damned boarding school has damaged your career."

"I have a new addition to my act that will change your mind." Mathilde unrolled the draft of a poster advertising her act.

After the manager read the poster, he just had one question for the singer.

"When will your accompanist be ready to start?"

On the train to Avignon, Chupin perused a letter that had been written to him by Irene in late 1885. She had sent it to him only a few months after her arrival at the College. The letter had ended with certain requests:

"When you have time, dearest uncle, you may wish to read Stowe's *Uncle Tom's Cabin* or Dana's *Two Years Before the Mast*. You will find them just as enthralling as *Nicholas Nickleby*. I pray for you every night. Please pray for my soul every night, too."

Chupin often wondered if Irene had experienced a premonition of the cruel blow that fate had in store for her. From her letters, it appeared that she had prospered. A select elite of female students functioned as assistants to the headmistress, Madame Fourneau. Irene had joined that select clique in late 1885. In 1889, she had been promoted to Fourneau's chief assistant. A year later, Irene nearly lost her life.

Fourneau had a son who suffered from asthma. His ill health prevented him from being sent to a boarding school for boys. He lived on the premises of the College. At 16, a bizarre idea had come into his head to become a modern Pygmalion. Rather than sculpt his vision of the perfect woman from clay, the boy had opted to use a more grotesque ingredient: human flesh.

He had murdered five girls over a period of four months in order to obtain supplies for his ghastly handiwork. He was able to hide his atrocities by creating the impression that the girls had run away from the school. Irene was his sixth victim. The killer had knocked her unconscious and then had mutilated her hands. The headmistress, who had been unaware of her son's butchery, had discovered her murderous offspring and Irene's comatose body in the school's attic. The sudden revelation of her son's abominable crimes had caused her to perish from a fatal heart attack.

Irene surely would have bled to death in the attic if not for a fortuitous coincidence. A doctor had arrived at the College late that night. He had forced the janitor of the school to let his carriage inside the gates. The doctor and the janitor had then searched for the headmistress. Their quest had taken them to the attic. The killer had attacked the janitor with a knife, but the custodian had easily disarmed him. The doctor had found the dying Irene and taken her to his carriage which rushed to the Countess Yalta Memorial Hospital. The doctor was Anatole Cerral.

The newspapers had ruthlessly exploited the horrific events. They dubbed the killings the College Girl Murders. Although journalists had howled for the execution of the youthful maniac, he was eventually judged to be mentally incompetent to stand trial. He would probably spend the rest of his life in an asylum for the criminally insane. Many lurid stories had circulated about the College Girl Murders. It was often claimed that the killer's sixth victim had perished. One popular story was that the butchering youth had completely severed both of Irene's hands.

Chupin knew that the latter story was totally false. He had seen Irene at the hospital twice. The first time was in late January 1890 when she was still comatose. The second was a month later when she was awake, but in a state of delirium due to her terrible ordeal. On both instances, her hands had been wrapped in bandages. Shortly after his last visit, Chupin had embarked on the case that caused him to make a lengthy trip to England.

When the train arrived at Avignon, Chupin took a carriage to the Countess Yalta Memorial Hospital. He was able to secure an interview with Dr. Cerral in his private office.

During his previous visits to the hospital, Chupin had only had brief discussions with Cerral. He was a tall, thin man with black hair and a short beard. His hands were soft and delicate. Cerral had been a talented surgeon who left Avignon to work in Paris in 1871. He eventually secured a position at a medical school, but a controversial proposal concerning surgical procedures had led to his resignation in 1885. Chupin was unaware of the exact circumstances, but he had heard rumors that Cerral's critics had compared him to Moreau, the notorious vivisectionist. Returning to Avignon, Cerral had risen to a position of authority at the Countess Yalta Memorial Hospital. Chupin had only had brief meetings with him during his previous two visits because the surgeon had been occupied with other matters in the hospital.

After thanking Cerral once again for saving his niece's life, Chupin took a chair in front of the doctor's desk.

"You have expected this visit, Doctor, because of several statements made by my sister during an altercation that you had with her. Let me assure you that I am not acting in her interests. I am merely concerned with my niece's welfare. My sister and I have never been very close."

"You claim to have no strong bonds to your sister, then why are you so concerned about her daughter?" asked Cerral.

"Doctor, I am over 40 and unmarried. I doubt very much that I will ever be a husband. Bachelorhood suits me. I have always possessed a special kinship for Irene. Perhaps it is because I always harbored a foolish hope..."

"I do not understand, Monsieur."

The detective noticed a photograph on the doctor's desk. It was of a middle-aged woman, five young girls and a boy. Victor gestured towards the photograph.

"You have a rather large family, Doctor."

"The oldest girl is 22. My son is only six years old."

"Do any of them show an interest in becoming a doctor?"

"The girls have no desire to seek a vocation in the medical profession. I hope that young Alexandre may follow in my footsteps, but he is too young to make such a choice now."

"Yet you would desire that he, too, become a doctor."

"I am conducting a line of research that will probably not reach fruition in my lifetime. The possibility that Alexandre could finish my work is highly attractive."

"I have established a small but profitable detective agency. I harbor the ambition of enlarging it to be a nationwide concern. I have capable assistants, but none of them could function as a possible successor. The thought that Irene might perhaps inherit my business has entered my mind. She is intelligent and perceptive. She may even possess managerial skills. Of course, I recognize that my idea may be naive. Irene had artistic aspirations. Most likely, she might want to be an artist, or a writer. In light of her recent trauma, it is now extremely unlikely that she would ever find my line of work appealing."

"If you felt so close to your niece, then why did you concur in the decision to send her to boarding school?"

"I was not involved in that decision at all. If I had been consulted in the matter, I would have opposed it. Of course, I understand the reason for it."

"What is your understanding?"

"My niece wished to study at a school in Southern France because it would be more conducive to her mastering the Italian and Spanish languages."

"You are under a misapprehension, I'm afraid. Your niece was enrolled in that school for a far different reason. She was accused of theft."

"Theft? What nonsense are you mouthing, Doctor?"

"I assure you that I am being quite serious. Madame Fourneau kept meticulous records. In 1885, she interviewed extensively the two ladies who brought Irene to the school."

"Was my sister one of these ladies?"

"No. The ladies were Henriette d'Andresy and the Duchesse of Dreux-Soubise. The Duchesse had visited the d'Andresy residence earlier. On that occasion, she was wearing a diamond brooch. After she left the house, she discovered that it was missing. She returned to the house and insisted that Henriette search the rooms of your sister and your niece. The brooch was found hidden under Irene's mattress. She was accused of stealing it."

"Did my niece offer any explanation as to how the brooch had gotten there?"

"She offered a rather intriguing theory. Irene believed that the brooch had been stolen by Raoul, Henriette's son. Your niece argued that he had temporarily hidden the brooch under her mattress planning to retrieve it later. Although Irene was warned that there would be serious consequences if she persisted in her denials, she refused to recant. Your sister declined to defend her. The Duchesse recommended that your niece be sent to the College as punishment. The headmistress of that institution had gone to convent school with the Duchesse and Henriette... I can see by your face that all this information comes as a shock. Do you believe the story that I have outlined?"

"Yes," stated Chupin bitterly.

"Do you feel that your niece was innocent?"

"Yes."

"May I ask your reasons?"

"Because I have a strong belief in my niece's character, and because I know Raoul's all too well."

The investigator reconstructed in his mind the probable significance of Cerral's revelations. Raoul must have hoped to repeat the success of his theft of the Queen's Necklace five years earlier. Victoire knew that the only way to protect Irene would be to expose Raoul. To pursue such a course would have made public both her and Raoul's involvement in the previous crime against the Dreux-Soubise. Irene had been made a scapegoat in order to protect both her mother and her half-brother. Chupin reasoned that Henriette d'Andresy sincerely believed in her son's innocence. He also concluded that Irene had no idea about her mother's role in the theft of the Queen's Necklace.

"I must be honest with you, Doctor. There is one thing that I can't explain." The detective reached into his briefcase and pulled out a packet of letters. "I do not understand why my niece never mentioned these events in any of her letters."

"May I see those letters?"

Chupin handed the letters to Cerral. The Doctor untied them and read the letter at the top of the bundle. It was Irene's very first missive, the same that Victor had been reading on the train.

"You may be correct, Monsieur Chupin, about your niece's potential as a detective. I wonder if Irene is as talented at discerning clues as she is as deliberately leaving them."

"Clues? Why did Irene leave clues?"

"In order to fool the censor. All of the mail that the students received or sent was read by one of the headmistress' assistants. She would never have been allowed to write you the truth about her situation at the College. The individual responsible for censoring Irene's mail must have been ignorant of English literature."

"I do not understand, dDoctor."

"Irene mentioned three books in this letter, *Uncle Tom's Cabin*, *Two Years Before the Mast* and *Nicholas Nickleby*. Have you read them?"

"Yes."

"The three books have radically different settings, but they all have something in common. Do you known what that is?"

Victor paused before answering. "They all deal with physical beatings. Slaves are whipped in *Uncle Tom's Cabin*. Sailors are beaten in *Two Years Before the Mast*. *Nicholas Nickleby* involves the flogging of boys in a boarding school."

"Your niece was in a boarding school similar to that portrayed by Dickens. The majority of the pupils were sent there because their families believed them to be guilty of crimes. Fourneau ran her school like a dictatorship. She had a tyrannical personality that must have sparked her son's madness. Corporal punishment was employed to maintain discipline."

"Doctor, you examined Irene. Was she ever beaten?"

"I regret that I must inform you that your niece has permanent scars on her back. She was beaten with a lash during her initial months in the school."

"But Irene accepted a position as one of Fourneau's student assistants!"

"Conformity is a convenient avenue of escape from constant persecution."

"Irene was later promoted to the position of chief student assistant. Did she try to mitigate the oppression?"

"By that time, your niece was a privileged member of the ruling regime. The chief assistant was responsible for censoring the mail and administering the flogging."

"I can't conceive that Irene would be capable of such acts!"

"Did you ever know an individual who was once a decent person but then was compelled by duress to commit a sinful act? And then became a habitual sinner as a result of that one act."

"I once knew a man named Baptiste Mascarot. He was a blameless teacher of algebra and geometry until those he loved were in danger of perishing from starvation. Mascarot committed an act of extortion to gain money to feed them. He gradually evolved into the most dangerous blackmailer in Paris."

"Your niece embarked on a similar downward path the moment she became one of ruling circle of the College."

"I still find your assertions about Irene's conduct impossible to accept."

"Did you ever hear of a student whose name was Teresa Grévin?"

"Mademoiselle Grévin was the College Girl Murderer's fifth victim. She was slain the night before my niece was attacked." Chupin recalled the grisly details in the newspapers of Teresa's corpse after it was found by the Avignon Police. The throat had been slashed and the hands and feet had been removed. There had been further mutilations as well.

"Teresa was a virtuous girl of 18 years," continued Cerral. "It is my misfortune that I never met her during her lifetime. Unlike most of her fellow pupils, Teresa had never been accused of any crime. Her offense was her mere existence. Her mother, Mathilde Grévin, was a singer at the *Tivoli* cabaret in Avignon. She is now over 40, but she likes to pretend otherwise. The presence of a daughter of Teresa's age called that subterfuge into question. Mathilde simply wished to place Teresa away from prying eyes."

Chupin knew the *Tivoli*. Female entertainers there would generally lose their audience as they grew older unless they were either exceptionally talented or able to develop an unusual gimmick that generated publicity.

"What about Teresa's father? Did he not object to Teresa's enrollment in the College?"

"Mathilde had her daughter out of wedlock. Teresa's father was a former lover who left Avignon before she was born. He was totally unaware of her birth." Cerral paused for a brief moment. "You have probably wondered what prompted me to arrive at the College. Teresa wrote a letter to her mother and arranged for it to be posted outside the normal channels of the school."

"How did she engineer that feat?"

"She befriended a fellow student named Suzanne Noel. Teresa gave the letter to her. There was a workman who delivered firewood to the school. He had arranged a romantic rendezvous with Suzanne. As a favor to her, he posted the letter after he left the school's grounds. The letter revealed that Teresa was being persecuted to join the coterie that functioned as the headmistress' 'enforcers.' Teresa had not been flogged, but she had been warned that constant refusals could result in such a penalty. When Mathilde received the letter, she became distraught. Not only did she decide to remove her daughter from the school immediately, but she also wanted a doctor to examine her. Mathilde wanted to make sure Teresa had not been further abused. She enlisted my assistance in retrieving her."

"Why did Mathilde come to you?"

"I had been a patron of the *Tivoli* early in her career. I hired a carriage and traveled with her to the College. I forced the janitor to open the gates and let us in. You know the rest, how I found your niece in the attic."

"Yes, and I will always be grateful for your heroic actions. What relevance does Teresa's letter have to my niece?"

"You probably assumed that it was Madame Fourneau who was persecuting your niece, but in fact she delegated much authority to her chief assistant. On her own volition, Irene was harassing Teresa."

"I can't believe that!"

Cerral reached into a drawer of his desk and pulled out a letter. "This is the letter, Monsieur Chupin. I will let you read it, but I must warn you that it concerns other unusual practices at the school besides the floggings."

Cerral handed his companion the letter. Chupin read it in silence for several minutes. When the sleuth had finished, he threw the letter on the desk in disgust.

"My Irene... Could she be that corrupt?" moaned Victor.

"Do not be so harsh in judging your niece, Monsieur Chupin. She was accused falsely of a crime and exiled to the equivalent of a penitentiary. She was victimized in the same manner as Teresa. If Teresa had not been slain, she could easily have succumbed to the same temptations that ensnared your niece."

"I do not blame my niece. I blame myself."

"How could you be at fault?"

"I failed Irene. I styled myself to be a solver of mysteries, but I couldn't see the cries for help that she was concealing in her letters."

"You had no reason to suspect that the letters had hidden meaning. If anyone failed Irene, it was her mother. Your sister refused to defend your daughter against the accusations made against her, and I suspect there are more complex motivations for her actions."

"What are you hinting at, Doctor?"

"Henriette d'Andresy died in 1886, one year after your daughter was enrolled in the College. The headmistress did not keep her pupils captive for mere spite. She was paid tuition by their relatives or guardians. After Henriette's death, there was nothing to prevent your sister from removing Irene from the College. Nevertheless, tuition to ensure her entrapment in that school continued to be paid for the next four years. I think you may know whose name was on those payments..."

"Théophraste Lupin."

"Quite correct. I have been very honest with you, Monsieur Chupin; I expect reciprocity. Who is this Théophraste Lupin?"

"My sister may have told you that she is a widow. She is lying. I cannot prove this, but I have long suspected that Théophraste Lupin is Irene's real father–and he is also the father of Raoul d'Andresy."

"Things are becoming clearer now, Monsieur Chupin. The father must have wished to protect his son from being exposed as a thief. Consequently, Théophraste Lupin paid to continue Irene's confinement. Your sister seems to have a stronger affection for her lover's son than for her own daughter."

Chupin wondered exactly what role Théophraste Lupin had played in Raoul's life. Most likely, he had assisted Victoire in disposing of the diamonds. The detective had never heard of any criminal named Lupin. Perhaps Théophraste Lupin was an alias, and Victoire's paramour was a swindler of the caliber of Ballmeyer and John Clay.

"Now that we have had a frank discussion, Monsieur Chupin, I can explain my refusal to allow your sister to see Irene. In a physical sense, your niece is in excellent health. The bandages have been removed. With the exception of some surgical scars near her wrists, her hands have healed perfectly. In fact, Irene has even been able to skillfully play a piano."

"I was unaware that my niece has any musical aptitudes."

"She learned how to play the instrument during her five years at the College. Despite her failings as a human being, Madame Fourneau did have some talent as an educator. It is not your niece's physical state that worries me. It is her mental health. She has nightmares."

"She must be haunted by her memories of the College Girl Murderer."

"It is not the spirit of that deranged youth that troubles Irene. It is the guilt of her conduct as Fourneau's chief assistant. Irene cannot live with the knowledge of how she tormented Teresa and other pupils at the College. Your niece views the defilement of her hands as a form of divine retribution. I could not allow a visit by Irene's mother to upset her. At the very least, it would add feelings of betrayal and resentment to her burdens."

"Will you at least permit me to see her?"

"Of course. I recognize that your only priority is Irene's well-being. She is in a therapy room practicing on her piano with Madame Grévin."

"Teresa's mother? Is it wise for the two of them to be together?"

"Madame Grévin has no desire to revenge herself on Irene. In fact, Mathilde views herself as Irene's benefactor. I must alert you to the fact that Irene has become emotionally dependent on both Mathilde and me. Your niece has adopted us both as substitute parents."

Cerral and Chupin left the office. They went to a room on another floor of the hospital. As the detective entered the room, he heard music. He saw a slender attractive girl with dark hair playing at the piano. It was Irene. Next to her was a middle-aged woman, whom he guessed was Mathilde Grévin. She was singing a ballad. Victor noticed the table with books by Madame Blavatsky. Tarot cards were arranged in a pattern next to the volumes. Irene immediately stopped playing and rose from the piano. Mathilde stopped her singing.

"Uncle Victor!" Irene cried with joy. She then stopped and raised her soft delicate hands. She stared at them and then began to cry. "You had better leave,

Monsieur Chupin. Irene no longer exists. She died in the attic of a boarding school." She then rushed towards Mathilde and embraced her. "Mama, have Papa tell this man to leave! I won't be ready for my debut!" she screamed.

Cerral responded by motioning Chupin to leave. The Doctor suggested that they confer in his office. When they reach it, Cerral closed the door.

"I am afraid that your visit has only upset your niece further. I don't think your continued presence will benefit her further."

"On the contrary, Doctor, I must insist that you discharge my niece immediately!"

"On what grounds do you make this demand?"

"You have not been totally truthful with me. I may have failed to utilize my deductive powers to help my niece five years ago, but I won't make that mistake now."

"I give you my word that I have not lied to you."

"But you omitted certain key facts. For example, there is the nature of my daughter's operation. You did not simply repair her hands. Irene's slender hands were strong and firm. They are now soft and delicate. Her original hands had been completely severed. You somehow grafted new hands onto her body!"

"Would you rather that I had equipped her with ugly appendages like hooks?"

"It would have been better for my niece's sanity if you had. You gave her the hands of Teresa Grévin. Her hands were soft and delicate, like your own. I suspected from your remarks that Teresa was your daughter."

"I swear to you that I did not know that they were Teresa's hands when I performed the operation. I found those hands lying in a darkened corner of the attic. I assumed they were Irene's. That monstrous killer must have severed Teresa's hands in order to practice for his later attack on your niece. I did not realize the truth until I saw Irene's reactions when I removed the bandages. She is an artist with a flair for anatomical detail. She recognized the hands as Teresa's."

"And that knowledge consumed her very being, drove her mad. She came to the absurd conclusion that the spirit of Teresa now lives within her. She must want to expunge her guilt by becoming another person. Mathilde Grévin has fed on that delusion for her own selfish purposes. She has augmented my niece's hallucination with occult paraphernalia such as Tarot cards and the absurd doctrines of Blavatsky. She is an aging cabaret performer who needs a gimmick to revive her act. She intends for my niece to be her accompanist on the stage. Mathilde will present her as the sole surviving victim of the College Girl Murderer. And she will also portray herself as Irene's rescuer, no doubt. Well, I cannot and will not allow my niece to be exploited in such a manner!"

"I had no choice but to acquiesce in Mathilde's stratagem. She threatens to reveal my illicit affair with her to my wife. I was foolish enough to write her letters and send her my picture years ago."

"Your domestic problems are your own affair, Doctor. You must immediately discharge my niece or I will bring you up on charges to the medical authorities!"

"The operation was a success!"

"It still was an operation not accepted by the medical community. You made my niece the subject of a potentially dangerous operation without the permission of her family. Do you agree to my demand?"

"Yes."

"I have another demand. I want Teresa's letter."

"Why?"

"I intend to burn it in order to prevent it from ever being used to blacken my niece's reputation."

"Please, don't do such a thing. It is the only memento that I have of my deceased daughter."

"I am afraid that I must insist."

Cerral reached inside his desk and retrieved the letter. He handed it to Chupin, who turned his back on the Doctor in order to light a match over an ashtray.

Cerral reached inside one of the side pockets of his jacket. He began to grasp the syringe filled with curare. It would be easy to stab the needle into Chupin's neck. The Doctor could then arrange to have the detective's death diagnosed as a heart attack. Cerral had hoped that he would never need to perform this action. It was regrettable that his plan to misdirect Victor without technically lying had failed.

"If you destroy this letter, you are no better than Mascarot," he finally said to Victor.

Chupin then extinguished the match. He turned around to face Cerral. The Doctor withdrew his hand from his pocket. It was empty.

"You are correct in your diagnosis, Doctor. I return Teresa's letter to you." Victor handed the letter back to Cerral.

"Do you still intend to bring charges before the medical authorities?"

"No. I will use cleaner methods to gain custody of my niece. She is only 19, and her mother is still her legal guardian. I should be able to gain a court order."

"You can't intend to return Irene to her mother!"

"No. Victoire is unfit to raise her, but I will coerce my sister to make me her guardian."

"There is no necessity for you to involve your sister. Mathilde will be leaving the hospital in about an hour. I will discharge Irene in your custody afterwards."

"What will you do to avert Mathilde's threats to tell your wife about your affair?"

"As you said earlier, Monsieur, my domestic bliss is my own concern."

103

Irene left the hospital in Chupin's carriage. The detective realized that he would need to place his niece in a nursing home in order for her to regain her mental health. He thought it best to remove her as far as possible from the rumors surrounding the College Girl Murders. During his stay in England, he learned of the recent opening of an excellent nursing home known as the Sanctuary Club. He would secret Irene there.

Chupin recognized that the history of her misdeeds as a disciplinarian at the College could eventually become public knowledge. Besides Teresa's letter, there must be police records. There also were over a score of former pupils who must have been cognizant of his niece's activities. If his niece ever returned to France, it would have to be under another name.

Chupin also intended to have a stern talk with his sister after enrolling Irene in the Sanctuary Club. Considering his knowledge of the Queen's Necklace affair of 1880, he possessed a powerful tool of persuasion. He would permit Victoire to see Irene on condition that his sister would prevent any contact between her daughter and Raoul. Victor Chupin bitterly blamed Théophraste Lupin's son for all of his niece's problems.

After spending a month with Irene at the Sanctuary Club, Victor returned to Paris. He searched for any news of Dr. Anatole Cerral. He read a report that the surgeon had given evidence at the inquest into the recent death of Mathilde Grévin in Avignon. She had died in the Countess Yalta Memorial Hospital on the day after Irene's departure.

The Coroner's verdict was that she died of a heart attack.

A Suite of Shadowmen

With the notable exception of Harlan Ellison's Dangerous Visions, *anthologies generally neglect to invite contributions from artists, as opposed to writers. Not so* Tales of the Shadowmen. *We are pleased to welcome here the talented Fernando Calvi, a brilliant young artist from Argentina, who contributes to this volume his own take on eight of the most iconic characters of French Pulp Literature. To complement Fernando's striking vision, we have selected eight short vignettes meant to counterpoint Fernando's depiction of our favorite Shadowmen. Serge Lehman, one of France's most gifted science fiction writers, has an impish sense of humor–he once confided to me that one of his youthful unfinished projects was a novel entitled* Langelot et les Martiens, *featuring the popular hero of a long-running French YA spy series. In a style reminiscent of Fredric Brown's, Serge tackles here the first two of Fernando's* Suite of Shadowmen.

Serge Lehman & Fernando Calvi: *A Suite of Shadowmen*

Rouletabille: *The Mystery of the Yellow Renault*

Rouletabille forced his way through the crowd of reporters; his still youthful silhouette was familiar to everyone and they let him through.

He looked at the yellow Renault 4CV. With a single glance, he grasped the essentials of the crime. He asked the mechanic who was standing by the vehicle with a worried face:

"Tell me, my friend, were you here when the horrible deed took place?"

"Yes," said the man. "I've been here all day. I'm not in the habit of leaving cars unattended."

"And you saw what happened from start to finish?"

"As I said."

"*Parbleu,*" said the young reporter with a triumphant smile. "We know there is only one body inside that car, and the mechanic told us he's been here all the time. Therefore, there can only be one conclusion..."

The Inspector looked at Rouletabille with expectant eyes.

"Yes?"

"*It's a locked room mystery!*"

The Policeman looked at the yellow cube of metal that had once been a Renault 4CV before its passage through the compactor and sighed. Damned amateurs!

Doctor Omega: *The Melons of Trafalmadore*

Doctor Omega and Hoppy Uniatz were the first spacemen ever to visit the planet Trafalmadore. After landing the *Cosmos* at the foot of a mountain made of beryl, the Doctor decided to leave Hoppy in charge of the ship and explore.

The next morning, when he got up, Hoppy was pleasantly surprised to discover that, during the night, someone had left a giant melon just outside the ship. He was delighted to realize that the planet's natives were obviously friendly and wondered if the Doctor had met any of them yet. He ate the delicious melon for breakfast while waiting for a delegation of Trafalmadorians–which never came.

The following morning, he found another succulent melon outside the ship, but still no other sign or word from the aliens. Hoppy decided that they might have expected an exchange of gifts, so he reciprocated by leaving a bottle of his best Glenfiddich outside.

This went on for a week: a delicious melon for a bottle of scotch, but still no emissaries. Hoppy was starting to get upset. Did the aliens think they were too good for him?

The Doctor returned ten days after his departure. The first thing he saw was Hoppy's body, with a note pinned on the corpse. It read:

"Why did your monkey eat all our ambassadors? This means war."

Thanks to Doctor Omega's legendary skills, a diplomatic incident with Trafalmadore was narrowly averted and Earth was saved again.

The aphorism "less is more" is generally credited to architect Mies van der Rohe. While not true in every circumstance, the very short story, or "short short," is a unique medium that allows the reader to focus on one aspect of a character and find something surprising and enlightening about it, as if he was looking at the shadow of a larger thing. Unlike prose poems, it is not purely about the language, and it should contain more of a plot than a mere character sketch. An acknowledged master of the "short short" was the late Fredric Brown (1906-1972), to whom this Suite *is respectfully dedicated.*

Jean-Marc Lofficier & Fernando Calvi: *A Suite of Shadowmen*

Arsène Lupin: *Arsène Lupin's Christmas*

Arsène Lupin was always early. He had often found it useful in his career. But this time, the girl, perhaps wiser, had not shown up for the hastily arranged rendezvous on the Grands Boulevards.

"Bah," said Lupin. Since he had a couple of hours to spare, he entered the children's theater. It was the week before Christmas and they were presenting a traditional puppet show. In the dark, among his own people, Lupin felt safe. Suddenly, just as Père Noël–Santa Claus–was shown coming down the chimney, he noticed that the child next to him, a little girl of ten, had begun to cry.

"Excuse me, Monsieur," said a woman who turned out to be the child's aunt. "I thought the show would help take her mind off of things, but you, see, the Police arrested her father last night..."

It turned out that the child's father, Monsieur Dubois, had been the *homme à tout faire*, handyman, employed, or rather exploited, by Baron d'H***. The heartless nobleman had fired Dubois, a widowed father, the week before Christmas, refusing to pay him his final month's wages. When Dubois had returned during the night through the chimney to steal something in exchange for what he was owed, the wily Baron, who had anticipated the move, was waiting with the Police.

The next day, a man impersonating Chief Inspector Ganimard signed for Dubois' release at the Prison de la Santé. That same night, Baron d'H*** was the victim of a daring burglary which robbed him of nearly half-a-million francs.

And in Canada, there would soon be a newly-emigrated French family whose little girl never cried again when she saw Santa Claus slide down a chimney.

Erik: *Figaro's Children*

Figaro was the only one in the Opéra not afraid of Erik.

Figaro was a cat.

Pardon, Figaro was a *chatte*, a lady cat (in every sense of the word), but it had always been a tradition to name the Opéra's cat Figaro, and gender had not been deemed important enough to upset that tradition.

Every rat the Rat-Catcher did not get was Figaro's to enjoy. She was welcome everywhere, above and below the Opéra.

And, as we said, she was the only resident of that prodigious building who was not afraid of Erik. She purred when he caressed her, came occasionally to visit him, begging for treats (she loved dates) and generally behaved like a proper little lady around him.

There was one man, however, who did not like Figaro: Antoine Manoukian, a *machiniste* who, unbeknownst to Management, raised rabbits in a hutch on the third level. Manoukian thought that Figaro ate his baby rabbits, and truth be told, not all baby rabbit disappearances could be blamed on rats.

When her time came, Figaro had kittens. In those days, the Rue Scribe was a notorious haven for cat dalliances.

Manoukian was prepared to put up with one Figaro, if only because he knew that to do otherwise would mean being ostracized by the rest of the staff, but he could not tolerate a chowder of Figaros.

So, stealthily, he managed to grab all the helpless little kittens and stuff them into a bag, weighing it down with a stone, intending to drown them into the Lake.

Mewling bag in hand, he approached the dark water's edge.

Antoine Manoukian's body was found floating in the Seine the next day. Cause of death: drowning, presumably accidental.

Figaro's children still roam free today below the Opéra.

Ask anyone.

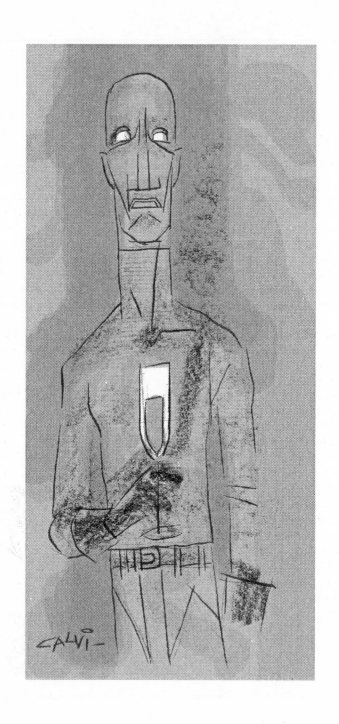

"Death. I see Death," said the gypsy fortune-teller laying out the seven major arcana of the Tarot on the table.

"Indeed," said Fantômas, quickly plunging his dagger into the woman's right eye socket.

The body was quickly undressed and stuffed inside the empty box that served as the support for a scratched crystal ball that had seen better days.

Then, dressed in the gypsy's robes, properly made up, a veil partially obscuring his face, Fantômas waited.

Juve and his men had pursued him to the Foire du Trône. By now, they undoubtedly had drawn a cast iron Police cordon around the Fair. Escape was chancy at best.

Fantômas looked at the cards the gypsy had laid on the table before her untimely demise: Death. *Well, we've seen to that,* he thought.

The Fool. Fandor, who had been sent on a wild goose chase down into the Catacombs. Fantômas smiled at the thought of the deadly trap he had set down there. Perhaps, this time, the pesky journalist would not be lucky.

Justice. Juve. Dull, plodding, but relentless. No surprise there.

The Devil in the middle. That would be him. *So far, so good,* he thought. *But how does the Devil get out of jail? Is there a card for that?*

The Wheel of Fortune, the Hanged Man and the House of God, struck by lightning. Fantômas smiled. He swept away the cards. He had the answer he sought!

The fire, which nearly destroyed the Foire du Trône, was attributed to arson. Eight people died, crushed in the panic; a dozen more had to be hospitalized. The fire had started near the Grande Roue. Luckily, it was put out before it could collapse, which would have killed even more people.

Police Commissioner Juve was found hanging by his feet in the snakes' pit inside the Pavilion des Reptiles. Only his knowledge of the ancient Hindu songs of the snake-charmers of Manganiyar had saved his life.

Fantômas remained an unbeliever in the power of the Tarot, but never criticized Lady Beltham anymore for spending her Wednesday afternoons with her astrologer.

116

Doc Ardan: *The Star Prince*

"If you please, draw me a dinosaur!"

Francis Ardan looked at the golden-haired boy. He was dressed in an operetta-style costume, wearing a long blue coat, white shirt, pants and shiny boots. The aviator had been forced to make an emergency landing in this deserted part of the Western Sahara and was busy repairing the engine when, suddenly, the boy had appeared out of nowhere.

"What are you doing here?" asked Ardan.

"If you please, draw me a dinosaur," asked the boy.

It seemed churlish to refuse. Ardan took out his logbook and pencil and began drawing.

"Who are you?" he asked.

"I come from above," said the boy, pointing at the starry sky. "I am so bored up there."

"How did you come here?"

"It is difficult. And very painful. When I leave, I die a little. So I only come when someone is around. I can only come here because that's where they are. The machines."

"The machines?"

"They're buried deep in the sand. There used to be a sea here, and dinosaurs and other children with whom I could play. But everything is gone now. And I am all alone."

Ardan had finished the drawing. He gave it to the boy.

"It is very beautiful," he said. "Just as I remember them. Thank you. I will treasure it forever. It was worth it."

"Can't you come more often? Reach other people?" asked Ardan. "There is so much we could learn from you."

"I don't have enough power. I'm sorry. I'm only a very little star," said the boy, as his made-up body slowly began to crumble into dust, mingling with the sand that covered the ancient machines.

The Nyctalope: *Marguerite*

Vichy had ordered a sweep of the region of Combefontaine, North of Lyon, for members of the Resistance. The Nyctalope was asked to go along; he was not happy because he despised the Milice, but when Jacques de Bernonville had told him that Mezarek might have returned, he felt he had no choice. He feared that the carnage Belzebuth might wreak far exceeded that of Klaus Barbie.

They had been searching the village for an hour when the Nyctalope entered the Loubets' house. The old farmer and his wife looked at him with the hostility he had come to recognize; in a corner, he noticed a small girl playing with a doll.

"What's your name?" he asked the child.

"Laurence," she replied.

"And what's her name?" he said, pointing at the doll.

"Marguerite."

"Can I hold her?"

The child reluctantly gave him the doll. He looked under its skirt. It was made in England.

"Where did you get it?" he said, giving the doll back.

"Yesterday was my twelfth birthday. The Tooth Fairy came in the middle of the night and brought me the doll. He said her name was Marguerite. He kissed me and told me to go back to sleep and not tell anyone."

The Nyctalope stood up. The Milice was about to enter the Loubet house. He looked at the child. He looked at Marguerite.

"Please, Monsieur, take Marguerite for your daughter," said Laurence, shyly handing him the doll. "Maybe she doesn't have a Marguerite."

The Nyctalope took the doll.

"I already searched this house," he told the Milice. "There's no one here except a couple of farmers and their granddaughter. False alarm." Then, he whispered to Laurence: "I'll take Marguerite but only because someone else might wonder what a British doll is doing here. Tell the Tooth Fairy that tonight, the border will be unguarded near Chaumont."

After the War, the Loubets–father and daughter reunited–received a package in the mail that contained Marguerite. They searched in vain for the Nyctalope to thank him, but he had vanished.

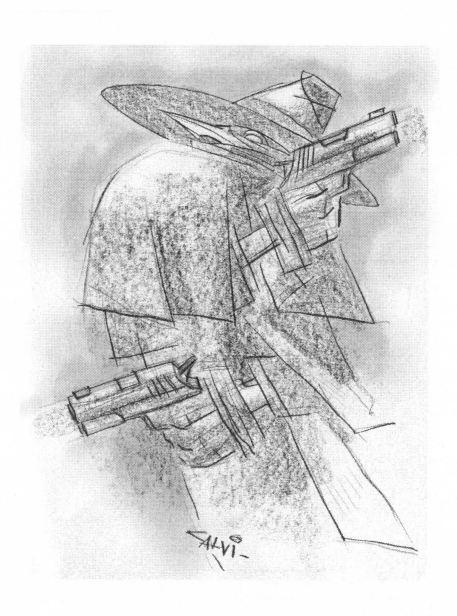

Judex: *Lost and Found*

Jacques de Trémeuse had sworn to destroy the banker Favraux, responsible for his family's ruin. Whatever he could not achieve by day under the guise of Favraux's discreet secretary, Vallières, he undertook by night as the black-clad Judex, an identity he had come to relish.

It was Vallières, however, not Judex, who sat across from the corpulent, sweating, 30-year old German in the *Brasserie d'Alsace*.

"I will come straight to the point," wheezed the interloper. "Information has come into my possession, Monsieur Vallières, that your employer, Monsieur Favraux, has purchased an important consignment of rare *objets d'art* from Turkey. Worth a veritable fortune, but only if properly appraised and sold to the right parties, of course."

"You are well informed, Herr...?"

"Gutman. Kaspar Gutman. That consignment happens to contain a treasured heirloom, which had been in our family for generations until the great earthquake of Izmir in 1883... I would like you to arrange for that special item to be sold to me privately. Of course, there would be a gratuity for you, Monsieur Vallières. A considerable gratuity, I might add."

"I am not in the habit of doing those kinds of transactions, Herr Gutman. I am sorry but you will have to talk to Monsieur Favraux yourself."

Gutman had told Jacques de Trémeuse what he wanted to know, which is why he had agreed to the meeting. Properly auctioned off, that mysterious consignment, the contents of which Favraux had kept secret, could provide an unexpected boost to the banker's fortunes, just as they were beginning to flag. That could not be allowed to happen. A plan was forming. As Vallières, he had access to all the shipping information, and it would be child's play, as Judex, to let these details fall into the hands of the Vampires, for example...

The news that the consignment had been stolen in Marseilles was a shock to Favraux, although not as much as Judex expected. The wily banker had gotten wind of the underworld's interest and purchased some last minute insurance.

"It's out of my hands now, Herr Gutman," Favraux told the German. "What was that item again?"

"A black statue in the form of a bird... A falcon..."

"Well, I'm sorry, Herr Gutman, but it's probably lost again. Forever, this time, I think."

A Tales of the Shadowmen *anthology would not be complete without, somehow, a mention of Sherlock Holmes. Xavier Mauméjean, an old hand at myth-making, as those who have read his* League of Heroes *may attest, breaks the usual boundaries of Holmesian fiction by throwing the Great Detective into a world very different from what he has, so far, encountered, a world which will undoubtedly be immediately familiar to any reader as the very epitome of the loss of freedom and dehumanization of the individual. A world where they took away his name and...*

Xavier Mauméjean: *Be Seeing You!*

The Village, 1912

The Most Dangerous Man in the Kingdom stepped out of his cottage to have breakfast. His features were drawn as he walked down the Village's flowerlined paths. When the residents passed his tall, lanky silhouette, dressed in a dark jacket with white trim, they saluted him, but only perfunctorily. They, too, were dressed in strange holiday accoutrements that would not have been out of place on Brighton Beach. The newcomer was known in the village as "Danger Man"– a man with whom it was better not to be associated. He, conversely, ignored them, not returning their salutes, not even that of the friendly cyclist atop his penny-farthing bicycle.

He sat down at the terrace of the Café. A waitress appeared almost instantly.

"A cup of tea," he asked, ignoring her overly ingratiating smile.

She went back inside, relayed the order to the Chef, then coded a brief message which she handed to the operator for immediate transmission. It said:

Attention: Number 1. Stop. Confirming Arrival of Mr. Sherlock Holmes in the Village this morning. Stop. Awaiting Instructions. Over.

The Detective had no recollection of his kidnapping. It had been an ordinary summer day in Sussex. In late afternoon, he had attended his bees as usual before calling it a day. He had gone to bed at home, in his bed, and had inexplicably awakened in this near-perfect, brand new Village, which still smelled of fresh paint. A kind of "Neverland" as James Barrie, one of Watson's literary agent's friends, might have called it. Good old Watson! No doubt he would move Heaven and Earth to find him. But where would he start? As far as anyone knew, he was just an ordinary retiree enjoying his golden years in solitude on the Downs.

A young man showed up. He carried an umbrella and wore a top hat and a formal black suit, the type one saw at the Foreign Office. Somehow, he reminded Holmes of his younger self.

"Where am I?" asked the Detective.

"In the Village," replied the young man.

"What do you want?"

"Information."

"Information?"

"Information about your brother."

"Ah. I see. And who are you?"

"Number 2."

"What a preposterous label! Why not 'Thursday?' "

The young man remained impassible. "If you cooperate," he said, "your stay among us can be quite enjoyable. You may even be trusted with a position of responsibility in this community."

"You won't hold me."

"Sooner or later, you'll want to tell us what we seek."

"I doubt it," said Holmes contemptuously.

"Anything else?" asked Number 2.

"Yes. I hope your new position here will not make you regret having resigned your post as Police Commissioner in Burma."

In the following days, Holmes found multiple other uses for his deductive powers. Even though the other residents were very guarded in their conversations with him, he did not fail to observe that most of them were retired or captured spies, some British, others not. There were Prussians and Frenchmen, Italians and Russians. Some, such as Von Bork and Azzef, he even recognized from files to which he had had access.

He gleefully shared his observations with Number 2 in order to show him that he was not fooled by the atmosphere of fake congeniality in the Village. Beneath its appearance of gentility, the place was as deadly as a nest of vipers.

"I disagree," said the young man. "We see this as a prototype for the World of Tomorrow. A blueprint for a new order, peace and enlightenment under the governance of the great western powers."

"If that is your new world, I might want to hitch a ride on Mr. Barbicane's next rocketship," said Holmes.

All the time, he had been planning, scheming, and now he was ready to make his move.

The darkest recesses of Her Majesty's Secret Service were a State within the State, a cancer growing on the Empire. Their "Number 1" was variously known as "M," "Control" or "Hunter." The current holder of that title was more dangerous that even the nefarious Professor Moriarty, more scheming than his predecessor, his brother Mycroft, who had been overthrown by a Whitehall cabal.

Funnily, he had had only to invert his initial to assume the title.

"W" had become "M."

Winston Churchill.

The ambitious First Lord of the Admiralty–a more effective cover than that of the Diogenes Club–was his enemy. Of that, Holmes had no doubt. He was the one who had had him arrested and transported to this ingenious, new Bastille that Churchill's fertile mind had devised to find out what was in the files Mycroft had entrusted to him before disappearing.

Holmes was pulled out of his musing by Von Bork's arrival. The elegant German agent sat near him.

"Do you have a light?" he asked. Then, as Holmes handed him a lighter, he grabbed the Detective's wrist and whispered: "Your plan is working–so far. Ned Hattison reached his father's medium, who in turn contacted *him*, as you suggested. He has now arrived. My men are ready. The watchers will be disabled at my signal. We've put all our hopes in you, Mr. Holmes. Don't disappoint us."

Then, like in a perfectly rehearsed musical number, Azzef walked into the Café, looking for all the world like a man who was hopelessly drunk.

The Russian anarchist bumped into the Prussian agent, who pushed him back forcefully. Azzef stumbled into the table behind him, where four residents were eating. It collapsed with a fracas of broken dishes and insults.

Soon, a general melee started; but a canny observer would have noticed that certain men were, in fact, ganging up on others, immobilizing them, preventing them from raising the alarm.

As soon as the scene had started, Holmes had jumped to his feet and run towards the beach. Some of the residents waved at him as he ran. A couple tried to stop him but there was an obliging umbrella swung by one or the other of the prisoners to put a stop to their actions.

As the Detective set foot on the beach, the not-so-friendly-anymore cyclist on his penny-farthing pulled out a gun and fired. The bullet whizzed by Holmes, missing him by mere inches. Suddenly, the cyclist fell to the ground, pushed by someone who had come out of a bush. It was Ned Hattison who pointed towards the distant surf.

"The tide is up. *He*'s waiting for you over there," he told Holmes. "Run! *And beware the Rover!*"

This was perhaps the hardest physical effort Holmes had ever undertaken. Running on wet sand, especially at his age, was like torture. He felt his heart pounding wildly in his chest, blood vessels throbbing in his temples. But he could not stop. He had to get away. He had to escape.

Suddenly, behind him, Holmes heard an inhuman, high-pitched whistle.

Without stopping, he turned his head to look back. What he saw almost froze him in place.

A huge sphere made of bolted metal plates was bouncing madly in his direction, propelled by jets of steam, uncannily defying gravity. *Another of Cavor's maddening inventions*, Holmes thought.

He had reached the water, soon waistdeep, and began swimming with renewed energy towards the small submarine which had just appeared. Its turret opened and *he* was there just in time to grab him and pull him inside.

But the *damnable Frenchman* could not just pack up and go. In his typical fashion, he had to indulge in a last act of Gallic bravado. He made a funny salute, thumb and index circled, hand tipped to his cap, and shouted:

"*Bonjour chez vous!*"

Then, Arsène Lupin slammed the hatch behind him, the submarine dived and disappeared.

"You might as well call back your guard dog now, Number 2," said Number 1, puffing on his cigar.

"I could still have one of our destroyers go after him," suggested the young man in the dark suit.

"You did not recognize that submarine. I did. That was the *Bouchon-de-Cristal*, Monsieur Lupin's own craft, built from Louis Lacombe's designs. We have nothing yet than can match its performance. I'm afraid we have lost our Mr. Holmes for good. We will have to be more careful in identifying and monitoring his type in the future. We need a special code... Hmm... Remind me already, what is Mr. Holmes' birthday?"

"January 6," replied Dennis Nayland Smith, the man who was the first Number 2.

"Let's call them Number 6 then," said Winston Churchill, the man who was the first Number 1.

Like Paul Féval, Alexandre Dumas is one of the founding fathers of modern popular literature. He is, for example, credited with the famous motto "Cherchez la femme," which first appears in his proto-detective novel, Les Mohicans de Paris. The first volume of Tales of the Shadowmen featured Dumas' notorious Count of Monte-Cristo, and this one drops us right at the center of the writer's most famous novel, The Three Musketeers. But as always is the case with our stories, nothing is quite what it seems. Sylvie Miller and Philippe Ward, who have already peeked behind the curtains of History in their novel Le Chant de Montségur, now reveal what really happened to D'Artagnan in London during the Affair of...

Sylvie Miller & Philippe Ward: *The Vanishing Diamonds*

London, 1898

"Another whiskey and soda, Mr. Jorkens?" asked Allan Quatermain, knowing full well that his fellow Club member always told one of his fabled stories when offered his favorite drink.

Joseph Jorkens grabbed an empty glass that rested on the coffee table next to him and offered it to Quatermain. While the famous explorer mixed the drink, Jorkens spun one of his yarns.

When he was done, he looked at the little group that had gathered around him near the great fireplace. That night, the Club had attracted a fine sampling of explorers and adventurers. In addition to Quatermain, there was Nemo, silent and brooding in the corner, Lord Baskerville, recently returned from Asia, Hareton Ironcastle, already planning his next expedition, Griffin, his face wrapped in bandages as usual, sipping a glass of port in a leather armchair, and the man they knew only as the Time Traveler.

The story Jorkens had just told them concerned Charles de Batz-Castelmore, Comte d'Artagnan. The real D'Artagnan. Or so claimed Jorkens.

"So, my dear fellow," said Baskerville at last, with a thinly veiled note of glee in his voice, "that pesky Musketeer never came to England to recover the Queen's diamonds from the Duke of Buckhingham after all."

"I didn't quite say that," Jorkens clarified. "What I said was that it was highly doubtful. I don't think Queen Anne would have fallen in love with the Duke anyway, and even if she had, I can't imagine she'd have given him the very diamond necklace King Louis XIII had just presented to her. It defies credibility."

126

"For once, I'm inclined to agree with you, Jorkens," said Baskerville. "I think that fat Frenchman Dumas invented the whole thing, lock, stock and barrel."

"It is a good yarn, though," said Ironcastle.

"An exceedingly good one, indeed," said Baskerville. "But wholly unsupported by historical evidence."

"I disagree."

The man who had just spoken stood, unprepossessing, leaning on the mantelpiece of the fireplace. His grey eyes shone and twinkled and his usually pale face was, for once, flushed and animated.

"D'Artagnan did come to London and did get the diamonds back to thwart Cardinal Richelieu," he continued. "Dumas may have embellished the story somewhat, but it is, nevertheless, true."

No one in the room knew the man's name. For some reason, known only to himself, he had refused to divulge it when he had first joined the Club. But he had been sponsored by Challenger, who had vouched for him, and that was enough. So, as per his wishes, he was merely–the Time Traveler.

"How would you know?" asked Quatermain. "No, don't tell me, you've used your... machine to check on D'Artagnan?"

"No, but I met Dumas once during one of my journeys. I asked him about D'Artagnan and the Queen's diamonds and he swore to me that the story was true. He is, er, was, a man of many secrets, but overall, he struck me as a truthful man. I'm inclined to believe him."

"How is it possible then," said Baskerville, "that no history books, no letters, no documents of the times mention these famous diamonds? How do you explain that?"

"I can't," replied the Time Traveler, "but just because the diamonds aren't mentioned in history books doesn't mean they didn't exist. Certainly, King Louis gave many presents to his wife. Richelieu's dislike for that foreign princess who consorted with the hated British is well-documented. Besides, why should anyone have written about the diamonds? The whole matter was shrouded in secrecy from the start and no one was eager to brag about their role in it. D'Artagnan brought them back in the nick of time, the King then saw them at the ball and must have instantly dismissed the whole matter as mere Court gossip. As for Richelieu, he had bigger fish to fry... The diamonds vanished between the cracks of history, that's all. That is, until Dumas somehow unearthed their existence."

"With all due respect, that's a rather preposterous argument, sir," said Baskerville. "You are relying on the word of a Frenchman of dubious morality, known for concocting yarns that even Munchausen would have been ashamed of."

"Are you calling me a liar or a fool?" said the Time Traveler, with barely repressed anger.

The two men looked at each other with undisguised hostility. It was not inconceivable that they might have come to blows had Nemo not stepped in.

"Please, my friends. Such arguments are not worthy of you. Especially when there is a much easier way to get to the bottom of this..."

"You don't mean?..." said the Time Traveler.

"Yes, I do," replied Nemo, twirling his moustache for dramatic effect. "Use your fabled Time Machine to travel back to the past and bring us back indisputable proof of the existence of these diamonds."

"I say, that *is* a jolly good idea," said Jorkens.

"Let's make a bet on it," said Ironcastle. "I love bets. Like when I bet Zephyrin Xirdal that..."

"I'm not afraid of any bet," interrupted the Time Traveler. "However, we must agree on what would constitute indisputable proof in your eyes. I can hardly bring the diamonds back as that might change the course of history..."

"Quite right," said Quatermain. "I think a good photograph would be satisfactory. What do you think, my friends?"

"Provided that it includes some recognizable background or historical figure to eliminate any possibility of trickery, yes," said Baskerville.

Everyone nodded his assent.

"Very well," said the Time Traveler. "I'll leave at once and will see you tomorrow, here, at the same time. You know what they say: there's no time like the present."

In the hallway, the Time Traveler bumped into Griffin who was going to the cloakroom. He had an instinctive dislike for the Invisible Man who was often selfish and arrogant. He had been let into the Club only at M's insistence, but was barely tolerated, if not ostracized, by the others.

On his way out, the Time Traveler was joined by Nemo, who put a large, leathery hand on his shoulder.

"Do not mind them too much, my friend," said the sub-mariner. "You and I are scientists, inventors. The lands that we explore are not of this Earth. We journey beyond the boundaries of the physical world. They can be a little jealous of that, at times."

"I know, but sometimes I wish they gave us a bit more credit..."

"It is hard for any man to believe in what he cannot see."

The Time Traveler nodded in silent agreement.

The Club's butler handed the Time Traveler his coat. As the heavy oak door closed slowly behind him, he stepped outside and sniffed the damp London night. He pulled up the lapels of his coat and started walking. Luckily, a cab was passing by. He hailed it and soon was on his way home.

Having paid the driver, the Time Traveler rushed towards the front steps of his house. As he crossed the front garden, he idly thought that his rose bushes needed some pruning and that he needed to oil the hinges of the gate which creaked horribly as it sluggishly shut behind him. But he had been so busy lately...

Once inside, he briskly walked upstairs and entered a large dressing-room. There, he kept a collection of costumes and accessories that enabled him to blend relatively unobtrusively into the various eras he visited. He selected an unremarkable 18th century suit and put it on. Then, he opened a drawer and found a purse full of period gold coins.

Thus properly attired, he went downstairs into his office, opened his note-book and began a new entry to chronicle his projected trip. He always liked to keep meticulous records of his journeys. Occasionally, he also used a camera especially designed for him by Edward Muybridge, the famous photographer, to take pictures of some of his most spectacular destinations. These had been the subject of a Special Exhibit at the Club.

Grabbing his "chronographic model B" camera, he then walked into his workshop where he kept his Time Machine.

It stood there, its glittering, metallic framework shining softly in the dark-ness. It was made of metal, ivory and some transparent crystalline substance. There was an odd twinkling appearance about the central crystal bar, as though it was in some way unreal. In front of the control chair were two small levers, one white, the other black, and what could best be described as a universal cal-endar.

The Time Traveler checked that everything was in order, made some last-minute adjustments, including depositing two teardrops of oil onto a delicate gear, then sat in the control chair. There was a faint breeze in the air, although the windows were shut. He set the chronometer to "1626," took a deep breath to get rid of the anxiety he still felt before each of his trips, and pushed the black lever.

The laboratory grew faint and hazy, then fainter and ever fainter. As he gained velocity, the palpitation of night and day merged into one continuous greyness. As usual, an eddying murmur filled his ears and a strange confusion descended upon his mind.

London, 1626

There was a sound like a clap of thunder. The Time Traveler remained in his seat, stunned for a moment. The confusion in his ears was gone. He looked around. He was in the damp basement of a Richmond house that had existed on the same location where his own house had been built 150 years later.

He had used the house before, so he did not waste any time. He gave his Machine a last check, noticing some rather unusual wear and tear on the intricate network of brass bars that supported the control chair. Some of them were slightly bent, as if they had buckled under an unknown pressure. He knew from past experience that the "time vortex" (as Doctor Omega called it) could inflict such strain on the outside of the craft. However, since it was nothing that would threaten the integrity of the Machine, or affect its performance, he decided not to worry about it until after his return.

He waited for nightfall before going out. The streets were deserted. He had visited the London of that era several times before and had no trouble getting to the palace of the Duke of Buckingham. There, a few small coins handed to a servant enabled him to learn of the recent visit of a mysterious French gentleman two days earlier. That, he deduced, must have been D'Artagnan delivering Queen Anne's letter in which she asked her lover, the Duke, to entrust the diamonds to the Musketeer. Thus having obtained the information he sought, the Time Traveler returned to Richmond and jumped back in time to the precise day when Buckingham and D'Artagnan would show up at the Palace to get the diamonds.

This time, the Time Traveler carried his chronographic camera with him, intending to secure a picture of the jewels with either the Duke or the Musketeer.

He waited patiently in the Palace's courtyard. Finally, after two hours, he heard the sound of a cavalcade. It was Buckingham and D'Artagnan. The Time Traveler blended into the courtiers and servants who always surrounded the Duke when the great man was in town, trying to appear invisible to prying eyes. He found some reassurance in the fact that Dumas, if not history, had recorded that the Duke had willingly given the diamonds back to D'Artagnan, who had then left for Paris without further incident of any kind.

The Duke walked so fast that even D'Artagnan had trouble in keeping up with him. He passed through several apartments, the elegance of which even the greatest nobles of France could not match, and at length arrived in a bedchamber, which was at once a miracle of taste and wealth. In the alcove of this chamber was a door concealed in the tapestry. The Duke opened it with a small gold key which he wore suspended from his neck by a chain of the same metal. With discretion, D'Artagnan remained behind; but as Buckingham crossed the threshold, he turned round and, seeing the hesitation of the young man, cried: "Come in! If you have the good fortune to be admitted to her Majesty's presence, tell her what you have seen."

Encouraged by this invitation, D'Artagnan followed the Duke, who closed the door after them. The Time Traveler, however, had seized the opportunity of the Duke's distraction to sneak unseen into the room.

They were in a small chapel covered with a tapestry of Persian silk worked with gold, and brilliantly lit by a vast number of candles. Over the altar, beneath a canopy of blue velvet, surmounted by white and red plumes, was a full-length portrait of Anne of Austria, so perfect in its resemblance that D'Artagnan uttered a cry of surprise on beholding it. On the altar itself, beneath the portrait, was a casket. The Duke knelt as a priest might have done before a crucifix, and opened it. Inside were the magnificent diamond studs

From his hidden place behind a confessional, the Time Traveler noticed that, unlike what Dumas had written–no doubt in an attempt to spice up the story–all 12 studs were present and accounted for.

"Here," said the Duke, drawing from the casket a large bow of blue ribbon sparkling with diamonds. "Here are the precious studs which I have taken an oath should be buried with me. The Queen gave them to me, the Queen requires them again. Her will be done, like that of God, in all things."

Then, he began to kiss, one after the other, those dear diamonds with which he was about to part.

D'Artagnan took the jewels and carefully slid them into a black velvet purse.

Suddenly, there was a commotion outside. The door burst open and five men, all dressed in black, burst into the room. Buckingham and D'Artagnan pulled out their swords and began fighting in earnest.

The Time Traveler was surprised by this unexpected assault that had not been mentioned by Dumas. Perhaps, he thought, the writer had covered up this incident by making up the more ludicrous story of the two missing studs? But why?

The five attackers, benefitting from their greater number, had the upper hand. D'Artagnan had killed, or severely wounded, one of them but was now backed against the wall by two of the men. The Duke fared no better.

The Time Traveler decided to step in. Silently emerging from behind the confessional, he grabbed his camera and slammed it hard onto the skull of one of the attackers. That, and the element of surprise, enabled the Musketeer to quickly finish the other man and then jump to the Duke's rescue.

"I don't know who you are, nor where you came from, Monsieur," said the Musketeer in a gravelly voice, "but I owe you my gratitude."

"I would consider myself repaid if you would let me see the Queen's diamonds," said the Time Traveler in rather clumsy French.

D'Artagnan grew immediately suspicious and his blade went up, threatening the Englishman. "Why?" he asked. "How do you know about this? Are you another of the Cardinal's spies?"

"No, not at all," said the Time Traveler, hurriedly. "I don't want the diamonds. I mean, I only want to see them. You can keep them in your hands all the time. In fact, it would be better if you did. Then I'll leave and..."

"I don't understand any of this rigmarole, but I have no time for it." D'Artagnan turned towards Buckingham who was slowly regaining his breath. "My Lord, I must leave immediately. The Cardinal must already have more men out looking for me."

"You're right," said Buckingham. "I will accompany you to the riverbank. There's a brig there whose captain is in my employ; he will convey you to a small port, St. Valery, where you are certainly not expected, and which is ordinarily only frequented by fishermen..."

The Time Traveler decided to make one, last appeal.

"Please, Monsieur," he began.

But Buckhingham had already summoned two of his own guards.

"Take away these bodies," he instructed, "and keep watch over that man. I shall want to question him when I return."

While one of the guards dragged the first of the five dead men out by their feet, the Time Traveler remained prisoner under the watchful eye of the other guard, who held the point of his sword to his throat.

Suddenly, as the other man came back to grab the second body, he somehow tripped and stumbled right on top of his fellow guard. Both men fell to the ground, swearing loudly.

The Time Traveler seized the opportunity and bolted from the chapel. Locking the door behind him to slow down his pursuers, he rushed to a balcony and jumped over its railing, managing to land onto a cart driven by a pair of oxen, carrying bales of hay for the stables.

A few minutes later, he was safely out of the Duke's Palace.

But he still had no picture of the diamonds. To return to the present without such a document would be an admission of failure, or worse. Instantly, his mind was made up.

There was really only one thing left for him to do.

Paris, 1626

On that morning, nothing was talked of in Paris but the ball which the Aldermen of the City were to give for King Louis XIII of France and Queen Anne of Austria, and in which their Majesties were to dance the famous *La Merlaison*—the King's favorite ballet

At six p.m., the guests began to arrive. As fast as they entered, they were placed in the grand salon, on the dais prepared for them. The Time Traveler was among them. He had used most of his gold to secure transportation to Calais, then across the Channel, and then by an express coach to Paris. He had arrived that very afternoon with little time to spare to rent a room, buy himself a presentable suit and secure an invitation to the night's festivities.

At midnight, great cries and loud acclamations were heard. It was the King, who was passing through the streets which led from the Louvre to the Hotel de Ville, and which were all illuminated with colored lanterns. His Majesty, in full dress, was accompanied by his usual coterie of Dukes, Counts and Chevaliers. Everybody noticed that Louis XIII looked subdued and preoccupied.

The Time Traveler had used the time to secure a safe spot for himself, from which he would be able to unobtrusively photograph the Queen wearing her famous diamonds.

Half-an-hour later, fresh acclamations were heard; these announced the arrival of the Queen. The Aldermen did as they had done before, and preceded by their sergeants, advanced to receive their illustrious guest. The Queen entered the great hall; and it was noticed that, like her husband, she looked subdued and weary.

At the moment she entered, the curtain of a small gallery which, until then, had been closed, was drawn. The pale face of Cardinal de Richelieu appeared. His eyes were fixed upon those of the Queen, and a smile of cruel joy passed over his lips.

Anne of Austria was not wearing her diamond studs.

The Time Traveler was thunderstruck. What could have gone wrong? Had D'Artagnan not made it back to Paris in time? Then, he remembered that Dumas had described the very scene that was now unfolding before his eyes.

The King had just made his way through the crowd. He went straight to the Queen, and in a strained voice said: "Why, Madame, have you not thought it proper to wear your diamond studs, when you know it would give me so much gratification?"

Anne of Austria cast a glance around her, and saw the Cardinal with a diabolical smile on his face.

"Sire," she replied in a faltering voice, "because, in the midst of such a crowd as this, I feared some accident might happen to them."

"You were wrong, Madame," said Louis. "If I made you such present, it was that you might adorn yourself therewith." His voice trembled with anger. Everybody looked and listened with astonishment, no one understanding what truly transpired, except for the Time Traveler, who, despite his knowledge, could not help but be gripped by anxiety.

"Sire," said the Queen, "I can send to the Louvre for them, where they are, and thus your Majesty's wishes will be fulfilled."

"Do so, Madame, do so, and that at once; for within an hour, the ballet will commence."

The Queen bent in token of submission, and followed the ladies who were to conduct her to her room. For his part, the King returned to his apartment.

There was a moment of disturbance and confusion amongst the assembly. Everyone had remarked that something had passed between the two monarchs; but both of them had spoken so quietly that everybody, out of respect, had withdrawn several steps, and had thus heard nothing. The violins began to sound with all their might, even as no one listened to them.

The King was first to emerge from his room. He was in a most elegant hunting costume that became him well. Suddenly, a cry of admiration burst from every mouth. For if Louis appeared to be the first gentleman of his kingdom, then Anne of Austria was, without doubt, the most beautiful woman in France.

She wore a beaver hat with blue feathers, a *surtout* of grey-pearl velvet, fastened with diamond clasps, and a petticoat of blue satin, embroidered with silver. On her left shoulder sparkled the diamond studs, on a bow of the same color as the plumes and the petticoat.

The King trembled with joy and the Cardinal with vexation.

At that moment, the violins sounded the signal for the ballet.

The King advanced towards the Queen and the ballet began. Everytime Louis faced her, his eyes devoured the 12 beautiful, sparkling diamond studs on his wife's pale shoulders.

The Time Traveler retrieved his camera discreetly and checked it thoroughly. It had captured no less than five pictures of the King and the Queen dancing, the diamonds clearly in evidence.

He had won his bet.

Tomorrow, he would return to London and head back to the future.

London, 1898

"These are beautiful pictures," said Allan Quatermain, looking at the glossy portraits spread over the coffee table. "What do you say, Baskerville? Has our friend won his bet"

"Yes, I must admit that he has." Then, addressing the Time Traveler directly. "I'll be happy to settle with you at your convenience, sir."

"So shall I," added Jorkens, "for I confess I never believed in that story myself. But I guess you have proven both of us wrong, eh?"

"Indeed, he has!" said Ironcastle. "Be a good sport, Baskerville. Your generous contribution will help finance my next expedition. A worthwhile use of funds if there ever was one. What about you, sir?" he asked the Time Traveler. But the latter remained silent, absorbed in thought.

"What's wrong, friend?" inquired Nemo. "You act as if you hadn't won the bet..."

"No, it's not that, but the diamonds..."

"What about the diamonds?" asked Quatermain.

"I haven't told you the end of my story. The next morning, just before I was ready to depart for Calais, my driver, who was a great gossip and whose brother worked at the Palace, informed me that all 12 diamond studs had been stolen during the night."

"What?" "How?" "By whom?" exclaimed the others.

"No one knows. They were taken from the Queen's own bedroom. No one saw anything even remotely suspicious. They just vanished. The Queen thought there was a curse upon the stones and that's why no one ever mentioned them again..."

"That is very strange," said Nemo.

"Even stranger still is, how then did that French Dumas learn of the matter?" added Baskerville.

"Do you think we will ever find out?" Quatermain asked the Time Traveler.

"I don't think so," the latter replied. "Unlike the saying, time doesn't always tell."

Paris, 1843

"That is nothing less than an amazing tale, Isaac," said Dumas to the tall, gaunt, bearded man sitting in front of him. "It will make a one hell of a rip-roaring yarn! I can't wait to start. There was nothing like it in D'Artagnan's *Memoirs*. Are you sure it happened exactly as you told me?"

"I beheld it with mine own eyes," the Wandering Jew said. "In exchange, you must remember your own promise to me."

"Yes, yes, I will write your story someday. I gave you my word," said Dumas peevishly.

"Sue is already working on..."

"Sue is a poseur, a maker of cheap theatrical melodrama. This Musketeer story will leave him behind, eating my dust. Trust me, Isaac Laquedem, your long, harrowing tale will be better served by someone such as me. I will write something for the ages. You will become the interpreter of man's thorny and twisted path in his slow climb towards progress..."

"But Sue said..."

"Enough about Sue already! There is one thing you haven't told me. What happened to the diamonds, afterwards?"

"They vanished."

"They vanished?"

"Yes. No one ever saw them again."

"How odd. Hm. I'll have to spice that part up a bit. Maybe a plot twist about two missing studs... Yes, that will do nicely. We can't have any loose ends. The readers wouldn't like it..."

London, 1898

Griffin sat alone in the modest room that had been assigned to him by Her Majesty's Secret Service.

Before him, on the table, sparkling like a river of fire, were the 12 diamond studs of Queen Anne of Austria.

At first, he had only sought to play a dirty trick on the Time Traveler, whom he loathed because he had been so readily accepted by the same Club members who barely gave him the time of the day.

He had followed him invisibly back home and ridden with him to the 17th century. But after beholding the diamonds, the temptation had proven too great to resist. Besides, if what that fool had said was true, hadn't he *already* stolen the jewels? Weren't his actions *already* written in the great tapestry of time?

With such a fortune in his possession, there was nothing he could not achieve, no dream was beyond his grasp, starting with freeing himself from the hateful yoke under which M had him.

Anyone who might have been unfortunate enough to peek inside the room at that very moment would have seen a sparkling river of diamonds being cradled and rocked gently into thin air and heard the sound of small kisses being lavished upon them.

The Invisible Man was scheming.

Jess Nevins' droll idea of bringing together nearly all of the most famous master thieves and criminals of their times was originally planned to appear in our first volume, but its execution was delayed by Jess' prodigious work on the two companion books to League of Extraordinary Gentlemen, *as well as his more recent* Encyclopedia of Fantastic Victoriana. *But like the famous dish that is better served cold, it was worth the wait and is, in fact, perfectly suited to a volume entitled* Gentlemen of the Night. *Join us now for a merry chase* à la It's a Mad Mad Mad Mad World *throughout France and Europe as the most notorious villains of all times compete...*

Jess Nevins: *A Jest, To Pass The Time*

Paris, Monte Carlo and London, 1921

It was, of course, the sensation of the season. The "Moonstone," that fabulous yellow diamond which was the subject of a Nine Day's Wonder two generations ago, anonymously donated to the Louvre! The Moonstone was to be granted a space to itself in the Galerie d'Apollon, the glorious Apollo Gallery, and would make its debut in a fashion guaranteed to leave lasting memories: an invitation-only unveiling, accompanied by a string quartet, and an introductory lecture by the noted gemologist Bernard Sutton.

Paris, still shuddering from the War and the new garden of white crosses at the Père Lachaise Cemetery, seized on the news with the avidity of *a demi-mondaine* near a bachelor millionaire. Invitations could not be had for love–but since we are being honest, we will call it "sex"–or money. A year's subscription to the Palais Garnier, a week with the Lady Wyndham, most delectable of the *haut monde*'s *colombes*, a private audience with Prime Minister Briand–all were politely laughed away as far, far too little. As the correspondent for *Le Temps* put it, "No debut since Princess Narda's has been so anticipated or exclusively attended."

The night of the stone's unveiling brought with it a storm of Wagnerian proportions; sometimes Nature is kind enough to provide the best accompaniment for an event. The gem's donor, who wished to remain nameless–for there was some question as to how the Moonstone had made its way from India to the West for a second time–inspected the security precautions an hour before the Louvre's doors were to open and pronounced them "sound."

Inspectors Jordan and Tony, two of the Sûreté's best detectives, had personally overseen the security measures. Flambeau, once notorious in the French underworld as a thief without peer but long since reformed, had as a personal favor to Inspector Jordan tested the museum's defenses himself. Flambeau was caught before he reached the second floor. The Police had men everywhere, officers at the entrances, watchers on the roof, plainclothes detectives among the guests–nothing could go wrong. All precautions had been taken. No thief could possibly come close to the gem, much less escape with it.

You may laugh now.

The local press accounts of the evening's events were broadly accurate, though erroneous in the particulars. As described in *Le Petit Vingtième*, M. Sutton was most eloquent about the Moonstone's beauty (on a par with the fabled Koh-i-tur), its size (rivaling the great Takawaja emerald), and its reputation (as dire as that of the Cosmopoli sapphires and the Gola pearls). The food was superb, especially the *cailles en sarcophage*, which had the older members of the crowd wondering if Achille Papin had somehow returned to his kitchen. The wine was a stunning array of rare vintages; an astonishing four bottles of the Branaire-Ducru Medoc '05 were available. The string quartet was flawless. Most of the guests were dressed in a fashion that, in a company less wealthy, would have been described as ostentatious. For this group of individuals, the adjectives chosen were "stylish" and "flamboyant." The women wore an array of custom-made silk Chanel and Patou gowns. The men were clad in bespoke tuxedos, white ties and silk cummerbunds. At its height, the party brought back memories of *la belle époque*, and the reporters, those vultures of the press, were complimentary to the point of obsequity in their descriptions. Even the Marxists fell prey to the allure of glamorous excess: M. Dicky, who could usually be relied upon for an "Oh, for a Chauchat and a wall to line them up against" quip about the *haut ton*, contented himself with a weak grumble about the starving children of Paris.

But then the lights in the Apollo Gallery went out. For all their acumen and attitude, the press of Paris did not report correctly what took place in the darkness and after the power was restored. *Le Matin* and *Le Figaro* were too busy flattering the egos of the Bencolins and the Trissons of the Sûreté to be bothered to accurately describe what took place. Perhaps unsurprisingly, only the foreign correspondents came closest to the truth in their accounts. But even they missed many relevant details.

I did not. Oh, yes, I was there. And that is why you may rely on my account of the events which followed.

Monsieur Sutton was concluding his remarks, quoting the Lama Samdad Chiemba to the effect that the Moonstone is "the heart of India, and where the Moonstone is, there also India is," when the lights suddenly flared and went out. The abrupt loss of the luminous glow created by the lights and the delicate colors of the paintings in the Gallery–*The Fall of Icarus* had never seemed so lush, nor Schalken's portrait of the Amayats so heartbreaking–created a sensation of almost physical shock, especially among the more refined women in the crowd, who were accustomed to nothing more distressing than an incorrectly mixed aperitif.

There was a second of horrified silence, broken by the triumphant shout of "Z is the life! Z is the death!" The reaction to this cry... you can imagine it, but to truly understand it, you had to have lived in Paris while the monstrous Zigomar–for the cry was his motto–was terrorizing the citizenry.

Wallion, in his article in the *København Aftonbladet*, caught something of the electric thrill of panic which ran through the crowd on hearing the shout. Elvestad put it well, in his account in the *Stockholm Boersen*, when he described the sounds of women fainting in the dark as "an arrhythmic percussion emphasizing the medley of screams." The reaction of the men in the Gallery–first, hearing the motto of the serial murderer Zigomar, then hearing their women faint, and all the while unable to see anything–as Hagen-Kander put it in the *Berliner Morgenpost*, "every man present was caught between the Jekyll of terror and the Hyde of fury."

After 30 seconds of panic and rage in the darkness–I tell you, I have heard nothing like it since the War, when Auguste Dubois, Miraculas and I blew up the castle at Styria and left Götz, Wormer and their men trapped inside to die by fire–electricity was restored to the Gallery and the lights came back up, and the men and women in the crowd immediately fell silent.

The guards protecting the Moonstone were on the ground, unconscious or dead, and a quite undistinguished man in a surprisingly tedious tuxedo was clutching the diamond. His face was so plain that even a Holmes would not have spared him a second glance–but to look that ordinary is a kind of genius, and in that way, this man was among the greats of our century. But even while his face betrayed nothing–besides a lack of hygiene and an appalling taste in facial hair–his eyes... well, they were cold, my friend, cold as the killing fields of Verdun. He held a gun on the crowd, his hand was steady and he had the manner of a man who has long passed caring about one murder. Or five. Or a hundred.

In ordinary circumstances, his manner, and his gun, which in the silence looked so very big, would have been sufficient to guarantee his escape. But as he opened his mouth to again shout, "Z is the life!" a knife, thrown from somewhere in the crowd, hummed through the air and knocked the gun from his hand.

(In retrospect it was foolish of him to expect this, of all crowds, to be daunted by the sight of a gun. He could not have known who he would face, but it was predictable that the debut of the Moonstone would attract an... unusual group of men and women).

He recovered quickly and grabbed for another gun, but before he could draw it, the front row of men was on him. No man, not even Dunot himself, can hold off an angry crowd for long, and the men in this crowd were both skilled and angry. The thief fell quickly to the pistoning arms and legs of the crowd. A moment of confusion followed, and then the most elegant man in the room emerged from the scrum holding the diamond.

I had spoken with him earlier during the wine reception (what my friend Countess Told calls "the miracle of reverse Transubstantiation: turning a heavenly red wine into dull, temporal water") and had been impressed by him. An Italian, he was a friend of Comte Etienne de Beaumont–you know of him, he of the "townhouse *le monde*," the intimate of Chanel and Cocteau, and by acclaim the best-dressed man in the city–and all observers granted the Italian the palme de soie as the Comte's superior in couture. The Italian wore a monocle, a double-breasted coat, and a cloak, all the superior of the shops of Milan. He claimed to be a Baron of noble lineage and even a descendant of Caradossa himself. The Baron had struck me as cultured, erudite and quite incapable of physical violence. He was tall and thin–"wiry," if you are feeling generous–but there were small (but visible) crow's-feet around his eyes, his hair was streaked with silver, and his mustache was waxed; experience has taught me that no man who waxes his mustache is effective in a fight.

But the Italian Baron was possessed of a surprising strength, enough to wrest the Moonstone away from a crowd of men desperate to possess it. The Baron held the Moonstone in one gloved hand and let the lights play off the diamond's facets and reflect off the mirrors of the Gallery. The light built in brightness until it seemed that the Baron held a tiny star in his hand, and the audience hushed and grew still as we shared his appreciation of the diamond's beauty. But scant seconds later the moment was ruined.

"You, there! Put that down!"

The speaker was a museum official who had made himself unwelcome during the reception due to his coarse manner and the distasteful way in which he drank his wine. (The wine server should have given him a spoon.) He was officious, had an offensive mustache, wore a remarkably unfashionable suit, and his voice was a marvel of abrasiveness. He advanced on the Baron.

"You, sir! I am Louis-Charles Picardet, Chief of Security for the Louvre, and I demand that you relinquish the stone at once!"

His chest puffed, his chins quivering; the man was the very picture of a petit-bourgeois official finally given the chance to hector one of the nobility. The Baron smiled with great geniality and with a flourish proffered the gem to Picardet. I was particularly impressed that the Baron's expression did not at all betray his disappointment at not being given the chance to swap the Moonstone for the glass duplicate cunningly concealed in his vest pocket.

Picardet swept from the Gallery in a cloud of self-importance. He snapped his fingers at two of the guards who were still conscious, and they followed him out of the Gallery and toward the Escalier Henri II. But once out of sight of the crowd in the Gallery, Picardet's stride lengthened, the heavy, clumsy clomp of his so-unsuitable shoes changed to a light, nimble tread, and a close observer would have noticed that he was suddenly four inches taller and somehow broader in the shoulder. Even an acute observer, however, would have been hard-pressed to have followed Picardet's fingers as he slipped the Moonstone into a sleeve pocket and exchanged it for a duplicate.

As Picardet reached the stairwell, he was beaming and almost skipping. So joyous was he, in fact, that he temporarily forgot that, behind him, were two armed security guards, both of whom might be as false as the duplicate Moonstone.

The first guard–his uniform read "Marcel Troyon"–was lean to the point of gauntness, and his Byronically pale skin bore a fascinating set of scars and tattoos. The second–his uniform read "Etienne de la Zeur"–was somewhat shorter, more muscular, though giving way to the comfortable bulk of middle age, and had a naturally glowering expression. A Policeman, seeing him, would immediately arrest him, simply on general principle; de la Zeur's was a face that guaranteed future violence.

Troyon moved first. Picardet was entering the stairwell when Troyon struck him on the back of his head with a nightstick. It was a clean blow, well-practiced, and he awoke a half-hour later with only a slight headache. De la Zeur, not having suspected his comrade of duplicity, was momentarily surprised; Troyon used the moment to unsheathe a stiletto from his boot and point it at de la Zeur, holding him off while Troyon rummaged through Picardet's pockets. Troyon found the Moonstone and then fled down the stairs.

He took the stairs two at a time and exited on to the Entresol. He ran through the Oriental Antiquities wing, not even glancing at the celebrated diorama of the Duke of Chin's approach to Knei Yang which looms over the Richelieu Wing. Perceiving that de la Zeur was close behind, and in possession of a knife of his own, Troyon tore down a Metzengerstein tapestry and threw it on top of de la Zeur, followed by the oversize frame containing Penniel's *The Hills West of Napa Valley*.

Troyon ran down the Escalier de la Victoire de Samothrace and into the maze that is the Louvre's sub-level, where the relics and damaged works are kept. He followed a series of chalk marks on the wall until he reached a janitor's bathroom. He locked the door behind him and waited. Several moments passed, and he still heard no sounds of pursuit. He grinned and stripped out of his uniform, removing his wig and facial makeup.

He was examining his hair and mustache in the bathroom's cracked mirror when the door was kicked open. De la Zeur leapt inside and fell on Troyon before the latter could reach his knife. Troyon managed to disarm De la Zeur, and the two were left to grapple for the Moonstone. A terrible struggle followed, each abandoning what martial skill they knew to resort to savagery and brute strength. I have seen rams fighting who had more subtlety, and feral cats with more mercy.

Behind them, unnoticed during their fight, a wall panel in one of the stalls silently slid aside, revealing a tunnel into the bedrock. Crouched in the tunnel, owlishly watching Troyon and de la Zeur grunt and strain to throttle the other, was a figure in heavy black robes and a hood and wearing a black ceramic mask which bore a severe expression and only exposed the eyes and mouth.

(Yes, you are correct–it was the "Phantom of the Louvre" himself. No, he is no myth; I have spoken with him myself).

The Phantom waited, unmoving and breathing shallowly, until the inevitable occurred: the Moonstone was jarred free. Troyon and de la Zeur were too occupied with their struggle and their pain–de la Zeur's arm was dislocated, and one of Troyon's eye sockets was fractured–to notice the gem rolling free. The Phantom scooped up the Moonstone and replaced the wall panel, and neither Troyon nor de la Zeur were ever the wiser as to the gem's disappearance while they fought.

There are many stories about the tunnels beneath and around the Louvre: that they connect to the catacombs of the city, form a spiderweb beneath the city, and reach even as far as Amiens; that a vampire once used them as his home; that the Masons and Rosicrucians use them now for secret rites; that they are hellish passages, covered in slime and home to spiders the size of cats and rats the size of mastiffs. Only the latter story is false. The tunnels beneath the Louvre are usually cool and dry and quite pleasant; centuries of feet have worn the stone smooth, and the regular passage of people have chased the vermin into the sewers.

The Phantom followed a twisting trail through these tunnels–even I would have been hard-pressed to follow him–until he finally exited into a sewage tunnel underneath the Rue de Rivoli. Those tunnels are as ghastly as rumor make them out to be; the Phantom was wise to wear black, as the unspeakable stains he rapidly acquired would not show against the fabric of his robes.

He crept to the intersection of sewage tunnels beneath the church of Saint-Germain-l'Auxerrois. I have, to my regret, been there (I had to have both my trousers and boots burned afterward), and it is a foul place. Picture a wide, rough-hewn cavern with a suffocatingly-low ceiling. Picture multiple pipes emptying their filth into the cavern. Picture a slurry of sewage, sometimes only ankle-deep, but over a foot high on this evening due to the torrent of rain. Now imagine yourself in this place, and imagine it enlivened only by the dimmest of lights, and imagine it bearing a smell only Arabic has the words to describe.

The Phantom was slogging through this cavern, no doubt holding his breath, when he became aware that he was not alone. He stopped, and out of the darkness a voice spoke to him, bearing the coarse accent of the *Apaches* of the streets.

"Good evening... What are you calling yourself these days? The Duc d'Arcachon? Belphegor? Mylord L'Arsouille?"

The Phantom did not respond but carefully drew a revolver–care more than speed was called for, for to drop the gun into the liquid at his feet would be to lose the gun (that is, you wouldn't want to try to get the gun back)–and began peering into the gloom, searching for the source of the voice.

"Never mind. It's not important. We bear a message for you from Margot."

The Phantom froze and stared to his right, in the direction of the tunnel which led to the Pont Neuf station.

"You remember Margot, don't you? She's no 'Lord of Terror,' and she's not known by a clever anagram, but she is our queen, and we feel kindly toward her. So when she tells us, 'Boys, go get this diamond for me,' why, we're happy to do so."

The Phantom pointed his revolver to his right and said, in an incongruously high-pitched voice, "If she's the queen, she should have sent rooks and bishops, not pawns. They're the first to get knocked off the board."

Small lights appeared around the Phantom. In the opening of each sewage pipe and tunnel stood several street urchins, holding lit matches in one hand and a knife or cudgel in another. They numbered perhaps two dozen, and under their filth and rags they were well-fed and healthy, sewer rats grown plump and sleek on a diet of *foie gras* and *mignon au poivre*. Their leader grinned ferally and said, "Oh, but we're not playing chess. We're playing *vingt-et-un*, and I've got 21."

The Phantom pointed his gun directly between the speaker's eyes. "But I'm an ace, boy, and that trumps everything."

Behind the Phantom one of the urchins, a girl, said, "Sigono, enough with the taunting. Let's just do him and get the stone."

Before the Phantom could respond, a huge gout of viscous, black liquid spurted into the cavern from one of the pipes. It splashed many of the urchins, and the force and weight of the discharge was enough to knock the Phantom over–and spare some sympathy for the Phantom, if you will: there does not exist enough cologne or perfume on Earth to conceal the stench of the Paris sewers.

But the *Apaches* did not leap upon the prostrate and flailing Phantom.

Sigono wrinkled his nose and hesitantly said, "Is that... oil?"

In answer came, from one of the tunnels, a gleeful, evil laughter. Panicked looks crossed the urchins' faces, and Sigono swore, "*Merde! Le génie!*" The children fled into the closest tunnels, and the Phantom forced his way to his feet and tried to follow them.

From the tunnel nearest the Phantom, a lit match pinwheeled through the air. When the match touched the surface of the liquid, it ignited, and flames and smoke instantly filled the cavern. The Phantom threw himself into the nearest tunnel, out of the flaming liquid, and hurriedly threw off his burning robes. Unclothed, but still wearing the mask, the Phantom could be seen to be a slim, athletic woman.

She was checking herself to make sure no burning oil clung to her body when a man quietly stepped out of the darkness behind her and struck her on the back of the head with a cosh. She dropped without a sound, and the man stepped over her, stamped out the flames from her robes, and withdrew the Moonstone from them. He tossed the diamond in the air and chuckled. He moved to leave, then stopped and covered the Phantom with his cloak. He tipped his hat to her, and returned to the Louvre via the sewage pipes and tunnels.

Before entering the Louvre, he paused to adjust his hat and cravat and then smoothed down his tuxedo. He placed a domino mask on his face–it is not that he particularly desired anonymity, you understand, but he is sufficiently well-known and recognizable, wearing the mask, that his vanity demanded that he appear in public wearing it.

He entered the museum through a concealed doorway in the Entresol and ignored the noise of the crowds piled up at the museum exit and enduring the indignities of a body search by the Louvre guards–so efficient now that the theft had already taken place! He climbed the Escalier Colbert to the Second Floor and into the museum's attic, where the curators store material not ready for display.

At this time, most of the material in the attic was South American, the results of the Forrestal-Littlejohn expedition down the Bermejo River, so the visitor to the attic was greeted by the grisly display of several dozen shrunken heads accompanying crude clay figures and two large, inexpertly-carved gold statues. (Hardly worth the effort to steal, which is why no one had bothered.)

The man in the domino mask paused on seeing the rows of shrunken heads, all placed on display sticks and arranged by some waggish student assistant to face the entrance to the attic. The effect was to put the visitor in mind of a macabre, expectant audience at some *valse funèbre*. I am told the man in the domino mask removed his hat, bowed, said, "Ladies and gentlemen, good evening," and continued onward to the roof.

Ahead of him lay the bodies of the Policemen he had killed and the small balloon which his men had constructed there earlier in the evening. But between the roof exit and the balloon stood another man, also in tails, insouciantly leaning on an ivory cane.

The interloper's skin and hair were snow-white, and his crimson-irised eyes glittered as they reflected the lights of Paris. The albino briefly inclined his head toward the man in the domino mask. "Monsieur Fantômas, I presume."

Fantômas smiled and bowed theatrically to the albino. "The Romanian Prince."

The albino smiled coldly. "Indeed."

Fantômas withdrew a long knife from an interior pocket of his jacket and held it ready behind him in a pose known and feared across Paris.

The albino's smile widened, although there was little humor in it. "Ah. You have spared yourself the farce of negotiation and have decided on a more basic language." He pointed his heavy ivory cane at his opponent, although he did not withdraw the sword from it. "It is a tongue I speak fluently."

Fantômas abruptly leapt forward, his knife swinging around to slash at the albino's throat. The albino leaned back slightly and deflected the blow with his cane. He elbowed Fantômas in the jaw and followed through with a stiff, powerful left.

The albino retrieved the Moonstone from Fantômas' unconscious body and was walking toward the exit when he heard whistles from below and the scuffling of boots on the stairs. He walked to the balloon, untethered it, shoved it off the roof, and hopped into its undercarriage as it took to the air.

The Police found the deflated balloon in the Gare d'Austerlitz several hours later.

The sequence of events which followed was not discovered by the Police. It is only by piecing together several different accounts that a clear picture can be drawn of the movements of the Moonstone over the next week.

Blanchard, in *Le Petit Vingtième*, described an event which provoked some mild, brief outrage among the reading public. An albino gentleman–foreign royalty, though Blanchard declined to identify which nationality–was walking toward the hotels along the Boulevard St. Marcel when he saw, limping in his direction, a veteran of the War.

He was horribly scarred–one eye covered by a patch, and a formerly handsome face permanently disfigured–and he was missing an arm. But the man was tall, broad, and seemed to have a great vitality, and on his chest he wore the Légion d'Honneur. He had clearly been reduced to penury–his uniform, seemingly his last piece of clothing, was soiled and had many rents–but he carried himself with pride and did not lower himself to ask the handsomely accoutered albino (returning, Blanchard said, from the previous night's entertainment at the Louvre) for any money.

It was perhaps this pride which caught the albino's attention and drew him to offer the maimed veteran first a cigarette and then the contents of his billfold– for, the albino Prince said, "the sadness of survival." It was this pride which kept the Prince still as he listened to an account of heroism at the Somme and then at the infamous "Loki" prisoner of war camp. And it was this pride, and the eloquence of the veteran, which–according to the albino Prince–distracted him and prevented him from noticing what the veteran was doing as he described the torments of the camp and emphasized his story with gestures from his remaining arm.

The albino Prince admitted–"in a face curiously rueful and almost admiring," or so Blanchard says–that after bidding the veteran farewell and wishing him "the honor of a dignified death," the Prince walked for several hundred yards before thinking to check his pockets. They were quite empty, of course, and the veteran had, by that time, vanished. Carlier, the officer handling the case, had no leads but shared the anger of many that a scoundrel should use the guise of a veteran to commit a crime.

The stories in the Parisian newspapers about Ténèbras, the infamous "Ghost Bandit," are almost as numerous as those about Fantômas, the "Lord of Terror," himself. One story, written by M. Courville in *L'Année 2000*, has received surprisingly little attention from those who track Ténèbras. The afternoon following the disappearance of the Moonstone from the Louvre, a body was found in the Jardins du Trocadero. An autopsy, performed by Dr. Cordat of the Sûreté, revealed that the man had been gassed, and a cab ticket found in the man's vest pocket led Inspector Walter, one of the Sûreté officers pursuing Ténèbras, to claim that the victim had been poisoned in a cab rigged to flood its compartment with poison gas–one of the trademark murder methods of Ténèbras.

Experienced observers of Ténèbras have seen this as but one more murder to his name and, truly, there are so many that, as with Fantômas, Zigomar, Satanas, Dr. Tornada and the many other madmen who have plagued our society, one gets the feeling that more men have died of crime in Paris than perished from German lead during the War. But these observers have slighted this particular murder victim. Among his possessions was a monogrammed handkerchief with the initials, "G.D.," a ticket to the Moulin Rouge, a yellowed newsclipping about the famous American Carter's defeat of a "School of Crime," and a small case, which might once have contained theatrical makeup. On the man's face were substantial traces of makeup, and beneath his coat was a rig which actors and beggars use to conceal a limb. (It involves a harness, a generously cut coat, and the willingness to put up with the discomfort of having one's arm twisted behind the body for hours at a time. It is most uncomfortable).

In the international edition of *The Daily Star*, an Italian reporter named Ruder Ox wrote a piece on the *Café Noir de Lune*. In this piece he–

What? You do not know of the famous *Café Noir de Lune*? I had thought every last Englishman and woman acquainted with it by now, and spending so many hours there that–you will forgive me saying so–the *Café*'s former patrons, good Frenchmen and women all, are prevented from taking any tables. The *Café* is located along the Rue de Nevers, named for the Duke of honored memory. Of late the *Café* has become renowned as the personal salon of France's wittiest raconteur, Emil Lupin (no relation to the infamous Arsène, you may be assured).

It is a café first, of course, and formerly it was famous for the quality of its food, but since the War, Lupin has, every night, taken a center table and entertained the guests of the *Café*, and now the *Café* is better known for Lupin's stories than for its food. I myself have spent several nights there, and Lupin's reputation is well-deserved. He is a master of both dramatic timing and the *bon mot*, and it is understandable that he and the *Café* would become so popular with tourists.

Lupin's stories are marvels of humor and irony, and his "Rupert of Graustark" is a favorite of tourists, not least because of its delightfully slanderous subject matter. Popular rumor has it that those described in the story actually brought suit against Lupin–but I am assured they did not, for fear of having Lupin's tale proven to be true. Among the locals, Lupin's "Fifi's Flight to Eucrasia" remains his most-requested tale. And quite amusing it is–but then, Parisians tend to have a dark and even savage sense of humor. To a more select clientele, Lupin is known for more mature material, including "The Last Draw on the Cigarette."

Alone among the cafés of the Rue de Nevers, the *Noir de Lune* is open all night. Should you care to visit it sometime, Lupin usually appears around 10 p.m. and leaves at 4 a.m. precisely. So it should be no surprise that someone in the mood to celebrate–say, the acquisition of a valuable gem, or perhaps a triumph over one's peers–would go to the *Café* for breakfast. Few tourists frequent the *Café* in the early morning, and it remains a popular spot with the locals for coffee and *oeufs Lyonnaise* or *saucisson à l'Anatole*.

Ruder-Ox describes how, on the morning after the Louvre contretemps, Emil Lupin himself made an appearance at the *Café*, much to the surprise of the regulars. He insisted on seeing that the customers were enjoying themselves, and was seen to pay particular attention to one man, a muscular tough in working-man's clothes. Ruder-Ox made much of the man's appearance by way of illustrating how popular the *Café* was with the locals; Ruder-Ox wrote, "This man seemed more appropriately the inmate of a hard labor camp at Toulon rather than the famous *Noir de Lune*, but Lupin himself treated him as family." Lupin even deigned to share a pot of tea with him–no small honor from the famous Lupin, whose distaste for dining with others was well-known.

The customer was flattered by the attention and delighted with the food, and it was only after leaving the *Café* that he thought to inspect his belongings. In place of his billfold, and what he claimed was a fake diamond of purely sentimental value, was the calling card of one "Professor Pelotard," on which was written one of Villiod's mottos: "One finds that the most suspicious of criminals are always the easiest gulled." The real Emil Lupin, naturally, denied most vehemently ever having been at the *Café* that morning.

A short time after the incident at the *Café*, a guard at the Place St.-Michel train station noticed a weathered Breton businessman being approached for directions by an English tourist, a handsome black-haired woman of indeterminate years and very determinate dimensions. Ordinarily, the Breton's reaction would have gone unremarked upon, for he would have taken her by the arm, spoken with her at length, urbanely flattered her dress and appearance, and then invited her to share breakfast with him in his cabin–English women are so enthusiastic in their consumption of *café au lait*, they are really quite inspiring.

But the Breton's reaction to the English tourist was peculiar, and so drew the guard's attention: he bowed politely to the woman and then backed away from her, never allowing her to come with an arm's length of him. The guard's assumption was that the businessman was a Gideist, but the man wore a wedding ring. Recently married, surely, to pass up the opportunity to flirt with a desirable woman. The Breton was similarly wary of a porter on the train and refused to leave his cabin until the train was well underway to Monte Carlo. Only then did he emerge, obviously well-satisfied with something, and venture to the dining car.

Subsequent approaches to the man by a female server–this one sharing the ample proportions of the English tourist, but blonde and speaking French like a Marseillaise–in the dining car were met with aplomb and invitations to dine with the man–perhaps not so recently married after all?–and a later attempt to burgle the man's cabin was laughingly dismissed. That, of course, is the sign of a burglary done quite incompetently.

The Breton was not so sanguine after awakening the following morning and realizing that the wine he had brought onboard the train–an exquisite Tokay Imperial–had been tampered with, and that he had been rendered unconscious for over 24 hours and his person thoroughly searched. The Breton lodged a futile complaint with the authorities and exited at Dijon in no good mood, though perhaps wiser in the ways of beautiful women, if not his own vanity. Of course, his ire might have been the result of the ruination of the Tokay rather than his scheme to gain the Moonstone.

Some hours later, outside Lausanne, the train made an unexpected stop and was boarded by the Police. A woman was taken from train and her cabin searched. The woman claimed to be a Spaniard by the name of Elena Acevedo; she had red hair the shade of a Sorraia colt, and it took five Policemen to restrain her.

The leader of the investigation, a fascinatingly ugly man–imagine a Shar Pei wearing glasses and a trenchcoat–whose papers identified him as "Bertrand Charon" of the Deuxième Bureau, claimed that the woman was a Catalan separatist and that she had a bomb in her cabin, so that he and he alone could search her cabin. The search took 90 minutes, although no bomb was found. Charon then took the woman to the Lausanne prison and left her in the care of the prison guards.

An hour later, in Chamonix, a man who called himself "Prosper Bondonnat" and who did not resemble Charon in the slightest boarded the train and stayed in his cabin until it reached Monte Carlo, at which time he headed for the Casino.

I am friends with one of the chemin-de-fer dealers at the Casino, and he told me of a game played there that evening. Five players took part: our friend Bondonnat, three English lords and one Russian woman. Véra Roudine is an adventuress infamous among the habitués of the Casino, not least for her intimacy with members of Cheka, who have often–quite forcefully–collected her debts for her, and only brave men dare to gamble with her. One of the Englishmen, Maxim de Winter, is almost as well known for his skill at chemin as for his magnificently sprawling mansion. I have myself visited it, and it is quite impressive. The second Englishman, Lord Lister–ah, you recognize the name. Yes, the same one who relieved the Duke of Norfolk of the burden of his diamonds. Needless to say, Lister is a master at cards, and those who know him do not risk their money by gambling with him. The third Englishman identified himself as "Lord Stuart." He was not known to the others at the table, and had the air of a none-too-bright member of the nobility who overestimates himself in every way. Such men, you may be sure, are frightfully common–it seems that one of the requirements for a title in England is an intelligence below the average Seine mudlark's–and are quite welcome at the tables of the Casino. They are better company than bank clerks, and are easier to get money from.

Imagine it: an empty-headed English lord gaming with Bondonnat, Roudine, de Winter and Lister. Heady company for a vain English lord, and surely Stuart kept both eyes on his own wallet far more than on his cards. Yet when the evening was over, Stuart emerged with the valuables of Lister and de Winter, the guarantee of one night's pleasure with Roudine–for, like her compatriot Mlle. Lazarre, whose company I myself have enjoyed on more than one occasion, the sultry Roudine was far more willing to gamble herself than to risk her money–and Bondonnat's chips, his cash, his watch, his silver cigarette case, and a particularly valuable yellow diamond which Bondonnat was forced to risk when the cards seemed to have turned against him.

Such events do not go unnoticed, of course, especially among the criminal fraternity, what my friend Yvonne Cartier calls "the Light-fingered League"–perhaps it does not translate into English? Many sets of eyes tracked Lord Stuart's movements around the Casino, and more than eyes followed Stuart on to the express to Calais.

But he survived the trip unscathed and was whistling as he entered his West End mansion, the so-called "House that 1000 Diamonds Built"–I have seen it from the inside, and the more apposite gem is the rhinestone. It is a typical nouveau riche monstrosity, all faux-silk *chinoiserie* and cheap copies of Japanese art. It was only while he was visiting his famous cousin Percy at Percy's club that Lord Stuart was reminded that a man's home may be his castle, but that all castles have cracks in their mortar. (You remember Percy Stuart–the "Savior of the Sunken City," the beau ideal of the foolish rich and the brainless press).

As Percy Stuart was toasting his cousin's success, and as Lord Stuart was accepting the acclaim of the club with a false modesty that ill became him, Lord Stuart's mansion was being carefully inspected by an unannounced visitor. Several dainties were removed from a concealed space beneath the floor of the bedroom, including a 17th century Bourdon painting of King Solomon confronting a demon, Hallward's *36 Views of Tyburn Tree*–and the Moonstone. Lord Stuart's visitor left no calling card–he lacked the panache of Professor Pelotard– but among the community of fingersmiths, it was soon known that the Englishman Raffles was discretely boasting about his possession of the Moonstone.

I have been asked about Raffles' claims, and I have always laughed and declined to answer.

I enjoy the occasional jape at my English friends' expense—though Holmes and Blake have not often seen the humor—and, one day, I shall let Raffles in on my little joke. Raffles—or whoever gains final ownership of the stone, for I'm reliably informed that several of Raffles' lesser-known and quite jealous compeers are on their way to London from Europe, America, and as far away as China to pay M. Raffles a visit.

You see, *I* have the Moonstone.

Raffles has only a glass duplicate. The Moonstone was never allowed to reside in the Louvre. I was the patron who wished to remain nameless, and I gave a cunningly-wrought imitation diamond—supposedly crafted by the hand of René Cardillac himself—into the keeping of the Louvre. The thought of my contemporaries expending their time and energy against each other and toward the end of gaining a chunk of glass amused me.

What else would one expect of Arsène Lupin?

Kim Newman was among the first writers to have different characters from popular fiction meet, love and do battle. His wildly imaginative and exceedingly well-researched Anno Dracula *series remains the model against which any crossover fiction must be judged. Kim is also unique in that he exhibits a refreshing knowledge of works from non-English-speaking countries and a daring willingness to mix genre boundaries. There could be no better demonstration of his wit and elegance than this cheerful, action-packed romp in which, once upon a time, there were three little girls who went to the Opéra...*

Kim Newman: *Angels of Music*

Paris, 1878

In the '70s–that colorful, hectic decade of garish clothes, corrupt politics, personal excess and trivial music–three girls were sent to the Paris Opéra. They could dance a little, sing a little more, were comely when painted and cut fine female figures in tights. Were the world just, they would have been stars in the ascendant, rewarded with fame, riches and advantageous marriages.

However, a rigid system of seniority, patronage and favor-currying then governed the house. Our heroines, no matter how perfectly they trilled audition pieces or daintily they lifted skirts from shapely calves, were of the "untouchable" caste, and fated to remain in the depths of the chorus. If critic or admirer or patron were to call public attention to their qualities, they would likely find themselves cast then as blackface slaves in the next production, holding the Queen's train at the rear of the stage. Such was the ruthless dictate of the house's reigning *diva*, Signorina Carlotta Castafiore.

Yet... Christine Daae had a Voice. Trilby O'Ferrall had a Face. And Irene Adler had a Mind. When they arrived at the Opéra, these girls were gems in the rough. To be revealed as brilliants of the first water, they required polish, cutting and careful setting. Without such treatment, they were likely to become dull pebbles, lost among so many other stones.

Many equally appealing girls have served years in the chorus as their brothers served terms in the armed forces (or prison), trying not to squander meager pay on *absinthe* or cards, hoping to emerge whole in limb from regular ordeals, dreaming of comfortable retirement. At best, they might end up the second wives of comfortable widowers; at worst, they might... well, *at worst* is too hideous to be dwelled upon, save to observe that such as they are found ragged on the cobbles or drowned in the Seine with a frequency that verges on the scandalous.

These *demoiselles* tended to attract the puppy-like devotions of decent, dull-witted youths and the carnivorous attentions of indecent, cold-hearted *roués*. Our trio, in their private dreams, yearned for quite a different stripe of suitor–mysterious, dominating, challenging. Without such a presence in their lives, the girls lacked direction. But, even kept outside the circle of the limelight, they had an unnerving tendency to sparkle. La Carlotta saw that shimmering in her wake, and made sure it stayed in shadow. Nevertheless, one by one, they were *noticed*, not by the stuffy and harassed management or the violently partisan audience *cliques*, but by a personage who saw into their secret selves.

This unique individual was at once Christine's Trapdoor Lover, Trilby's Mesmerist Genius and Irene's Mastermind of Intrigue. All Paris knew him as the Phantom of the Opéra, though most deemed him a true phantasm, conjured by stagehands intent on throwing a scare into pretty little ballerinas. Those who knew more, who had cause to believe the Phantom of the Opéra a man of flesh and bone, knew better than to speak of him overmuch.

His *protegées* came to know him by his true name, Monsieur Erik.

Among the very few who shared this privileged information was the Persian–a long-faced, astrakhan-capped fellow whose exact function at the opera house was hard to determine but evidently essential. The girls flitted through a surface world of upholstered finery, fashionable *cafés* and society engagements, of grand opening nights and merry madcap balls; the Phantom of the Opéra confined himself to the decaying, watery labyrinth beneath Garnier's great building, among the tombs of tortured men. Only the Persian could pass easily between the two realms. It was said he was the only man living who had seen the true face behind mirror and mask, though some claimed to have glimpsed a hollow-eyed, noseless specter in Box No. 5, upon which he had a permanent lease.

From behind the mirror in their shared dressing room, Erik gave "music lessons," whispering for hours to his songbirds–his French nightingale, Irish thrush and American eagle. He first discovered Daae, his most naturally-gifted pupil, calling from her a voice to rival the angels. Moreover, he taught her to *feel* the music, to imbue the polite perfection of her natural tones with the rude turbulence of her young heart. Thanks to Erik, Christine's voice could reach and affect in a manner those who heard it would never forget, though for her finest performances her only auditor was a single, tattered soul weeping under his mask. O'Ferrall, near death after a spell under another mesmerist-tutor, was cracked in voice, body and spirit when she was brought to Erik. He repaired her voice if not to its former, artificial magnificence–once, briefly, she had performed at the highest level–then at least to pleasant adequacy. Not a natural singer like Christine, Trilby was, if properly presented, the greatest beauty of her era, an attainment involving at least as much sacrifice and special exercise as musical distinction. Adler, the American, was warier, less obviously gifted, too strong-willed for the special tutelage Erik bestowed upon her comrades, but prodigiously gifted in a surprising range of skills. Irene's involvement with the

Agency was a matter of negotiation towards mutual advantage rather than submission to the will of the Phantom of the Opéra.

Each, in her own way, benefitted from Erik's work with them, and grew when they all worked together. Collaboration went against the instincts of the potential diva in each girl but made them more effective as a trio than they would have been as three solo turns.

It was circulated in the proverbial circles that those who wished to engage a certain Agency must first make contact with the Persian or, for more delicate matters, Madame Giry, the Keeper of Box No. 5. These loyal operatives would convey the details of the case to the Phantom himself. Often Erik was already well-apprised of matters in which prospective clients wished him to take an interest. Thanks to an intricate array of tubes and shutters, he could eavesdrop on gossip uttered in any box, dressing room or lavatory in the house–and few matters of moment troubled the city without being discussed somewhere within the Paris Opéra. Once a case came to Erik's attention, it was his decision–unaffected by the scale of fee on offer–whether a commission was accepted or declined.

If accepted, a bell sounded.

Bells were always ringing around the house, to summon *artistes*, dressers, musicians, commissionaires, wine-waiters, clerks, servants, composers, scene-shifters, rat-catchers, chorus girls, washer-women. Bells were sounded to alert the audience when a performance was about to commence or resume. Not to mention the cow-, sheep- or goat-bells used by the percussionists when pieces with rustic settings were given. Only the most finely-tuned ear could distinguish individual sounds among such tintinnabulation. But our three girls knew *their* bell. When it sounded, anything they happened to be doing–no matter how important–was set aside in their haste to make their way to a dressing room at the end of a basement corridor which had apparently been abandoned as too far from the great stage for convenience.

When Erik rang the bell, Christine Daae was in a scuttle-shaped bathtub, all a-lather, singing scales... Trilby O'Ferrall was posing in a sunlit upper room for a class of impoverished art students who'd pooled meager funds to purchase an hour of her time... and Irene Adler was practicing her lock-picking blindfolded, working away with hairpins and clever fingers.

Within moments, the tub stood empty, the students disappointed and the lock unpicked. The girls nipped swiftly to answer the summons, using dumb-waiters, trapdoors and other byways known only to the intimates of Charles Garnier. They arrived simultaneously at Dressing Room 313. The Persian, who was perusing the latest number of *La Petite Presse*, looked up and flapped a hand at them, the smoke from his Turkish cigarette making a question mark in the air. The trio arranged themselves on a divan before the large, green-speckled mirror: Christine and Trilby still wriggling into suitable clothes, helping each other with hooks and buttons, Irene coolly fanning herself with the scarf she had been using as a blindfold. When the Persian turned down the gaslight, it was possible to discern a chamber beyond the thin silvering of the mirror. A thin shadow stood there, extravagantly cloaked and hatted, violin tucked under his chin. Erik extemporized the sort of "hurry up" trill used to encourage unpopular acts to get off the stage as the French and Irish girls concluded their business with a minimum of pinching and tutting.

"What's the ruckus this time, Bright Boy?" asked Irene, whose speech still bore the pernicious influence of her native New Jersey. "Is some mug tryin' ta knock over the Louvre again?"

"Could it be a plot to bring down the Government?" asked Trilby.

"Or detonate dynamite under Notre-Dame?" asked Christine.

The Persian exhaled a smoke ring. "Nothing so everyday, ladies."

There was a pause, and all eyes turned to the mirror. Trilby, by a smidgen the prettiest of our trio and a long chalk the most vain, fussed a little with her short brown curls, accompanied by a teasing little violin tune, then noticed the others looking at her, smiled sweetly and put her hands in her lap as if about to listen dutifully to a sermon.

The violin was set down and a sepulchral voice sounded, conveyed into the room through a speaking tube with a woodwind tone.

"Our client," said Erik, "is most exalted. In fact, a President."

"The President of the Republic!" exclaimed Christine, saluting.

With the shortage of male chorus in the years since the war and the commune, the boyish Daae frame was often gussied up *en travestie* in braided uniform. She was better at close-order drill than anyone else in the company. Off duty, as it were, she often favored military-style tunics. Though her parentage was Swedish, she was a true French patriotess, who could have posed for the image of Marianne if, unlike Trilby, she were not addicted to the fidgets.

"It can't be that fathead in the White House!" said Irene Adler.

"Ireland hasn't got a President, more's the pity," muttered Trilby–born in Paris of an Irish father and a French mother, never to set foot on the green sod from which she inherited complexion and accent. "Just the cursed God English, and their fat little German Queen."

"Our client is far more respected than a mere head of state," said Erik. "She is *la Présidente*. Apollonie Sabatier, *née* Aglaé Savatier. Her *salon* may be more vital to *la Vie Parisienne* than any Government building, museum or cathedral."

"*Salon?*" queried Christine.

"He means whorehouse," explained Irene. "What Miss Potato's Limey oppressors call a 'knocking-shop.' "

Trilby good-humoredly stuck her tongue out at Irene.

"I've heard of Madame Sabatier," said Trilby. "She's one of those 'Horizontal Giantesses.' "

154

"Indeed," continued Erik. "The most upstanding, indeed paradoxically vertical, of the Nation's *Grandes Horizontales*. You will have seen her portrait by Messonier, her statue by Clésinger."

"That Beaudelaire freak was nuts about her," said Irene.

There was a pause. It would be too easy to conceive of a yellowish, skeletal brow wrinkling in a frown, a lipless mouth attempting a *moue* of displeasure, a glint of irritation in sunken eyes.

"What did I say?" whined Irene. "Everyone knows the guy was ga-ga for the dame. Did you ever see Beaudelaire? Weirdest-looking turkey this side of the state fair, mooning over this overpriced sporting gal. Most ridiculous thing you ever heard of. Just like *Beauty and the Beast!*"

An exhalation of impatience hissed through the speaking tube.

Irene thought over her last comments, looked again at the silhouette beyond the mirror and paled into rigid terror, awaiting the wrath of her employer. She had spoken without thinking, which was unlike her.

Without the benefit of "music lessons," Irene was less schooled than Christine and Trilby in the disciplines expected of Erik's operatives.

Eventually, the hissing became a normal susurrus, and Erik resumed.

"It is true that the *Salon Sabatier* has been the haunt of poets and artists. *La Présidente* has admirers among our greatest creative minds."

"I know all about the minds of poets and painters," said Trilby. "Filth and degeneracy is what goes around in their clever little brains. Enough scribblers and daubers have trotted after me. Ought to be ashamed, so they should."

Trilby spat in her hand and crossed herself. It was something her father often did when pledging to creditors that funds would be available by the end of the week, just before the O'Ferrall *ménage* moved to a new, usually less salubrious address.

"Our client requires us to display great sensitivity and tact," decreed Erik.

"None of the tittle or the tattle," said Christine.

"Exactly. In the course of this investigation, you might well become privy to information which *la Présidente* and her particular friends ..."

"Johns," put in Irene.

"... would not wish to be generally known."

"Have you noticed how these fancy fellers *always* think their wives don't know a thing?" said Trilby. "Bless their hearts. They're like tiny children. Wouldn't they be surprised if they knew what their missuses got up to while they're tomcatting about the town?"

All three girls laughed. Christine, it had to be said, often did not quite "get" the meaning of her friends' comments–especially when, as often, they spoke in English–but was alert enough to conceal occasional ignorance by chiming in with musical giggles. Her chief trait was adorability, and foolish fellows were already composing remarkably poor sonnets about the smallness of her nose, with ambitions towards epic verse on the subject of the rest of her anatomy.

Trilby was older than the others, though no one would ever tell to look at her, and her greater experience of the artistic life inclined her to be protective of her baby sisters. Foolish fellows in her presence tended to be struck dumb, as if she were a vision at Lourdes. Sometimes, a glazed look came into her eyes, and she seemed a different, more ethereal, slightly frightening person. Irene, in years the youngest, was a harder nut to crack, and men thought her handsome rather than pretty, as dangerous as alluring. The story went that she had fled her homeland after knifing a traveling preacher for whom she had been shilling. She often imagined returning to New York on the arm of one of the crowned heads she had seen in the *rotogravure*. In her copy-book, she had already designed an Ad-ler coat of arms–an American eagle, beak deep in the side of a screaming naked Prometheus. A foolish fellow who stepped out with her tended to find some un-known *Apache* had lifted their note-case, snuff-box, cuff-links and watch.

"It is a matter of a man and his wife which has been brought before us," announced Erik. "The man of some distinction, the woman an unknown."

The Persian undid the ribbon on a large wallet, and slid out clippings from the popular press, a wedding brochure, photographic plates and other docu-ments. These were passed among the girls.

Some excitement was expressed at a reproduced portrait of a handsome fellow in the uniform of a Brigadier of the armies of the late Emperor Napoleon I. There was cooing among the doves, of admiration for a curly moustaches and upright saber. With a touch of malice, the Persian handed over a more recent likeness, in which the golden boy was all but unrecognizable. These days, the soldier was an enormous, shaggy-browed, weathered hulk, a pudding of flesh decorated with innumerable medals.

"You recognize Etienne Gerard, retired Grand Maréchal of France, still reckoned one of our most influential citizens," said Erik. "No one is as canny as he when it comes to badgering the right politician to change a procurement pol-icy or effect a strategy of preparedness."

"He started shouting 'the Prussians are coming, the Prussians are coming' just after Blucher bloodied his nose at Waterloo," said Christine. "I had an uncle like that."

"Of course," said Trilby, "the Prussians really were coming."

"That doesn't make the old man any less a lunatic."

"You're behind the times, Chrissy," put in Irene. "Gerard stopped tooting that particular trumpet a few months back. He's a changed man since he got hitched to this little social-climber. Now, he's big on beating swords into ploughshares and insisting the French people have no bigger buddy than Bis-marck."

The wedding brochure commemorated the joining-together of Grand Maréchal Gerard with his bride, Poupée Francis-Pierre.

"He's over 90 and she's what ... 16?" said Trilby.

"Precise details about Madame Gerard's age, background or qualities are hard to come by," said Erik. "Such information is one objective of our investigation."

"I heard she was a dancer," said Christine, looking at a studio photograph of the bride. "Looks like she's made of porcelain. You'd think she'd *snap* if the old goat so much as touched her."

"Is she one of *la Présidente*'s dollymops?" asked Irene. "Some addlehead dotards go for that rouge-cheeked widdle girlie act."

"Madame Gerard is *not* a former ornament of *Salon Sabatier*," said Erik. "Indeed, she is the cause of some consternation among the girls there. Before his nuptials, the Grand Maréchal, despite his advancing years, was an especially favored and enthusiastic regular customer."

"Tarts like 'em old and rich," said Trilby. "They can't do much, but pay well over the odds."

Irene laughed, and Christine joined in.

"Though not of an artistic temperament," continued Erik, "Grand Maréchal Gerard found Madame Sabatier's establishment more to his liking than many rival houses run to cater to more military tastes."

"Boots and whips," shuddered Irene.

"Subsequent to his wedding, he has not visited the *Salon*."

"No wonder. He's getting poked for free at home."

"*La*, Irène, you say such things," tittered Christine.

"Madame Sabatier reports that losing a longstanding patron to marriage is an accepted risk of her business. However, she takes pride in the fact that, with this single exception, her clients have returned within three months of their honeymoon, and been more generous than before in the matter of recompense and gifts, usually with an added exhortation to increased discretion."

Christine laughed out loud, musically. "The Madame is deluded. Look at Gerard's life, all the way back to the last century. All those exploits and adventures. He's obviously a reckless romantic."

"I agree," said Trilby. "The old idiot's probably in love with the minx."

"I'll bet nuggets *Petite* Poupée has been down to the dressmakers to see how she looks in black," said Irene. "Then steered by the apothecary's on the way home. If used in excess, those boudoir philters for the use of senior gentlemen have fatal side-effects... so I hear."

"If that is the case, we are required by our client to intervene," said Erik.

"I'll say," put in Trilby. "Can't let some filly get away with murder. We've got a reputation to think of."

"Does Madame *la Présidente* fear for Gerard's life?" asked Christine.

There was a pause. Breathing could be heard through the tube.

"It may come to that. At present, she is more concerned that the old fellow is not 'acting like himself.' She takes a keen interest in the defense of France..."

"Sausage-eaters are notoriously rough on whores and stingy about paying."

"Thank you for that insight, Irene. 'Adler' is a German name, is it not? As I was saying, Etienne Gerard's change of mind on matters military and political troubles Madame Sabatier more than his absence from her customer register. She believes the Grand Maréchal might have been 'got at' in some way..."

"Hypnotized," said Christine, thrilled.

"Mesmerized," said Trilby, dreamily.

"Doped," said Irene, cynically.

"She wonders if the Grand Maréchal even *is* the Grand Maréchal."

"Murdered and replaced by the mad twin from the attic," suggested Christine, who read a great deal of sensation fiction, avidly following every *feuilleton* in every periodical in Paris. "Possessed by one of those invisible *Horlas* one hears of and forced to do the bidding of some creature from beyond the veil."

The Persian gathered back all the documents, and resealed the packet.

"Erik," said Irene, "are you *sure* this is a job for the Agency? It sounds mighty like some scorned popsy, sulking because Sugar Dad has cut off the cash-flow, out to do dirt to the chit who has stolen him away. Shouldn't they settle it with a decent knife-fight and leave us out of it?"

The Persian produced several more wallets.

"The Grand Maréchal is not an isolated case."

The Marriage Club had international members, though all were often found in Paris. Aristide Saccard, the daring international financier, a man who would never escape the sobriquet of "shady;" the Duke of Omnium, an English cabinet minister whose speeches were rumored to have the mystic power of sending entire Houses of Parliament into restful sleep ("if Planty ever had to declare war," sniped one critic, "we'd have to wake up the enemy to shoot at him"); Chevalier Lucio del Gardo, a respected banker no one outside the Phantom of the Opéra's Agency would have believed moonlighted as a needlessly violent burglar known as the "Spine-Snapper;" Walter Parks Thatcher, the American statesman and banker; Georges Duroy, the social-climbing journalist who had risen through marriage and inheritance to a position of influence as a newspaper publisher; Simon Cordier, behind his skirts called "M. Guillotine," a magistrate and sculptor, renowned for cool, balanced and unsympathetic verdicts in capital cases; and Cardinal Tosca, the Papal Legate, reputedly the greatest virtuoso of the *boudoir* to come (or be chased) out of Italy since Casanova.

All were getting along in years, widowed or lifelong bachelors, and had recently taken to wife much younger, socially-unknown women, or–in the Cardinal's case–brought her into his household as official servant and unofficial bed-warmer. All had reversed long-held public positions since their happy unions, made peculiar public statements or financial transactions, been far less often seen in society than before (Gerard was not the only old bridegroom to be missed at his favorite brothel) and were reported by estranged friends and relations to have "changed their spots." All, it transpired, had first encountered their current spouses at *soirées* hosted, on an absurdly well-appointed barge in the Seine, by one Countess Joséphine Balsamo. Some said the Countess was a direct descendant of the mountebank and purported sorcerer Cagliostro. It was believed among the peers of *la Présidente* that the Countess was directress of an unofficial wedding bureau, schooling girls plucked from orphanages or jails in the skills necessary to hook a prominent husband, arranging discreet disposal of the lovestruck old men, then taking a tithe from the widows' inheritances. A flaw in the theory was that none of the husbands, as yet, had died in the expected mysterious circumstances–several long-term moaning invalids had leaped from apparent death-beds and taken to cavorting vigorously with their pixie-like sylph brides.

Christine held, against experience, to the possibility that nothing more was amiss than a collection of genuine May-December romances ("more like March-Next February," commented Irene) which should be protected from the jealous wiles of Erik's client. Trilby considered malfeasance was likely on the part of these men of wealth and influence, and that the Countess Joséphine was simply a well-dressed procuress with a dubious title. She felt the true victims of the Marriage Club were the unfortunate, nearly-nameless children given over into the beds of men who purchased them as others might a hunting dog or a painting. Irene suspected everyone was up to no good, and wondered what their angle on the *Affaire* Balsamo ought to be. She was as much magpie as eagle and it occurred to her that this case should afford access to households where valuables might be carelessly strewn about for the filching.

The Persian, through his Police and Government contacts, had obtained a list of the Countess's holdings. Few of her interests were in the name she most commonly used. These papers were passed through a shutter, to the chamber behind the mirror.

"This seems the most likely 'lead,' " said Erik, after a perusal. "*Ecole de Danse Coppélius*. The Countess is a 'sleeping partner.' Young women of barely marriageable age and malleable personality might be found in a dancing school, *hein?*"

The Persian showed again the photograph of Poupée Gerard. In the corner of the picture were scratched the initials *E.d.D.C.*

"It's a perfect front," said Irene, getting the talk back on track. "Haul 'em in, paint 'em up, sell 'em off."

A lever was thrown, and two wardrobe doors sprung open, disclosing three varied sets of female attire and one suit of male evening dress (with turban). The girls knew at once which were their costumes. The Persian took the turban.

"Christine, Trilby," said Erik, close to the glass, eyes shining. "You will try to enroll at the *Ecole Coppélius*. Christine, at least, should be able to pass an audition if dancing is actually required, while Trilby can certainly be passed off as bride-to-be material."

159

The girls looked at each other, not sure whether to be offended by Erik's implications. Then Christine was struck by the loveliness of her new dress, and forgot any sleight.

The shutter opened again. A newly-struck, gilt-edged invitation card lay within. The Persian picked it up by forefinger and thumb, careful not to smudge the ink. Erik had a printing press in his lair–along with much other apparatus somehow smuggled below street level for the use of the Agency.

"That," said Erik, "is for the Countess's Summer Ball, to be held tonight on her famous barge. She expects the pleasure of the company of Rhandi Lal, the Kasi of Kalabar, and his daughter, the Princess Jelhi."

Irene held up a silken sari, pressed her hands together in prayerful submission, and bowed mockingly at the mirror, eyes modestly downcast.

"Do try not to overact, Miss Adler."

With her jeweled head-dress, scarlet forehead dot, exposed midriff, kohl-lined eyes, near-transparent costume and sinuous walk, "Princess Jelhi" was instantly popular, attracting a platoon of admirers in white tie and tails or dress uniform. Most of the men had swords: as a consequence of jostling for position among the upper ranks, several duels were likely.

As Irene flirted and fluttered, the Persian scanned the ballroom.

The dancing floor was not the classic square, but an oblong. Brassbound porthole-shaped windows above and below the waterline reminded guests that they were on the river. The mooring was secure and the barge heavy in the water: only the slightest motion reminded guests they were not on dry land. The theme of the ball was Childhood Remembered, and the room was dressed as a giant's playroom. Ten-foot tall wooden soldiers and other outsized toys stood around, as conversation pieces or to excite wonderment. In the center of the floor, a gigantic, stately top spun on its axis, ingeniously weighted not to stray from its spot or fall over.

Irene lifted a bare foot, showing off her painted nails and oddments of paste jewelry from the Opéra's vast store of dressing-up kit. The motion parted her sari, affording a glimpse of her shapely inside-leg. Gasps rose from her admirers and she tittered modestly at the "slip," chiding the gallants in delightfully broken babytalk French.

The Persian looked about for anyone *not* enraptured by the Princess. If the business of this ball was fishing for *fiancés* and an uninvited interloper was raiding the stock, the fleet who held rights in these waters would be out of sorts. Countess Josephine had not made an entrance, but the Persian knew she would be watching. Erik was not the city's only addict of secret panels, two-way mirrors, listening tubes and portraits with removable eyes. Any descendant of the mountebank Cagliostro would be mistress of such matters.

Irene Adler could be relied upon to glance at a crowd of gentlemen and single out the most distinguished victims–taking into account inherited or acquired wealth, ancient or modern title, achievements on the field of battle or in the arts, and degree of commitment to their current marital state. At a masquerade where everyone was dressed up as what they were not, she could spot a Crown Prince through a throng of mere Viscounts and chart a course which would lead inevitably to taking the prize. Within minutes, she had dismissed the also-rans and narrowed the field down to the three men in the company worth bothering with.

The choice picks were Count Ruboff, the Russian military *attaché* (which is to say, spy) and a cousin of the Tsar, Baron Maupertuis, the Belgian colossus of copper (and other base metals), and "Black" Michael Elphberg, Duke of Strelsau, second son of the King of Ruritania (a mere unmarried half-brother's death or disgrace away from succession to the crown). Any or all of these might be candidates for the Marriage Club, though only the Baron was elderly.

Count Ruboff asked the Princess to demonstrate the dancing style of far-off Kalabar, and Irene obliged with a shimmy she had learned as warm-up for a snake-oil salesman in the Wild West. As a well-developed 13-year-old, her tour with a medicine show had been her first attempt at escaping from New Jersey. Of course, the moves that had dried mouths and stirred vitals in Tombstone, Cheyenne and No Name City were still effective in Paris, though the crowds were cleaner and, on the whole, had more of their original teeth. Some women simply gave up, collected their wraps and went home in huffs, leaving behind befuddled gentlemen who would find home lives difficult for the next week or so. Others took careful note of Irene's steps, and resolved to learn them.

A five-piece orchestra provided ever more frenzied accompaniment in what they must have fondly imagined was the style of far-off Kalabar. The musicians were dressed as a strange breed of clown, with ridiculously stack-heeled boots, lightning-pattern leotards immodestly padded with rolled-up handkerchiefs and cut low to reveal thick thatches of chest hair (not entirely natural), faces painted with celestial maps so eyes and mouths opened disturbingly in purple moons or stars, and shocks of bright orange hair teased up into jagged peaks. The band made a lot of noise, and even more fuss–sticking out gargoyle tongues, making obscene advances to their sparkle-patterned instruments, capering grotesquely like dressed-up apes with their rumps on fire.

Irene began to unwind the interlocking scarves that constituted her sari, wrapping them around admirers' necks, brushing the trail-ends across their faces to raise their color. The Kasi of Kalabar, suspecting this might go too far, was on the point of stepping in to administer reprimand to his "daughter" when the Princess was flanked.

Two pretty girls, similar enough in face and figure to be taken for sisters, assumed positions either side of Irene, clicked fingers, and fell in step, mimicking exactly her dance moves. There was a ripple of applause from those who supposed the Countess had brought in a choreographer. A frown of surprise briefly passed across Irene's tinted forehead. She left off the Salomé business, concentrating on energetic, elaborate footwork, with snake-moves in her hips and back. Out West, the crowd would have been discharging Colts at the ceiling. The sisters, however, were not thrown. They perfectly matched her, not even seeming to follow a lead.

The Persian considered the bland, shiny faces of the girls. They showed no emotion, no exertion, scarcely even any interest. Irene was, in polite terms, "glowing"–and thus in danger of sweating through her betelnut makeup. The caste mark on her forehead looked like an angry bullet-hole. It was harder and harder for her to keep up with the dance.

Everyone in the room was watching this trio.

The band were murdering the "Jewel Song" from Gounod's *Faust*–la Carlotta's signature number, as it happens. One of the clowns sang like a castrato, inventing new lyrics in double Dutch.

Irene made a tiny misstep, and lost her lead. Now, she had to follow, to mimic, to copy–and the Terpsichorean sisters began to execute a series of balletic leaps, glides and stretches which were too much for the New Jersey Nightingale. Her bare foot slid, and she had to be caught by a nobody–her former admirers were now enslaved by the sisters.

For a moment, it seemed there would be a problem–three swains, two dancers–but Irene was instantly replaced by a third girl, darker-haired but sharing the family resemblance. The debutante locked at once into the dance, and the three tiny, strong girls performed like prima ballerinas prevailed upon to share a leading *rôle*. Now, there was a sister apiece, if sisters they were, for the Count, the Baron and the Duke.

The Princess was helped, limping, out of the circle by her rescuer, Basil–a homosexual English painter with only academic interest in the female form. Even he deserted her as soon as she was dumped on a couch, and was drawn back to the circle around the dancing girls.

"They ain't human," the Princess said–through angry tears–to the Kasi.

The performance concluded, with a tableau as the darker girl was held high, pose perfect. Thunderous applause resounded. The girls' pleasant smiles did not broaden.

"It must be mesmerism," said Irene. "Trilby's old tutor is probably behind it. He put her to sleep with a swinging bauble and fixed her croak so she came out an angel. Those witches have had the same treatment, only for dancing."

Irene stood up, putting weight on her foot. Her ankle was not turned or sprained. Only her dignity was really damaged.

"The patsies are lost," she told the Persian. "While no one's watching, let's sneak out. There must be something on this tub to give the game away."

He nodded concurrence.

"*Zut alors*, Trilbee," said Christine. 'We have wasted our time. This is not a dancing school…"

"This is a mannequin factory," concluded Trilby.

"That fool of a Persian must have made the mistake. And we have come all this way by fiacre. Erik should not put his trust in such a person. So the trip is not a wash-out complete, we should go to a café and have some pastries."

"The Persian's not a fool," said Trilby, concentrating.

"He has sent us to the wrong address."

"But the name is correct, look. It may not be *Ecole de Danse Coppélius*, but–see–here on the board. *Fabricants des Mannequins*–M. Coppélius & Sig. Spalanzani. Perhaps the dance school failed, and the Countess' partners found a new use for the building."

They had hoped to enroll in evening classes.

"Chrissy, now it's time for subtle fuge."

"Subtle what?"

"Fuge. You know, sneakin' about."

"Ha! But you are ill-suited for such, with your hopping-of-the-clod Irish feet and so forth."

"Never you mind my feet. It's your own slippered tootsies you should be thinking on."

Christine arched her leg, displaying her fine calf boot and its row of buttons.

"Lovely," said Trilby. "Very suited for sneakin'. Now, if you'll climb up over this fence–mind the spikes on the tops of the rail, looks as if they've been sharpened–I'm certain you'll be able to get that chain loosened so I can follow. This is a task much more suited to your delicacy."

For a moment, Christine wondered whether she had not been manipulated into taking an uncomfortable risk. But she knew the Irish girl was too simple-minded for such duplicity.

"Careful," called up Trilby. "You'll tear your..."

There was a rip, as Christine's skirts caught on a spike.

"Never mind. It'll set a new fashion."

Trilby looked both ways, up and down the alley. They had sought out a side entrance to the factory, away from passersby.

Christine dropped from the top of the fence and landed like a cat, with a hiss. She had a fetching smear of grime on her forehead and her hair had come loose. From her reticule, she found a hand mirror and–angling to get moonlight to work by–effected meticulous repairs to her appearance, while Trilby waited for the chain to be seen to.

As it happened, the chain was draped incorrectly around the wrong railings. The gate had been left unfastened. It swung open with a creak.

"I suppose we should have tried that first."

Christine frowned, a touch pettishly. "Now is not the time to bring up this matter, Trilbee."

"Perhaps not. Now, the fastenings of that little window, eight or ten feet up the wall, look to me to be similarly neglected. Let me make a cradle with my rough Irish peasant hands and hoist your dainty delicate French footsie like so…"

With a strength born in hours of holding awkward poses while undressed in draughty artists' garrets, Trilby lifted Christine up off the ground. The French girl pushed the window, which fell in with a crash.

"Perhaps we should announce our arrival with 24 cannons, *hein*?"

Trilby shrugged, and Christine slipped through the window. She reached down, and Trilby was pulled up after her.

They both stood in a small, dark room. Trilby struck a lucifer. All around were racks of unattached, shapely arms and legs.

"*Bonne Sainte Vierge!*" exclaimed Christine, in a stage whisper. "We have stumbled into the larder of a clan of cannibals!"

Trilby held the match-flame near a rack. Porcelain shone in the light, and a row of arms swayed, tinkling against each other.

"No, Chrissy, as advertised, this is a mannequin factory."

Against the wall sat a range of womanly torsos, with or without heads. Some were wigged and painted, almost complete. Others were bald as eggs, with hollow eye-sockets waiting for glass.

"What would doll-makers have to do with these Mystery Brides?"

"I've a nasty feeling we're about to find out."

A light appeared under the crack of the door, and there was some clattering as a lock was turned. Then bolts were thrown, and several other locks fussed with.

"What are we to do, Trilbee?"

"Take off our clothes. Quickly."

Christine looked aghast. Trilby, more used to getting undressed at speed, had already started. The clattering continued. Christine unfastened the first buttons of her bodice. Trilby–already down to stockings, drawers, corset and chemise–helped with a tug, ripping out the other 98 buttons, getting Christine free of her dress as if unshelling a pod of peas. The door, so much more secure than the gate or the window, was nearly unlocked.

Trilby picked up Christine, and hooked the back of her corset on a hanger.

"Go limp," she whispered.

Christine flopped, letting her head loll.

Trilby sat against the wall, making a place among a row of mannequins similarly clad in undergarments. She opened her eyes wide in a stare, sucked in her cheeks, and arranged her arms stiffly, fingers stretched.

The door finally opened. Gaslight was turned up.

A gnome-like little man, with red circles on his cheeks and a creak in his walk, peered into the room.

"Cochenille, what is it?" boomed someone from outside.

"Nothing, Master Spalanzani," responded Cochenille, the gnome, in a high-pitched voice. "Some birds got in through the window, and made a mess among the *demoiselles*."

"Clear it up, you buffoon. There will be an inspection later, and the Countess does not take kindly to being displeased. As you well know."

Cochenille flinched at the mention of the Countess. Christine and Trilby worked hard at keeping faces frozen. Slyly, the little man shut the door behind him, listened for a moment to make sure his master was not coming to supervise, then relaxed.

"My pretties," he said, picking up a bewigged head, and kissing its painted smile. "Lovelier cold than you'll ever be warm."

Cochenille tenderly placed the head on the neck of a limbless torso and arranged its hair around its cold white shoulders. He passed on, paying attention to each partial mannequin.

"Alouette, not yet," he cooed to a mannequin complete but for one arm. "Clair-de-lune, very soon," to another finished but for the eyes and wig. "And... but who is this? A fresh face. And finished."

He stopped before Christine, struck by her.

"You are so perfect," said Cochenille. "From here, you will go to the arms of a rich man, a powerful man who will be in your power. You will sway the fates of fortunes, armies, countries. But you will have no happiness for yourself. These men who receive you, they appreciate you not. Only Cochenille truly sees your beauty."

Christine concentrated very hard on being frozen. As an artists' model, Trilby was used to holding a pose, but Christine's nerves were a-twitch. She worried that the pulse in her throat or a flicker in her eyes would give her away. And the urge to fidget was strong in her.

"What these men know not is that they take my cast-offs," said the gnome, rather unpleasantly. "Before you wake, before you are sent to them, you are–for this brief tender moment–the Brides of Cochenille."

With horror, Christine realized this shrunken thing, with his withered face and *roué*'s face-paint, was unbuttoning his one-piece garment, working down from his neck, shrugging free of his sleeves.

She would do only so much for Erik!

Cochenille leaned close, wet tongue out. Suddenly, he was puzzled, affronted.

"Mademoiselle," he said, shocked, "you are too... warm!"

Christine gripped the rack from which she was hung, taking the weight off her corset, and scissored her legs around Cochenille's middle. Trilby leaped up, tearing an arm from the nearest doll, wielding it like a polo mallet. She fetched the gnome a ferocious blow on the side of his head as Christine tried to squeeze life out of the loathsome little degenerate.

Cochenille's head spun around on his neck, rotating in a complete circle several times. He ended up looking behind him, at the astonished Trilby.

"He's a doll," she gasped.

Something in his neck had broken and he couldn't speak. His glass eyes glinted furiously. Christine still had him trapped.

"And he is a disgusting swine," she said.

Trilby lifted Cochenille's head from his neck and his body went limp in Christine's grip. She let go and the body collapsed like a puppet unstrung.

His eyes still moved angrily. Trilby yanked coils and springs from his neck, detaching a long velvety tongue with a slither as if she were pulling a snake out of a bag. She threw the tongue away.

Christine got down from her rack and uncricked her aching back.

Trilby tossed the head to her, as if it were a child's ball. She saw lechery in those marble eyes, and threw the nasty thing out of the window, hoping it wound up stuck on one of the fence-spikes.

Outside, dogs barked.

Christine, conscious of her *déshabillé*, looked around for her ruined dress.

Then the door opened again.

They looked at the guns aimed at them. Christine slowly put her hands up. Trilby did likewise.

"Who have we here?" said the tall old man with the pistols. "Uninvited guests?"

"Snoopers," said his smaller partner. "Drop 'em in the vat."

The tall man smiled, showing sharp yellow teeth.

Irene and the Persian had doffed their Kalabari disguises. Now, they wore close-fitting black bodystockings with tight hoods like those popularized by the English soldiers at Balaclava. The lower parts of their faces were covered with black silk scarves; only their eyes showed.

They crept along the deck of the barge, conscious of the music and chatter below. The clowns were performing some interminable Rhapsody from Bohemia, which made Irene vow to avoid that region in the future. The full Moon and the lights of the city were not their friend, but they knew how to slip from shadow to shadow.

On the Pont du Caroussel, a solitary man stood, looking down at the dark waters and the barge. Irene saw the shape and laid a hand on the Persian's arm to stop him stepping into moonlight. They pressed against the side of a lifeboat, still in the shadow. Irene first assumed the man on the bridge was a stroller who had paused to have a cigar, though no red glowworm showed. She hoped it was not some inconvenient fool intent on suicide–they did not want attention drawn to their night-work, with lanterns played across the water's surface or the decks where they were hiding. The figure did not move, was not apparently looking at the barge, and might as easily have been a scarecrow.

Irene slipped away from the lifeboat, did a gymnast's roll, and found herself next to the housing of some sort of marine winch. Heart beating, she looked up at the bridge. The possible spy was gone. There had been something familiar about him.

The Persian joined her.

The Countess Cagliostro's barge was armored like a dreadnought, which was one reason it sat so low in the water. Aft of the ballroom were powerful engines, worked by dynamos which hummed. The barge was fully illuminated by electrical Edison lamps, and mysterious galvanic energies coursed throughout the rubber-clad veins of the barge, nurturing vast sleeping mechanical beasts whose purposes neither of Erik's operatives could guess.

"She could invade a country with this thing," said Irene.

"Several," commented the Persian.

"Do you think it's a submersible?"

The Persian shrugged. "I should not be surprised if it inflates balloons from those fittings, and lifts into the skies."

"You've an inventive turn of mind, pardner."

"That is true. It is part of the tale of how Erik and I became associates, back in my own country… but this is not the time for that history."

"Too true. Let's try and find the lady's lair."

Beyond the engines, the deck was featureless plate but for several inset panes of thick black glass. Irene reckoned this was Erik's trick again–transparent for the sitting spider, opaque for the unwary fly.

From the pouch slung on her hip, she drew a cracksman's tool: a suction cup with an arm, attached to a brutal chunk of diamond. The tool was worth more than most of the swag Irene had used it to lift–the cutting gem had been prised from a tiara and shaped to order by a jeweler who nearly balked at the sacrilege of turning beauty into deadly practicality.

Irene cut a circle out of the glass, and placed it quietly on the deck.

The space below was dark, a pool of inky nothing. Working silently, the Persian unwound a coil of rope from his torso and Irene harnessed herself. After a tug to test the line, Irene stepped into the hole and let herself fall. The Persian, anchored strongly, doled out measured lengths of rope, lowering her by increments.

Once inside, the hole above was bright as the Moon, and all around was cavernous dark. Irene blinked, hoping her eyes would adjust–but the gloom was unbroken, the dark undifferentiated.

Then there was a musical roaring, as if a steam calliope were stirring, and a thousand colored jewels lit up, dazzling her. Incandescent lamps fired, and Irene found herself dangling inside what seemed like the workings of a giant clock. Gears and wheels, balances and accumulators were all around, in dangerous motion, scything through the air. She had to twist on her rope to avoid being bashed by a counterweight.

Music was playing–mechanical, but cacophonous, assaulting her ears.

The Persian began to haul her upwards hastily, out of the potential meat-grinder, and she climbed, loops of rope dangling below her. A razor-edged wheel whirred, slicing through loose cord.

Irene was pulled up on deck. By more than two hands.

Light streamed upwards from the hole.

She was held by men in striped jerseys, their faces covered by metal half-masks. The Persian, scarf torn away and hood wrenched off, was caught by a stranger character, one of the ten-foot toy soldiers from the ballroom, miraculously endowed with life. Its tin moustaches bristled fiercely and its big wooden hands gripped like implements of torture. Slung on its back was an oversized musket with a yard-long bayonet. Stuck out of its side was a giant key. The Persian, lifted completely off his feet, was crushed against the soldier's shiny blue tunic.

"Messieurs," said Irene, "you're taking liberties. Get your paws off the goods if you don't intend to buy."

The half-masked sailors were briefly confused, and relaxed their ungallant grip on her person. Irene darted and her slick leotard slipped through the hands of her would-be captors. Like an eel, she was out of their grasp, heading towards the side of the barge. If she got over, she would have a chance. The Persian could be rescued later, if that were possible.

Something rose from the shadows and took a much faster hold.

Three swift blows to the stomach knocked the wind out of her. She doubled up in pain, and was recaptured by the sailors, who were less considerate about how they kept her now.

The thing that had struck her emerged into the light.

It was a woman–of course–wearing a costume modeled on Elizabeth of England, with a red lacquered moon-face mask and towering head-dress. Dozens of pearls studded bodice and face, exciting Irene's larcenous instincts. Getting her breath back, she sighed at such extravagance.

"Countess Cagliostro, I presume."

"Your hostess," said the woman. "Though I don't remember putting your names on the guest list. What were they again?"

"I'm Sparkle and he's Slink. We're desperate *Apache* thieves. You've bushwhacked us properly, so do us the courtesy of summoning the *Gendarmes* and handing us over to French justice so we can start plotting our escape from Devil's Island. We accept this as an inevitable reverse of our chosen profession, sheer crookery. And there's no need to be unpleasant about it."

The Countess's mask seemed to smile, its eyeslits narrowing.

She glided, on invisible feet, to the side of her toy soldier, and twisted the key as if winding a clock. Then she stood back, and the key turned as–with big, jerky motions–the soldier raised the struggling, bleeding Persian above its head, then dropped him over the side of the barge. After a long scream, there was a splash.

Irene's heart leaped. This was not what had been planned.

The soldier stumped away from the edge of the barge, and the Countess paid attention to Irene.

"Now that's taken care of, let's talk about you."

Irene deemed it politic to swoon.

"She's with us now," said Trilby.

"Irène," said Christine.

"Eh... what?" said Irene.

Irene blinked, awake and uncomfortable. Her wrists were tied above her head, and she hung from an iron hook. To her sides dangled Trilby and Christine, similarly trussed, wearing only undergarments.

The air was warm. A fragrance swelled upwards.

"Don't look down, dear," advised Trilby.

Of course, Irene could not help herself.

Below her feet was a vat shaped like a giant-sized witch's cauldron, heated by a bellows-fuelled furnace. Pink, molten mass bubbled angrily, smelling of paraffin and cinnamon.

"A coat of wax does wonders for the complexion," said one of the men who stood below.

Irene looked up at her wrists. She could probably saw through her bonds by swinging on the hook, but then she risked a death-plunge into boiling wax.

"Who's your friend?" she asked Trilby.

"Coppélius," said the Irish girl.

"Spalanzani!" insisted the man who had spoken. "He's Coppélius!"

Spalanzani was the taller of the pair. With them was the Countess, who had kept her mask but changed into male evening dress spectacularly tailored to fit her figure.

"Three pretty girls, with unusual talents," said the Countess. "Only one Agency I know of in Paris can lay claim to such employees. You are the Angels of Music? The creatures of... One Whose Name is Seldom Spoken. I have heard of your previous exploits. It will almost be a shame to write *finis* to such a *feuilleton*. Almost."

Spalanzani and Coppélius laughed, unpleasantly.

"Naturally, ladies, I should delight in attending your final performance," said the Countess, "but pressing business elsewhere summons me. I have been absent from my Summer Ball for too long. Matters there are coming to a head. My doll-makers and I are required to oversee the course of true love. A trusted servant will remain behind to supervise your fatal immersion."

The Countess snapped her long fingers.

A small creature lurched into the circle of light. Christine and Trilby groaned. Irene knew that was not an encouraging sign.

"Poor Cochenille," said the Countess. "He has been fearfully mistreated this evening."

The little man's head did not fit on properly, and several of his limbs dragged. He would not have been especially attractive at the best of times, and now he was a complete quasimodo. The Countess patted his head, and withdrew–the doll-makers trailing after her.

"They're mannequins," said Trilby. "The brides. Poupée Gerard and the others. Automata."

"Clockwork," said Christine.

"I guessed as much."

"That lump isn't real either," said Trilby, nodding at Cochenille.

"I heard that," he shrilled. "Soon you won't be so particular. When the wax hardens, the Countess will give you to me. As toys."

"Toys shouldn't have toys," said Christine. "It's absurd."

Cochenille manipulated a winch, unrolling chain from a drum, humming to himself.

The girls were lowered, by inches.

Christine and Trilby took deep breaths, and twisted, knees up to their chests, feet tucked against their rumps. Irene, who'd had quite enough perilous dangling for one evening, tried her best to imitate her colleagues' tactics, straining her shoulders and back. She yelped.

Cochenille lowered them further. They could feel heat boiling off churning wax. Spits painfully dotted their bodies, forming solid specks on their garments. It seemed the advantages of hot wax for the complexion were decidedly overrated.

They were hung from hooks fixed to a bedstead-sized frame which was attached at the corners to four chains which gathered up through an iron loop affair to wind around pulleys fixed to the factory ceiling. The more chain was extended to lower them, the more give there was.

Irene looked up, and saw a dusty skylight and the roofs of Paris. For an instant, she thought she saw the billow of a cloak.

From somewhere, three sharp notes sounded.

Christine and Trilby threw their weight backwards, taking Irene with them, so she could see skylight and cloaked figure no more. The girls extended their legs, feet pointed like trapeze artistes. Their eyes were open, fixed nothing in particular. They concentrated on becoming living pendulum weights.

It was a side-effect of the "music lessons," Irene thought–the way Christine and Trilby sometimes started acting in concert like the Corsican Brothers or (and this chilled her) the mannequin dancers at the Countess' ball. She knew her colleagues were flesh and blood, but Erik had tinkered with their minds. At times

170

like this, she regretted not also having submitted to the special tutoring, though she usually shrunk in cold terror from the idea.

"Stop that swinging, at once," shrieked Cochenille. "Naughty naughty girls."

Irene again did her best to imitate Christine and Trilby, throwing her weight in parallel with theirs. The frame swung in a long arc, up and back, then down and forward, as if tossed on a great wave. It seemed for a moment that the girls' feet and legs might dip agonizingly into hot wax, but their heels barely brushed the furious surface. It was fortunate that Christine and Trilby were divested of their dresses, for skirts would have trailed in the wax and anchored them in the deadly cauldron. Irene's leotard was close enough to a circus aerialist's costume to be suited for this venture.

Cochenille frantically worked the winch, which seemed stuck.

On the next pass, the frame took the girls past the rim of the cauldron, over dizzyingly empty space. Then they crossed the deadly gulf again, higher still at the height of the swing, and were pulled back.

Irene saw what was intended.

She hoped they wouldn't break their legs, though that would still be better than becoming a prize exhibit at the grand opening of the Musée Grévin, the new waxworks which would supposedly rival London's Madame Tussaud's if it ever got finished.

On the next pass, as they looked down, the girls stuck out their legs, bracing themselves for a shock. Their feet slammed against the lip of the vat, which rang like a bell, and their swinging stopped. They bent at the knees and waists, but stretched out as if standing up at a 45-degree angle, held by their chains but safe, feet planted on the hot metal, their weight tipping the cauldron.

Another note sounded from nowhere.

Christine and Trilby were out of their useful trance.

All three girls complained of discomfort–strain on their muscles, searing against the soles of their feet, damage to their stockings.

Cochenille hopped in frustration. If he loosened the chain more, the girls would be able to slip their bonds. He must reverse the winch and raise them higher, dragging them over the lip of the vat.

The gnome took hold of the wheel of the winch.

"Give it a bit of kick," said Trilby.

Irene strained with her thighs, putting more weight against the cauldron. The others did too.

The vat was on an axle set in housings, so wax could be poured into moulds. By inches, the girls tipped the vat with their feet. Liquid poured out of a spout-like groove in the rim.

The first pink gush splashed against the floor.

A wave broke against Cochenille's ankles, and froze solid on cold flagstones. He was trapped.

"Harpies of the Inferno!" he shouted.

A greater cascade fell all around him, and he broke into pieces.

Irene took her feet off the cauldron and swung upwards, hooking her legs through the frame, taking weight off her wrist bonds, which she freed and twisted apart. She climbed the chains, as feeling came back to her fingers. Monkeylike, Christine managed the same trick, leaving Trilby to take the strain of keeping the vat, now lighter for the loss of most of its contents, in pouring position. Then, in concert, Irene and Christine lifted Trilby free.

The vat clanged back on its axle.

Wax spread on the floor, solidifying.

The girls swung wildly on their frame, comparing bruises to their skin and damage to their costume. They picked deposits of wax out of each other's hair.

"That was horrid," said Christine.

"I've got aches in places where I didn't think I had places," said Irene.

"We're not out of the woods yet," said Trilby. "We've got to get down from here and finish the job. Some men have to learn that their brides are life-size dolls without minds."

"Some men might not care," observed Irene.

Fortunately, the mannequin factory had an extensive store of suitable costumes for their products. The trio found playroom clothes which would pass among the giant dolls and toys at the Summer Ball: Irene as a buck-skinned cowgirl of the Wild West, Christine as a bold Brigadier of Napoleon's army, and Trilby as a parti-colored Harlequin. .

In the factory's stable, they found a light carriage, with a pair of horses tethered and ready. Pinned to the seat was a hand-drawn map showing the best route between the factory and the barge's mooring, signed *P.O.*, for Phantom of the Opéra.

"He thinks of everything," said Christine.

"Always watches over us," said Trilby.

"He might have been more help when we were about to be dunked in the boiling wax," said Irene.

Her colleagues looked at her, shocked.

"Irène, Erik works best in the shadows," said Christine. "This you know."

Irene shrugged and climbed up onto the box.

She knew now who had been up on the rooftops. She wondered about those strange, skull-piercing musical notes and their effect on her colleagues.

"Yee-hah, giddyup," she shouted, taking the reins.

The vehicle charged out onto the street, knocking over a brazier at which a night-watchman had been warming his hands. Hot coals spilled on the cobbles.

The watchman made an impertinent gesture at the departing carriage.

Christine and Trilby argued over the map, feeding Irene instructions at each turn. The horses seemed to know their way already, which Irene didn't find all that comforting.

The Angels of Music tore through the streets of Paris.

At midnight, three happy couples were escorted by creaking wooden soldiers from the ballroom of the barge into a smaller, equally well-appointed chamber where the company was far more select. Here, music was provided by intricate automata whose instruments were parts of their bodies. The orchestra had been constructed by skilled Venetian craftsmen a century earlier.

A stiff-backed, golden-faced toy conductor–a marvelous engine in itself, clad in a gold swallow-tail coat with jewel-studded epaulettes–precisely ticked off the seconds with a baton.

The Count, the Baron and the Duke each escorted a tiny dancer. Barbée, Cyndée and Dépenaillée Annette had entirely captivated their newfound *fiancés* with artificial charms, augmented by certain drugs administered through tiny scratches from sharp glass fingernails. Nothing was left to chance.

Each couple joined the dance, moving elegantly to the automata's tinkling. The other couples on the floor would have been familiar to Erik's Agents, for their documents had been examined. Here was Grand Maréchal Gerard, the Duke of Omnium, the Chevalier del Gardo, Magistrate Simon Cordier, Mr. Thatcher of New York, Cardinal Tosca and all the other "husbands," partnered with–and, in some cases, propped up by–deceptively fragile, hard-eyed wives. Indeed, a careful observer would have noticed these men were led around the floor by their painted dolls, in an advanced state of befuddlement verging on somnambulism.

At length, the dance concluded, and the couples stood in neat rows as if for inspection, male heads hung, female faces turned up. A trap slid open and a podium raised, upon which stood the masked Josephine Balsamo, swathed in pure white furs, from arctic wolves and polar bears. She presented a savage, commanding aspect–like the chieftain of a marauding tribe clad in the skins of fallen enemies.

"Tonight, at last, our company is complete," she announced. "The men in this room can claim between them to control the world. Every sphere of human activity is represented–politics, finance, arms, faith, letters, industry, science. Beside you are your perfect wives, so demure, so devoted. You are theirs, entirely. Through them, you are mine entirely. You serve the Cause of Cagliostro. I have played a long game. You all had to be in place. Nothing in this world cannot be decided among the men in this room. Wars can be arranged. Fortunes shifted. Governments changed. On my whim, I could choose what people will say, think, eat, hum in the bath. This has been my goal for more years than I care to remember. My sole regret is that, at this moment, I am essentially talking to myself, for you, the wives, are but my instruments, unliving tools who express only my will. And you, the husbands, are sleeping, dreaming what I have deemed you will dream, dancing at the end of strings I control. Shall I feel lonely? Is this game *solitaire*? Earlier tonight, it was revealed to me that forces–pathetic, perhaps, set beside this company, but not to be despised–were set against me, against us. Agents have been dealt with. But there may be others. Believe me, I am glad of this. For we must test our strength. We must seek out the other players of this Great Game and destroy them utterly."

China palms clapped together, in approval.

Beneath her moon-mask, the Countess smiled on her creatures.

From the Pont du Caroussel, Christine, Trilby and Irene watched as carriages ferried away the Countess' lesser guests. Thus was the chorus dispensed with, ejected from the Ball–only members of the exclusive Marriage Club remained on the barge with the Countess and her minions.

"Is that an unwound turban floating by the bilges?" asked Trilby.

Irene had not had time to explain fully the fate of the Persian.

Christine gasped and clutched her throat, apprehending at once that something dreadful had transpired.

Irene drew six-shooters from her leather hip-holsters, and thumb-cocked the hammers.

"Come on, Angels," she drawled, "a gal's gotta do what a gal's gotta do!"

The trio advanced through the barge's ballroom, stepping tactfully over drunks and suicides, avoiding staff clearing away the *débris*, posing briefly among giant toys when it seemed they might be noticed. They came to a locked door. Irene put away her guns and picked it. The party was continuing, inside, in more select fashion. Christine, Trilby and Irene crept in, and sat at the back without attracting attention.

The Marriage Club was in session.

All around, on the polished wood floor, sat tiny artificial brides, cradling husbands like babies, whispering musically into their ears, caressing them intimately, giving tender orders.

The automated orchestra played a lullaby. The toy conductor swiveled on his podium, seeming to stare at the interlopers–then turned back to his musical machines.

The Countess sat on a throne, weighed down by white furs.

Irene drew a bead on the Countess' forehead and fired.

A bullet spanged against the red mask, cracking the face of the moon–but the Countess did not flinch. None of the husbands reacted to the shot, but all the wives looked up at once, glass eyes fixed malevolently on the newcomers.

Irene sighted with her other Colt, aiming for the spot where the Countess ought to have a heart. Knowing it wouldn't be any use, she fired again. A black, smoking patch appeared on the Countess' furs.

"It's just another doll," said Trilby.

They looked around the room, wary. So many automata, so many painted eyes.

Christine had drawn a sword, which she held up like an expert ready for attack.

In concert, the wives got to their feet, letting husbands fall or roll where they might. One or two of the men groaned, scratched their heads and tried to stand–then sprawled again.

There were at least 30 mannequins, clockwork-and-porcelain-and-wax sisters, costumed in high fashion finery. As they moved, clicks and whirrs suggested their interior workings.

"I'll wager they do more than dance," said Christine.

"I'd not take that sucker bet," said Irene.

The Countess' throne revolved. The puppet Countess' broken head fell unnaturally. On the turntable dais were two identical thrones, back to back. The Countess had been hiding behind a mannequin in her own image. She wore a fresh mask, a rainbow-winged butterfly of silk over steel, and a suit of scarlet, lightweight armor decorated with Chinese dragon motifs. Quantities of loose dark hair fell over her shoulders and down her back.

Irene fired at once, but the Countess–with supernatural swiftness–bent one way and then the other, avoiding the bullets which smashed into her throne or the wall behind her. She struck elegant poses as Irene missed with several more shots.

In the end, in frustration, she pitched the guns at the Countess as if she were shying horse-shoes. With mailed gauntlets, the Countess knocked them out of the air, and they skittered uselessly across the floor.

The pack of brides took a march-step towards the three girls.

"You escaped the wax," said the Countess. "Well done. I could use ladies like you in my service."

Irene knew that was not going to work. And so did the Countess. She shrugged, rattling the shoulder-pieces of her armor.

"What do you think you look like, dearie?" asked Trilby.

"Red Jeanne, evil twin of the Maid of Orléans?" suggested Christine.

The Countess seemed to consider the idea.

"She dyes her hair," said Irene. "You can always tell."

The Countess made angry, spike-knuckled fists.

"What say we do this fair and square?" said Trilby. "Just you and us. One to three. Not bad odds for a supposed immortal."

"That's just how it will be," said the Countess. "I don't count these puppets as people. But as tools."

Christine, Trilby and Irene were backed against the wall. Only Christine had a usable weapon. She extended her sword-point.

One of the wives stepped out of formation and walked up to Christine. The sword dimpled against her chest, then slid through her torso. She stepped calmly up to Christine's face, blade emerging from her back, sword-hilt against her copper-wire ribs. She angled her head from side to side, looking into Christine's face–then reversed her walk, like a music box wound backwards, wrenching the sword from Christine's grip.

The orchestra still played, but the tinkling tune was running out, as if the music box were winding down. The conductor's baton slowed.

The Countess made a gesture, and there was a whooshing sound.

The wives' fingernails extended by an inch, razor-edges glinting.

"This is probably where we get cut to ribbons," Irene told her colleagues.

Trilby and Christine held hands. Irene took a fighting stance–she'd had an afternoon of boxing lessons from a bare-knuckles champion. Before she went under, she'd break a few toys.

The music stopped. The baton was still.

"Goodbye, Angels," said the Countess.

Then the automaton conductor twisted, suddenly loose-limbed, on his podium, baton falling from gloved fingers. A curtain tore away from the complex works underneath the clockwork musicians and the real conductor could be seen–faceless, broken and stowed away under the bandstand. Several barrels were wired into the workings of the grand Venetian device, marked "gunpowder."

The girls just had time to realize who had taken the place of the mechanical music master.

The golden face-plate was lifted from a lipless horror of a mouth.

The girls' hearts leaped. The Countess whirled, enraged but still confident of victory. The mannequins attacked.

Clawnails passed Irene's face, and she took hold of cold, unliving wrists. An implacable mask of beauty loomed close to her, chin dropped to show rows of sharp ceramic teeth. These dolls were designed for murder as much as marriage.

Erik–for it was he!–raised a tube to his mouth. It was about the size of a piccolo, but with fewer holes. He sounded three distinct notes, shrill and dissonant, unknown to music or nature. Irene had heard them once before this evening, and again her teeth were set on edge.

Christine and Trilby reacted at once to the signal. Their eyes became fixed, almost as glassy as the mannequins'. Ignoring aches and bruises, they cartwheeled into the fray, arms and legs scything through the cadre of wives, fetching off dolls' heads and limbs, spilling clockwork innards and horse-hair stuffing.

Irene, whose head hurt from the shrilling, concentrated on wrestling the contraption which was trying to shred her. She battered its wax-and-china face with her forehead, and tried to break its wrists.

Erik had his temporary mask back in place. He threw a lever, and the clockwork orchestra began to play Tartini's *The Devil's Trill*–but with strange lapses and lacunae, filled by the crackling of electrical arcs.

The Countess looked at Erik, mask to mask.

From the podium, Erik picked up a box, which trailed wires deep into the orchestra's innards and the barrels of explosive. Surmounting the box was a metal switch in the form of a frog.

Christine danced, whirling swords taken from a toy soldier's wooden fist and a sleeping senior officer's scabbard, cutting through mannequins. She fought like an eight-armed Hindu goddess with a scimitar in each hand. She heard music, and the music directed her actions. Lady Galatea, Duchess of Omnium, hurled herself at Christine, foot-long porcupine spines stuck out of her chest and back, arms wide for a deadly, skewering hug. Christine stepped under the embrace and used her swords like scissors, snipping the Duchess in half length-wise. Without breaking her movement, she hurled the two halves of the broken thing at two more of the wives, sticking them through with the spines, then stepping down with a heavy boot-heel on their fallen faces.

Trilby fought less elegantly, with feet and fists, delivering *savate* kicks and powerful fist-blows. She wrenched the arms off Madame Venus de l'Isle del Gardo, and whirled them about, raking their claws across the toys. Madame del Gardo hopped comically from side to side, off balance, trailing wires from her shoulders twitching and sparking, lubricational fluids spurting from ruptured rubber tubes like yellow blood. The armless doll, momentarily the image of a more famous Venus, collided with a toy soldier, and its head flew apart in a puff of flame, burning wig shot across the room, metal and china shrapnel ripping through the soldier. With Venus' arms, Trilby battered away several more of the wives.

It was a dazzling performance. Within moments, the floor was strewn with spasming, broken things. Springs and cogs scattered underfoot. Pools of yellow liquid formed, and electrical sparks set light to them. Flames ran quickly, spreading from doll to doll, melting wax prettiness away from metal skulls, crumpling lacework and human hair wiggery in instants, taking hold on torn and oily dresses. Some of the husbands sat up, awake, patting at scorching patches on their evening clothes, yelping in pain at the rude disturbance to their dreams.

Irene still wrestled with her single opponent, Madame Gerard, née Francis-Pierre.

Trilby stepped up, and wrenched off Poupée's head. Her body went limp.

Irene looked at Trilby, holding the head up like Perseus with the Medusa. Its eyes still rolled and it tried several sweet smiles before its internal mechanisms wound down and the lids fell shut.

The last of the wives had fallen back to the throne, to protect the Countess, who was trying to make herself heard above the racket. The orchestra broke down, and the Tartini shut off. The wives were assembling themselves into some many-legged war machine, directed by the Countess.

The trio stood before the throne. Trilby and Christine opened their mouths and ululated, a high, clear, pure, penetrating sound that rose. Irene clapped her hands over her ears, but couldn't completely shut out the sound.

The Countess halted her work on the machine, a trickle of blood leaking from one of her eyeholes.

The voices soared, a wordless sound, two tones entwined. Edison bulbs burst. Champagne flutes flew to splinters. The faceplates of the last brides shattered, showing the intricate works beneath. Even their glass eyes burst.

Irene jammed her fingers into her ears, trying to shut out the pain.

Trilby and Christine, unaffected, seeming to be able to do without breath, took the sound up to a peak. Somewhere on the barge, something major broke.

Another shrill note came, from Erik's flute–cutting through his *protegées'* voices, shutting them off.

And Christine and Trilby were fully awake, bleeding and puzzled.

"What happened?" Trilby asked Irene.

"You went away for a while," she said. "Everything's fine now."

Trilby realized she was holding a broken head, had a moment of disgust, and dropped the thing.

"*Zut alors,*" said Christine. "What a shambles!"

The Countess was gone, her throne descended into a trapdoor, a smear of thick blood marking her trail. Erik was vanished too. During the *mêlée*, he had fixed his detonator-box to a clockwork percussionist, wiring its hand to the frog switch and setting an hour-glass timer which was already close to running out.

"Abandon ship," ordered Irene.

Most of the company were in the main ballroom when Erik's explosives went off. There was a vast grinding sound as the greater works of the barge misaligned and tore themselves to pieces, wrecking whatever purpose they might have had. More explosions followed.

Christine, Trilby and Irene were in a corridor, which ought to lead up to the deck and safety. They found the doorway barred and bolted. The Countess evidently took the ruin of her schemes personally. The incandescent lamps wavered, and they were ankle-deep in cold water. Then the floor listed, and the water flowed away. The girls found things to hang onto.

"I think our music master might have planned this phase of the evening rather better," observed Irene. "We're quite likely to drown."

"Have more faith, Irène," said Christine, cheerfully. "Something will turn up."

They were looking at a foaming torrent advancing up the corridor. Something broke the surface angrily–one of the toy soldiers, or at least the top half of one. It thumped against a wall, turned over, and sank.

"How sad," said Christine. "I love a man in uniform."

One of the porthole windows broke inwards, and a rope ladder descended. A familiar face loomed through the aperture, a beckoning arm extended. It was the Persian! Alive!

"Ladies, time leave this playroom."

He did not have to say it twice.

Only two or three of the Marriage Club were drowned, and they weren't among those who'd be most missed. The hero of the hour, *fêted* as such in the popular press, was the aged Etienne Gerard. Shocked to his senses by cold water, the one-time Brigadier labored fearlessly at great risk to his own life to aid his fellow guests in their escapes from the fast-sinking barge. Some wondered why such a noted gallant managed only to rescue wealthy, famous, *male* members of the party from the depths, leaving scores of poor, obscure, young wives to the Seine. No corpses were ever recovered, though broken mannequin parts washed up on the mudbanks for months. It was another of the Mysteries of Paris, and soon everyone had other scandals, sensations and strangenesses to cluck over.

The Persian reported that he had been fished out of the river by his old friend, Erik–who effected emergency medical assistance, before taking the unusual step of venturing himself onto the field of battle.

Back at the Opéra, quantities of brandy were consumed, and repairs were made to the persons of the lovely ladies who had done so much for a world which would never know what services had been rendered. As dawn broke, baskets of fruit and pastries were delivered, with a note of thanks from Madame Sabatier, who also enclosed a satisfactory bankers' draught.

After hauling cardinals and bankers out of the cold water, the newly-widowed Grand Maréchal Gerard–if one could be widowed after marriage not to a human woman but a long-case clock with a prettily painted face–repaired to the *Salon Sabatier*, paid in advance for the exclusive company of three of *la Présidente*'s most alluring *filles de joie*, and promptly fell into a deep sleep that might last for days. That certainly counted as a happy outcome.

The only pall cast over celebrations came when Irene announced that she felt it was time she quit the Phantom of the Opéra's Agency to venture out on her own. Christine and Trilby wept to hear the news, and bestowed many embraces on their friend, not noticing that she was unable to control a shudder when they touched her. Irene could not look at their active, lovely, characterful faces without recalling the expressionless, bloodied masks of skin that took their place when three shrill notes sounded. Not to mention the proficiencies in arts devastating and deadly they exhibited under the fluence.

The Persian understood and conveyed M. Erik's good wishes.

"He suggests, however, that you limit your field of operations."

"I should stay out of Paris?"

"He thinks... France."

"Very well. There's Ruritania, and Poland and London. All a-swim with opportunities."

Irene left the building.

Behind his mirror, Erik knew regret. But he understood the American was not like his other girls. There was a steel in her core, which made her unsuitable for "music lessons," the specialized training he deemed necessary in his most useful Agents. That steel would never be bent entirely to his purpose, and might eventually bring them into conflict... as he had been brought into conflict with Josephine Balsamo.

The Countess Cagliostro was, of course, still at large, and liable to be unforgiving now her carefully-contrived plan of world domination was sunk. She would quite probably be suffering from a splitting headache, too, and be unhappy at the loss of her marvelous barge and so many toys, either. This was no time for the Agency to be under-strength.

This *feuilleton* was not over.

For days, Christine and Trilby moped, and were inconsolable. Everything said to them was a reminder of something Irene had said or done, and would set them off in further floods of tears. Other ladies of the chorus assumed their hearts had been ordinarily broken, and dispensed wisdoms about the untrustworthiness of the perfidious male sex.

Then, the bell sounded. Not for "music lessons," not for an exploit, but a simple summons.

As they walked down the corridor to their dressing room, they came upon a familiar, shambling, bent-over figure. Christine, acting on instinct, took him by the throat and shoved him rudely against the wall.

"No more, please," said Cochenille, squirming.

Temporary repairs had been made to the mannequin, and he was coming apart again. As Christine pinned him, Trilby rolled up her sleeves, intent on smashing his face to bits again.

"Ladies, let him be," said the Persian, looking out of the dressing room. He had been in a conference with Spalanzani and Coppélius. "These gentlemen have split with their former employer."

Christine dropped the gasping Cochenille. His hand came off, and he picked it up and stuck it into his pocket. Trilby gave him a kick, and he scurried away, followed by the doll-makers, who gave the girls a wide berth as they passed out of sight. Trilby gave their backs the Evil Eye Stare.

"We have come to an arrangement," said the Persian. "Advantageous for our Agency."

Trilby and Christine entered the dressing room.

On the divan sat a small blonde girl, dressed all in white, posed like a ballerina in a tableau.

"She's not a doll," said Christine. "She can't be."

The girl's head moved and she blinked. There was no clicking or whirring.

"She must be the original, from which the mannequin-makers copied," said Trilby.

The girl's chest swelled and contracted with breath. She gestured, showing the suppleness of her fingers. She picked up an apple from *la Présidente*'s basket, flicked out her nails and rolled the fruit in her hand, letting the peel slither away from the flesh in an unbroken ribbon, then crushed it to juice with a sudden, powerful squeeze.

Christine and Trilby walked around the divan, observing the newcomer from all angles, wondering at the ingenuity of her manufacture.

"This is Olympia," said Erik, from behind the mirror. "She will be joining us for 'music lessons,' and taking the departed Miss Adler's place in our roster of agents."

Olympia curtseyed.

"It is a pleasure to meet you," she said. "I hope we shall be the best of friends."

John Peel continues to thrill us by crafting clever little crime thrillers. After his story, last year, of the duel between the Count of Monte-Cristo and the Black Coats, this time, it is the sagacious Rouletabille, the most Cartesian of all French detectives, that warrants his attention. Gaston Leroux's detective here shares the limelight with master showman Serge Diaghilev, impresario and manager of the famed Ballets Russes, *which entranced the West with their revolutionary and exotic performances. And, as Peel demonstrates, in this instance, they are quite dramatic...*

John Peel: *The Incomplete Assassin*

Paris, 1910

The premiere of any new form of art in Paris is always an occasion for extravagance and celebration, and that of the 1910 season of the celebrated *Ballets Russes* was certainly no exception. As the grand evening dawned, I considered myself quite fortunate in having a friend who had secured us tickets for this new production, but as the evening drew on and the fresh corpse turned up, I was no longer as certain of my good luck.

Nothing of this will be found in the official accounts of the premiere, for reasons that will shortly become apparent. Not even a hint of it can be delved from the report delivered by my good friend Joseph Rouletabille, reporter, who was the prime mover in resolving the strange mystery.

I had known my peculiar friend some ten years before these events, and had never noted in him any particular love of music. Oh, on an evening in Maxim's, he would enjoy a gypsy violinist, or a performance of the can-can, but they can hardly be considered serious music–more frivolity than virtuosity. So when he mentioned to me that he had two tickets, and asked me to accompany him, I was both pleased and surprised. Naturally, I questioned his motives, and he smiled at me over his freshly-lit briarwood pipe.

"Music is always interesting," he explained. "Though I am not certain that I quite like the trends some composers are taking. But this performance is reputed to be something quite special. As you know, in their first season, the *Ballets Russes* took Paris by storm, so the second is a highly anticipated event, which in itself makes for news. Add to that the fact that this production, *The Firebird*, is their first with freshly-composed music, and it becomes more important. And since most of the people, including the composer, are still young, my editor felt that a young man's opinions on the night's performance would be of interest. And I am to be allowed backstage after the performance to conduct interviews, which I felt you might enjoy." He laughed. "There really is no mystery in this at all, my friend."

In that prediction, he was to be proven quite incorrect.

It seemed that everyone who was anyone in Paris was at the Théâtre du Châtelet. Though not as well-known as the Opera House–or as infamous, as the celebrated case of the Phantom of the Opera has shown–it is to my mind one of the most pleasing of the city's many temples of culture. Set a little back from the Seine, it is perhaps a trifle square and straightforward by day. But at night, illuminated from within and without, it captivates the senses. The main entrance, through five arched doorways surmounted by five equally-large arched windows, greets with warmth and a promise of the grandeur within. Pass the steps crowded with the elite of Paris society, festooned in jewels, perfumes and expensive clothing. Go through the throng in the lobby indulging in their last cigarettes before taking their seats, and into the sumptuous hall–well, it raises the excitement level, and hones the anticipation of a grand evening.

And such it proved to be. It was perhaps a trifle *avant-garde* for my tastes, but the staging could not be faulted. Parisiennes have become accustomed to horses upon their stages, and the *Ballets* used theirs sparingly. But at the point when the magician's spells are broken, and the long-frozen, gray, cobweb-festooned statues came to life, a collective gasp sped through the audience. Michel Fokine, the young choreographer, also danced superbly. I was a trifle disappointed that it was not the prodigy Nijinsky who was dancing–as, too, were many of the women in the audience. Anna Pavlova, my companion informed me, had been intended to dance the title role, but had refused, claiming the music to be undanceable. True, the music I found a trifle grating, but the main themes were certainly harmonious enough. Pavlova was replaced by Tamara Karsavina, who may not have had the same reputation, but who clearly did not find the ballet unperformable. At the end of the performance, the audience gave vent to its pleasure, and Rouletabille and I cheerfully joined in the applause.

"What do you think, Sainclair?" my companion asked me.

"Another triumph, of course," I replied.

"But not quite your taste, I take it?"

"I'm not as young as you, my friend," I replied honestly. "And consequently, I am a little stuck in my ways. Tschaikovsky is about as advanced as I can thoroughly enjoy these days." We had seen a performance of *Swan Lake* by the Kirov whilst on a recent adventure in Russia, and that still lingered favorably in my memory.

Rouletabille laughed. "And this upstart Stravinsky simply will not do, eh? Well, shall we go and hear what the upstart has to say about his success?" He led me through the maze of corridors out of the public areas of the theater and into the performers' and managers' sections. To my surprise, we were not challenged by any of the attendants whose task it was to prevent the over-zealous from mobbing Nijinsky or any of the other performers. As had happened before, it seemed that the staff here knew my companion by sight. Naturally, Rouletabille did not explain, and I knew that questioning him would be fruitless. Doubtless he had performed some service here in the past.

Champagne was flowing in the performers' rooms. Laughter, ribaldry and other slightly-coarse comments were also flowing. I had once discovered that the artistic community tends to flout accepted behavior, sometimes quite scandalously. Diaghilev himself, the manager of the *corps*, made very little secret of his own passion for his leading man, and Nijinsky made little secret of his passions for almost anyone. It must be difficult for a young man, not yet out of his teens, who is the toast of Paris, to restrain his impulses, so I do not judge him–I merely observe.

The composer, it turned out, was a smallish man, with nervous habits and a penetrating glare. He responded readily to my companion's request for a few words about the successful performance.

"This is merely the start of a revolution," he declared. "I envision more and greater ballets that will take Paris–nay, the world–by storm. I will overthrow the old, and bring in a new era." He went on in such a vein for quite some time before Rouletabille and I could make our excuses and go in search of Diaghilev for his opinions.

"What do you make of our young composer?" Rouletabille asked me, a twinkle in his eyes, as we elbowed through a crowd of stage hands. "Is he capable of such a revolution?"

"It seems to me that far too many Russians are trying to foment revolutions in too many spheres," I replied. "That young man may succeed in starting something, but whether it will ever catch on is another matter." After a moment's consideration, I added: "He is a shortish man, and I have noted that many such people like to make up for their lack of stature by seeking to make a large impact in the world."

"The Napoleon of music, eh?" Rouletabille laughed again. "I suspect he will be one of the voices of the future, my friend. Whether for good or ill–who can say?"

The crowds seemed to be thinning out, finally, as the house was getting packed back into trunks and boxes ready for the following day's performance. Dancers, now without makeup and in their normal attire, had started to filter out into the Paris streets. No doubt the crowds were also on their way for nightcaps, or a late-night meal. Things were winding down–or so I imagined. One's imagination can be so often very wrong.

Movement in the corridor ahead of us caught my eye. An elderly gentleman, quite distinguished-looking and dressed with modest but excellent taste, stopped walking when he caught sight of us. It was clear from his manner that he was expecting us to come to him, and we did not disappoint him.

"Monsieur Rouletabille, I believe?" the gentleman asked. "I have been looking for you."

"It appears that you have found me, Monsieur..."

"Strogoff," the man replied, with a formal bow that my companion returned. "I have two favors to ask of you–though it may seem presumptuous of me to ask any, since we have not been formally introduced."

Rouletabille laughed. "It is hardly necessary for Michel Strogoff to introduce himself," he commented. "Knowing your name, I also know that you are the Tsar's man, and that, if you seek me out, it is so that I may perform another service for Tsar Nicholas. I should be more than happy to offer such services."

Strogoff smiled back. "It would appear that your reputation is deserved, Monsieur." He glanced at me, clearly weighing me up. "I think I will be able to find something to occupy your companion in the meanwhile," he offered. "Some of the ballerinas have not yet departed..." It was a wonderfully polite way of saying that he could not be sure that he could trust me to hear whatever he wished to tell my friend.

Rouletabille shook his head. "It will not be necessary to trouble the young ladies–though I am sure they would be, as you say, his glass of tea. Monsieur Sainclair is a longtime friend and companion of mine, and can be relied upon utterly–as I have often done."

The Russian nodded. "If you vouch for him, then I, too, shall trust his discretion. If you gentlemen would be so kind as to follow me..."

He led us through the corridors with their thinning crowds, and into the backstage area of the theater. Here, I noticed, there were more people concentrated, and one man standing outside a closed door was clearly performing guard duty. He moved aside as we approached, and allowed Monsieur Strogoff to open the door and usher us inside.

Diaghilev himself was there, tall, distinguished and resplendent in his tails. We were in some sort of scenery storage room, and there were several of the stage hands about. There was also one corpse laid out on a long table. Rouletabille, knowing now why he had been summoned, rushed forward to examine the body. I was a trifle more reluctant, but went to do my duty as my friend's observer.

The victim was in his late twenties and dressed as a stage hand. He had been shot, once, in the chest, the bullet puncturing a lung, but narrowly missing the heart. I observed blood on the table, but there was a pool of it on the floor, closer to the door, clearly where he had been shot. There were drag marks made in the blood from the original spot behind the door, to the table, which was in the center of the room. I could tell nothing else from the body, but the smile that flickered on my friend's face told me that, as ever, it educated him far more.

He turned to Strogoff. "What can you tell me of this event?" he asked.

"Little enough, I am afraid," the Russian replied. "He was shot and killed perhaps 20 minutes ago. He lingered a short while, being found on the verge of death by the other stage hands. One of them was dispatched to find me, and the others, intelligently, barred further entry to this room. He died shortly after I arrived."

"This is a disaster," Diaghilev wailed. "When news of this reaches the newspapers, this production will become a scandal."

"It is my desire that such an event will not happen," Strogoff said, firmly. He looked at Rouletabille. "For the first of those favors I mentioned, can I ask that this even be treated as if it had never happened? The *Ballets Russes* represents the Tsar and our country, and a scandal such as murder would not help our diplomatic mission here in Paris."

Rouletabille smiled slightly. "I am not certain that I agree with you there," he said. "I suspect that if all of Paris knew of this killing, it would induce many more people to flock here for the ballet. Parisiennes can be drawn by the ghoulish. Nevertheless, I understand your request, and I am willing to abide by it. The killing will need to be reported to the Police, of course, but I can suggest a few names of those who will be willing to be most discrete."

"That would be acceptable," Strogoff agreed. He turned to the impresario. "Your reputation will be unharmed, and your performances will continue unhindered–at least, by any breath of *this* scandal."

"Thank you!" Diaghilev exclaimed, delightedly shaking my friend's hand. "Now, I must be off–if Diaghilev does not party this night, some tragedy will be suspected. I shall force myself to be witty and gay." He rushed from the room.

Rouletabille smiled at me. "I suspect he will not need to force himself too strenuously," he observed. Then he turned to Strogoff. "And the second favor you wish of me?"

The Russian gestured at the table. "To uncover who did this deed–and why. I have always been more of a man of action than a man of deliberation, I must confess, and I can see nothing here to help me understand this tragedy."

"Each to his own *métier*," my companion said. "I shall see what effects my own small skills may have." He turned to the stage hands. "This man was one of your company?" he asked. "But it is clear that he has been with you only a short while."

"Barely two months," one of the others agreed. "His name is Zhadikov. But how could you know that?"

"His hands," Rouletabille said, casually. "I see that the four of you have calluses from your work; this man is barely starting to form them. Hence, he joined you recently. Also, he clearly did little manual work before this, which would be odd in a man as old as this."

"He spoke little of his background," a second man offered. "Nor did he socialize with us."

"That is understandable, since he did not come here to find work."

Strogoff looked curiously at my companion. "How can you be so certain of that?"

186

"His hands, once again, Monsieur," Rouletabille said. "Always examine the extremities, for they will tell you much about a man. In this instance, if you look at the hands of these good workers, you will see that their fingernails are broken, due to the work they perform." He held up the left hand of the dead man. "Zhadikov, by contrast, has hands that were clearly manicured recently, as his nails are unbroken and filed. Hence, he is a man with his own income, and therefore he did not come here because he needed work. Rather, he came here because there was something here for him." He looked at the workers again. "Did he speak at all before he died?"

"A little," the first stage hand said. "But he was delirious, and his words made no sense. I asked him who had done this to him, and he replied, simply, *More...*" The man shrugged. "He was having great difficulty breathing, and spoke no further."

"That is understandable." My companion considered for a moment, and then looked at Strogoff. "I take it that these four good men may be relied upon to say nothing of what they have witnessed?"

"They may be French and not Russian, but they are reliable," Strogoff replied.

"Good. Then all that needs be done now, I think, is to summon an ambulance."

Strogoff looked astonished, as well he might–he did not have the advantage I had of knowing my friend often made suggestions that at first might appear more than a trifle odd, but that, eventually, would make perfect sense. "An ambulance?" he repeated. "But this man is dead."

"Perhaps he is," Rouletabille agreed, examining the body once again. "*But he may not necessarily remain that way*–at least, not to the murderer. He is a young, well-built man. If you can aid me with a little of the stage makeup here and a wig, I imagine that I might be mistaken for him, especially at this time of night."

Strogoff's eyes sparkled. "Ah! You are laying a trap?"

"Indeed I am." Rouletabille smiled. "I must confess that I am, from time to time, a lazy man. I don't see why I should race all over Paris searching for the man when I can force him to come to me." He turned to the four workmen and myself. "Now, I require of you all to be consistent in this story. When the ambulance arrives, it will cause some curiosity in passersby outside the theater. If anyone should ask you, tell them merely that a stage hand has been injured, and is being taken for emergency medical aid. If asked for further details, say only that the man is expected to recover fully. Then say no more."

I nodded. "You expect, of course, that we shall be asked."

"I rely upon it. And if I understand the murderer correctly, it is inevitable." He clapped me on the shoulder. "Stay at the theater here no more than a quarter-hour after the ambulance leaves. Then hurry at once to the hospital. Dr. Génessier is on duty tonight, and I believe I can rely on his skills to ensure that I–as the injured stage hand–will make a surprisingly wonderful recovery."

Most of the audience and the performers had left the theater by the time that the ambulance arrived. It departed a few moments later, with my friend on a stretcher in the back. A small crowd only had gathered, mostly of the well-dressed in no hurry to return to their homes after an evening out. As Rouletabille had predicted, several of them wondered aloud what was happening. As per my instructions, I said only that a stage hand had been somewhat injured.

A well-dressed young man asked casually how this could have happened.

I shrugged. "I know few details," I said. "Only that his wound is apparently not severe, and that the medical attendants believe he will recover after surgery at the local hospital." I tipped my hat. "Now, really, I must be off. A glass of cognac will steady my nerves." I hurried away, and three blocks later I hailed a cab.

It deposited me at the hospital a few minutes later. I hurried to the admitting station, and discovered that a M. Zhadikov had been rushed into surgery, and that Dr. Génessier was operating. After this, he should be taken to room 301. I would be allowed to wait there, as Dr. Génessier had already approved this.

Hurrying to the room, I found that there was already a patient in the bed–my friend Rouletabille, naturally. The room was dimly-lit, and with a wig and a little applied makeup, he did bear a passing resemblance to the murdered man. There was with him an elderly attendant, arranging water and flowers beside the bed.

"Sainclair, excellent," my friend said, happily. "Everything went as expected?" he asked me.

"Indeed," I agreed. "I was questioned after I left the theater by a group of onlookers, and then left to come here and join you." I knew his methods well by this time, and yet I could not help but wonder how he could be so certain that the murderer would follow along. But there was little point in questioning him–Rouletabille explained what he wished only when he wanted.

"Good. Then come, sit by my bedside as if you were some concerned relative, and we shall await events." He glanced at the attendant. "I think that will be all."

"As you wish," the old man said, and he left the room, closing the door behind him.

"Turn down the light a trifle, if you would," Rouletabille suggested. "Shadows are our friends when we are in such a rough disguise as this."

We sat quietly together, and listened, whilst pretending to do nothing of the sort. It was by now past midnight, and the hospital was fairly quiet. From time to time footsteps approached the room, and we both tensed. But on each occasion, they passed on by. We had sat there almost an hour when we heard further foot-steps–only these stopped outside the door instead of moving on.

I glanced around as the door opened. It was difficult to make out details, as we were in such gloom, but I could see our visitor was the well-dressed young man I had spoken to outside the theater.

"So," he said, harshly, "despite my efforts, you still thwart me, Zhadikov. But no more!" He raised his right hand, which held a pistol. "This time, fare-well!"

The events of the next few seconds were quite confused. I launched myself from my chair, hoping to intercept the man before he could fire, despite the dis-tance between us. Rouletabille, with his customary agility, threw himself from the bed toward the floor. And the elderly attendant sprang onto the assassin from behind.

The bullet passed over my head, and impacted in the now-vacant bed. With surprising skill and strength, the old attendant wrestled the pistol from the young man's grip, and then Rouletabille and I helped to subdue the now crazed and screaming man. A few moments later, several strong policemen joined in the struggle, and the howling assassin was dragged off to a cell. Rouletabille prom-ised to be along shortly to explain the charges against him, and the corridor was soon almost empty again.

"Dr. Génessier has, as I instructed, kept the hospital staff from this area," Rouletabille explained to me.

"Except this attendant," I said, "who proved to be of such valuable assis-tance."

The attendant laughed, and drew off his own wig, and wiped his face. I saw with surprise that under the makeup it was none other than Michel Strogoff. "It has been a long time since my duties have been quite so physical," he admit-ted. "And I am sure I shall pay for it by waking aching in the morning. But it has been worth it." He reached out a hand to my friend. "Monsieur Rouletabille, your aid has been invaluable. But perhaps you would now explain how you knew that this would happen?"

"By all means," he agreed. "But it was all quite obvious from the scene of the murder–if only you knew how to interpret the facts."

Strogoff looked at me in astonishment. "You are his colleague–do you know what he means?"

"Rarely ever," I confessed, with a smile. "Until he expounds, and then you wonder how you could have missed it all along."

Rouletabille laughed. "Come, Sainclair, you are an intelligent man–was all of this truly baffling to you?"

"It was, as you know it always is," I responded. "I cannot see the link be-tween the theater and here–save for the obvious. You made the killer believe that his murder had not be accomplished, and so forced him to try a second time. But how could you know that he would do so? After all, it might have been a crime of the moment–that Zhadikov had stumbled over the killer committing some crime and been killed for it."

"No, the facts did not admit to that as a possibility," my friend replied. "Though the murder *was*, indeed, a crime of sudden intent. The first clue was the dying man's last word."

"He said only *More*," I protested. "That means very little."

"It means everything. Zhadikov was Russian, and the stage hands who found him were French. What he wished to say had to be translated for them to understand. As you know, there are a number of revolutionary groups involved in Russia politics at the moment. Many feel that their country needs a change in rulership, often through violence. Zhadikov, a wealthy man, joined this company here in Paris as a stage hand? Why? Clearly because here he had contacts with people allowed to travel freely to and from Russia. I am certain that it will be found that Zhadikov–under another name–was on a list of know activists, and would not be allowed there himself. Here, at the *Ballets Russes*, he could work unknown and meet his contacts for intelligences.

"Our assassin, attending the *Ballets* himself, must have seen and recognized Zhadikov. How and why? Just seven years ago, the Russian Social Democratic Labor Party split on matters of policy. One branch became known as the Bolsheviks, the other as the Menshehviks. No love has been lost between the two factions. Bolshehvik, of course, means *more*, because they demanded more; Menshevik means *less* because they are less extreme."

The matter was starting to become clearer. "So!" I exclaimed. "Both men were revolutionaries, but on opposite sides of the issue."

"Quite so. And their chance meeting here led our killer to a swift decision. Seeing Zhadikov in the theater, he knew he had stumbled onto a spy ring belonging to his opponents. The only one he recognized was Zhadikov, so he would have to act to close down the ring. How? By making the others think they might become his next victims. He followed Zhadikov into the backstage change room and killed him. It then became important that Zhadikov be discovered swiftly, and his death become a warning."

I frowned. "But why was the shot itself not heard?"

"The backstage areas are well soundproofed," Strogoff interjected. "It would not do to have activities there heard on the stage." That I could understand.

"But you no doubt noticed that the place where Zhadikov had been killed was behind the door," Rouletabille said. "That did not suit our killer's purpose– it was always possible that in the bustle and confusion of a premiere that the body might not be found immediately. He needed to strike instant horror into his quarry, so the body *must* be found before the end of the evening. So he dragged the dying man across the room and then positioned him on the table–in clear view of anyone who opened the door."

"But how did you know it was the killer who dragged the poor man, and not the stage hands?" I objected.

Rouletabille smiled. "My friend, they are four strong men, used to moving heavy pieces of stage equipment. If they had stumbled across the dying body of their friend, they would not have *dragged* it—they would have picked it up and carried it to the table. So, no, the killer moved the body, and clearly so that it would be seen. Most killers *hide* their victims—this one did the opposite, so it obviously was in order that the corpse should serve as a warning."

Strogoff smiled. "And, of course, you made the killer think that his plan had come apart, and that the victim was still alive. He then *had* to follow, and attempt the murder again—and so we have him." The Russian shook his head. "I cannot believe that we saw the same things as you, and yet understood so little."

"As I remarked before," my companion said, "each of us to his own *métier*. Fortunately for you, you had on hand the one man in all of Paris who would be able to resolve your mystery. If you will allow me to intrude just a fraction on your profession, though, I would suggest that you begin to search through the personnel of the *Ballets* to discover Zhadikov's co-conspirators."

"Indeed I shall," Strogoff agreed. "And I should like to meet with both of you gentlemen again, to discuss the thanks my Tsar will undoubtedly wish passed along to you." He bowed formally to us both, and left.

I turned to Rouletabille, who had by now shed his disguise and recovered his evening clothes. "Well, my friend—now what?"

He examined his pocket watch. "Well, with a little luck, the crowds may have started to thin. Perhaps we might do well to see if either of us has sufficient influence to get a table at Maxim's? All of this mental activity has left me quite famished."

The notion that Man was not alone, and further that, thanks to the new discoveries made possible by science, he would soon visit his planetary neighbors, became common place in 19th century science fiction. In 1865, 12 years before Italian astronomer Giovanni Schiaparelli thought he saw canals on Mars, Baron Alfred d'Espiard de Colonge, in La Chute du Ciel ou Les Antiques Météores Planétaires, *hypothesized that life on Earth had originated on another world, and may have started as the result of deliberate seeding by aliens. Three years prior, French astronomer Camille Flammarion had begun to discuss the physiological properties of extraterrestrial life. Amidst the plethora of fictional scientists harnessing imaginary energies and building new and bigger craft, one figure stands alone: the mysterious Doctor Omega, created by Arnould Galopin in 1906. In this story, cleverly inserted between chapters two and three of Galopin's novel, Chris Roberson takes a closer look at what lurked behind the apparent miracles of space age technology of the 19th century.*

Chris Roberson: *Annus Mirabilis*

Le Creusot and Bern, 1905

In the still dark hours of the morning, while the town of Le Creusot slowly rubbed the sleep from its eyes and woke to another spring day, the old man ambled along aimlessly through the foothills of the Morvan. He was lost in thought, a dark mote drifting along the green Bourgogne countryside in his black cloak, a long striped scarf wrapped round his neck, a peaked fur hat atop his head, which could scarcely conceal the snow-white hair and rebellious forelock that swept back from his high forehead.

As the Sun pinked the eastern sky, and Le Creusot began to hum with life and activity, the old man came back down into the township proper, passing the gates of the Château de la Verrerie, since the last century the residence of the Schneider family, the masters of the forges. At this early hour, dark smoke already bled into the lightening sky, billowing up from the smokestacks of the foundries. Arriving at the metal-works unmolested, the old man flung open the door, and a wave of heat from the forges rolled toward him like a solid wall. Within, directing the workmen of the Schneider foundry, the old man found his companion already hard at work, crescents of sweat darkening the arm-pits of his crisp white shirt, his trouser legs stained and scuffed.

"Borel," the old man said, then had to repeat, raising his voice over the tintinnabulation of metal striking metal. "Borel! How goes the assembly?"

"What?" the young man shouted back, cupping his hands around his ears like a listening trumpet. The old man repeated his question, raising the pitch of his voice even higher. "Oh, well enough, Doctor! We seem to be proceeding on schedule."

"In that case," the old man said, quite unconcerned now whether his companion could hear him further, "I shall find a bite to eat, hmm?"

On a side table was laid out the makings of a simple breakfast, for the use of the foundry's workers. The Schneiders had evidently learned that providing such simple amenities, though a notional expense at the outset, meant that their laborers had a shorter distance to travel to sate their appetites, and would perforce be the quicker to return to their duties. The old man, considering himself in some regards as the workers' employer–he had, after all, contracted the foundry's services in the construction of the large craft which Borel now oversaw– had no compunctions against helping himself to their board.

Selecting an apple, a hunk of cold cheese, and a small loaf of fresh bread, the old man seated himself on a nearby straight-backed chair, on the back of which was folded some sort of newspaper or journal. As he bit into the apple, the old man unfolded the periodical, and scanned the contents. It was a copy of *Beiblätter zu den Annalen der Physik,* and the old man concluded that it must have been left by one of the foundry's engineers. Absently chewing on a bite of apple, the old man began to read, idly.

After finishing no more than half of the apple, having hardly touched the bread, the old man's eyes opened wide, and he jumped to his feet, clutching the journal.

"Borel!" he shouted, racing across the foundry floor, waving his arms for the young man's attention. The old man's companion, seeing his approach, gave a shout of alarm, and rushed to his side, his labors forgotten.

"Doctor, what is it?" the young man said, his expression suggesting that he feared the worst.

"What is the date, my boy?" the old man asked, his mouth drawn into a tight line.

The young man's forehead wrinkled momentarily, as he did some quick mental calculation. "March the sixth," he finally answered. "A Monday."

"Yes, yes," the old man said impatiently, waving his hand. "But the year, man, what year?"

The young man was a bit taken aback, but it was clear he'd grown used to the old man's eccentricities in recent weeks. "Why, it's 1905, naturally."

"Oh dear, oh dear." The old man began to pace back and forth, his expression grave, his eyes flashing. "No, this won't do. This won't do at all."

Before the young man could speak, to ask the old man what was the matter at hand, the old man stopped short, straightening.

"Borel, I'm leaving you in charge. See to it that the three components of the craft are appropriately joined together."

"Certainly, Doctor. But where will you be?"

"I'm sorry, my boy, but I have vital matters which must be attended." With that, the old man shoved the journal into the young man's hands, turned on his heel, and stalked from the foundry.

The young man watched the retreating back of his companion, baffled. He glanced at the journal the old man has been reading, hoping there to find some clue to what had set the old man off. It was open to a review of a Professor Wellingham's paper, "*On the role of panergon in the relationship between electricity and light,*" by one A. Einstein. The young man could see no reason for excitement with either the names or the subject and, tucking the journal into his trouser pocket, shrugged and returned to his labors.

Two days later, on the morning of Wednesday, March 8, the old man appeared at the reception area of the Swiss Patent Office, in Bern, Switzerland. Not bothering to doff his fur hat, nor unwind his striped scarf, he marched up to the clerk behind the reception desk, leaning forward like a man walking against a heavy wind.

"I insist on speaking with one of your technical assistant examiners," the old man said, before the clerk had the opportunity to ask.

The clerk sighed, a long-suffering, resigned sort of sigh, and pushed his glasses up on the bridge of his nose. "And does this concern a pending patent application, I assume?"

"You may assume what you like," the old man said, brusquely, "it makes no difference to me. However, I dare say that the matter on which I have come will impact a great many future patents and discoveries which might one day pass through this office."

The clerk sighed a second time, if anything more dramatic and expressive than the first. "And whom should I say is calling?"

The old man straightened, grabbing hold of his lapels with either hand.

"I am the Doctor."

"Who?"

"What?" The old man blinked, a bit perplexed, as if suddenly asked by a stranger the dimensions of his inseam. "Oh, Omega will suit under the circumstances. Doctor Omega."

The clerk looked the old man up and down, suspiciously. After a considerable pause, he gave yet another sigh, rose from his desk and moved to open a low gate for the old man. "This way, Herr Doctor."

The old man followed behind, as the clerk escorted him through narrow, musty hallways, grey and grimed. Finally, they came to a small room, smelling of old tobacco and mold, dimly lit by sunlight filtering in through heavy glass panes that hadn't been washed since the previous century. There, seated at a low, wide desk, was a young man, bent low over a great stack of papers, a pen in hand.

"Albert," the clerk said, motioning the old man forward, "this gentleman has some inquiries for you."

"Ah," the old man said, brightening. He strode forward, smiling broadly, his hand extended before him. "Mr. Einstein. Precisely the man I wanted to see. I am Doctor Omega."

Albert Einstein was a week shy of his 26th birthday, with dark, curly hair and a full mustache, and though his eyes seemed sad, he smiled easily and often. There was a certain unearthly quality about him that reminded the old man of someone, though it took a moment to recognize something of his granddaughter's look in the young man's expression. The old man wondered, idly, if there might not be a trace of his "countrymen" somewhere in the young man's ancestry. It wouldn't be the first time.

"It is about your recent review concerning panergon that I have come," the old man explained, once he'd arranged himself on a chair opposite Einstein's desk. "In it, you discussed panergon's capacity to produce 'secondary electricity,' with which one can control the movements and qualities of projected light."

"Yes, that's correct," Einstein said, folding his hands in his lap, looking more than a little surprised that someone had sought him out to discuss his avocation and not his vocation. "And it is Wellingham's contention that panergon is also the cohesive force that keeps the molecules of matter from falling apart from one another."

"Mmm." The old man rubbed at his lower lip. "And in your remarks, appended to your review, you made mention that this put paid to your own theories on the nature of photoelectricity."

Einstein nodded. "I had made careful study of Heinrich Hertz's writings on the subject, and had begun to formulate an equation that might address the causes of the so-called 'Hertz effect.' This effect concerns the production and emission of electricity from matter upon the absorption of visible or ultraviolet light..."

"Yes, yes, I know all about that," the old man said, impatiently. "What, specifically, was this theory of yours, impacted by the discovery of panergon?"

"Well, my thinking was influenced by Joseph Long Thomson's theoretical 'corpuscles.' Thomson argued that these subatomic components constitute cathode rays and, under certain conditions, that these 'corpuscles' could be excited in such a way that they would be emitted singly, and thus detected. It occurred to me that light, which since Maxwell has been assumed to be a wave phenomenon like electromagnetism, might be constituted of small, discrete packets of energy, which I thought to name 'light quanta.' "

The old man leaned forward, pulling his fur hat from his head and worrying it between his hands. "But you no longer believe this to be the case?"

"Clearly not," the young man said, shaking his head sadly, "as the demonstrated nature of Welligham's panergon clearly precludes the existence of the quantum."

"Hmm." The old man shook his head, eyes narrowed and lips pursed. "Something is very much amiss here, Albert."

Over the course of the next hours, the old man picked through Einstein's thoughts, questioning him at length about the reading he'd done into the study of energy in recent years. In addition to his summary of Wellingham's panergon studies, it transpired, Einstein had also written recent reviews of Professor Mirzabeau's work on violent flame, and Henry R. Cortlandt's paper on apergy, and had just begun a survey on recent findings concerning *vril*.

The old man was interested, specifically, in the ways in which recent discoveries about these energies had affected Einstein's understanding of the fundamental laws and forces which governed the natural world.

As Einstein spoke, the old man scribbled strange notations on his cuff with a laundry marker from time to time, deep in thought.

At length, the old man pushed off his chair and stood. He set his fur hat back on his head and wound his long scarf around his neck. "I thank you for your time, Herr Einstein. I'm afraid, based on what you've told me, that I haven't a moment to lose."

The old man turned and started towards the door, but Einstein jumped to his feet, taking hold of the old man's elbow.

"Please, sir, I now find I have many questions for you."

"For me?"

Einstein was breathless, eyes wide. "From your questions and comments, it's clear to me that you have a stronger grasp of theoretical physics than any individual it has been my pleasure to encounter."

The old man's mouth formed a moue of distaste, and he waved his hand, shooing away the compliment as though it were a horsefly. "I've no interest in your flattery, sir. It means as little to me as the praise of a child first learning his alphabet complimenting Flaubert's penmanship."

The old man tried to extricate himself from Einstein's grip, but the young man was insistent. "Wait! You say that you find some peril in this talk of energies and fundamental forces?"

"Yes," the old man said, nodding slowly, "grave peril."

"I won't pretend to have any notion what you might mean; however, I can't but trust a man with your grasp of physics. If there is anything I can do to assist, you have but to ask."

The old man responded with a tight smile and, as Einstein released his grip, swept towards the door, his long cloak billowing around him. "Well, come along, young man, don't dawdle. There is work to be done."

That night, on a hilltop some distance from Bern, the two men bent low, their attention on a small assemblage of iron rods, copper wiring and ceramic vials.

Einstein connected the components as the old man directed, while the latter busied himself with strange objects he pulled from the inner folds of his coat. They were small, glittering objects, flashing in the moonlight like gems.

"There," the old man said, once the apparatus was assembled to his satisfaction. "Now, step back a moment, my boy. Were these to be misaligned, even a fraction, neither of us would survive long enough to attempt a correction."

Obligingly, the young man stood, and took a few paces backwards. Only when he was safely out of reach did the old man kneel down, placing the objects one by one at key junctures of the assemblage.

When the old man finally rose and stepped back, a low humming noise began to fill the night air around them.

"Doctor, what precisely is this we have constructed?" Einstein looked down on the strange assemblage, a worried expression tugging down the corners of his mouth. "What is its purpose?"

"This device emits a sort of resonance pattern," the old man said, as though it were the simplest thing in the world, "specific to this region of space-time, which should be anathema to anything which resonates at a different frequency. Like positive and negatively charged plates drawn together, or matter being forced into a vacuum, this emitter will serve to attract any non-resonant objects, pulling them here to us."

Einstein blinked, and slowly shook his head. "I can scarcely begin to understand the principles involved."

"I'm sure they will become clear to you," the old man said. "In time."

"But supposing that this device does function as you suggest," Einstein said, "what is its purpose? What is the utility of attracting objects with a different resonance frequency that this... what did you call it? Space-time?"

The old man rubbed his lower lip, and then wagged a finger in the young man's direction. "I believe I've worked out the cause of anomalies you have noted in recent years, those involving these strange energies which seem to contravene the expected laws of physics. It would appear that your continuum has been infected by influences from outside what you would consider the natural world. These strange energies, resulting from the presence of beings from beyond the dimensions of space and time that you know, over the course of decades, has been perverting the fabric of reality, slowly transforming it into a replica of some other plane of existence."

"Towards what end?"

"Why, to colonize your world, of course. My boy, you are being invaded, and you don't even realize it."

The night wore on. The assemblage before them continued to hum, setting their teeth on edge, and the stars wheeled in their slow courses overhead.

The two men discussed energy and matter and space and time, passing the hours, until finally falling silent, simply staring up at the clear night sky overhead.

"It just occurred to me, Doctor," Einstein said at last, breaking a lengthy silence. "Should these beings you seek appear, what do you intend to do?"

"Hmmm?" The old man raised an eyebrow, a contemplative expression on his face. "Do? Oh, yes. Well, that is a good question, isn't it?"

"But, I thought..." Einstein began, alarmed, but the rest of his words were cut off, as the air around them suddenly began to vibrate, and a soft blue light suffused the hilltop.

"No time for that now, my boy," the old man said, raising his voice above a sound like a hundred violins tuning up at once. "I believe our guests have arrived."

Suddenly, the sound ceased, and just as suddenly the empty air around them was filled with a riot of shapes and forms.

"*Donnerwetter*," Einstein whispered.

Circled around the two men and the strange apparatus, these unearthly shapes appeared to fall into one of three categories. Cones, which varied in color from blue to green, and which were about half the size of a full-grown man; cylinders, some tall and thin, others low and squat, which range from bronze laced with green, to purple, to black; and layers, vertical shapes patterned almost like the bark of a birch tree, which seemed to resemble virgin copper. Each of them was translucent, shifting in color and size continuously, and at the base of each is a dazzling light. As the two men watched, the shapes shift from one form to another, cones becoming cylinders, layers becoming cones, undulating endlessly.

"As I suspected," the old man said, as the undulating figures circled around them.

"What are they, Doctor?" Einstein asked, his voice a tremulous whisper.

"On most worlds in which they have appeared, they are known simply as 'The Shapes,' but my people have long known them as the Xipéhuz."

"Doctor!" Einstein said urgently, grabbing the old man's elbow and attempting to drag him away from the device. "We must flee."

"Flee?" The old man snarled briefly, his eyes momentarily flashing. "What do you take me for?" He calmed, and then added, "Besides, each of the Xipéhuz is capable of emitting radiant energy in a concentrated burst, sufficient to reduce either of us to ashes."

"What?!" Einstein blanched, and regarded the strange floating forms in horror intermingled with amazement.

"But this is not a contest to be won by fisticuffs and feet, my dear boy," the old man said, patting Einstein's shoulder. "No, we must reason with these creatures. They are quite simple, when you get down to brass tacks."

"But what are they?" Einstein asked, eyes wide.

"They are three dimensional intrusions of multidimensional beings, naturally." The old man shook his head, a distasteful expression curling his lip. "But really, they are little more than pests."

One of the floating cones flashed red, angrily, and advanced towards the old man, the star-like light at its base dazzling.

"There we are. An invitation to parley." The old man stepped right up to the advancing cone, his chin held high. "You know who I am, don't you?" he said, a hard edge to his voice.

The cone seemed to vibrate in the air, and a black symbol appears on its front. It resembled nothing so much as the Greek letter omega, but then quickly transformed into what appears to be the Greek letters theta and sigma, which then turned sideways before fading from view.

"That's right," the old man said, nodding slowly, as though coaxing a simple answer from a slow child. "And you know what I'm capable of doing, I would bargain."

Einstein was confused, and grabbed hold of the old man's elbow. "Doctor, what is happening?"

"The shapes and lines which sometime appear on the surface of the Xipéhuz"–the old man pointed to the symbols now coming into view on the surface of another of the forms–"are complicated signs used for communication. But though they hate to admit it, they are capable of understanding the spoken word, perfectly, and could probably even vibrate the air around them sufficient to create spoken language, if they weren't so pig-headedly obstinate."

Another of the Xipéhuz now displayed a new symbol, a complex figure-eight design inside of a circle.

"I have left my people," the old man answered, as a cloud passed across his features. He shook his head. "A minor difference of opinion. But don't think for an instant that I've surrendered any of my power in doing so."

A floating cylinder shifted like sand through an hour glass, going from tall and thin to short and squat, and flashed a quick sequence of black shapes on its forward edge.

"This is my home, for the moment," the old man answered, crossing his arms over his chest, "and I won't have you muddying the place up."

One of the vertical layers moved from side to side, and flashed a single, incredibly complicated symbol on its surface.

The old man glowered, and shook his head. "That's all well and good, isn't it, until you've pushed things too far, and then decoherence is the least of our problems. At that point, there's no more particles, no more fundamental forces, and no more arrow of time."

One of the cones shifted from blue to green, and displayed another set of symbols.

"Good for you, perhaps," the old man said, stabbing a finger in the cone's direction, "but not good for me, nor for any of the natives of this continuum. And if you think I'll stand idly by, and allow myself to be marooned in a little bubble of distorted four-space, you are sadly mistaken."

Several of the Cones clustered together, raising slightly off the ground, and moved closer to the two men, menacingly. The one in the lead displayed one, simple symbol.

"What will I do about it?" the old man said, repeating the question.

After a lengthy pause, the old man smiled, darkly, and answered.

"You know who I am, and you know what I'm capable of doing. The question you need to ask yourself, Xipéhuz, is what I won't be willing to do about it."

The old man and the patent examiner stood in silence as the shapes appeared to communicate amongst themselves, rapidly shifting shapes, sizes and colors in a dizzying array too quick for the human eye to follow.

Finally, they all adopted the same form, and the two men were ringed by dozens of translucent blue cones, each about half the size of a man.

As one, the cones all displayed the same symbol on their surfaces, and then with a mighty inrush of air, they disappeared from view.

The air was still around them, as the sky began to pink in the east, the first signs of the coming dawn.

"What happened?" Einstein looked around him, turning this way and that, as though suspecting the strange forms of sneaking up behind him. "What did they say?"

"They have gone, leaving this continuum for less... troublesome climes. As for what they said? Well, let us say that they expressed displeasure at my intervention, and leave the matter at that."

The old man leaned down, and collected the small gem-like objects from the assemblage they had constructed, and the faint humming which had persisted through the night suddenly stopped.

"Had I not seen it with my own eyes," Einstein said, rubbing his hands together, "I'm sure I wouldn't believe a bit of it. I came following you seeking answers, and find myself now with even more questions than before."

"The important thing is not to stop questioning," the old man said, smiling. "Curiosity has its own reason for existing."

The old man pocketed the glittering objects and started down the hill, leaving the assemblage of copper and iron and ceramics behind.

"Come along, my boy," the old man called back over his shoulder. "You have work to which to return, I'm certain, and I have matters requiring my attention back in France. But first, a hearty breakfast seems in order, don't you think?"

Over a stout Swiss breakfast of fresh bread, cold meats and cheeses, sweet rolls and coffee, the old man and the patent examiner discussed all manner of things, most often with the old man listening attentively as the younger man worked his way through any number of his half-formed hypotheses. The old man nodded appreciatively, asking leading questions from time to time, the bones of their meal lying forgotten on the table between them.

Near midday, when the young man could delay going to the Patent Office no longer, the two men shook hands and parted company. Each headed into history, each in his own way.

By week's end, Doctor Omega was back in Le Creusot. Though Borel plied him with repeated inquiries about what had so commanded his attention that he traveled to another country, the old man remained tight lipped about the affair.

Five weeks later, though, on their return to his residence near Marbeuf in Normandy, the old man found a parcel waiting for him. It contained the finished draft of a paper, *"On a Heuristic Point of View concerning the Production and Transformation of Light,"* along with a note from its author, indicating that the work would see publication in the June 9th edition of *Annalen der Physik*. An analysis of the photoelectric effect which disregarded the notion of panergon–recently dismissed by the scientific community as nothing more than a hoax–it introduced the author's notion of quanta, discrete packets of energy which, in the aggregate, behaved like a wave.

Over dinner, having spent a long day attaching plates of pandimensional metal to the surface of their still-unnamed vessel, shipped by rail from Le Creusot, the old man showed the journal to Borel, and tried unsuccessfully to explain its significance, saying as much as circumstances and decorum would allow.

That Borel failed to recognize the import of those few pages was hardly surprising. It would be many years to come before any but a select few would recognize what a year of wonders this had been.

*As George Orwell observed in his article "Raffles and Miss Blandish" (*Horizon, *Oct. 1944), amateur cracksman Raffles is not just "a honest man who has gone astray, but a public-school man who has gone astray. His remorse, when he feels any, is almost purely social; he has disgraced the old school." Lupin, on the other hand, was not born a gentleman and, despite all his attempts to pose as one, will never truly be part of High Society. He is, at heart, a street urchin, an anarchist of the salons, a true man of the people. That quality is wonderfully emphasized in this remarkable contribution by Canadian writer Jean-Louis Trudel, which is a fitting almost-conclusion to a volume which was entitled, after all,* Gentlemen of the Night...

Jean-Louis Trudel: *Legacies*

Paris, 1924

In the gardens of the Palais-Royal, a cold rain was falling. Oblivious to the drops, a lone stroller skirted the patches of yellowed grass. There was no mistaking his national origin. Under his black umbrella's shelter, he was from head to toe the very picture of an English gentleman in Paris. Bowler hat, bespoke suit from a Savile Row tailor, real leather shoes waxed by a Crillon bellhop... All that he lacked was a proper coat, especially since the late October weather had turned bitter.

Withered leaves crunched under the man's feet, the sound cutting through the patter of raindrops. The gravel paths of the Palais-Royal were deserted. Even the hardy British nurses were nowhere to be seen. They had sought the protection of the arcades, taking along their young Parisian charges. The rosy-cheeked young women from Hull or Perth were waiting for a break in the weather, holding on tightly to the boys in sailor suits and the girls in heavy skirts who still hoped for a chance to play.

Though the lines of the man's face betrayed a life already rich in adventure and high drama, he fancied many a youth would have envied the spring in his step and the slimness of his frame. As he approached the far corner of the public gardens, he tipped his umbrella to sneak a glance at the dormer windows lining the edge of the zinc roofs. Grey skies glowered back at him.

"Poor Ganimard!" he whispered to himself. "A mere garret. It's a poor reward for so many years of service. The Republic owed you more. But I may be able to do something about that... if you'll let me."

Once inside, he climbed a series of stairs. The higher he went, the rattier the carpeting. The last flight was bare wood, stained and worn in the middle. A card pinned to the third door allowed him to knock confidently.

"Who is it?"

"Inspector Lestrade, from London."

The door opened.

"Come in, Monsieur Lestrade. But please excuse the state of the premises."

Justin Ganimard was showing his age, thought the visitor. Retirement had not been kind to the former Chief Inspector. The white hair was unkempt and the sunken cheeks showed a pitiful stubble. The suit he'd hastened to put on shone at the elbows, nearly threadbare. And the room was small, with hardly enough space for a bed, a table, a couple of chairs and a folding screen to hide the washstand.

"To what do I owe the honor? Everybody knows Scotland Yard's finest, but I don't believe we've met."

"Oh! But we have, and many times besides."

"I really can't recall..."

The visitor swung his furled umbrella at the humble room.

"So what happened to that little house you were saving for?"

"I put all my money in Russian Bonds. How was I to know..."

The old Policeman shrugged eloquently. The demise of Tsarist Russia had left thousands of French citizens with nothing but worthless paper to show for their pre-war savings.

"But wait... Who told you about the house?"

Laughter burst forth. Ganimard stared, amazed, at the unexpected sight of a London Police Inspector besides himself with mirth. Unable to speak for laughing, the man was holding his sides and wagging a finger reprovingly at him. At length, he caught his breath and spoke again.

"Truly, Ganimard, it is a wonder that you still can't recognize me. You've been running after me long enough."

The visitor leaned forward. In that instant, his face changed. His gaze sharpened, losing the weary vagueness of the London Policeman's eyes. As muscles unclenched and age lines disappeared, the man in front of Ganimard appeared to make the years vanish from his expression. He smiled mockingly.

"You!"

"Ah, Ganimard, I'm glad to hear you say that with such obvious pleasure. I was worried you might bear me a slight grudge. No, don't bother being polite, you have the right, I admit it readily. I did play you for a fool once, perhaps twice. And it was unfailingly delightful to give you the slip. The old cops and robber routine only works if the Police is left dumbfounded... but I'm rubbing it in, am I not."

"You!" growled the old man, unwilling to pronounce the name of Arsène Lupin aloud. "Are you here to torment me?"

"Never. Wouldn't dream of it. In fact, I'm here to ask you for a favor."

Ganimard was, true to form, dumbfounded. Lupin smiled wanly.

"You want my help?"

"I need an invitation to the next ball at the Soviet Embassy."

"But why?"

"Why do you think? A lady fair and worthy of my acquaintance... if I'm allowed in."

Ganimard sighed.

"You and your petticoated friends. What's her name?"

"Well, she said she was the Grand Duchess Anastasia, but I don't know whether I should believe her."

"If she is that, I doubt she'll be welcome at the Embassy."

"Indeed she won't, but she asked me to go."

"And what did she ask you to do?"

"Nothing much. The new Russia is in dire straits. It would seem, my old enemy, that if the workers run the country, nobody is left to work. The Soviets desperately need money. Well, Ganimard, what does one do in such a case? Perhaps you know how it is now, if you never did before... You pawn what you have. Family heirlooms, if necessary. Jewels, for instance."

"Jewels!"

"The Romanov jewels, if you prefer. Diamonds, emeralds, Fabergé eggs, and the like... The Commissars wish to use them as collateral to negotiate an international loan of some sorts, and they've brought them to Paris for appraisal. On the other hand, the Grand Duchess wants them back."

"I can't help you steal!" the old man protested despairingly, for he knew he was fighting a losing battle.

"Is it theft? Surely, the Romanov jewels belong to the Romanovs. The Grand Duchess Anastasia is a Romanov. Ergo, this is not theft but restitution. QED. The law should approve. And you should applaud. You're surely not going to tell me the Bolsheviks have any right to them? They massacred the rest of the family to get their hands on them. They are thieves themselves, and worse than thieves."

Lupin straightened and shook his head fastidiously.

"Ganimard, there is blood on those pretty stones. I will not soil my hands with them."

"It's true you never were a murderer," Ganimard whispered. "Still..."

"Think of it as poetic justice, with you in the role of Purity guiding the hand of the Blind Goddess. Or is that Innocence? The Soviets left you with nothing. Now, I shall leave them with my card in exchange for the Romanov jewels they were kind enough to bring to Paris."

Ganimard glanced at his surroundings. Outside, the rain had stopped, but the sky was still clouded over. The leaden light did not show the room to its best advantage, if there was such a thing. Suddenly, hatred flashed across the old man's face.

"I'm not saying I accept or that I can promise you that invitation, but if I call in a few favors... What name shall I put on the invitation?"

"That's the spirit! Later perhaps, I can help you get that little house you dreamed of..."

The Gentleman Burglar gave Ganimard his instructions. When he left, the Sun was peeking through the clouds.

"And so ends the first act," muttered Lupin, going down the stairs.

The Police were nowhere to be seen.

The Soviet Embassy had never hosted such a throng, if only because Paris had steadfastly refused to recognize the new regime. Now, top hats and evening dresses shone in the gathering gloom as guests tarried inside the central court-yard. They pointed to each other the architectural features of the Hôtel d'Estrées. ("Built in 1713, don't you know?" "Wait till you see the inside!" "I know, I re-member how it was before the war." "We had some grand times here, didn't we just?") Whether or not it was politic to display one's acquaintance with the building before the time of the Soviets.

Out of respect for Parisian *étiquette*, a decent number of footmen lined the stairs leading inside the building, holding flambeaux to show the way. Inside the ballroom, more footmen stood at attention between the windows. Electric light streamed through the broad, Regency-style casements and turned the garden's white gravel paths into shimmering ribbons while deepening the shadows stretched out behind the trees and hedges.

Names rang out at regular intervals.

"The Marquis de Saint-Loup."

"Prince Pavel Chernin, Grand Duke of Kurland and Semigallia."

"The Prince of Guermantes."

"La Comtessa di Cagliostro."

Footmen also moved through the crowd, offering fluted glasses sparkling with the best champagne–Mumm's, not Louis Roederer–and *canapés* daubed with the blackest caviar. Conversations didn't pause. Both champagne and *can-apés* were designed to be taken in small doses, without interrupting gossip or banter.

In one corner of the room, two men watched the guests coming in.

"I didn't expect to see so many aristocrats at a Soviet ball."

"It's not just a ball. It's an occasion, even a double occasion: the 50th an-niversary of the acquisition of the Hôtel d'Estrées and the prelude to renewed diplomatic relations between France and the Soviets."

"Was that enough of a reason to invite class enemies?"

"No, but then they had another reason for inviting *le gratin*. Though there are fewer thrones in Europe than before the war, the aristocracy is never far from the seats of power. Gaining its goodwill is worth a few invitations."

"Goodwill?"

"A measure of neutrality, then."

Joseph Joséphin, known to readers of *L'Epoque* as the intrepid Roule-tabille, was one of the few journalists to have received an invitation. The Soviets professed to care little for the bourgeois press, but they were extending an olive branch to the Paris *crème de la crème*. They didn't want it to go unnoticed.

"I think you're right," Rouletabille admitted. "The *Tout-Paris* is here."

"Half the Gotha," Lupin said. "Even Baron Karl and that White Russian Countess of his. I was hoping to see them."

"Those scoundrels? Why?"

"The Police will need to arrest somebody. In a pinch, they'll do."

"It is true, then? I'd heard the rumor about the Romanov jewels, but if you hadn't told me I'd see you here, I would have dismissed it."

"In fact, you read the story I planted. So did Baron Karl, I suspect. Which is what I intended."

"But, wait, are you really in league with Kutepov and the White Rus..."

Lupin bowed without answering, half turning to greet the newcomer he'd spotted in the crowd. As he did so, he overheard Rouletabille's whispered curse. The journalist was used to keeping others off-balance, not to be the one taken by surprise. Joséphin hailed the familiar face, peeved but hiding it well.

"Ah! Marcel, how nice to see you here."

An aging dandy nodded, moving to greet Rouletabille. Lupin did not miss the chance to get away discreetly. It had not escaped him that the Baron had al-ready slipped out. The actors were taking their assigned places. It was now up to him to make his entrance and play his part.

He made his way unremarked through the throng with an acrobat's agility. He left the room so quietly that his parting words hung about the doorway like ghosts rather than physical sounds.

"And so ends the second act."

By this point in his career, Lupin no longer stole for gain. He had set aside enough riches to live out several consecutive lives as a gentleman of leisure, whether in the guise of a countryside correspondent of the Académie des Sci-ences, an eccentric artist in Balbec, a wealthy retiree in a villa on the shore of lake Léman or a peaceful philanthropist ensconced in a Paris suburb.

He no longer stole for the challenge of it. He had solved enigmas that had defied the ages, when lives not his own depended on it. He had appropriated historic treasures and compelled the greatest men of the world to acknowledge his genius. He had conquered an empire, helped defeat another and outwitted the darkest designs of villains half-mad with greed or lust.

He no longer stole for the sheer, physical thrill of it. The exhilaration of walking in forbidden places and eluding the traps set for the unwary remained, but it had faded, its force blunted by repetition. He no longer sought it. How-ever, each expedition allowed him to recapture something of the original experi-ence. A thrill that had never been edged with nervousness or fear. What he enjoyed most was the heightened clarity of his thoughts and the intense awareness of his surroundings that came with the keying of his senses to their highest pitch.

And so he now stole for the remembrance of thrills past.

This did not exclude planning. It never had. When Lupin made his way to the offices in the back wing of the embassy, he knew exactly where he was going.

A door at the top of the stairs had been left open for him. On the way up, he stepped over the eleventh step, for its plush carpeting hid an alarm. He picked a small key placed atop the doorjamb and then pulled the door shut behind him. He strolled down the corridor, unhurried, and he counted under his breath the nameplates in Cyrillic, until he bent over a lock and forced it to give way.

Inside the office, he pulled the drapes together and turned on the desk lamp. No good work could be done in the dark. This, Lupin had always believed. In any event, he would need the light to read the documents hidden away.

The little key served him well, as did his long experience with trick desks. Soon, he was leafing through the most confidential letters and personal papers of Commissar Varishkin, and setting aside those he could read.

Another man might not have heard the sound of the door opening, but age had only taken the slightest edge off his carefully trained senses. He flung himself in the armchair turned away from the entrance, hoping to remain unseen, but the cushion creaked. Steps crossed the floor, muffled by the Persian carpet.

"Dear me, are we interrupting anything?"

When he looked up, it was into the muzzle of a gun and the face of Baron Karl von Hessel. By his side stood Lily Bugov, Countess Idivzhopu, tall and slender and unusually ravishing.

"Really, Lupin. You must think everyone is as thick as the French Police. It was not exactly a stretch to match Pavel Chernin with that old nom-de-guerre of yours, Paul Sernine. Check to see if he has a gun, Lily."

"I rarely carry any. They're liable to fall in the wrong hands."

The willowy Countess came around the other side of the armchair. She patted Lupin down before turning the desk lamp on him to have a better look at their catch.

"But he's not the Prince!"

"Are you sure? Look harder. Remember that Lupin is a master of disguise."

"I was dancing with Prince Chernin ten minutes ago, my dear Karl. I was close enough to breathe his *eau de toilette*. There is no resemblance. And he was still in the drawing room ten minutes ago, in a dinner jacket. This man is dressed like one of the footmen. How could Lupin have changed his clothes and his whole appearance in so little time?"

"If he's not Lupin, who is he?"

The Countess did not offer an answer. The Baron pondered the mystery, his brow creasing like a cheap pair of pants. His gaze took in his captive's attire, flickered to the champagne bucket left by Lupin on the chimney mantle, and pondered the open desk. Lupin watched him intently.

"Unless..."

"What?"

"Unless Chernin was a decoy. Whether they believe he's a White Russian *émigré* or Lupin himself, he's got the attention of all the NKVD and GPU agents downstairs."

Lupin applauded.

"Very good!"

"You see, Lupin, you're getting too old for this."

"Artistry never ages. You may yet get the chance to observe how I outthink my enemies. But then, Policemen are equally dim the world over... As for you, I'm willing to watch you at work. Tell me, do you know where the diamonds are?"

"Not in the basement room they've set half their men to guard, I'm certain of that."

"Indeed. I asked Ganimard for an invitation to make sure of that. I knew his sense of duty would win out over any personal feelings about the Bolsheviks. Let me take a bow: I killed two birds with that one stone. Because the Soviets expected me to use the invitation, all their attention would be on the guests downstairs. Just like that of any Sûreté agents called to the rescue. And I also knew that once the Soviets heard I was coming, they'd move the jewels."

"But where to?"

"Really, Baron, do you expect me to tell you?"

"Then don't tell him," the Countess said, "tell it to the gun that will kill you if you don't speak. Trust it to be a good listener. It's used to hearing last-minute confessions."

"Ah, it is so hard to resist the sweet entreaties of a beautiful lady..."

"I promise you I'll be impressed. It's not like the Baron has any leads."

"Countess!"

"I shall put it to you as a riddle, then, so the Baron too has a chance to shine. Among the Romanov jewels, there is a trove of diamonds. In the parlance of the professional fence, diamonds are known as 'ice.' Where would you look for ice on a night like this?"

"In the kitchens."

"Bravo! Take a bow, Countess. The meat locker is protected by a door that would stop a tank. It's as good as a bank vault. The Soviets have assigned their best men to guard it, along with enough fur coats to make it through a Siberian winter night."

"What about the rest of jewels?"

"You've got the brains of a pumpkin, Lily!" said the Baron. "The Soviets are smart enough to have kept them all together. But I do have one question, Lupin. If the jewels are downstairs, what are you doing upstairs?"

"If it is improper for a butler to steal from his employers, it is doubly so for a footman. I am here to make sure things happen, that is all. You could say I'm supervising."

"From up here?" The Baron pushed the gun's end into Lupin's cheek. "I don't believe that!"

"I don't like guns, especially in the hands of people like you. And I don't like tainted jewels. Every day, the Bolsheviks kill more people in the name of the Revolution and the Romanov jewels sink deeper in a mire of blood. I promised the jewels to a friend, so I thought I'd see what else I could find up here."

"He might be telling the truth, Ka..."

Lupin heard the sound of the door opening behind them, before it registered with Baron Karl and the Countess, their attention focused on him. When a primly enunciated "What is this?" sang out, Lupin took advantage of the Baron's momentary distraction.

A quick elbow to the solar plexus was followed by a chop to the Baron's forearm. Lupin grabbed the gun from the man's nerveless fingers and shoved back the aristocrat into his companion's arms.

He got up from the armchair, his gun trained on the Baron. It was time for him to take his leave.

"You fool, he's Arsène Lupin!" exclaimed the Baron, gasping as he caught his breath.

His appeal to the newcomer did not go unheeded.

"Don't move or I'll ring."

Lupin's gaze assessed coldly the young woman clutching the bell-cord used to call servants. If the English inflection of her French hadn't told him so already, Lupin would have identified her instantly as one of the guests from downstairs.

Her hair was bobbed in the latest flapper fashion and her frock was a scandalously short tunic that clung to every perfect curve of her lanky body. A heavy brass wristlet did not so much weigh down her left arm as point out its aristocratic shapeliness. And she wore the three rows of her pearl choker with the natural grace of a peeress of the realm, not the vulgar pride of a demi-mondaine.

"Lady Diana Wyndham," breathed Lupin. "How kind of you to drop by."

"The pleasure is all mine," interjected the Baron.

Karl von Hessel had taken advantage of Lupin's look away to leap for the door, pushing the Countess ahead of him. There was no point in shooting, and Lady Diana was still clutching the bell-cord.

Lupin sighed and pocketed the gun.

"So ends the third act."

The peeress stared at him.

"And what do you mean by that?"

"That I'm having fun. The play is proving to have unexpected pleasures."

"Is it true you're Arsène Lupin?"

"Indeed, it is the name I'm famous for." He left it at that, the shorter the better to play on her curiosity. "So, may I ask why you strayed from the ballroom?"

"I was looking for my future husband."

"Here? All the eligible bachelors are downstairs, surely."

"I'm talking about my *fiancé*, Leonid Vladimirovich Varishkin."

It was Lupin's turn to stare.

"What is an English peeress doing with a Soviet Commissar, in the name of Lenin?"

"I am ruined, Monsieur Lupin. More than that, I am a hunted woman."

Lupin bowed.

"I can well believe you are sought by all."

"You don't understand. Whether in Bathgate or Brighton, Dover or London, creditors hound me. My *fiancé* has promised me clear title to the Georgian oil wells bought by my late husband, Lord Wyndham. They may or may not make me wealthy again, but they will allow me to pay off my creditors."

"Do you care so much for your creditors and so little for yourself, Lady Wyndham?"

"Marriage is never dishonorable for a woman, Monsieur Lupin, and a Wyndham pays her debts, come what may."

He stared at her for several seconds, as if unwilling to accept what he had just heard.

"You are the best judge of your family's honor," Lupin said slowly, appearing to struggle with himself. "But are you so sure it is your family?"

"What do you mean?"

"You believe yourself to be Lady Diana Mary Dorothea Wyndham, born in Glenloy Castle, Scotland, on the 24th of April, 1897, do you not? The only daughter of the Duke of Inverness? Married in 1916 to Lord Wyndham, former ambassador of His Majesty to the court of the Tsar in St. Petersburg?"

"I am!"

"Your mother, Guinevere, loved Tennyson and Rossetti and Burne-Jones. She was a tireless horsewoman, able to ride all day through the heather of Scotland and be home in time for tea. She often visited the poor, leaving small, tactful gifts that could not be refused."

She blinked.

"How is it that you know so much about me?"

He had her attention now. The bell-cord was forgotten. Lady Wyndham came closer, feeling a dread she could not have named. Lupin did not answer, gazing off into the distance as if he could peer into the past.

"It's funny that you should ask, Lady Wyndham. I spent most of the summer of '96 in Scotland. I wrote my beloved that a broken ankle was keeping me from making the trip back to France. In the beginning, that was true enough, but your mother soon nursed me back to perfect health."

"What are you saying, Monsieur Lupin?"

His smile had turned tender, almost protective.

"Didn't you think it strange that I recognized you as soon as I saw you?"

"I am not unknown in society circles. If what they say is true, we may have met before..."

Her voice was uncertain and trailed off.

"It's true we have been introduced before. You might recall Señor Avista, the son of Peruvian shipping magnate, at the charity ball of Great Ormond Street Hospital, for instance. But I've been keeping track of you for a much longer period of time. Though rarely from so close... You do not take much after your mother, as you surely know. But you do remind me of my own mother."

"Ridiculous!"

"On the contrary, Lady Diana, it was marvelous," he said gravely. "I will remember that summer with Guinevere till the day that I die. Even riding in the rain had its charms when it was with her... But I won't insist. Most of those who knew the truth are dead. I know that it is true, and it is surely known to your heart, if only you dare look into it."

She glared at him. Because he had never stated outright that she was his daughter, she could not bring herself to deny it. It would have meant saying it out loud.

"I don't need to convince you," he added, "but you haven't convinced me you were looking for Varishkin. There is no reason for him to be here at this late hour, tonight of all nights... You didn't ring for help. Could it be that you did not wish to be found here?"

"Think what you will. Now, you'd better go before I do call somebody."

Lupin did no such thing. He thrust his hands in his pockets and produced the sound of paper crinkling between his fingers.

"Are you sure? I might take away something you were looking for."

She faltered and fell silent, uneasily aware that he had seen through her. Lupin waited for the truth to come out, but she surprised him. Out of desperation, she filled the quiet with a question he did not expect.

"And what are you doing upstairs, Monsieur Lupin?"

"I was headed for the kitchen when I heard somebody coming, so I ducked into the first open office."

"Open?"

"How could I be here if the door was not open?"

"Don't toy with me. I know you found the oil concessions."

"I wasn't looking for them," Lupin confessed. "With most of the embassy staff downstairs, either assigned to the ball or guarding the jewels in the basement vault or in the kitchens, I knew there would be nobody left up here. Nobody could ask for a better opportunity to go through the secret papers of the embassy. The right ones will fetch a good price from the French Government. At least if it sets any value on knowing the names of GPU and NKVD agents in this country."

"What about the oil concessions?"

"They're signed in all the right places by the Soviet authorities. The name of the beneficiary has been left blank. Quite convenient. I think it's time for Arsène Lupin to go into the oil business. It would be a chance to meet new people."

"My late husband..."

"Do you really want these oil wells, Lady Diana? If you claim them, you'll just entangle yourself some more with the very unpleasant people who run Soviet Russia, whether or not you're able to break off with Varishkin. Why not make it a clean break?"

"You may be right..."

She left it at that. As she turned away, she threw him a playful smile over her shoulder.

"Well, Monsieur Lupin, I'll take my leave. But one last thing. You're a poor excuse for a footman. No properly trained servant would be taking an unopened bottle of champagne back to the kitchens."

She grabbed the champagne pail off the chimney mantle, overturned a settee and was out of the room before Lupin could hurdle the obstacle and reach the door she had shut behind her. As he did so, his mind flashed through some of the formidable women he had known. Had he met anyone to equal her?

He ran after her down the corridor, but she reached the stairs leading down into the ballroom before he managed to close the distance. He stopped and laughed softly.

"And so ends the fourth act."

Rouletabille was growing bored. In spite of the ballroom's expanse, he felt like a lion penned in too small a cage. Even the rented musicians showed signs of flagging as couples left the dance floor to speak quietly, go outside for a breath of fresh air or join the conversations in neighboring rooms. No scandals so far. Not even a White Russian attempt on the ambassador's life. Rouletabille sighed. Where was the excitement that Lupin had promised him?

Of course, Lupin had said very little. A general in the midst of a battle does not confide his plans to foot soldiers. By all accounts, Lupin was only talkative after the fact–as long as things went his way.

For a moment, Rouletabille entertained the thought he might not see Lupin again. If the thief's schemes did not work out, that would leave the journalist no other option but to resort to the time-honored solution of the harassed scribe. He would make up something.

He idly set about composing a headline, with details to be filled out later. If he claimed there had been a heist at the embassy, the Soviets would deny. But nobody would believe the denial...

Around him, the guests fell silent. Heads swiveled. Rouletabille looked up in turn, recognizing the notorious Lady Wyndham. Everybody watched as she swept down the stairs. She nearly missed a step and caught herself on the railing. Yet, when her voice rang out, Rouletabille could detect no hint of slurring.

"Ah, friends, Parisians, countrymen! How glad I am to see you here. This *soirée* has been enjoyable enough so far, considering the questionable past of our hosts, but I promise you more if you come with me."

"More what?" asked someone in the crowd.

"More fun!"

"Come with you where?" hollered another.

"*Maxim's*, to start with. Quick now, before I run out of champagne!" She was cradling possessively a pail with a bottle of Mumm's. She uncorked the bottle with one practiced hand, crying: "One for the road! *Za vashye zdorov'ye!*"

The cork popped out with a bang. She took a swig from the bottle and the sight of her lips fastened to its neck roused several of the younger men's attention. A few cheered lustily, the more thoughtful ones dashed off to get their car, and others flocked around Lady Diana, shouting suggestions.

Rouletabille was struck by the sheer glee on her face. No, it was no ordinary tipsiness. There was something strikingly free about her manner, as if she had been liberated from a long-shouldered burden. She surveyed the young people gathered around her with the fearless gaze of a pirate captain choosing a crew for a jaunt into a hurricane, past a Royal Navy warship, and into the cannons of a galleon or two. Undaunted by some less than honorable propositions from the onlookers, she then pushed past the footmen and skipped down the stairs, trailed by her admirers and swinging the champagne bucket like Little Red Riding Hood off to see her grandmother.

The remaining guests took up again the conversations interrupted by the British aristocrat ("Disgraceful!" "She's a free spirit, isn't she?" "Lord Ralph must be spinning in his grave."). Rouletabille took out his notebook. It was not the kind of news that made the front page of the morning papers, but it would be grist for the gossip mills in the society pages. He'd only gotten to the lead when a new tumult broke out.

A man ran out from the direction of the kitchens, yelling in Russian. He crossed the dance floor and only skidded to a halt in front of the ambassador. His words tumbled out, but he kept his voice so low that Rouletabille was forced to sidle closer.

More men burst forth. Rouletabille spied old Ganimard himself, followed by a couple of Policemen escorting Baron Karl and Countess Idivzhopu, their clothing in obvious disarray.

The journalist did not need to strain to hear Ganimard confirm the disappearance of the Romanov diamonds. The rest of the trove was untouched, but the diamonds were gone. Baron Karl and his accomplice had been caught red-handed trying to overpower the guards stationed in the kitchens. They had been searched before being handcuffed. Nothing had been found on them.

Soon, the entire crowd was abuzz with the rumor that all of the Romanov jewels had been stolen. Lupin's name had been mentioned by no one, but it was soon being muttered in amazement.

As Ganimard sent off his agents with orders to keep people from leaving the grounds, Rouletabille came up to the old Chief Inspector.

"Ah, Monsieur Rouletabille..."

"May I leave?"

"You're going to run straight to your newspaper, of course."

"I have a car. It'll be faster."

Ganimard stared at him like a maddened animal.

"Your scoop will be out of date before you get there," he said roughly. "I will catch him this time, I swear. When your rag comes out with the news of Lupin's successful robbery, the others will be announcing his arrest."

"So be it."

"Béchoux!" thundered Ganimard, calling to one of his assistants. "Please take this man to his car. And pat him down before he goes; Lupin could have slipped some diamonds in his pockets without anybody realizing it."

Rouletabille did not object. A petty humiliation was a small price for getting out with such a scoop. Afterwards, Béchoux shadowed him all the way to the courtyard and his waiting car.

The driver was finishing a cigarette, but he stubbed it out quickly when he saw Rouletabille hurrying towards him. Showing commendable initiative, Béchoux also searched the car rapidly before walking off to the gate. When the car rolled up, the Police Inspector waved it out, all the while watching the courtyard for any attempts to take advantage of the gate's opening.

As the car sped off into the darkened streets, the journalist breathed out.

"I've rarely been this nervous," Rouletabille admitted, "even under fire."

Lupin pushed back his chauffeur's cap and tore off the nicotine-stained moustache he had been wearing all night.

"Think of the scoop!"

"I was thinking of my father. Since there was no other way I could repay you... But I will use the scoop, too. Can you tell me more? How did you do it?"

"Ganimard helped. He provided me with an invitation to the ball."

"But you knew Ganimard would betray you?"

"I was counting on it. The fools never learn that Lupin does nothing in vain."

"And the invitation?"

"Was to focus their attention on the guests. I gave the invitation to an old friend, a perfectly honorable gentleman who really is the Grand Duke of Kurland and Semigallia. He couldn't resist an opportunity to tweak the nose of the Soviets."

"Aren't they going to interrogate him?"

"He left an hour ago."

Lupin chuckled. Once, he might have stopped the car to celebrate, jumping up and down benches, or twirling around streetlights. He'd grown more reflective with age, and it was enough to imagine the utter confusion of the opposition.

"How it must have galled Ganimard! Just think of it, my goodness. Ganimard coming to the rescue of the Bolsheviks! A bitter pill to swallow for a man sworn to defend the public peace and uphold the rights of property owners. But a pill sweetened by the chance to work again for the Police. I hope Justin realizes what he owes to me."

"Weren't you playing with fire? He knows you so well."

"It was part of my plan. When the Ambassador was told by the Sûreté that I was showing an interest, he thought twice about his hiding-place–and that was one time too many. I had an ally inside the embassy and I was told the jewels had been moved."

"Your friend witnessed the move? I'm sure our spymasters would love to know how you managed to find such a highly-placed source!"

"He didn't actually see the move, but he was among those the ambassador chased out of the kitchens before posting guards outside the meat locker."

"Weren't you lucky your informant happened to be working in the kitchens?"

"Luck is a woman. If you wish to be favored by her, you must court her assiduously. I told Ganimard that I had paid off a member of the embassy's security staff and I asked him to find me a contact among the kitchen staff. Once Ganimard reported this to the Soviets, they were bound to doubt their current arrangements and to consider the kitchens to be the most secure section of the embassy."

The car reached the boulevards and picked up yet more speed. Rouletabille concentrated on his questions, hoping that they wouldn't distract Lupin from his driving.

"So, how did you get inside? Surely, after Ganimard's warning, the Soviets did not hire any help from outside, or at least none that the Sûreté hadn't vetted?"

"Of course. I showed up disguised as one of the regulars, though a relatively recent hire. I haven't spoken Russian very often since Sonia's death, but it proved sufficient. In any event, nobody had time to chat this afternoon. It was a perfect frenzy of errands and last-minute preparations."

Rouletabille sighed happily as he stretched, thinking back to their exit from the embassy.

"Thankfully, Béchoux did not think to ask if I'd come in with a driver at the wheel of my car."

"Béchoux is a dunce. He doesn't even speak Russian."

"Still, the real challenge was in getting the diamonds out of the meat locker. How did your accomplice manage that?"

"It took the two of us working together. Understand: the diamonds were not just dumped inside the locker. The kitchen staff still needed to have access to the frozen meat and the ice trays. The strongbox inside which they were stored was moved to the locker as a unit."

"Go on," Rouletabille said, scribbling feverishly in the dark and hoping that it would produce something readable the next morning.

"My collaborator lost his whole family to the GPU. For him, it was not just a matter of financial gain. He was ready to run any risk. He distracted the guards while I was in the meat locker, dealing with the strongbox. Not that I tried leaving the kitchen or even the locker with the diamonds in my pockets. The Soviets had posted two men to search anybody who left the kitchen, and it was no good trying to hide something outside the meat locker. There were people running all over the place. So, I just went in, cracked the strongbox, and threw the diamonds inside a block of congealing water. I then went out, clean as a whistle."

"I think I know how you did it, but..."

"Don't interrupt. A few minutes later, my friend took out a block of ice larded with Romanov diamonds. He attacked it with a pick to fill an ice bucket for chilling the champagne. The next time I came to the kitchens, I was handed the diamonds. In a silver bucket bearing the hammer and sickle. The guards searched me from head to toe, but they did not go through the pieces of ice in the pail."

Rouletabille frowned.

"So, do you have the diamonds or not?"

"No. They went out in front of you. Not that I'm accusing Lady Diana Wyndham, a peeress of the realm, of having absconded with any part of the Romanov jewels..."

"Indeed not!" Rouletabille cried, pocketing his notebook with a curse. "I can't print anything of the kind. Not without proof. And your say-so isn't enough. But... but how did she end up with them?"

"She's no Constance Bakefield and she's no accomplice of mine. Don't think that. Let's just say that I was too chivalrous for my own good. I wanted to knock away some of her scruples and I succeeded beyond my wildest hopes. Once she spotted the diamonds, she was too quick for me."

Lupin told Rouletabille what had happened between Lady Diana and him.

"She got away with the diamonds, then. Like father, like daughter?"

Lupin laughed delightedly.

"She could be my daughter. I truly was in Scotland that year, or at least in Britain. But I never met her mother, though I may have paid a midnight visit to the castle grounds. I had some information about an undiscovered Jacobite cache of gold in the vicinity..."

"So why did you lead her to believe she is your daughter?"

"I told her that because I could see she was too stubborn not to go through with that mad, mad plan to marry Varishkin if she could not get her hands on those oil wells. I wanted to shake her up, and shake out of her head the 'Death before dishonor' code. I have met beautiful creatures who lived by that code, but not happily."

He paused.

"And so ends the final act."

He laughed.

"What's so funny?" Rouletabille asked.

"Fate's little joke on us... I came for the Romanov diamonds and she came for the oil wells. But she got the diamonds, and I got the oil wells. Come to think of it, it probably makes more sense that way."

"So, now that you can be the French Rockefeller, what are you going to do with your oil?"

Lupin pondered, but only a moment.

"I may keep a well or two, to sell back to the Soviets."

"But what will the Grand Duchess Anastasia say?" Rouletabille asked.

"If she wants to fund the Counter-Revolution, there's more money in oil wells. In fact, it's probably better this way. My hands will be cleaner. There's less blood in oil."

We close this volume with a mammoth contribution by Brian Stableford, who embarks here on an ambitious multi-part serial entitled The Empire of the Necromancers. *Although this novella can be read independently, subsequent pieces will add to the tapestry begun here. We asked Brian to introduce his story for the benefit of readers unfamiliar with the characters in Paul Féval's* John Devil, *perhaps one of the most seminal works in the history of popular literature.*

Brian Stableford: *The Grey Men*

(Being the first part of
The Empire of the Necromancers)

The Grey Men *is a sequel to Paul Féval's* John Devil. *More precisely, it is the prologue to a vaguely-conceived but hopefully extensive series of sequels to my translation of* John Devil–*which is not exactly Féval's version, because it includes a long supplementary essay pointing out the inconsistencies in the novel's plot and making some suggestions as to how those inconsistencies might be resolved. The* Grey Men *assumes that my interpretation of what "really" happened in* John Devil *is correct.*

Forty years ago, Kyril Bonfiglioli (the editor of Science-Fantasy) *rejected an early story of mine on the grounds that it was "too recherché"–which was a polite way of saying that the vast majority of readers would be unable to figure out what it was supposed to be about. Earlier this year, a publisher's reader killed off a much more recent book with the brutal judgment that "Nobody is interested in this stuff...there is no point in publishing it"–which proves that I have not changed my ways in the interim. One could certainly argue that no one but a lunatic would bother to write a sequel to a novel that practically no one has read in the last 100 years and practically no one is likely to read in the next 100, but I've done it anyway, because the whim took me.*

Anyone who wants to read John Devil–*together with my analysis of its enigmas–is very welcome to do so in the Black Coat Press edition. It is, in my opinion, a very interesting and historically significant book, but I must confess that my own particular fascination with it arises from the fact that I kept such close company with its slowly-unfolding narrative for several months while translating it–an experience that is mine alone. It was a strange thing to stand in Féval's shoes, as it were, following the course of a story that he was making up as he went along (under some external pressure from the editor who was serializing it, it seems, and the readers to whom the editor was pandering), using narrative techniques that he was also improvising anew, in his capacity as one of the exploratory pioneers of popular fiction. Such an experience gives one a whole new perspective on the craft and business of writing–but no one else is likely to care about that, so the point of this introduction is to provide some prefatory information that will make* The Grey Men *easier for its potential readers to understand.*

John Devil *is the story of a long and complicated duel of wits between its eponymous anti-hero and an English police detective named Gregory Temple. John Devil is a legendary figure, whose name is assumed during the story by a remarkable person who might, in fact, be two people. Its primary wearer is certainly Comte Henri de Belcamp, the son of a French aristocrat and an English thief named Helen Brown; in my interpretation, Henri is also Tom Brown, Helen's notoriously villainous son, although he claims that Tom Brown is actually his half-brother–a claim to which various other characters, including Gregory Temple, eventually lend their support. Comte Henri's objective in* John Devil–*which is set in 1817–is to build a powerful steamship with which to rescue Napoleon from exile in St. Helena and spearhead the building of a French empire in India.*

Although he contrives to negotiate an amazing series of obstacles–some of which seem curiously self-imposed–Henri de Belcamp fails to bring his plan to completion (as known history requires him to) and he shoots himself in the head, apparently fatally, although he is such a master of disguise and deception that one is free to doubt the result. Along the way, he frames Temple's assistant and prospective son-in-law, Richard Thompson, for murder, but then contrives to take his place in his cell in Newgate–shortly before Temple arrives with the intention of working the same trick, thus bringing about a highly dramatic confrontation, in which Henri drives Temple to the brink of madness.

John Devil *cries out for a sequel, and I suspect that, if Féval had ever managed to work out to his own satisfaction who had actually done what in the interstices of his plot, and exactly why, he might have attempted one. He would have been faced, however, with one intractable narrative problem:* John Devil *is simply too accomplished, and his plans too grandiose, to be hidden away in a secret history. In Féval's day, the genre of alternative history had not yet been invented, and it would have seemed inconceivable to him that his character might return with a plan worthy of his talents and ambition, which really could change the face of the world. Fortunately, I have no such inhibition. I can do what Féval could not, and give John Devil an opportunity worthy of his talent and* élan–*thus providing his mortal adversary, Gregory Temple, with a corollary challenge worthy of his.*

I ought, perhaps, to mention one more observation I was able to make while standing in Paul Féval's shoes as his translator, and that is his astonishing ability (which must, I think, have astonished him too) to identify with whichever of his characters happens to be occupying center-stage at any particular point in his story. It seems extremely probable that when he began John Devil *he intended Gregory Temple to be its hero and Henri de Belcamp its villain, but things did not work out that way. When he brought Temple to center-stage, Féval inserted himself wholeheartedly into Temple's character–but he did ex-*

actly the same with Henri, so the contrast between them became utterly con-
fused, first morally and then logically. More than that: when the author had oc-
casion to bring other characters temporarily to center-stage, he identified so
forcefully with them that they too became forceful and heroic, even if–like the
vertically-challenged petty criminal Ned Knob–they had initially been designed
to provide comic relief. I liked that, so much that I decided that Ned Knob must
continue on his accidentally-destined road, and become more heroic still–per-
haps even more heroic than either of his supposed masters (who are, at the end
of the day, a little too deeply embedded in the history of their time to welcome
the kinds of changes to which it might be subject if something really big were to
upset it).

  Now, as they used to say in the days of serial fiction, read on...

London, 1821

Chapter One
In Jenny Paddock's Parlor

Ned Knob was sitting opposite Sam Hopkey in one of the new booths in the parlor of Jenny Paddock's Cabaret Theater when the grey man walked in.

  Sam was on the upholstered bench, with Jeanie Bird at his side. Ned was on a stool with his back to the door, so he did not see the grey man immediately. The first he knew of the miracle was the expression on Jack Hanrahan's face.

  Hanrahan had just sidled over to the booth, reaching out a hand to support himself against the post while he leant down to mutter in Ned Knob's ear. He had got as far as "I'd very much like a word with you if I may, Master..." when his eyes–which were flickering from side to side, as was their habit–were arrested by the sight of something that made all the color drain instantly from his face. He stopped in mid-sentence, as if his throat had been cut.

  Ned knew that the sight that could do that to Jack Hanrahan must be an exceptional one. Jack Hanrahan was a *burker*, whose business it was to haunt mortuaries and churchyards, seizing the dead from their slabs or hauling them out of their graves so that they might serve the ends of medical science on the dissecting table. A sight that could make Jack Hanrahan blanch was a sight indeed, and Ned was as anxious to see it as he was to score a point off the body-snatcher by conserving the color in his own cheeks. He just had time to see Sam Hopkey turn white in his turn, and Jeanie Bird arrive on the brink of a fainting fit, before he glanced over his shoulder to see what had occasioned such dread.

He had to admit, when he found himself looking straight into a mono-chrome image of Sawney's face, that there was reason enough for a certain amount of mental disturbance.

Sawney had been hanged not quite six weeks before, despite all that his friends could do for him. When a man is charged with being the most prolific supplier of false witnesses that London has ever known, there is little that can be done by way of mounting a convincing defense with the aid of false witnesses, even if his professional shoes have been filled by as clever and articulate as Gentleman Ned Knob.

Had Sawney returned from the dead, Ned wondered, or was this some kind of strange doppelganger?

Ned knew that he would need all his famed articulacy if he were to rise to such an unexpected occasion, but he was never daunted by a challenge. He spun around on his stool, glad for once that his legs were not long enough to reach the ground when he was thus seated. He leapt to the floor, throwing his arms wide as he went to greet his old friend.

"Sawney! What a joy it is to see you!" he cried–although he would have been clearly audible had he spoken in a whisper, so profound was the silence that had fallen on the Saturday-night multitude. The crowds packed Jenny's es-tablishment every night now, from newly-whitewashed wall to wall, but Satur-day always attracted a surplus.

Sawney's grey face showed no sign of immediate recognition, so Ned went on. "We thought you dead, you know," he said, "and it has to be said that, save for your evident ambulatory capability, you certainly have the look of a corpse."

Ned heard a chorus of sharply intaken breaths, but the simulacrum of Sawney did not seem offended. The shade of grey that now possessed the old man's face–and his hands too–was somewhere between the color of clay and the color of slate, but it did not have the glutinous sheen of freshly-dug clay or the leaden glimmer of freshly-cut slate. It was, as Ned had frankly observed, a *dead* grey. What was more distressing still was that the eyes slowly scanning the room had no color in their irises, nor any tiny red blood vessels in their whites; the pupils were like black points set upon on two billiard-balls.

Sawney's hair had been greying before he went before the judge, but it was a paler shade now. If the suit he was wearing was the one he'd been buried in, though, it had certainly sustained a deal of wear in the coffin.

"Don't you know me, Sawney?" Ned asked, taking the old man by the arm. "It's Gentleman Ned–or Republican Ned, as they're as likely to call me nowa-days. Here's Sam, do you see, to whom you've been a second father–and Jeanie, his lovely leading lady. Sit down and have a drink with us, old chap. Jenny! A brandy for Sawney–it's raw outside and the cold has got into his bones."

Sawney reacted at last. He looked Ned in the face, and his lips moved. The sound that came out was not his old acting voice, with which he had been able to reach every last corner of an auditorium, but it was clearly audible. "Ned," he croaked, his voice as dry and grey as his face. "In the parlor. And Sam. Wanted to see Sam. Jeanie too. Cold in my bones."

"That's all right, Sawney," Ned said, pulling him toward the booth. "We'll soon have you warm. Take my stool. Do you know Jack Hanrahan, Sawney?" It was mostly mischief that made him ask that question, because he had gathered from Jack Hanrahan's reaction that the two had met before. He was curious to know whether Sawney would recognize the burker, assuming that they had met for the first time *after* the hanging.

Sawney did not look at Jack Hanrahan–for which mercy the burker seemed relieved. Hanrahan beat a hasty retreat, his expression readable as blind terror. Sawney, meanwhile, continued to look at Sam Hopkey and Jeanie Bird. "My friends," the grey man said, in a strangely tender manner, given the neutrality of his tone. "Wanted to see you."

Sam and Jeanie, to their credit, were actors enough to mask their own superstitious dread as Sawney took Ned's stool. Ned fetched another from a neighboring table.

"Not on stage, Sam?" Sawney murmured, as if making conversation.

"Tonight's performance is over, Sawney," Ned told him, as he hopped up on to his new seat. "You're late, I fear–but you'd be a good few days late for All Soul's Eve, if you really were a ghost. You're not a ghost, are you, Sawney? How did you cheat the hangman, old friend?"

Sawney's papery brow furrowed slightly at that, as if he were puzzled, or searching for a lost memory.

Jenny Paddock arrived with a jug of brandy, four glasses on a tray. It was not her habit to wait at tables, but she was not a woman to hang back when something extraordinary needed to be done.

"Thank you, Mistress Paddock," Ned said, politely. "You may pour, if you don't mind."

"You can pour yourself–and I'll take the money now, if you don't mind," was Jenny Paddock's retort. Ned thought the demand a trifle rude–and quite unnecessary, given his status in the establishment and the fact that Sawney showed not the least sign of running amok or strangling anyone. He handed over threepence, and then poured brandy into all four glasses. He glanced sideways to see how far Jack Hanrahan had retreated.

The burker had paused a dozen paces away; he had his own glass in his hand, having just taken a liberal gulp of gin. Hanrahan was staring at Ned now, not at Sawney. Ned liked that; he always gloried in the admiration of tall men.

Sawney had still not replied to Ned's last question, and Sam seemed uncharacteristically tongue-tied, so Ned decided that it was up to him to keep the conversation going. "We miss you, Sawney," Ned assured him, "but we're keeping things going, exactly as you would have wished. Jenny Paddock's Cabaret Theater is the talk of the town, always packed out. We're a success, and we owe it all to you." He thought it best not to add that the publicity given to Sawney's hanging had done the troupe no harm.

After a pause–while Sawney continued staring at Sam and Jeanie, with what might have been affection in his grey features and disconcerting eyes–Ned went on. "Perhaps that's as well, given that the witness racket hasn't picked up at all. Business is bad all around, I fear–except for burking, where there's said to be a boom. There's hardly a grave from Highgate to Dulwich that hasn't been raided these last three weeks, if you believe the gossip–which we don't, of course. I wish you'd tell me though, that you aren't dead at all, and never were. I think there's many a mind hereabouts would be set at rest by that assurance."

Sawney lifted his glass to his colorless lips, and sipped the brandy. Having tested it, he drained the glass and put it down, obviously hopeful of another.

Ned poured.

"How did you escape, Sawney?" Sam Hopkey whispered.

"And where have you been these last forty days?" added Jeanie.

"Forty days," Sawney echoed, as if slightly surprised by the figure. "Forty days and forty nights, in the wilderness. Wanted to see my friends."

"If you've been fasting," Ned said, "we'd best get you something to eat–if there's anything left, that is." He raised his voice to shout: "Jenny, my love! Have you some mashed potato and gravy?" He took the absence of a rude reply as an affirmative.

"How did you get away, Sawney?" Sam repeated. "I couldn't bear to go myself, you know, but there are people in this crowd who went to your hanging, and saw it done. Are you a ghost? Tell us, I beg of you."

"Ghost?" Sawney repeated, quizzically. "Am I a ghost?"

"No!" said Ned. "Let's not have superstitious talk at this table! You're as solid as you ever were, Sawney, although you seem a trifle thinner. I've seen you play a ghost, mind, up there on that stage Mistress Paddock built for you. That's what you're doing now, isn't it? You're playing games with us, because you knew we thought you dead. You've made yourself up as a ghost, and you're playing the part to the hilt, as ever. Bravo, Sawney, bravo! But Sam's right, you know–it would be a kindness if you'd explain to us exactly how the hanging failed to kill you."

While he was speaking, the door opened again–but Ned's back was still to the door, and he did not turn around immediately. Sam and Jeanie did not react as they had to the sight of Sawney, with awe and terror, but they did react. Ned realized that the *dramatis personae* in the unfolding drama was not yet fully assembled. He turned to look at the newcomers–and Sawney turned too.

This time, only one of the two men who had come in was grey enough to seem dead, and he was no one that Ned Knob had ever met. This grey man was so tall as almost to qualify as a giant, and powerfully built. His head seemed slightly out of proportion to his body, but that might have been a trick of the light cast by the lantern he was carrying–which he was still holding up at head height, even though Jenny Paddock's was reasonably well supplied with candle-sticks.

The grey giant had the same white-irises eyes as Sawney. Their strange gaze picked Jeanie Bird's face out of the crowd, but there did not seem to be any menace or recognition in them. Ned's stare, by contrast, was drawn by a similar magnetism to the other new arrival.

The giant's companion was as wondrously short as the giant was tall, and seemed as vividly alive as the giant seemed dully dead. Had the short man been 25 years younger, Ned Knob might have felt that he was looking at a long-lost brother. Age aside, he and the shorter newcomer were very similar in their phy-sique. The newcomer's good suit was a better quality than Ned's, even though Ned tried as hard to live up to his first-chosen nickname as to his second, but that only served to emphasize that here were two dandies in miniature. The shorter newcomer was carrying a large suitcase in his gloved left hand, sturdier than any bag Ned had ever needed to carry his own meager portables. He was presumably a well-traveled man.

The smaller newcomers was looking at Sawney, having quickly scanned the room. It seemed that the exotic pair had come looking for Sawney–but the small man hesitated before coming forward to claim him. He was evidently wary of a place so crowded, into which he had never stepped before.

Ned spun around again and hopped down to the ground. He went directly to the shorter of the two men, and marveled at the fact that he could look the fellow straight in the eye without tilting his head at all. "Welcome to Paddock's Cabaret, my friends," he said. "You're a little late for the performance, I fear, but I hope you'll have a drink with us. Would you care to join my party? I'm Ned Knob, by the way. May I know who you are?"

The short man only hesitated for a moment before setting down his suit-case, pulling off his brown glove and reaching into an inner pocket. He took out a silver card-case, drew out a visiting card, and handed it to Ned without saying a word.

"Germain Patou," Ned read, aloud. "A physician–from Paris, I see. Well, Monsieur Patou, if you're the man responsible for our friend's uncanny state of health, you're doubly welcome." Then, on an impulse, he leaned forward, and whispered in the other's ear, so softly that he could not be overheard even in the general hush: "*A l'avantage, mon ami!*"

Patou's eyes gave him away, although he tried to hide his surprise. "I am pleased to make your acquaintance, Monsieur Knob," he said, his pronunciation very precise despite his French accent, "and I am sure that everything is indeed *for the best*. I am your friend's doctor, as you have deduced–and he is not yet fully recovered from his ordeal, as you can plainly see. We have come to take him back to the ward, if you will kindly permit it."

"Sawney doesn't need my permission to go where he will, Monsieur Pa-tou," Ned said. "You'll forgive my familiarity, I hope, but I don't meet many men whose stature is similar to my own, and never one from Paris. You're a man of 40, I suppose–tell me, is it true that the Emperor Napoleon was no taller than you or I?"

Again he heard a chorus of gasps, but none of them was Patou's. Patou smiled before replying: "I had the honor of meeting the Emperor on more than one occasion, when he was the First Consul," he said. "I had a dear friend who knew him very well. Alas, he was taller than I–and therefore taller than you–by twice the width of my thumb." He held up his hand as he said it, by way of illustration.

"Alas," Ned echoed. "Will you have a drink with me, Monsieur Patou–and your friend too, of course. I have just ordered a meal for my old friend, who seems a trifle thinner than when we saw him last. What is your companion's name, by the way? Has he too passed through the hangman's noose and survived to tell the tale?"

"John," said Patou–addressing the giant rather than answering Ned's question, although the name provided one item of the information for which Ned had gone fishing, "will you take your fellow patient by the arm and guide him to the door. I'm sorry, Monsieur Knob, but I am fearful for the well-being of both my patients. No one should be wandering abroad on a night so cold, even to see his old friends. He will come again when he is fully recovered–you may be sure of that."

"I'd dearly like to know the hospital in which he's lodged at present," Ned was quick to retort as the giant moved forward. "We'd all like to visit him, wouldn't we, Sam? With your permission, doctor, of course. Is he in Guy's, perhaps, or St. Thomas's?"

"You may be sure that I shall send word to you when that is possible," Patou said, his voice still purringly polite, although there was a slight edge of steel in it now. "Mine is a private sanatorium. As you can see, your friend has been very seriously ill, and he is far from himself at present. When he is well enough, I shall be very glad to admit visitors to see him."

"But where?" Ned retorted. "Your card has only a Paris address."

Patou bowed, and reached out his ungloved hand to take back the card. Then he produced the stub of a pencil from the pocket of his trousers, and scribbled on the back of the card. "You may reach me via that address," he said.

Ned glanced down. The address was in Stepney; Ned did not know the street, but he did not know of anything in that neighborhood that could pass for a private sanatorium. He had taken note of the fact that the Frenchman had not said that he was actually in residence there. Ned wondered how many men it would require to immobilize the giant. There would be no shortage of volunteers if he called for help on Sawney's behalf, and the two newcomers could not possibly stand off a multitude. On the other hand, Ned did not want to start a fight in which Sawney might get hurt. The old man's condition was obviously very delicate. If this physician really had revived him after a hanging, even if the executioner had been careless, it was the next best thing to a miracle–and it would be a great pity were the work to be carelessly undone.

"You're very kind," Ned said, insincerely. "Are you sure that Sawney would not be better if he were fed before he braves the night again?"

"Quite sure," Germain Patou replied. "But I hope that you'll permit me to pay for the wasted supper." He rummaged in his trouser pocket again, and this time hauled out a sixpence. He threw it on the table, saying: "Please let me buy you a drink, Monsieur Knob–and your friends too. Are you ready, John?"

"Won't you stay a little longer, Sawney?" said Jeanie Bird, courageously. The giant was still staring at her; there was no hostility in the stare, but it was intimidating nevertheless.

Patou moved around Ned with surprising agility, and laid his hand on Sawney's shoulder. "We must go back, now," he said. "You will see your friends again, I promise."

Sawney stood up. "Wanted to see you," he said, regretfully. "Must go back now." His voice had faded to a broken whisper, and his grey brow was deeply furrowed, as if the memories he had been trying to recover were proving perversely evasive.

The Frenchman guided Sawney back to the giant named John, who took Sawney by the arm. Sawney looked up at the giant, trustfully. "Wanted to see..." he repeated–but this time his voiced drained away to nothing, and he seemed to be on the point of collapse. The giant took firmer hold of him, supporting him as he took a step towards the door. Ned did not imagine that there would be many in the hall who would be sorry to see him go. He did, however, observe that the giant cast a long backward look at Jeanie Bird.

"You must come back and see us again, Monsieur Patou," Ned said, softly. "You have our undying gratitude, for what you have done for dear Sawney. Do you hear me, Sawney–we love this man, for what he has done for you, as we have always loved you. Send for us when you can, I beg you."

Sawney roused himself in response to this speech. "Ned," he said, weakly. "Gentleman Ned. Wanted to see..."

"You shall see us all, old friend, when you're well," Ned assured him. "Depend on it."

The giant was already guiding Sawney through the door. Patou bowed and tipped his hat before picking up his suitcase and following them.

Ned was so confounded by the event that he did not even try to prevent Jenny Paddock from scooping up the sixpence as she laid down the unnecessary mashed potatoes, or complain when she did not offer him any change. "Stay here, Sam," he said–although Sam had not given the slightest sign of getting up. "I'll follow them all the way to Paris, if I must. I'll meet you here tomorrow, as usual." He paused just long enough to make sure that Patou's visiting card was safely stowed in his breast pocket before setting off for the door. By the time he got to it, the hubbub of conversation had risen behind him to twice its normal volume.

The night was very dark, and there was enough fog to stifle the meager lamplight that shone at either end of Low Lane. That was not to Ned's disadvantage, though, for it made the giant's lantern that much easier to see, and to follow. The exotic company made slow progress, for the giant was still supporting Sawney and was by no means light on his feet himself.

Ned had followed better men than these and gone undetected. He was on his home ground, and knew how to hide himself away whenever Germain Patou glanced behind–which he did quite often. Ned had hoped that they might turn north but they went south, towards the Thames, and then turned east. They went under Blackfriars Bridge and continued along the embankment towards Southwark Bridge.

If they had a boat waiting for them, Ned knew, his boast that he would follow them to Paris would be so much wasted breath.

The route that the three men followed was not a safe one for a man dressed as Patou was dressed, even if he had not been carrying a bag, but they went unmolested. If the giant's size were not deterrent enough, the lantern-light still displayed the corpse-like pallor of the Frenchman's two companions. The hawks patrolling the rookery and the shore were very prone to superstition, and there had been all kinds of eerie rumors abroad since the recent epidemic of burking had begun. No one imagined that the surplus of snatched bodies was merely being piled up in some cellar beneath St Thomas' Hospital, and everyone had his own hypothesis as to the use to which they might have been put.

So far as Ned knew, there had been not an atom of evidence available within the bounds of the city to support any of those hypotheses–until now.

Despite its slowness, the journey was not a long one–but the three men *did* have a boat waiting. Nor was the ferryman's skiff the craft that would take them all the way to their destination–in which case Ned might have been able to follow it along the bank. The ferryman took them no more than 30 yards out into the watercourse and 100 yards downstream, where a two-master was waiting on the far side of Southwark Bridge, on the edge of the navigation channel. There were men waiting too, to haul Patou's two companions up to the deck–ordinary men, so far as Ned could judge, not grey ones. The lantern in the stern cast just enough light for the vessel's name to be read: *Prometheus*.

The giant passed his own lamp down to Patou before climbing up, and Ned hoped that Patou might keep it lit, but the short man snuffed it out before he was lifted in his turn. Ned was doubly annoyed when someone else came out on to the bridge to look down at the new arrivals. Ned's heart began to pound within his breast, and not because of his exertions in following the three strangers from Jenny Paddock's. It was pounding because the man on the bridge was wearing a Quaker hat.

Ordinarily, Ned would have remained deep in the shadows, anxious not to be seen by the men he had been following, even though that no longer mattered. The sight of the Quaker hat changed his mind. He stepped forward on to the quay, deliberately setting himself beneath an oil-lamp, where he knew that he would be seen–and having done that, he raised his arm, as if in a salute.

The man in the Quaker hat did not return his gesture–not, at least, before a blanket was suddenly thrown over Ned's head from behind, and he was grabbed by at least two pairs of hands.

Throwing a blanket over someone's head to cushion the cudgel-blow that would lay them out was a burker's trick. Ned just had time to curse the name of Jack Hanrahan before the anticipated blow landed on the back of his head and knocked him insensible.

Chapter Two
A Cell in Newgate

Ned knew that he must have stirred and tried to sit up before becoming fully conscious, because the first thing of which he became fully aware–apart from the thundering pain in his head–was someone pressing a cup to his lips and bidding him drink.

It was laudanum, but diluted to a concentration that would do him more good than harm. Once he was sure of that, Ned drank meekly. He wanted his headache gone as soon as possible; wherever he was, he was in trouble, and would need his wits about him.

"Lie down!" a voice urged him. "Wait just a little a while, and you'll be well enough to talk."

Ned managed to open his eyes a little, in spite of the pain–but the light, such as it was, made the speaker a mere silhouette. He was tall, though not as tall as the grey giant, and he was not wearing a hat. Ned did not recognize the voice.

Ned did as he was told and lay back, keeping as still as possible to aid the relief of his sore head–but he kept his eyes open by the merest crack, so that he could study his surroundings. It was difficult to concentrate, but he knew that he had to try.

He was in a bare-walled cell whose walls had been recently whitewashed–although some of the old graffiti still showed through as a series of enigmatic blurs. It had no window but it did have a small ventilation-shaft let into one of the corners and a grille in the sturdy door. The wooden pallet on which Ned was lying was obviously intended as a bed although it had no mattress. The only other furnishings the cell boasted were a rickety table and two chairs. The table bore a medicine-bottle, a jug of water and a freshly-lit candle in a cheap tin tray.

The silhouette drew away, and resolved itself into the form of a man. He was better-dressed than Ned–though not so well as Germain Patou–but there was nothing of the dandy about the cut of his black jacket or his burgundy cravat. If this was a gentleman, true or feigned, he wore his status casually.

It was not until his captor finally sat down at the table that Ned saw his face, in profile. For a moment, he failed to recognize the face just as he had failed to recognize the voice, but then he realized who it was.

"Well," he said to himself, silently, "I must be in Hell or Bedlam, and it may not matter which. If the dead are walking abroad tonight, they have come out in full force." He had to make an effort to pronounce the words clearly inside his agonized skull, and was proud of himself for holding on until the end of the sentence.

Ned was doubly resolved, now that he knew who had power over him, to do exactly as he had been instructed, and lie as still as he possibly could until the laudanum calmed his raging headache. While he did so, he tried to calculate exactly how much trouble he might be in, and of exactly what sort.

He could not do it; events had moved too rapidly, and had taken too many strange turns.

"But I am Republican Ned Knob," he reminded himself. "I have more wits about me than any common enemy of the crown. If I do not appear on stage with Sam and Jeanie, it is only because I would be taken for a clown by virtue of my size. I can act as well as Sam, though not as well as Sawney could. If this man is determined to send me after Sawney, I must best him by cunning. It can be done. It has been done!"

A few minutes later, he sat up, and made a show of dusting himself down. "Well, Mr. Temple," he said, "I'm very glad to see you. I thought I'd been attacked by an eager burker, adapting to the excess of demand over supply as any orthodox political economist would. Perhaps I was, and you came to my rescue? Where am I, by the way?"

"Newgate," Gregory Temple replied, brutally. "Where you've long belonged, Master Knob–and where you'll likely stay, if you do not give me satisfaction."

"Newgate," Ned echoed, trying to sound no more than pensive. "My memory is at fault, then, for I do not remember being arrested, let alone charged, tried, convicted and sentenced–or has the law lost sight of such niceties, now that it must cope with determined radicals as well as the rabble?"

"You've not been charged with any crime as yet," Gregory Temple told him. "You should not congratulate yourself on that score, though, for I can think of half a dozen if I need to, and make every one of them stick."

Ned was annoyed by that. "You are addressing me with naked contempt, Mr. Temple," he said, getting off the bed and coming to sit at the table, opposite his captor. His head reeled but he took himself firmly in hand and resolved to sit very still while he faced his adversary. "I do not deserve that. If either of us has

229

any cause for resentment against the other, it is me. You did me a very bad turn once, by means of shabby trickery–but that was a long time ago and I'm not a man to hold grudges. I've forgiven you, for your lovely daughter's sake. If you wanted news of her, you did not need to have me kidnapped–you had only to seek me out and ask."

He realized immediately that he had made a mistake in mentioning Temple's daughter. His captor's face had been quite bland until then, considering that he was reputed to be a madman prone to apoplectic fits, but it became exceedingly furious now. "My daughter!" Temple cried, explosively. "What would a foul worm like you know of my daughter?"

Ned was taken aback, and honestly puzzled. "Did you not know that I know your daughter?" he asked, in frank surprise. "I have not seen her as often lately as I did in the wake of... the unpleasantness, but I spent three months at the chateau this summer. I know that you have not visited her there for years, but I assumed that as you are now up and about..." He broke off, frightened in spite of himself by the way that Gregory Temple was staring at him. "I appear to have misunderstood," he murmured, "I apologize."

Temple seemed to be fighting his own anger, with more than a little difficulty; it was his turn to be silent, and to wait until he was better able to speak. Eventually, he said: "How was she?" Evidently, he had cut off all communication with his offspring, although Suzanne Temple had been too proud to confess that to Ned.

"She is well," Ned said. "Richard, too–both Richards. The Comtesse is also well... and her son. You do know that the Comtesse has a son?"

"That I knew," Temple said. "What I do not know is how and why you have been her guest."

"Ah," Ned said. "I'm sorry–your reputation as a detective led me to assume that you would know everything. I carried a message to the new chateau on the night of the Comte's acquittal. Many of the guests awaiting him there thought it politic to withdraw in a hurry, but I stayed with Lady Frances–Countess Boehm, as she became, or Sarah O'Brien, as you knew her–to be of what service I could. As things turned out, there was a great deal I could do... not so much for Lady Frances, but for Jeanne Balcomb, whose position as the Comtesse de Belcamp needed to be proved, and regularized. I was Mr. Wood's clerk once, you know. There were a great many documents to sort through, a great many commissions to carry out, necessitating a great many trips back and forth across the channel. I'm quite the seasoned traveler now, Mr. Temple." He stopped, anxious now because he did not know exactly how far Temple's ignorance extended.

Temple was silent for a few moments before he said: "I see. But that's not the reason you're here, Master Knob–not directly, at least. You're here to answer questions about Jack Hanrahan and Alexander Ross."

"Hanrahan!" Ned exclaimed. "What do I know about Jack Hanrahan? And who on Earth..." He broke off again, cursing himself for not having remembered soon enough that Alexander Ross was the name Sawney had been given at birth–and the name under which he had recently been hanged.

"You were seen talking confidentially to Hanrahan last night at Sharper's," Temple stated, baldly, "just before your friend Ross came in–startling you as much as everyone else. I understand."

"Hanrahan said that there was something he wanted to talk to me about," Ned admitted, remembering the fact belatedly, "but I never found out what it was because Sawney came in just then–and Hanrahan backed away, like a frightened rabbit."

"But you do know Hanrahan–and you know his profession."

"I know him as well as any of the regulars at Jenny's–which no one calls Sharper's any longer, by the way, though the old plaque still hangs outside the door. He, I dare say, knows me a little better, since I'm now in charge of Sawney's old troupe–his actors, I mean, lest you should think I mean something else. I can't replace him on stage, of course–no audience could take a man of my status seriously in the kinds of roles he used to play–but I can write and direct, and ever since Sawney persuaded Jenny to take down Tom's old boxing ring and make a stage instead, we've gone from success to success. You should come and see my boys and girls perform, Mr. Temple–although it might be as well to come as Solomon Green. Some of the old hands are better by far at holding grudges than I am. What *are* you doing nowadays, by the way? I never really believed the rumor that said you were in Bedlam, let alone the one that said you were dead–although I think Suzanne might be very grateful for some proof of their falsity, if she really has none."

"That's not what you were brought here to talk about," Temple said, sharply. "And so far, you've told me nothing at all. How did Ross cheat the rope?"

"A very interesting question, Mr. Temple," Ned said, "And another I might have the answer to, if only I hadn't been interrupted. He seemed confused when I asked him, and I was trying to help him remember when his physician arrived to take him away. I fear that Sawney's memory isn't what it used to be, since he doesn't seem to remember that my poor Pretty Molly is long dead. I could have detained him, of course, but when a friend you took for dead shows unexpected signs of life, it's hard to be vexed with his physician."

Gregory Temple produced something from his waistcoat pocket and threw it on the table. It was Germain Patou's visiting card. "Who is he?" the former head of Scotland Yard demanded, as if he still had every right to do so.

"If you've read the card," Ned said, "you know exactly as much as I do. If you had a spy in Jenny's last night, who saw Jack Hanrahan come to talk to me, he must have heard every word that was spoken between us."

"Every word except one," Temple retorted, as if he had caught Ned out in a tremendous lie.

"Oh, *that*," said Ned, disdainfully. "I merely said *à l'avantage*. That's what the Knights of the Deliverance used to say in France, you know, instead of the *for the best* they whispered when they met in London. Patou did not give the customary reply–but he probably thought it unnecessary, given that the Emperor is dead and the Deliverance disbanded."

"That being the case," Temple said, coldly, "Why did you say it?"

"Because he is French, and because I've found it a very useful way to ingratiate myself with a certain kind of Frenchman. I told you just a few minutes ago, if you recall, that I carried a vital message to the Brotherhood at the new chateau. They have cause to be grateful to me, even though their cause is lost, and I'm a man who knows the value of gratitude. I can admit that safely, can I not, Mr. Temple? You cannot have me hanged merely for knowing a defunct password, and using it a trifle promiscuously."

"And this Patou recognized the Deliverance's watchword?" Temple queried, "Even though he did not make the approved reply?"

"He admitted openly to having met Bonaparte before he was Emperor, and to having a dear friend in common," Ned pointed out. "As to who that friend might have been, your guess is as good as mine."

Temple stood up, as if he wanted to pace around the room, but he thought better of it. He sat down again, but he held himself upright so that he could look down on Ned in spite of the fact that they were both seated. "Don't play games with me, Master Knob," he said, apparently trying to sound menacing. "As yet, you have not given me a single item of useful information."

"I'm aware of that, Mr. Temple," Ned agreed, wondering what the times were coming to when a man like Gregory Temple had to make an effort to sound menacing, and could not be entirely convincing in the role. "Just as I'm aware that you haven't told me why I should. The truth is, alas, that I have no such information to give you, and I'm not playing games with you at all. I'm as curious to get to the bottom of this matter of the grey men as you are, and would be glad to trade facts with you, if you had information to give me in exchange– but I'm an honest man, and will not try to trick you into telling me what you know without having anything to offer in return. I'm sorry that my knowing your daughter seems to offend you, but I'm not ashamed of being her friend, any more than I'm ashamed of being a radical and a man of some reputation at Jenny Paddock's. You may try to terrify me with your power and authority if you wish, but I repeat that I do not deserve your contempt, and you have no right to hold me here without charge."

Gregory Temple stared at him in open amazement, astonished to be addressed in such a manner by a man like Ned Knob. Ned felt that it was time to seize the initiative.

"I think I can guess, now," Ned aid, "why I was knocked on the head last night–it was last night, I presume? Your spy wanted to take possession of the card that Patou gave me, to discover what he had written on the back. You're ready to move against the body-snatchers whose increased activity has begun to cause alarm in Westminster–but I'm not part of that conspiracy. I'm an innocent bystander, who merely happens to be a friend of one of the men this Germain Patou seems to have brought back from the grave."

"You're a rogue and a liar, Master Knob," Temple said, his snarl still unconvincing. "*Who was the man you saluted from the quay near London Bridge?*"

Ned's head had been quiet for some little time now, thanks to the laudanum and the care he had taken to be still, and he felt that he had learned more from his present situation than Gregory Temple had learned from him. He felt that he was a step ahead of his captor now–which was exactly where he liked to be, in every situation.

"Ah!" he said softly. "So that is what this is *really* about. That is why we are here *à deux*, I suppose. No subordinates, no superiors–just poor Ned Knob and the once-great Gregory Temple. You should have lied to me, Mr. Temple, and told me that I had indeed been seized by burkers, and that you really had dashed to my rescue. I might have believed you, at least for a second or two. These are dark days for men of your kind, are they not? The government is direly anxious, since the gagging acts have made things worse instead of better. This is London, of course, not Paris–we are more careful to keep the existence of our secret police as secret as their names. You were the top man at Scotland Yard, I know, but that was before your supposed madness and public disgrace. You take orders now, I dare say, but you're not the sort of man to follow them to the letter, and if personal matters should intrude on your inquiries... well, once again you know as much as I do, Mr. Temple. The man wore a Quaker hat, as I'm sure you've been told. I saluted the hat, for old time's sake, although I could not see who wore it. Your guess is as good as mine."

Temple clearly had not liked this speech, but he had a tight rein on his temper at present. "And what is your guess, Master Knob?" he asked, with feigned politeness.

"If it is *him*," Ned replied, without hesitation, "then I suppose he too might have been brought back from the dead. Indeed, I can hardly suppose otherwise, since I know for a fact that he has not been in contact with his beloved Jeanne since the day he was reported to have shot himself in the head."

"You're teasing me, Master Knob. Why do you not name him?"

"Because I hardly know what name to give him. Should I call him Comte Henri de Belcamp, or James Davy, or Tom Brown... or simply John Devil the Quaker?"

"I had to carry a message to his father that another Tom Brown had been captured and hanged," Temple said, stonily, "having confessed to the murders of Maurice O'Brien and Constance Bartolozzi."

233

"I know," Ned replied, unable to stop himself although he knew that it might be unwise. "I sent that message."

Temple scowled. "You flatter yourself a little, Master Knob," he replied, almost calmly. "Ross was still the puppet master then, I think. Ross persuaded the boy to do it, and coached him in his speech."

"And I persuaded Sawney to persuade him," Ned replied. "Would you like to know why?"

Temple hesitated, but eventually said: "Ross refused to tell me the reason. I would have done better to ask him before he was condemned to hang, rather than afterwards, but I had no suitable opportunity."

"He would not have told you no matter how much force or cunning you exerted," Ned said, "but I will tell you, if you wish. Then I shall have told you something you did not know, and you'll have no more reason to be annoyed with me."

Temple did not like that, but he nodded his head. "*Touché*," he conceded. "Why did you do it, Master Knob?"

"Because your daughter asked me to–oh, don't be angry! She didn't do it on her own behalf, let alone to strike a blow at you. She did it for the Marquis, and for Jeanne. They had such a fervent desire to believe–such a fervent *need* to believe–that Henri was not the assassin of Maurice O'Brien and Constance Bartolozzi that Suzanne asked me to help them in that, just as I was helping them in other ways. It was a small thing–there's no shortage of men who are to be hanged, alas, and the lad would have done it merely for the jest and the noto-riety, even if we hadn't been able to offer help to his mother. He loved his mother, that boy–who was not Helen Brown, of course, no matter what he said in his little speech. You always knew that, I suppose... and yet you carried the message anyway, and offered it without comment. You're right; I did take a lit-tle of someone else's credit–not Sawney's, but yours. If you had called the lie a lie... but you loved the old Marquis too, didn't you? So you see, Mr. Temple, that we were allies once, even though you're now a member of Lord Liverpool's secret police, while I'm a steadfast reader of the *Black Dwarf*."

"Don't play games with me, Master Knob," Temple said, stiffly. "The Marquis is dead now, and if John Devil really has returned from the dead, he's your fast friend and my deadly enemy. I *can* keep you here, you know, for all that you haven't been charged with any crime. You might not be a man to bear grudges, but you have never been subject to the pressure that was put on me. Believe me, Master Knob, I would not hesitate to kill you here and now if I thought that it would bring me one step closer to the real Tom Brown."

"But it wouldn't," Ned pointed out, disdainfully. "And when you say that you *can* keep me here, you mean that you have the power, not the right. I am no longer the kind of man who bows down to power, Mr. Temple, but only to right. There was a time, I believe, when you were that kind of man yourself, and I hope that you still are. I have done nothing wrong, Mr. Temple. It is not a crime to stand on a quay and salute a Quaker hat, no matter what you might think of the man who might have been wearing it."

"No, it isn't," Temple conceded. "But if I let you go, you'll try to seek him out–and that will surely lead you into wrongdoing."

"I am interested to know what has become of my friend Sawney," Ned Knob said. "I am interested to know how he cheated the hangman, and how many other grey men there are in London just now. If Monsieur de Belcamp is responsible for Sawney's rescue or resurrection, I shall be very pleased to make his reacquaintance–but I'm my own man now, Mr. Temple. I follow right, not power."

"I'm interested to know how Ross cheated the noose myself," Temple admitted. "Hanrahan and his sinister brotherhood have been far too busty of late, and the situation is getting out of hand. When rumors of the living dead reach the palace of Westminster, even the Luddites seem mere scarecrows. You might be useful to me, Master Knob. Will you work for me, if I let you go–until we discover the secret of the grey men?"

Ned had expected this, and had known for some time exactly what he ought to say, but when he opened his mouth to speak, he found that he could not do it. "No, Mr. Temple," he said, as honesty got the better of him. "I won't work for the police, secret or otherwise, in this or any other matter. If all men were equal before the law, I could respect it–but until they are, I'll not assist it."

Temple clicked his tongue. "All you had to do," he said, resentfully, "was lie. I'd have expected you to betray me."

"I'm sorry to have disappointed you," Ned said, sarcastically. "But if you let me go, you'll have to do it for the right reason, not because I've provided you with a sly excuse. If you want to connect Jack Hanrahan to Sawney, and prove that Germain Patou is the buyer for all the corpses ripped from their graves these last few weeks, you'll have to do it yourself. And if you want to neglect your actual orders to go chasing after your old employee James Davy, who crushed your career and broke your system–and left you here in Newgate to explain why Richard Thompson had gone missing, even though you hadn't had the privilege of freeing him–you'll have to do that by yourself as well. I won't report to you, Mr. Temple, and I won't make false promises to you."

Temple was no longer holding himself stiffly. Indeed, he had slumped so far down in his seat that he seemed little taller than Ned Knob–who had drawn himself up under the pressure of his bombast. Silence fell, and Ned moved his head from side to side to stretch the muscles in his neck. If the worst came to the worst, he thought, at least he'd be able to lie down until his headache was completely gone. If Temple released him, he'd not be able to allow himself to rest.

"If I were you," Temple said, bitterly. "I'd be wondering why John Devil the Quaker has come to London without sending for his favorite messenger-boy. Perhaps he's heard that you are now a man of principle, and is too delicate to offend you with a new offer of employment."

"I know that you only mean to insult us both," Ned replied, proudly, "but I could believe that. The Comte de Belcamp was always honorable in his dealings with me. I tried to blackmail him once, and he struck back at me as I deserved, but afterwards, he treated me as a man–and that was not the way I was accustomed to be treated, in those days."

"His name," Gregory Temple said, dourly, "if he really is still alive, is Tom Brown. He lost the moral right to be the Comte de Belcamp long before he pretended to shoot himself in the head in his father's presence. You might have provided another Tom Brown to take the blame for some few of his crimes, but that was mere sham. If he really is alive, he is–as he has always been–a common criminal nurtured and raised by Helen Brown."

"He is far more complicated than that," Ned riposted, "and always was. That was his gift–whereas other men played parts, while remaining the same in secret, he lived all his roles wholeheartedly. When he was playing the assassin, he was the ultimate assassin; when he was playing the cavalier, he was the bravest and most chivalrous knight there ever was. Jeanne would not understand, of course–she could not begin to comprehend how such a perfect lover could vanish from her life completely, if he were not actually dead–but I am a wholehearted man myself, Mr. Temple, and I have a very good understanding of stagecraft, thanks to Sawney. I understand how plays are made, and how they ought to grip their audience. I understand how *this* scene is supposed to go. given your character and mine. You should let me go, Mr. Temple. Tell yourself, if you must, that you will always be able to find me again, if and when you think further interrogation might be valuable. In the meantime, you can go after Jack Hanrahan, or investigate Germain Patou's address in Stepney, as you please."

"This is no more a play than it's a game," Temple told him.

"*All the world's a stage*, Mr. Temple." Ned replied. "Now that we've each said our piece, it's time for us to move back into the wings. I don't doubt that we'll have other scenes to play, in later acts, but this one is surely done. Am I free to go?" He got down from his chair as he spoke, and as glad to find that he could stand upright without feeling dizzy.

Gregory Temple stood up too, not too proud to take full advantage of his height in looking down upon his insolent prisoner. He needed every inch to make himself convincing, as he said: "I can find you when I need to, Master Knob–and I can bring you back here at the snap of my fingers. I can put a noose around your neck, if the whim takes me. Next time we have occasion to talk, you really ought to be ready and willing to answer my questions."

"Yes, Mr. Temple," Ned said, content to be meek now that he had made his point. "I know all of that–and I think we understand one another. Will you take me to the turnkey now, and instruct him to let me go free, so that I may go about my business?"

Chapter Three
The Burking Business

Ned did not know whether to be glad that he was released into broad daylight, or annoyed that he had been kept all night in prison. He consoled himself with the thought that it was not the first night he had spent in a cell, and was highly unlikely to be the last, given that he had declared himself an enemy of the Crown and all injustice. He bought himself a good breakfast and a mug of beer–which seemed to clear away the drowsiness imparted by the laudanum without bringing his headache back in full force–and then he went to the public baths to wash himself.

Afterwards, he went to the market in Covent Garden, and asked for news of Jack Hanrahan. No one knew where he was, but there were plenty who could give him the names of people who might. The burker's trail was not an easy one to follow, but Ned was a persistent hound, and he finally tracked his quarry to the Sunday afternoon market in St. Paul's Yard. Hanrahan was wearing his good suit, but Ned was not convinced that he had been to church. He had already been busy, though; he was carrying a large haversack stuffed with what seemed to be tattered sheets and remnants from a textile mill.

"Hunting for a good book, Jack?" Ned said, as he came upon the burker loitering near a stall selling tracts and almanacs.

"Not here, Master Knob," Hanrahan replied, making a show of his contempt. "There's a far better stall further along, as you presumably know, where a man can buy *The Rights of Man* if he knows the right password."

"You wanted a word with me last night, Jack," Ned reminded him, drawing him into a gap between a heap of rugs and a rack of second-hand suits. "I've come to collect the message."

Hanrahan's wariness was leavened with slight surprise. "When I tried to deliver the message," he said, "I had no idea that the gentleman would come to you himself. Did he not write what he wanted on the card he gave you?"

Ned did his best to hide his own surprise. "Ah," he said, as if he had half-expected it. "When Patou gave you the message to pass on, he obviously had no idea that he would soon have occasion to set foot in Jenny's himself. I've been slow on the uptake I fear–I should have gone straight to the address he scribbled on the card, instead of looking for you. I'm sorry, Jack."

"No trouble," the body-snatcher replied. "I hadn't realized that the gentleman wasn't known to you. Perhaps he was working on behalf of someone else?" Ned had been wondering whether it might be polite to mention that Gregory Temple was keenly interested in the burking business, and Hanrahan's business in particular, but he decided that since Hanrahan was prepared to fish for information so blatantly, he might as well take the opportunity to do likewise.

"I imagine that he was," Ned agreed. "He's a physician, it seems, and must be in charge of the grey men in that capacity, but he's not the mastermind behind the scheme. How did Sawney give him the slip, do you suppose?"

"I couldn't say," Hanrahan replied, dropping his load and making a show of searching through the suits on the rack while the tailor peered at him from the other side. "As you must have guessed from my expression, Master Knob, last night was the first time I clapped eyes on one of *them*. I've heard talk, mind–but you know the kind of fancies that spring up whenever rumors fly. I'm just an honest tradesman, trying to make a living. What happens to the goods after I deliver them isn't my business–but I tell you straight, Master Knob, I'd far rather imagine that someone might breathe new life into them than know that they'd only be cut up and thrown away."

"I'm with you on that, Jack," Ned agreed. "I know that you're just a cog in the machine, collecting the goods and passing them on to the physician, with no questions asked–that's just as it should be. But you're an honest radical, as I am, and I know how glad you must be to know that you're doing good as well as making a living. If the dead are being brought back to life, Jack, then those who take them from their graves are saints, working in the great cause of progress. You have my congratulations–and my sincere thanks, for what you've done for Sawney."

"I was startled to see him, that's all," Hanrahan said, gruffly. "I wasn't scared. I was as glad as any of you to see him walking and talking." He hauled his cargo back on to his shoulder and moved off abruptly, in the direction of the bookstall where one could purchase banned books, if one knew the password.

Ned followed him. "You weren't as startled as I was, I can tell you," he said, companionably. "At least you knew that he wasn't safely tucked up in his pauper's grave. Are you perfectly certain that he wasn't still alive when you sold him? You know your business far better than I do, of course, but one hears much nowadays about catalepsy and premature burial, and one hears plenty of tales of half-hanged men revived by their friends when the law has been careless."

Hanrahan did not pause at the bookstall but pushed on until he was clear of the market, obviously reluctant to say more while they might be overheard. He set off northwards, towards the old wall, striding energetically in spite of his burden. Ned glided effortlessly by his side.

"You're right, Master Knob," the burker conceded, when he was sure that no one else was in earshot. "I've opened coffins that have been torn up inside, to find men who were supposed dead with their fingernails bloody and torn. I've seen men snatched early from the rope at Tyburn and carried off, with the stewards unable to interfere, or even turning a blind eye. Not everyone's dead who's supposed to be, it's true. But Sawney... I was certainly convinced that he was gone, else I'd have handled him a good deal more tenderly than I did. You followed him, didn't you? Do you know where they took him?"

"I followed Patou and the grey men down to the quay," Ned admitted, knowing that he would have to share his own information if he were to get a full return from the burker. "He took a ferry out to a ship in midstream–the *Prometheus*, as I said–where his master was waiting. I showed myself, so that they could come and pick me up if they wanted to, but someone threw a blanket over my head and smacked me hard on the back of my skull. To tell the truth, Jack, I thought for an instant it might be you, intent on making a delivery."

Hanrahan seemed genuinely offended. "I know they call me a burker," he said, "but I'm no common murderer, however fresh the Frenchies might want their goods. I have my methods, Master Knob, and I can lay my hands on the genuine article easily enough. I'd have sworn on St. Paul's, St. Giles' and St. Luke's that Sawney was the genuine article when I bought him from the undertaker's cart for half a crown–and you can be sure the undertaker thought so too, else he'd never have sold him to me. His neck wasn't broke, or I'd have got him for two shillings, but I never saw a tongue so black or a throat so deeply grooved on a man who still had breath in him. Anyway, if I'd taken it into my head to collect you, you wouldn't be walking about today as bright as a button. How did you get away? Fought them off single-handed, did you?"

"Oh, it wasn't burkers–nor even common cut-throats. When the fellow in charge found out that he's got the wrong man, he apologized."

"Wrong man?" Hanrahan repeated, incredulously, as he came abreast of a small high-sided cart with a horse between its hafts that would not have fetched a shilling to be boiled down for glue. The back of the cart was generously furnished with rags too filthy to attract even the meanest thief,

Ned turned his nose away, saying: "I hope you're not going to render the new ones as foul as that, Jack."

"No fear," said Hanrahan, as he threw his latest purchases into the back of the cart. "I've got my good clothes on. I'll take them down the cesspit another day, when I've sorted out the pieces that'll make good winding-sheets. These will do for this afternoon's job."

"Right," said Ned. "You're working. I didn't answer your question, did I? Yes, they got the wrong man. They were after Patou, of course. An easy mistake to make, in the poor light. I must say, though, that they seemed a far better class of nighthawk than one normally meets south of Covent Garden at midnight on a Saturday. I don't know what the physician had in his bag, but I imagine that's what they were after. Do you mind if I ride a little way with you? I won't come into the graveyard, mind–that's the kind of work best done in private."

"I'll not be doing any digging today, Master Knob," Hanrahan replied, rather scornfully. "I know people think that I spend every night digging down through freshly-turned soil, when I'm not out cutting throats, but that's not how the business works. I have dig down on occasion, it's true, but I prefer to get the bodies before they're laid to rest, if I can. I like to purchase them fair and square–from the next of kin, if that can be arranged, although I'm not excessively particular. These days, it can be arranged more often than you might think. Dissenting's been a boon to the business, and no mistake–except for Methodists, of course. The Clapham sect's the worst of all. Give me Unitarianism any day–godlessness that likes to keep up appearances. Better hop up smartly–that's the half-hour chiming and I'm due at St. Luke's in less than 30 minutes. Mustn't be late, or the little girl might end up underground regardless. Can't entirely trust the grieving, you know, if things don't go exactly to plan.

Ned did as he was bid, hoping that he would get used to the stink soon enough. His head had started to ache again, and he felt a pang of regret at not having purchased a phial of laudanum from the market while he had the chance.

Hanrahan untethered the horse, got up on to the bench beside Ned, and took up the rein and the whip. There was no need for the whip, though–the horse moved off obediently in response to a twitch of the rein.

Once they had made their way out into the traffic, Ned said: "It's possible, of course, that they weren't out to rob Patou at all, Jack. Maybe he has enemies, who want to do him harm–or who want to claim his services for a rival master. I ought to warn him, ought I not? Would you carry a message for me?"

"The Frenchie already knows that he has enemies, Master Knob," Hanrahan told him. "He lies very low, except when circumstances force him out–as they must have done yestereve. I never saw his master at all... although I've heard the name *John Devil* muttered abroad, as it always seems to be when anything remarkable is going on. You'd probably know more about than I would."

Ned shook his head wearily. "I never had the pleasure of knowing Mistress Paddock's husband," he said, with a sigh. "That was before my time."

"Not *that* John Devil," the burker said, giving his nag a flick of the whip for amusement's sake. "The Quaker, Tom Brown–the one who murdered Noll Green and Lochaber Dick in Paris. I heard tell you were there, and saw the whole thing."

"Pretty Molly used to put the story about when she was in her cups," Ned admitted, "but I fear that she was only trying to make me out a better man than I am. I did know Mr. Wood, though, who was Tom's solicitor, and he always said that Tom wasn't near a bad a boy as gossip painted him. Always loved his mother, you know."

"So did everyone else, the way I heard it," Hanrahan observed. "Many a tear shed when she shipped out for Botany Bay. She was married to a Frenchie once, wasn't she?"

"Yes, she was," Ned said. "I knew her husband slightly, although I know the present Comtesse much better. I've been in Paris a fair bit these last three years–but I never heard of a doctor named Germain Patou."

"I'll wager there's hundreds of doctors in London you never heard of," Hanrahan observed. "He's a doctor all right, and no mistake, if he brought

Sawney back from the dead–and that giant too. I wish he'd warned me that I might bump into the goods again walking and talking."

"I don't suppose he intended you that you should," Ned opined. "Sawney wasn't supposed to wander off on his own, whatever he was doing on the boat. Was the giant one of yours, by any chance?"

"No. You'd need a big heap of foul rags to hide a body like his–have to fold him up, see, or his feet'd stick out of the cart. Ever tried to fold a body when rigor's set in, Master Knob?"

"Can't say I have, Jack. Is that St. Luke's off to the right, along Fann Street?

"Yes it is–and we're still in good time." Hanrahan paused for just a moment before saying: "I suppose he *might*'ve been alive–old Sawney? The dead can't *really* be brought back, can they, Master Knob? This is all some kind of mummery, isn't it?" His voice was level enough, but Ned knew that there must be a deep anxiety as well as an honest uncertainty in the burker's words. He was glad to think that such a tall man was unashamed to seek reassurance on such a weighty matter from Gentleman Ned Knob.

"Well," Ned said, carefully, "There's a story–which is in print, not just idle chatter, so it might be true–about a gentleman scholar in Switzerland who found a way to reimpart the vital spark to a patchwork of dead flesh. Electricity is said to be the key–and now that men like Benjamin Franklin and Humphry Davy have begun to bring the fire of lightning down to Earth, who knows where it'll end?"

"Not the Methodists, that's for sure," Hanrahan muttered, as he turned the horse and maneuvered the cart into Fann Street. "Before your time, I know, Master Knob, but did you ever hear tell of a doctor named James Graham?"

"As a matter of fact, Jack, I did," Ned said, taken completely by surprise by the question, and wondering whether he might be getting somewhere at last. "He had a connection to Helen Brown too, you know, when she was taken up by the Duchess of Devonshire back in the '80s. Graham was the Duchess's pet quack–ran a so-called Temple of Health and Hymen in Mayfair, with an electric throne and a celestial bed and all manner of silly gadgetry. Would have been as famous as Mesmer, they say, if he hadn't got himself thrown in jail in Edinburgh. Why do you ask?"

"I happened to run across some of the equipment sold off when the Temple went bust," Hanrahan replied. "No sort of bed, mind–baths, they were. Do you know who he called his Goddess of Health? That woman who was Horatio Nelson's mistress–Emma Hamilton."

"I didn't know that," Ned lied. "That's amazing, Jack–to think that Graham's old equipment is still in use. Mr. Davy and Mr. Faraday would certainly be interested to know that–and I'll wager they'd be able to put it to very good use, in the cause of Radical Enlightenment. Where is it, if I might ask?"

"Shipped down river," Hanrahan told him. "It was on a quay near South-wark Bridge when I saw it, about to be loaded up–probably on to the same ves-sel you saw last night."

"Downriver," Ned repeated, thoughtfully. "But they bring the ship upriver at regular intervals, to collect all kinds of cargoes. Sawney must have slipped ashore last night, and made his way back to his old home-from-home. What was he doing on the ship in the first place, I wonder?"

Hanrahan had no answer to that, and tried to signify as much by shrugging his shoulders as he jumped down from the cart, which he had driven round to the vestry door of St. Luke's Church. Ned could see a funeral party wending its slow way to the northernmost part of the churchyard, into the shade of a clump of wych-elms. There was a coffin at the head of the procession, shouldered by four pall-bearers, but Ned had a strong suspicion that the corpse had been re-moved before the lid had been screwed down.

The vestry door opened, and a black-clad man came out, wearing a pol-ished top hat and carrying a small bundle tightly wound about by a dirty sheet. Hanrahan handed over a few coins and accepted the bundle into his own arms. Then he slid it gingerly into the back on the cart, using a pole and a pair of tongs to cover it with the filthy rags that no one would be eager to displace. Ned esti-mated that it weighed no more than four stones; it was the body of a child, no more than ten or twelve years old.

The man retired into the church. "That was no grieving next-of-kin," Ned observed. "That was the undertaker, or one of his mutes."

"I only said what I preferred, Master Knob," the burker said, defensively. "I can let you ride as far as Fleet Street, if you want, but I can't take you all the way. Guarantees given, you understand–but I'll deliver your message to Patou. He has enemies, who thumped you on the noggin thinking you were him, and apologized when they found you weren't. That's good, in a way. If a man has to have enemies, best to have civilized enemies."

"Very kind of you, Jack," Ned said, "Fleet Street will be ideal, and I thank you wholeheartedly. If Monsieur Patou asks after me, will you tell him that my success at Jenny's doesn't prevent me from taking other commissions, provided that they're lucrative enough. I'm a versatile man, and a good friend to have when a man is a stranger in the city and finds himself beset by enemies."

"I'll tell him that too," Hanrahan promised. He was silent until he turned back on to the North Road at the end of Fann Street, and then he said: "Do you suppose this one will be back too, Master Knob? She's only a kid–can't be as much as eleven. Never had a chance to live a life, although I dare say she did her fair share of skivvying."

"I don't know, Jack," Ned said, soothingly. "But if Patou can give her a second chance, you're surely doing a hero's work. If there's an alternative, anything's better than leaving a little girl to rot in a grave."

"You're right, Ned," Hanrahan said. "You've a good head on your shoulders, and a good heart too. There's not many men who've asked to ride with me on my cart, you know. You're no Methodist, that's for sure–but then, you're a satirist. I'm a radical myself, you know, in my heart, and I used to be more ardent than I am now. I was there when they pilloried Dan Eaton back in 1812, ready to defend him–not that he needed any defending, as it turned out."

"Why, Jack, we're practically twin souls," Ned said, brimming over with camaraderie. "I was in court to see Tom Wooler argue the toss with Sam Shepherd–the Attorney General himself. And what a fine fist he made of it! These are great times, Jack, for revolutionaries like us. The aristocrats have their past and their tradition, but we have our future and our hope... and a better hope for the resurrection, it seems, than the Clapham crowd. Not that I've anything against Wilberforce, you understand. He'll have slavery abolished in England before the decade's out, and that's a great thing... but they say that there are islands in the Caribbean where the dead serve as slaves. Slow of wit, I've heard, but very docile, and never need to sleep. Now then, what do they call them?"

"*Zombies*," said Jack Hanrahan, promptly. A man in his trade would be bound to pay attention to such tales, Ned knew, and Limehouse had more than its fair share of sailors who'd seen the Americas, even though Liverpool and Southampton were the ports of choice for the Atlantic trade.

"That's right," Ned agreed. "But they don't use electricity there, so rumor has it. It's all done with magic and the power of the will."

"They call it *voudun*," Hanrahan supplied. "African magic, Frenchified."

"That's right," Ned said. "Toussaint l'Ouverture led the slaves of Haiti to revolt against Bonaparte himself when he tried to bring slavery back after the Jacobins abolished it. I wonder if Germain Patou has ever been to the Caribbean?"

"More likely to have been in Paris while Mesmer was there," Hanrahan opined, "given what I saw on the docks that day."

"Or both," Ned said, thoughtfully. "Ben Franklin was on the committee appointed to evaluate Mesmer's claims, as I recall–and Antoine Lavoisier too. Humphry Davy knew them both–I've heard him say so–and he was well received in Paris when he visited with Faraday. I wonder if Mr. Davy knows Germain Patou."

"That's not the kind of question I can ask Patou," Hanrahan said, perhaps fearful of being asked to carry yet another message. "If you know Humphry Davy, you'd best ask him. *Do* you know Davy?"

"Only slightly," Ned admitted. "I was a regular at the Royal Institution's open lectures at one time, although I've grown a little lax of late. So was Tom Brown, I understand, before he was transported–but that, of course, was before my time. Perhaps I should have tried a little harder to understand the lectures, but I went there as a good radical, to show my support for Jacobin science, never thinking that I could fully understand the wonders of electrolysis..."

"They brought him water, you know, and food," Hanrahan said, nostalgically. "Dan Eaton, I mean... when he was in the pillory, for printing *The Rights of Man*. Now, if Patou could bring Tom Paine back to life–what a triumph *that* would be!"

"So it would, Jack," Ned agreed. "So it would."

Chapter Four
The House in Purfleet

When Jack Hanrahan let Ned Knob down from his cart in Fleet Street, Ned made a considerable show of going away, because he knew that the burker would be wary of being followed. Given that he had a strong suspicion as to where the cart was headed, though, he did not need to trot along behind it. He merely had to take up a convenient point of vantage once or twice along the way, to make sure that Hanrahan was still headed for the river.

He was not unduly surprised when the burker went around the Tower on the north side and made his way to the St. Katherine Dock. Patou was bound to be more careful now, having been seen at Jenny's and the quay near Southwark Bridge, in company with two grey men.

The cart skirted the docks and made its way to the edge of the Thames, to a jetty not far west of Tower Hill. Ned ran on ahead, as fast as he could go, to the Hermitage Stairs. There he found a ferryman whose boat was twice the size of a common skiff, and was fitted with a sail.

"Can you slip across to Cherry Garden Pier and wait in its shadow?" Ned asked. "There'll be a ship along in a matter of minutes–an hour at the most–riding the stream and the outbound tide. She's a two-master, but she won't be carrying much sail, given the flow. If you can keep pace with her till she docks again, without her master knowing he's being followed, there's half a guinea in it."

"There's six shillings now and another six when we get there," the ferryman relied, "provided that we go no further than Gallion's Reach."

"Six now, six then and another six if we have to go further than Hornchurch Marshes," Ned said, showing the ferryman a generous handful of coins that he had pulled from his trouser pocket.

"You're a gentleman, and no doubt," said the ferryman, only a little sarcastically–but he did as he was asked, and waited under Cherry Garden Pier on the south bank until Ned nudged him and showed him the vessel he was to follow.

"Right," said the ferryman, unenthusiastically. "Should've known it'd be *her*. If it weren't broad daylight, sir, I'd hand your money back–but it's only at night that she's said to be haunted. I'll follow her for you, but you needn't fear that I'll get too close. "

244

"If you know for certain where she's headed," Ned said. "You can take me there at your leisure. Do you know her regular berth?"

"Not far this side of Hell, I'd imagine," the ferryman opined. "I don't want to know–but I'll do as I promised, provided that I can keep my distance, and darkness doesn't fall."

"Why do you say that she's haunted?" Ned asked. "She seems very ordinary to me."

"You don't ply your trade between the Tower and Westminster after dark, sir," the ferryman said. "I've seen strange things in my time, and learned to keep my eyes averted from all kinds of skullduggery... but those eyes! If you'd seen those eyes looking out over the water..."

"Does her master have *those eyes*?" Ned wanted to know.

"I don't know," the ferryman admitted. "He shields them with that Quaker hat he wears–but when a ship is carrying the souls of the damned, its master is bound to be a demon. That's just common sense."

More common than sense, Ned thought, but he held his tongue.

They eased into the stream when the *Prometheus* had passed by. There was plenty of traffic on the river, and Ned did not think that anyone aboard John Devil's craft would think their sail suspicious, but he fretted nevertheless as they negotiated Woolwich Reach and Gallion's Reach, and kept on going past Crossness and the Erith Marshes.

Ned wondered, as they went, whether Gregory Temple had discovered anything at Germain Patou's Stepney address. He suspected not. Whatever message had been waiting there for Ned Knob would not be given to anyone else– and now, it would not need to be given to Ned Knob either. If Temple had drawn a blank, he would presumably redirect his attention to Jack Hanrahan, but that wouldn't matter either, now that Ned had satisfied himself that Hanrahan was on the very periphery of the affair. In time, Temple was certain to find out where Patou was, and where the grey men were normally kept, but for the time being, Ned had at least a day's start on the secret police.

He wondered, too, how many other people were of the opinion that a vessel crewed by monsters and captained by a demon was making daily trips up river into the Port of London. Ferrymen were not known for keeping close counsel, and they carried a great many passengers by day and night–even in the heart of the city, where there were bridges a-plenty–but there had been so many other stories of a fanciful sort abroad in the last 20 years that no one paid any of them serious heed. The Thames would be choked with ghostly pirate ships and rotting sea-serpents had all the tales been true.

The ferryman was beginning to grumble that he could not possibly go any further than the bend at Grays when the vessel they were tracking finally put in to Purfleet. Ned handed over the last of the promised coin, and begged the ferryman to set him down as quickly as he could. The ferryman was glad to oblige, and Ned set off at a sprint to catch up with Germain Patou's landing-party.

Half a dozen seamen–none of them grey-skinned–were loading up a cart far sturdier and more capacious than Jack Hanrahan's. Although the transferred cargo contained ordinary supplies as well as corpses, the number of parcels packaged in dirty winding-sheets told Ned that Jack Hanrahan was far from being the only supplier to this particular buyer. It occurred to him that when people spoke of a burking "epidemic," they were only referring to bodies that had been reported missing. Who knew how many more there might be like the little girl from St. Luke's, whose posthumous disappearance would never attract the slightest attention?

Ned did not know how far he might have to go when the cart set off and he set off in pursuit. He hoped that it would be no more than a few hundred yards, given that the masters of the grey men seemed to find the river so convenient for their purposes. So it transpired; on the eastern edge of Purfleet, there was a three-story house with two stubby swings and a hectic multitude of gables, set in high-walled grounds. The only obvious means of access was a sturdy steel gate that was locked as soon as the cart had vanished inside, but Ned wasn't in the least worried by that.

He made a tour of the walls, looking for the most convenient point of entry. There was ivy on the walls to the rear, but the bulk of it was inside and would not lend him much support. Fortunately, the wall was old and the mortar between the stones was crumbling. With the aid of his clasp-knife–which he plied with great care, not wanting to blunt the sharpness of the blade as well as the point–he was able to hollow out a sequence of footholds that would take him to the top. Once he was there, the ivy made the descent much easier.

There were birch-trees within the wall that hid his descent from the windows of the house, so he did not think that there was any possibility of his having been seen as he slid over the wall. He felt entirely confident of his invisibility as he crept through the undergrowth towards the house.

The ground was lower at the back of the house than at the front, so the rear door gave access to a basement whose floor was considerable lower than the floor of the front hallway. There was no one in the kitchen garden, but Ned saw movement in several of the windows on the floor above the basement and the floor above that. The house seemed to be abundantly tenanted–and he understood very quickly what the ferryman had meant by *those eyes looking out*. Grey faces were continually appearing at one window or another, merely in order to look out. They were not keeping watch as sentries might: they were simply staring into the garden, as if they had nothing better to do than contemplate the tawdry wilderness.

Sawney might be the best of them rather than the worst, Ned thought, *for all that he could not seem to string his thoughts together. Whatever has been done to these people, it has let them weak in body and in mind–but Patou seemed genuinely concerned for Sawney's wellbeing, and he a physician, not some Caribbean slave-holder.*

246

Ned rested for some little while when he reached the extremity of the useful cover, wondering whether he ought to wait for darkness–which would come soon enough, given that All Souls was more than a week past. If he intended to play the spy and make his escape without his presence ever being suspected, that was undoubtedly the wisest course–but how much could he learn by peering in through windows? The weather was cold, and it would get a good deal colder when night fell–and what would he do when he went back over the wall, given that he was so far from London?

In the end, the fact that Gregory Temple could not be very far behind him was the deciding factor. There was only one way that he could stay ahead of Temple–and only one way to put the mystery beyond Temple's reach, if that seemed to be the right thing to do.

"I'm a gentleman, after all," he murmured, dusting his sleeves, "and I'm an old friend of the family. Why should I be shy?"

Even so, he hesitated for five more minutes before he marched out of the copse, strode resolutely to the kitchen door and knocked.

When the door opened, he tensed himself, expecting to find himself face to face with a grey man, but the woman who answered was ruddy in the cheeks and bloodshot in the eyes. She was wearing a cook's apron.

"Who are you?" she demanded, in a tone more worthy of a fishwife. "What do you want?"

"Forgive me for coming to the tradesmen's entrance, Ma'am, if I should have presented myself at the front door," Ned said, cheerily, "but I have not been a gentleman all my life, and I am still at something of a loss when it comes to country house etiquette. My name is Ned Knob, and I'm here at the invitation of Monsieur Germain Patou, physician. I wonder if you could send a message to say that I'm here. He knows me, and is expecting me–though not, I confess, precisely at this hour."

"Wait!" commanded the cook–and slammed the door in his face. Five more minutes passed. When the door opened again, there was no sign of the cook; a footman had been sent to welcome him in.

"Would you come this way, sir?" the footman asked.

"Certainly," said Ned–and followed the manservant through the kitchens and up a dozen steps to the ground floor, then up two more flights of carpeted stairs to the very top of the house. The candles had not yet been lit, and the corridors were very gloomy; all the doors ere carefully closed, and he met no grey men on the way.

He was shown into a room that seemed to him the very image of what a scholar's study should be. Germain Patou was there, but it was not Germain Patou's study. The blond-haired man sitting behind the desk was younger than Patou, and slimmer. He looked very well, and very much alive–which was a little odd, considering that he was supposed to have blown his brains out in the summer of 1817, but not odd enough to astonish Ned Knob.

"Ned," said Comte Henri de Belcamp, alias Tom Brown, alias John Devil the Quaker. "It's good to see you again–I'm glad you got our message in spite of all the confusion, and were able to respond despite your mishap on the quay. Do sit down. May we offer you something to drink?"

"Cognac, if you have it," Ned said, taking the seat he had been offered, across the desk from the Comte. Patou went to a cabinet, poured brandy from a decanter and meekly brought it to him.

Ned raised his glass, and said "*A l'avantage!*" as if it were a toast.

"We no longer need all that," the Comte said, affably. "The Knights of the Deliverance would have served their purpose, had things gone well–but things did not go well. Indeed, I do not think I ever had a day in my life when things when so awry as the day when I thought it politic to die–and that was not for want of healthy competition."

The cognac was good–far better, at any rate, than Jenny Paddock's *eau de vie*. "Why did you not call for me sooner, old friend?" Ned asked. "I am quite offended. Was I not your most trusted lieutenant in England?"

"We only knew one another for a few weeks, Ned," the Comte reminded him. "It was a significant passage in your life, I know–and I am very grateful for all that you have done for my grieving widow–but you should not overestimate the extent of our actual acquaintance. Even so, you're absolutely right. I should have called for you sooner, and I was very disappointed to see you seized so rudely when you waved to me from the quay. I sent the boat back, of course, to see if there was anything to be done, but the blackguards had carried you off into the dark streets. I'm very glad to see that you're all right. Germain says that you told Hanrahan to tell him that he has enemies, but we already know that. Would you mind telling us how you got away from them?" His voice seemed light enough, but the suspicion behind the question was palpable.

"I pointed out that he had no right to hold me," Ned said. "He accepted the justice of my case, and let me go."

"Indeed?" the Comte said. "It seems that his moral progress is as rapid as his intellectual progress. He would not have been so gentle had he actually man-aged to capture Germain... although I had not thought him likely to make such a silly mistake, give that we were clearly visible from the shore. Was it living men who took you, or grey men?"

"I fear that we're talking at cross-purposes," Ned told him, apologetically. "I misled Hanrahan slightly when I said that my captors were after Monsieur Patou. They were only after the address he wrote on the card. I imagine they have investigated it by now. I did not go there once I knew that it had been com-promised–I followed the *Prometheus*. I could not see anyone else doing like-wise, but you might not have much time. Gregory Temple isn't a man to under-estimate."

Ned had seen Comte Henri de Belcamp astonished before, and had even had the honor of causing such astonishment himself, but he still thought it a feat worthy of congratulation–and so he congratulated himself, albeit a trifle reluctantly, when he saw the expression on the other man's face.

"Temple!" exclaimed the Comte, running his fingers through his blond hair. "I thought that I had put him in Bedlam for once and for all. Is *he* on my trail, then?"

"He is now," Ned told him, moving on swiftly to add: "Not my doing, I assure you–but his men saw your hat, just as I did, and he drew the same conclusion. Prior to that, he was only on Hanrahan's trail, trying to follow it back to the buyer who had created such a busy market in dead bodies. If you desire to work in secret, you really shouldn't advertise yourself. There are Quakers by the thousand in London, but they don't sneak up and down the Thames in a ship that every ferryman on the water believes to be haunted."

"That was bound to happen," Patou put in. "We should never have taken any of the grey men aboard the ship."

"How shall we–or they–ever find out what their capabilities are, if we do not try them?" the Comte complained, allowing his attention to be distracted. "How will they ever recover their old selves, if we keep them cooped up here with nothing to look at but unfamiliar walls and a mediocre garden? They need stimulation, Doctor, as you yourself have aid a hundred times. If we're to beat Mortdieu, we need to accelerate our progress. It was a mistake to send Ross, I'll admit... but in all fairness, he made more progress in the hour that he was gone than he'd done in the previous month, despite all your efforts. That's what they need if they're to recover their memories completely: to see familiar faces in familiar places, to converse with people they loved. How else can they recall themselves, or *be* themselves?"

"There was one who had no trouble," Patou said, grimly–but the Comte was already looking at Ned Knob again, his troubled eyes questioning.

"Until last night," Ned went on, "Temple had no idea of your involvement. He's with the secret police now, chasing radicals... especially radical burkers. He knows now, though–thanks to a stroke of mischance. Hanrahan came to deliver the doctor's message to me just as Sawney made his grand entrance, and Temple had a spy in the parlor, who jumped to the conclusion that I knew far more than I did. Temple still knows nothing, except that I saluted a Quaker hat– but that's all he'll need, given that he has no trouble with his own memory, and his burning desire for retribution. But I must know, before we decide how to deal with Gregory Temple–did you really bring Sawney back from the dead, or was the hangman careless?"

His urgency was in vain; he got no immediate answer. Instead, the blond man turned to Patou again. "If Ned could follow the ship, Temple won't be far behind," he said. "We have two sets of enemies now, Doctor, and they're both too close for comfort. I'm not sure which of them is more to be feared at present." He turned back to Ned. "The *secret* police, you say? England has secret police now, and Gregory Temple is working for them? I do not know which is

249

the greater scandal... but I suppose I must take some of the blame. I left him ruined as well as broken in that Newgate cell, and I dare say that he had little choice in matter of employment, once he was released. Damnation! You've changed, Ned. You were little more than a boy back in '17, so I suppose it's only to be expected... I should have reckoned on that, and come to you much sooner."

"I had a good teacher," Ned said, "if only for a matter of weeks. I'm here now–who is after us, apart from Mr. Temple?"

Again, the Comte did not reply immediately. Ned let loose a little sigh. It seemed that Helen Brown's son had not changed at all; he still fancied himself the master manipulator, who used everyone, trusted no one and never under any circumstances told anyone the whole truth, or anything at all until he had to.

"We'll have to move again," Germain Patou said. "There's been no sign yet of Mortdieu, and he's less capable than we are of moving unobtrusively, even though he probably has as many living men in his employ as we have. The secret police are a different matter. I'm as reluctant as you are to cut the experiments short again, but what choice do we have? The setback to our work will be far greater if they find us now."

"*Prometheus* can't carry all the materials we've gathered here," the Comte said. "We'll need a bigger ship–one that can carry us across the ocean, to some quiet island in the Caribbean. Do you have money, Ned? Money enough to charter a clipper?"

Ned laughed. "I had enough to charter a vessel from the Hermitage Stairs to Purfleet," he said, "but not enough to take me much beyond Grays. The cabaret at Jenny Paddock's is a great success, but the bulk of the profit is Jenny's. Your widow..."

"I cannot go to Jeanne," the Comte said, flatly. "To her, I am dead, and so it must remain. If you see her again, Ned, you must not tell her that you have seen her husband. In fact, you have *not* seen her husband. Jeanne's son is the Marquis de Belcamp now; until he has a son, there is no Comte de Belcamp."

"Sawney and I killed Tom Brown," Ned observed, "who died with his conscience clear. Mr. Wood and I had already disposed of the phantom Percy Balcomb once and for all. So who are you now, my friend? I cannot imagine that James Davy or George Palmer is a suitable candidate for resurrection."

"In Purfleet," said the *ci-devant* Comte Henri de Belcamp, "I am Arthur Pevensey, a Cornishman–but I can't say that I like the name as a permanent fixture. My adversary, as you heard just now, has taken the name of Mortdieu, although I call him ungrateful Lazarus... but we have no time to waste on such fancies. If the secret police are on to us, and have Gregory Temple for their bloodhound, we must move quickly. If we cannot buy or charter a better ship, we must do what we can with the one we have."

"I asked you a question a little while ago," Ned reminded him. "Are you really raising the dead?"

250

This time, the *ci-devant* Comte condescended to reply. "Yes," he said. "We are. Nor are we the only ones, for our monopoly was cut short far sooner than we'd planned. Of the first dozen we brought back from the dead, eleven were doltish–and most of them still are–but one was not. If only he had been as docile as the rest! He stole the secret from me... although I have to confess that it was not actually mine by right of discovery. Now he is our rival–our enemy. We've clashed a time or two already, but he seems to grow stronger every time, while our progress is frustratingly slow. Your friend Ross is now our most promising pupil, having overtaken John–although John had the finer mind while he was still alive, and may yet surpass him again." He stopped suddenly. "You're having difficulty believing this, aren't you, Ned?"

"A little," Ned confessed. "Jack Hanrahan couldn't quite believe it, even though he saw Sawney dead *and* resurrected. I told him that electricity must hold the key–and I suppose it must, since you have bought James Graham's magical electric baths."

"Well done," said the *ci-devant* Comte. "I used to attend Humphry Davy's lectures at the Royal Institution, you know, when I was Tom Brown–I called myself after him, in one of my many impostures. I *could* have made the discovery myself, if only I'd dedicated myself to such work... but I had to go to Australia as you know. How's *your* mother, Ned?"

"Quite well," Ned said. "I've heard Mr. Davy myself, although Faraday is the man of the moment now. I don't have your intellect, but I'm a great admirer of what the Tories call *Jacobin science*. You ought to be aware, Monsieur, that I'm a radical now, and a man of conscience. I'm all in favor of slaying the dragon of death, but there's a..."

The *ci-devant* Comte cut him off. "Would you like to see Monsieur Patou raise the dead with your own eyes, Ned?" the blond man asked. "Would you like to make certain of the truth of what we're doing?"

"Is that wise?" Patou objected, twisting his lips into a frown. The physician pulled out his watch and looked at it. "Is it even time?"

"Yes," said the *ci-devant* Comte, rising decisively to his feet. "It is wise, and it is time. Ned has been sent to us by Providence, in our hour of need, and he needs to know what we are about if he is to commit himself to our plan and bring us more recruits. As for the time, we have no leisure left to let them simmer, and we have a new batch ready to bathe. Lead the way, my friend."

Patou put his watch away, and went to the door. Ned stood up and followed him, with the former Comte bringing up the rear. The candles still had not been lit on the top floor, but the corridors below were illuminated. There was a murmur of noise from most of the rooms they passed, but no one came out as they passed by, and the only other people Ned saw were servants, of every common hue but grey.

They went down from the ground floor to the level where the kitchens were, but Ned discovered then that there was a further set of cellars even further below ground, sealed by a heavy door with a massive iron lock. Patou did not have the key, and had to let the blond man pass him by to open it.

There was a glimmer of light within the vault, but it was rather distant, and Ned waited on the threshold until Patou had lit a lamp. When the physician had done that, he led the way again, into the bowels of the Earth.

The cellars were damp, and had the reek of the salt-marshes that confused both shores of the estuary from Rainham to the Isle of Grain. They were not cold, however. There was a massive fireplace at one end of the chamber into which they had come, where a fire was burning behind an iron grille. It vigorous flames provided the light that Ned had glimpsed from the corridor outside the doorway, but it was only Patou's lamp that showed him the other contents of the room.

Forewarned by Jack Hanrahan, Ned was not entirely surprised to see six capacious bathtubs, each one equipped at one end with a fearsome mass of supplementary equipment. Ned cast his mind back to the demonstrations he had seen at the Royal Institution, but the Voltaic cells and Leyden jars he had seen there bore little enough resemblance to the lumpen masses gathered here; only the wires that sprang from their earthenware crowns assured him that they must be generating powerful electrical currents, which were being fed into the fluid in the baths.

The fluid was not water; it was far more viscous, and far more active. It bore some slight resemblance, in its texture and transparency, to frogspawn–but instead of tiny huddled tadpoles, it held human bodies. The bodies must once have been white, or brown, or black, but they were now the same shade of grey that Ned had seen the night before, in Sawney's exposed flesh and that of the giant.

Ned barely noticed that there were more bodies heaped up in an unseemly fashion in the corner of the room most distant from the fire, presumably awaiting their turn in the baths. He was far more interested in the corpses floating beneath the surface of the uncanny fluid, as if suspended between Heaven and Earth, mortality and eternity.

Patou handed the lantern to his taller companion, then rolled up his sleeves. He went to the first bath. The physician carefully pushed his right hand into the fluid, and touched the neck of the thin man who lay there, naked and seemingly asleep. "No pulse," he reported. "No revitalization of the skin. Irrecoverable, I fear."

Patou moved on to the second bath. This too was a man–only one of the six vessels held a female–but one of sturdier build. The Frenchman did not seem optimistic as he began his examination, but his face brightened almost immediately. "Yes!" he said. "The fluid is flowing in his veins, and his flesh has recovered its consistency. He'll be ready..."

"Wake him now!" his master commanded.

Patou pursed his lips, but he did not complain. Nor did he delay. He plunged both arms into the slimy mass, and took the floating man by the shoulders, slowly but firmly altering his attitude. After ten or twelve seconds, the man's feet were on the floor of the bath, and Patou pulled the head free from the fluid. The stuff clung to the grey man's face, but Patou immediately set about brushing it away, exposing the strange skin to the air.

The man who had been lying peacefully asleep in the bath spluttered and coughed, and fluid vomited from his mouth–although Ned guessed that it was coming from his lungs rather than his stomach. Patou tried to force the man to lean slightly forward, while making sure that he could not slip and fall, but he was too short to carry out the task effectively. The lantern was abruptly thrust into Ned's hands, and the man who had once been Tom Brown lent his own height and his own hands to the work of waking the man who had been dead.

More than a minute passed, but the grey man's eyes eventually opened. All the color had gone from their irises; the pupil was set in a globe unreddened by the least blood vessel. Ned inferred that the resurrected dead no longer had red blood in their veins but something else–something gifted to them by the fluid that had revivified their necrotic flesh.

While Ned struggled to hold the lantern steady, the *ci-devant* Comte looked the living dead man straight in the eye, and said: "What is your name? Can you remember your name?"

The man returned from the dead did not look around, as a man waking from an ordinary sleep would surely have done. He did not say: "Where am I?" or "Who the Devil are you?" He looked back at the man who had been Comte Henri de Belcamp and John Devil the Quaker, and he furrowed his colorless brow, trying to do as he had been told, and remember his own name.

Time went by; the question was repeated.

In the end, the former dead man spoke. "John," he said, in a voice thick with the effects of the fluid still clogging his mouth. The syllable was clear enough, though.

His interlocutor did not seem entirely pleased with the answer. "John," He repeated, scornfully. "Can no one find a way back from the Underworld but men named John? Can all the burkers in London not find me a Theophilus or a Walter? Or is there some infection spreading from brain to brain, which fills them all with the same false identity? What surname, dolt? What is your family name?"

The man raised from the dead made no protest at the abuse heaped upon him–quite unfairly, Ned thought–but only tried meekly to do as he was bid. Alas, it seemed that the task was too much for him, at present.

Germain Patou reached out to take his friend's arm. "Relax, *mon ami*," he said. "Best to wash and clothe him while he's still as tractable as a new-born. Your old friend has seen what he needs to see–he might be more use to us talking to Ross, continuing the good work he began last night. Ross has been asking incessantly for his old friends Sam and Jeanie, and that's a healthy sign, although it's become a trifle tiresome. If we only had time..."

Perhaps that was tempting fate too far, Ned thought, as the footman who had taken him upstairs came hurrying through the door in great agitation.

"You must come at once, sir–there's trouble at the dock, aboard *Prometheus*. Someone's trying to seize the ship!"

Chapter Five
The Battle for Prometheus

Minutes later, Ned was bundled on to the back of a cart with a dozen other men–none of them grey–while weapons were brought from the house and handed out. Patou had been instructed to stay behind, but the footman had climbed aboard. Ned was offered a brace of pistols, but refused–pistols, he knew, made very inefficient clubs once they had been discharged. He refused a saber too, for being too unwieldy for a man of his height, but he accepted a cutlass whose blade was no longer than the length of his forearm.

What he wanted to know, however, was against whom he might be wielding it. He asked, but only received a single word by way of an answer: *Mortdieu*.

Even when the cart moved off into the gathering darkness, its two horses having been whipped to a rapid trot, there was too much confusion about him for Ned to do anything profitable–except to keep his head down, lest he take an accidental blow from a cudgel. Once the hubbub calmed, however, and a sense of purpose overcame the mob, he was able to make his way to his commander's side.

The streets of Purfleet were poorly lit, even by comparison with Low Lane, and the sky was cloudy, but there was no fog hereabouts and the air seemed crisp and clean.

"This is more than I bargained for," Ned said, candidly. "I'm a good messenger, but a terrible soldier. Stealth is my forte, not swordplay–and to be honest, I don't know enough as yet to know what cause I'm supposed to be fighting for. Why is this Mortdieu attempting to steal your ship?"

"I told you–he's my ungrateful Lazarus," said the *ci-devant* Comte. "Germain's greatest triumph, and bitterest defeat. You've seen enough to know that the brain is not as easy to revitalize as the body. It seems that the flow of the mind is much harder to regenerate than the flow of the blood. Patou has brought 50 men and women back to life in those baths of his–more here than in Portugal, though three in every five we buy are too far gone even now. Of those 50, barely half can construct a coherent sentence, and only a dozen seem able to remember

254

who and what they were in life. Germain is gaining in skill with every day that passes, and he has worked more miracles than you have so far seen, but there is a very great deal to be learned, and his successes have been as unpredictable as his failures. Mortdieu is the only one, so far, who was capable of understanding what we have done for him–but instead of being grateful, he tried to steal our secret for himself, to make his own grey army."

"I see," Ned said. "You have stolen the fire of Heaven in order to make an army of angels, but you have spawned a rebel Satan who is amassing a demonic army of his own."

"Don't mock me, Ned," whispered the *ci-devant* Comte de Belcamp, with a quality of menace in his tone that Ned had savored before. "You must fight for me now, if you're with me still–but if you prefer to cut and run, I'll understand. I should have come to you earlier if I wanted time enough to explain my cause and my plan. There is no time now, alas–but I'd dearly like your help, if you're willing to offer it. Not as a fighting-man, for you don't have the stature for that kind of work, but as a trusted aide."

"I have a good life now, Monsieur," Ned murmured, after a moment's thought. "I'm as curious as a cat, it's true, and not without ambition–but I need to know what your purpose is, *mon ami*. To free Bonaparte from St. Helena and build an empire in the Indies, that I understood... but I'm a radical now–a red republican in my heart of hearts–and I'm no longer prepared to sell my conscience as easily as I once was."

"This is no mere matter of empire-building," said the former John Devil, his voice so slight now that Ned was sure that none but he could hear it. "This is greater still, and will change the world forever, if it is not nipped in the bud by foul treachery. It's immortality, Ned, if we only have time to master its evolution. It's the end of the empire of death and the empire of fear. Tell Gregory Temple that, if and when he questions you again. Tell him that I'm the least of his enemies now, and can save him from the worst if I can only win the necessary time and he can put the past behind him. Tell him that I can help him live forever, if only I can overcome my nemesis, and he can overcome his bitter heart. Tell him that Mortdieu's the one who needs to be stopped, if he can do it..."

The man who had been John Devil the Quaker–and still kept up the pose, on occasion–allowed his voice to trail off. The cart was already drawing to a halt on the quay, which was only slightly better lit than the streets.

Ordinarily the docks would still have been at work at this hour, but *Prometheus* was the only sizeable ship at the dock tonight. If she had the same reputation here as she had among the watermen of the city, that was not at all surprising.

The living men jumped down one by one, lifting up their weapons. The *ci-devant* Comte de Belcamp leapt over the side of the cart and landed like a predatory cat, ready to lead them. There was little or no time to evaluate the situation. Ned stood up, and craned his neck in order to see what he could of the brawl that was taking place on the deck of the *Prometheus*. It was mostly a play of shadows, but there were lanterns attached to each mast. He could not tell whether the white, brown and black faces on deck were outnumbered by grey ones, but there was a considerable struggle going on. Having counted heads, though, Ned concluded that the recently-arrived reinforcements would be more than enough to win the fight in a mater of minutes. It seemed that Mortdieu's raiders had been held at bay long enough.

The reinforcements in question did not hesitate in their charge. They were met on the gangplank, and had to fight their way aboard, but Ned could see that the resistance was weak, and that the would-be pirates knew that they cold not win. The erstwhile attackers were retreating now, scattering as best they could. One or two contrived to leap ashore, and Ned heard a sequence of splashes as others tumbled into the water–perhaps including some of the ship's defenders as well as its attackers. He squinted into the gloom, trying to identify grey faces among those of more vivid color, but the light was too poor.

Ned wondered how hard it might be to kill the resurrected dead for a second time, given that they no longer had red blood to bleed–but he deduced that it could not be as hard as all that, given that they still had beating hearts to stop, and throats to cut. The might be grey, but they breathed air, and must take in sustenance. They could not be immortal.

Could they, he wondered, produce children of their own? Could they produce grey children of their own? That question might, in the long run, be the key to their potential relationship with humankind.

Ned dropped his cutlass, and jumped down from the cart in his turn. He poised himself on his toes to run off into the streets of Purfleet, asking himself how much it would cost him to hire a fiacre to take him all the way to Covent Garden–but he could not hold that thought. Instead, he climbed back on to the cart and craned his neck again, anxious to know how the fight was going.

He picked up the cutlass absent-mindedly, simply because it was there–but he was glad that he had when he felt the cart lurch as someone stepped up behind him.

He turned to face the new arrival, perversely relieved to discover that the grey man was not a giant, nor even a man of average height. Ned realized that he had not the slightest idea whether this was one of the resurrected dead from the house in Purfleet or one of the others, raised from the grave by his own sinister kind. He was, however, somewhat reassured by the fact that the grey man was not carrying a weapon.

"I don't suppose, by any chance, that you know your name, *mon ami*," he said, as lightly as he could.

"I have not forgotten it," the grey man said, speaking far more coherently than Sawney had, "but I have discarded it. Do you know yours?"

"I do," Ned confirmed. "Have I, then, the honor of addressing Monsieur Mortdieu, the general of the great army of the dead?"

"I have not forgotten sarcasm either," the grey man said, apparently lacking nothing in intelligence or articulacy, "but I no longer find much use for it. Would you like to be raised from the dead, *mon ami*, when your time comes?"

"I'd rather it didn't come for a while yet," Ned replied. "And if the occasion should arise sooner than I hope and expect, I think I'd rather be among friends."

"You might find," the grey man observed, "that the friends you had before are no longer your friends, and that it will be to your advantage to make new ones."

"I might," Ned agreed. "You don't seem to be afraid of me, even though I have a sword, while your height and reach are almost as meager as my own. Would you care to tell me why that is?"

"You did not charge with the others," the grey man pointed out. "You're evidently a man of extreme discretion."

"So much for having no further use for sarcasm," Ned said. "You're evidently a man of discretion yourself. Your army might stand a greater chance of victory if you were at their head, leading by example."

"Do you think so, *mon ami*?" the grey man said. "That would depend, would it not, on exactly what their objective is?"

As the grey man pronounced the last two words, as neatly as any living man could have done, Ned was deafened by a mighty bang. He was hurled forward by the blast-wave that spread out along the quay from the *Prometheus*. He sprawled face-down on the floor of the cart, and felt the cutlass plucked from his hand. The two horses reared and neighed, but they could not break the tether that had secured them to a windlass, and were thus unable to bolt. The cart continued to rattle and jolt, but the grey man was not thrown out of it.

Ned tried to get up, but a heavy boot came down on the back of his right hand and pinned him.

The grey man knelt down beside him, but did not cut his throat. "The house is mine, now, *mon ami*," he said, "as it should be. The dead-alive imprisoned there are mine, now, as they should be. Fear not–I've a ship of my own at Tilbury, and I'll be gone in less than 48 hours, as soon I've gathered everything I need. You won't see me again, if you have no wish to do so–but you ought to remember what I tell you, and mark it well. *I have nothing against the living, if they do not seek to rule the dead-alive.* Indeed, I love the living, for they are the seeds of my own kind. If the living will only let me alone, and leave me to my work, I and my kind will let the living alone, but if your kind takes up arms against me, or tries again to usurp the privilege that is mine, I shall be an enemy more terrible than any you have ever faced before. I have no wish to harass the living, and every hope that your kind and mine will be able to share this world in amity, but I have observed the reactions of your kind to the sight of mine, and I thin it politic, for the time being, to be a man of *extreme* discretion. If anyone should ask you what took place this evening, tell them that the dead-alive have won the liberty that is their right as human beings, and hope to use it peacefully and productively. Tell them that we have no wish to go to war–but that if we are forced to do so again, as we have in the past, we shall do so with all the might we can muster. Can you remember all that?"

"I can remember the gist of it," Ned told him, resentfully. "I've the mind of a living man, and have no need to be taught to think all over again–but if you want your message to be heeded, you would probably have done better to confide it to a taller man. People of our humble stature are rarely taken seriously, as you may well remember."

"I remember everything," Mortdieu assured him. "I never had the slightest difficulty in being taken seriously, and I beg you not to underestimate your own potential. I'm truly sorry to have lured so many of your friends aboard the doomed ship, and to have left them without the slightest help of resurrection, but you can be sure that I'll treat Germain Patou far more gently, for old time's sake. Please don't return to the house, tonight or any time tomorrow. Go back to London, and retire to your bed for a while. It will be better for both of us if I am gone before you tell your tale."

The cart lurched drunkenly as the grey man jumped down, and then continued to vibrate as the horses twitched and fretted.

Ned got down himself as soon as he felt able, nursing his bruised hand. He raced to the water's edge, where the gangplank leading to the *Prometheus* had been. The gangplank had been blown apart, and one of the two hawsers securing the ship to the dock had been severed. The one at the bow had held, though, so the ship had merely changed its attitude as the stern drifted away from the quay. The upper deck was ablaze, although the furled canvas had not yet caught alight. The hull had been holed at the waterline, and the cargo-holds were filling up with water, but the ship was going down slowly.

There were men still on deck–living men, not grey ones–and two of them were howling for help. Ned found a rope and threw it to them, but could do no more. He found a lifebelt, though, and hurled that into the dark water, where there were heads bobbing amid all manner of debris. He hunted for more ropes to let down the side of the dock. He called for help too, but none came from the shoreward side.

There was no sign of the *ci-devant* Comte de Belcamp. Three men had gained the base of a flight of stone steps leading up to the quay, but there the fight broke out again, although none of them was grey. The one who was beset by two was hurled back into the water, but he seemed well able to swim, and struck out towards another place where he might climb up. Not everyone in the water was as fortunate–several were injured, and were having difficulty keeping afloat, let alone striking out for the dock.

There was a mighty gout of steam as the weight of the water in *Prometheus'* holds pulled the upper deck level with the water. The fire died, and the best of the light with it. There was a man directly below Ned, who had grabbed one of the ropes he had let down, but his arm was injured and he could not climb. Ned set his legs and began to pull hard, calling down to the man to set his good hand and his feet in whatever nooks and crannies he could find, so as to take as much of his own weight as he possibly could. Ned was small, but he was strong. After five minutes of struggling, the man grasped the rim of the dock with his good hand, and Ned caught hold of him while he scrambled for footholds, eventually wriggling over the edge on to the apron.

"Thanks, mate!" the sailor said, spitting out a quid of tobacco and a mouthful of river-water. "Never thought I'd make it."

"Some didn't," Ned said, regretfully, peering over the edge to see if there was anyone else who might benefit from his immediate assistance.

"Tricked and bested by a handful of men–and half of them walking corpses, by God!" the sailor went on. "I wish I could be sorrier to see her go, but she's been about the Devil's work since we shipped out of Lisbon. If I'd had any sense, I'd never have signed back on–but I've always been a fool for money."

The sailor was looking back at his ship as he spoke. *Prometheus* was sinking into the harbor now, although she hit bottom long before her masts were fully submerged. The arms carrying the topsails were level with the waterline, and Ned saw two swimmers grasp them gratefully, desperate to rest.

"They've a ship of their own at Tilbury, if Mortdieu wasn't lying," Ned said. "If Henri can regroup his forces, there might be time for a counter-attack."

"Who's Henri?" the sailor demanded, as he came to his feet, wringing wet.

"The erstwhile master of the *Prometheus*. Pevensey, is he calling himself now? The pretended Cornishman."

"He's not my master any more," was the sailor's curt reply. "I've lost my ship and must find another. This time, I'll stick to the tea trade if I can. If I must, I'll ship convicts to Botany Bay–but I'll have no more of demonkind, that's for sure."

"Best of luck to you, then," said Ned, sincerely. "What chance would we have, do you think, of finding a boat to carry us upriver, if we walk westwards?"

"Little or none," the sailor opined, hugging his wounded arm to his chest. "Far more chance of getting stuck in a bog. We'd best seek shelter for the night–I need to dry my clothes by a roasting fire and find out if my forearm's broken. I know an inn, if you'd like to come with me–I don't think they'll turn us away, even though they know we've been trafficking with the Devil, if we plead our innocence loudly enough."

"No," said Ned, with a sigh. "I'm dry, and there's always the road. But you might pass the message along, if you see any of Master Pevensey's servants, or the man himself. Mortdieu says that he has a ship at Tilbury, waiting to carry him away, once he's seized Patou and plundered the house. If he's lying, then his ship is somewhere else–but he certainly intends to be gone as soon as he can. Once he's at sea, Henri will never catch him, and probably won't find it easy to locate him again."

"I'll pass the word along," the sailor agreed, "If I have the chance. I owe you that much."

"Thanks," Ned aid, sincerely. "Good luck to you."

As it turned out, he had more than one opportunity to pass his message on himself before he quit the quay. He gave the same intelligence to the footman who'd brought the deadly warning to the cellar, and to another soaking wet sailor from the *Prometheus*. Ned formed the impression, however, that the footman and the second sailor were of much the same mind as the first, firmly resolved to be done with the Devil's work forever.

"Perhaps it's for the best," he murmured to himself, as he went in search of a hirer's or a coaching stop. "If Mortdieu withdraws from England, and takes Patou with him, it'll put an end to the burking epidemic and things will soon return to normal."

By the time he was fortunate enough to find a stop with a mail-coach expected imminently, however, Ned had changed his mind about that final judgment. Things would never return to normal. How could they? However slowly matters might evolve, a crucial bridge had been crossed that had delivered the human race into a new era. The greatest of all the old certainties had fallen by the wayside. Death was no longer the end–not, at least, for everyone. Whether Mortdieu contrived to hoard the secret or not, it had been discovered and would be again. Science was a method, after all; what one scientist could do, another could repeat–and another and another, *ad infinitum*. The day of the grey men had come, and there was no way to turn back the clock.

"Have you come from the docks?" asked one of the businessmen waiting to board the London-bound coach. "I heard an explosion over that way, not half-an-hour ago, and saw flames in the sky."

"Nothing to worry about," Ned assured the tall man, looking upwards to meet his eye. "Just the living and the dead-alive fighting over the dubious privilege of controlling the process of transition, while it's still esoteric. The *Prometheus* was blown up, but there were at least a dozen survivors, probably more. I don't know how many were killed, but probably not as many."

The man, inevitably, looked down at him as if he were mad. When the coach eventually came, the man and his fellows climbed up inside, while Ned was forced by the leanness of his resources to take a place on top, where stouter men than he had frozen to death on journeys not much longer. By the time he dismounted–in Fleet Street yet again–he was chilled to the bone. He jogged all the way to Jenny Paddock's.

Because it was Sunday there had been no performance that evening, and the parlor was half empty. There was no sign of Jack Hanrahan, but Sam Hopkey and Jeanie Bird were snuggled together in their favorite booth.

260

"Buy me a brandy, Sam, for God's sake," Ned croaked, as he sat down on the bench beside Jeanie, forcing her to move into even closer proximity with her leading man, until he jumped up to obey his director's command.

"Did you find Sawney?" Jeanie asked, eagerly, while Sam was at the counter.

"I found the place where he was, an hour ago," Ned told her, glumly, "but how long he'll be there I don't know. He's among his own kind now–I doubt that we'll be seeing him again, although I'm sure we could have done him a power of good, between the three of us."

"And what is *his own kind*?" Jeanie asked, fearfully.

"I believe they like to style themselves the dead-alive," Ned said. "It wasn't the hangman's carelessness that spared Sawney, or a miracle that brought him back to life. It was science, like Mr. Davy's and Mr. Faraday's."

"Science?" echoed Sam, as he set a generous brandy down in front of Ned and took the stool where Ned would normally have sat. "What kind of science can bring the dead back from beyond the grave?"

"I've see it done," Ned told him, before swilling the brandy down. "It'll cause trouble, I don't doubt, but in a hundred years' time, it will be the destiny of every living soul–and I, for one, will welcome it."

"You've seen it done by the Frenchman who was here last night?" Sam said, just to make certain.

"The very same," Ned said. This time, he did not have his back to the door, so he knew as soon as anyone else what was happening as the Constables and Town Sergeants poured through it with their truncheons at the ready. There were a dozen in all. They had not come to start a fight, though, but merely to make sure that no one else would. A single man strode in behind them, with his head held high and the air of a man who had just recovered something that was rightly his. Given that he could not have been reappointed Chief Superintendent of Scotland Yard, Ned had to assume that it was his dignity, or his sense of purpose, or both.

Gregory Temple marched straight to the booth, where Ned Knob only seemed to be cowering because his limbs were so infernally cold.

"Edward Knob," Temple said, taking less relish in the pronouncement than Ned might have anticipated, "I arrest you in the name of the law, on the grounds that in St. Luke's Churchyard, at three o'clock this afternoon, in company with John Hanrahan, you purchased the dead body of a young girl for use in unspeakable practices."

Ned heard the chorus of gasps that greeted this announcement, and could imagine the whispers that would follow it. Ned Knob a burker! Ned Knob a necrophile! Who would ever have thought it? Well, what can you expect from a miserable dwarf?

"Mr. Temple," he said, unable to suppress a shiver as he stood up to meet his fate, "you don't know the half of it, or even the tenth. Jack Hanrahan is a hero, and not only because he went to see Dan Eaton pilloried, in order to defend him against anyone wishing to do him harm, but because he gave that little girl a second chance to live–exactly as he did for Sawney Ross. You'll not find a man or woman in here willing to chide him for that."

A silence fell then, as profound as the one that had greeted the sight of Sawney's grey face, but Ned knew that it would not last.

"And before you take me away," Ned went on, striking the best leading man's pose that he could contrive, without the benefit of Sam's or Sawney's height, "I have a message for the world from General Mortdieu of the Necromantic Empire, which is this: *He has nothing against the living, provided that they do not take up arms against the dead-alive.* Indeed, he loves the living, for we are the seed of his own good folk. Nor should we hate or fear him, since he offers us the hope and expectation of a better resurrection–a *radical* resurrection. Down with King George, and long live the Republic!"

The audience was too dumbstruck to cheer him, but he knew that they would remember what he had said for a long time to come. They were living people, after all; they needed no help to learn to think for a second time.

Chapter Six
The Interrogation Cell at Bow Street

This time, Ned was not taken to some secret covert in Newgate Prison, but to Bow Street Police Station, where he was immediately lodged in an official interrogation cell. This one was better furnished than the one in which he had been entertained the previous evening, although it had neither bed nor window. Its table was much sturdier, it was far better lit, and it had two uniformed constables in attendance. On the other hand, the chair in which Ned was placed could not be described as well-upholstered or comfortable. Gregory Temple remained standing, obviously feeling that no height was too great from which to look down on a man like Ned Knob.

"You should not have arrested me, Mr. Temple," Ned complained. "I was not a accomplice to Jack Hanrahan's crime–if it can still be reckoned a crime, now that we know what we know. Had you let me at liberty, I'd have got to the bottom of this mystery in no time at all, and you may be sure that I'd have told you everything."

"You will forgive me if I doubt you," Temple said, curtly. "You will be doubtless be glad to know, since you say that you are innocent of any crime, that I have been seconded to Scotland Yard, and am able once again openly to wear the title *detective*. You may be less delighted to know that Jack Hanrahan has agreed to testify for the Crown against all his old associates, including yourself and Germain Patou. He has told us everything."

"And a great deal more, I don't doubt," Ned said, with a wry smile. "You couldn't possibly order me a cup of tea, by any chance? I'm still cold, having been forced to sit on top of a mail-coach in highly unsuitable weather, with the wind blowing in my face all the way from Purfleet to Fleet Street. A bite to eat would be nice, if it wouldn't overburden or hospitality. I was just about to order supper at Jenny's when you burst in with your guard of honor."

Temple turned to one of the Constables. "Fresh tea for the four of us," he said, "and find something toothsome for this man to eat."

The Constable's moustache twitched, but he dared not let the scowl spread across his features. He left without uttering a word of protest.

"You know as well as I do, Mr. Temple," Ned went on, "that I never spent more than a few minutes in Jack Hanrahan's company until this afternoon, when I ingratiated with him purely and simply to obtain information–information which will be of just as much interest to you as it was to me, and which I'm perfectly willing to share, in spite of the ungrateful and insulting manner in which I've been treated. I can now give you a more accurate sketch of the causes of the burking epidemic than can possibly be contained in Jack's fancies and fabulations–although I repeat that I could have given you a far more complete account had you only let me pursue my inquiries further."

"That's as may be, Master Knob," Temple said. "But Hanrahan has got in first, and he's given us enough to pack you off to Australia–and enough to hang Germain Patou, if his own people do not want him for the guillotine."

"This is all very silly," Ned told him. "Sit down, Mr. Temple and listen. I've seen *him*, and he asked me to give you a message. I've also seen his new arch-enemy, who was equally enthusiastic to find a reliable messenger. There's a great deal I still don't know, but if you want to hear what I do know, you'd do better to talk to me man-to-man than continue this charade of bullying."

"Did I not hear one of your messages just now, in Sharper's?" Temple parried.

"Only part of it–you seemed to be in a hurry, and I didn't want to be cut off in mid-speech. That would have been poor stagecraft, and Sawney would never have forgiven me. But you're right–that was the core of the message given to me by Patou's ungrateful Lazarus, who seems to be trying to reserve the privilege of restoring the dead-alive entirely to himself, at least for the time being. It was intended for the whole world, so I proclaimed it as loudly as I could. The message I was given by the man you once knew as James Davy, on the other hand, is for your ears alone, which I shall be glad to pass on in exactly that fashion, if you would care to ask the other Constable to leave us alone for a minute or two."

Temple shook his head. "This is an official interrogation, Master Knob," he said, "which must be conducted under formal rules of guidance." Ned realized, a trifle belatedly, that Temple's manner was not entirely of his own choosing. The produce of Jack Hanrahan's squealing had obviously made its way higher up the chain of command. Temple was still constrained by circumstance, even though he had been seconded to Scotland Yard.

"Ah," Ned said. "I see. My apologies to you, Mr. Temple–although you really did seem to be enjoying yourself just a little, back at Jenny's. I had forgotten how good you are at playing a part, once you have the determination to do so. Very well–within the framework of an official interrogation, what would you like to know?"

The first Constable came back in then, carrying a tin tray. It bore a teapot and four mugs, with a sugar-bowl and a jug of milk. There was also a plate bearing some day-old bread and a few slices of ham. Ned sighed, but he was hungry enough to attack the meager meal with some enthusiasm. Temple poured the tea, and passed two of the mugs to the Constables, who nodded in acknowledgement of his generosity. Temple asked all three of them whether they required sugar. The Constables requested two spoonfuls each, so Ned asked for three, calculating that his tour of duty must have been a good deal more laborious than theirs. Temple contented himself with one, but heaped it more generously than he had heaped any of the others, apparently unaware of the insight he was providing into the essential perversity of his character.

Temple sat down, and waited until Ned had finished the bread and ham. "Where was the girl's body taken, Master Knob, and by what means?" the detective asked, formally.

"Purfleet," Ned said, unhesitatingly. "Aboard a vessel named *Prometheus*, which sank in Purfleet harbor not three hours ago. You'll be getting your own reports of that very shortly, I dare say, but it won't make the *Morning Post* until the day after tomorrow."

"The ship sank?" Temple echoed, already forced to deviate from his planned agenda, though not from his formal manner. "How did it come to sink?"

"It was attacked by a party of raiders, including both living and dead-alive," Ned told him. "To begin with, the crew thought it was an attempt to seize the ship, but it wasn't. The fighting was a mere diversion, to distract attention from a petard placed at the water-line. The intention was to sink the vessel, in order to prevent its further use."

"Its further use in the stealing of corpses?"

"No–its use as a means of escape. When the master of the *Prometheus* found out that you were on his trail, Mr. Temple, he immediately decided to pack up and leave. No matter how great his need for an abundant supply of dead people was, I doubt that he would ever have come within 50 miles of London had he not assumed that you were a broken man, incapable of taking any further interest in him."

"Who are you talking about?" Temple demanded, bluntly.

"I told you–the man you once knew as James Davy. The viper you nursed in your bosom, who extracted all your secrets by stealth and turned them against you. The man also known as the bandit Tom Brown and as Comte Henri de Belcamp–being fully entitled to both names, by reason of his rather remarkable birth and upbringing, although he appears to have renounced them forever. I believe that he was calling himself Arthur Pevensey at the time of his probable death, masquerading as a Cornishman."

"What do you mean by *at the time of his probable death*?" Temple asked.

"He was lured aboard the *Prometheus* two or three minutes before it blew up. There were survivors, but I didn't see him among them."

"Did you see his corpse, then?"

"No–but I doubt that General Mortdieu will consent to revive him, even if it is still in good condition. General Mortdieu does not seem to me to be the kind of person likely to repeat his predecessor's worst mistake."

"And who is this General Mortdieu to whom you refer?"

"The cleverest and most ambitious of the dead-alive, resurrected by Germain Patou and Arthur Pevensey in Portugal, probably not far from Lisbon. He had another name when he was alive, of course, and claims to know what it was. I have a suspicion of my own regarding that item of information, but I doubt that it matters any longer. *Now* he is General Mortdieu, hero of the Revolution against Death and Emperor of the Dead-Alive. He says that he has no wish to make war on England, or on any nation of the living, and I am inclined to believe him, for now. As to the future... I have given that matter some thought while I was *en route* to London, in spite of being frozen half to death, and it seems to me that it depends on whether the dead-alive can breed. I did not have the opportunity to consult Monsieur Patou on that question."

"I don't understand what you mean," Temple said.

"You will, when you've had time to think about it. Point one: the dead can now be brought back to life–not all of them, but some. Point two: the dead-alive have trouble remembering who they were before they died, and most seem in need of considerable re-education–but at least some can recover all of their memories and the power of their will. Point three: in consequence of points one and two, the world has changed, utterly and irrevocably. Point four: at present the so-called Arthur Pevensey and the so-called General Mortdieu are squabbling over the secret of reviving the dead, evidently having different views as to how the advent of the new race should be managed. I do not know what either of them intends, but I know that it is a matter of small importance. Point five: *if* the dead-alive can reproduce their own kind, they are a new species, potentially capable of replacing humankind as overlords of the Earth. If not, then we are the larvae from whose corpses they must hatch as flies–in which case, they must continue to indefinitely cherish us as we cherish our children, if ever they do wrest political control of civilization from our hands. Point six: for the moment, you probably think that I am mad, and may even wish that I were–but that does not matter in the least. Whether you believe me or not, the world has changed, absolutely and forever."

There was a brief silence, while Ned and Gregory Temple each took several sips of sweet tea.

"You are perfectly certain that the dead can be resurrected?" Temple said, with only the slightest inquisitive inflection.

"I have not seen the process from beginning to end," Ned admitted, "but I did see the factory in which the dead are prepared for their return to life, and I witnessed a key stage in the resurrection process. I am far more certain now that it can be done, and has already been done a hundred times over, than I was last night after seeing Sawney Ross turned grey." As he finished this speech, Ned felt his breath catch in his throat, and he coughed to clear it.

Temple shook his head. "If you were to repeat this story in court tomorrow, you'd be presumed to be a madman," he observed.

"Tomorrow," Ned agreed, "denial will still be possible. In the longer term, it will not. More than a hundred people saw Sawney come into Jenny Paddock's last night, some of whom had seen him hanged. There are ferrymen sheltering beneath London Bridge and Blackfriars Bridge who'll be glad to tell you about the passengers the *Prometheus* sometimes used to carry after darkness fell. There'll be crewmen from the *Prometheus* herself trying to find new berths tomorrow morning, who'll be more than pleased to explain why. And even if all of those people should happen to be more anxious than I am to avoid being called a liar for telling the truth, we may be certain that General Mortdieu does not intend to hide his Empire of the Dead-Alive forever. If nothing else, they will want... well, I suppose I ought not to call it *new blood*, since the dead-alive have something other than blood in their veins, but I dare say that you can follow the logic of my argument now that I've set it out for you."

"It sounds impossible," Temple said, flatly.

"Yes, Mr. Temple," Ned replied. "It does. Indeed, it *was* impossible just a little while ago, but it is impossible no longer. We stand on the threshold of a new era, and all the firepower in the British Empire cannot hold it at bay. Ours will be a century of multitudinous resurrections, and we might as well try be proud of the fact."

Temple hesitated again, then said: "Where exactly, in Purfleet, was the girl's body taken?"

"To a house on the east of the town, standing in its own grounds and surrounded by a high wall. It has three stories at the front, four at the back, because the ground falls away so steeply. It also has a further set of vaults beneath the basement, where Germain Patou's equipment was sited until this evening. You will recognize the equipment easily enough if you can get there in time; as Jack Hanrahan has probably told you, it once belonged to James Graham's Temple of Hymen and Health. Not that I'm endorsing anything else he may have told you, mind."

"What do you mean by *if you can get there in time?*"

266

"Mortdieu is stripping the place as we speak, of anything useful to his campaign," Ned told him. "He has a ship of his own–at Tilbury, he said, although I would not put it past him to tell a fib or two in the interests of putting his adversaries off his trail. I have no idea where he will steer his ship once it sets sail, but he said he would be gone within 48 hours, of which at least five must now have elapsed."

"You seem to take a remarkable relish in all this, Master Knob," Temple observed, perhaps speaking entirely for himself for once.

"Do I?" Ned riposted. "Well, perhaps I do. I am a radical, you see, Mr. Temple, and a great enthusiast for Jacobin science and the philosophy of progress. I like to think of the order of things being upset, in the hope that it might make way for something better. Is that really such a crime, even in the eyes of a loyal lackey of the state?"

"If the reawakened dead really were stalking our streets last night," Temple said, leadenly, "and are about to overrun the world in years to come, I could not call that progress."

"That is because you are an old man, Mr. Temple," Ned said, cruelly, "and a man of the old order. I, on the other hand, am a young man of the new order. Perhaps our positions will be reversed in a short while, if you should choose to join the ranks of the dead-alive, or are rudely press-ganged into their company. Perhaps you will be able to think of it as progress then."

Temple shook his head, as if to clear it of unwelcome ideas. "You really are serious, aren't you?" he said, wonderingly. "I never had a moment's doubt that Hanrahan was lying through his teeth, but you actually mean what you say. Either you *are* mad, or you're telling the truth."

"I'm an honest man, Mr. Temple," Ned told him, regretfully. "Too honest for my own good, on occasion. He promised that he would bring you back from the dead, if you can put the past behind you and make a new start. That was the message he asked me to give you."

"Mortdieu?"

"The man who once posed as John Devil the Quaker, and still takes some pride in wearing the badge of that office. He might be able to fulfil the promise– Germain Patou may have been a vital element of the partnership to begin with, and Mortdieu will presumably take the opportunity to capture him, but *he* must know more than enough to set up in business again, provided that he still alive."

By now, Temple had ceased to make any pretence that this as still a formal interrogation, conducted under official rules of guidance. "You cannot possibly know how difficult it would be," the old man whispered. "To put the past behind me, I mean. You do not know what that man tried to do to me."

"Yes, I do," Ned assured him. "I don't know exactly how he set about it, but I know he did whatever he could to leave you in Newgate a broken man. You were too strong for him, though. You came back from the dead, just as he did, without the necessity of Germain Patou's magical fluid and electric shocks.

He's a different man now—and I think you know as well as I do how utterly he can change, when he steps from one role into another. It wasn't you who defeated him, remember—it was the burning of his steamship by riotous natives in Africa. That, and love."

"Love!" Temple spat out the word as if it were an oath.

"Yes, love. If he had not loved Jeanne, and wanted so much to be worthy of her love... he really did want to change history, you know, so that he might be innocent of the murders of Maurice O'Brien and Constance Bartolozzi—not for his own sake, but for hers. He really did want to annihilate Tom Brown: not to be him any longer, and never to have been him at all. He really is a man who can put the past behind him and make new starts—but then, he's a younger man than you, and one who believes in progress. Perhaps his belief is not yet as strong as it might be, but I think I might be able to help him in that respect, if I were given the chance."

Gregory Temple closed his eyes. The expression on his face was impossible to fathom, but it was not that of a man who could yet begin to believe in progress.

"What did you find at the address in Stepney?" Ned ventured to ask.

"Enough to tie Patou into half a dozen burkers," Temple told him, willingly enough. "But we didn't find the address of the house in Purfleet—you did better there."

"I probably did better with Jack Hanrahan too," Ned said. "I persuaded him that I was his friend, so he talked to me as honestly as he talks to anyone. I still won't be your spy, Mr. Temple, but that doesn't mean that I can't be useful to your inquiries. I haven't joined forces with John Devil either—I'm still my own man, and I'm more curious than ever to know more about the world that is to come. If you release me, I'll do what I can to find out more about Mortdieu's plans—and John Devil's too, if ever I see him again."

Gregory Temple shook his head again, this time very tiredly. "The interview is over," he said to the two silent Constables. "Take Master Knob down to the overnight cells—he looks as if he's in dire need of a good night's sleep."

"I'd be a deal more comfortable in my own bed, Mr. Temple," Ned opined.

"I doubt it," Temple said. "I know where you live—but I don't doubt that Hanrahan was lying about your involvement in his crimes, trying to reduce his own guilt by imparting it recklessly to others. I'll try to persuade my superiors that you're too useful to lock away. With luck, I'll be able to release you in the morning. In the meantime, you probably do need that good night's sleep. I hope the cells won't be too noisy for you."

"Mr. Temple," Ned said, "you're a gentleman, and a wise one too. I always thought so. That's why *he* admires you so."

"*He* tried to destroy me with a series of lies," the detective murmured, "and very nearly succeeded."

"The extent to which a man will go to wreak destruction," Ned said, soberly, "is the most accurate measure of his fear. Oddly enough, no one ever tries to destroy me–their first instinct is always to give me messages to carry. I wish I could be proud of that, as well as glad."

Chapter Seven
The Road to Greenhithe

The beds in the cells at Bow Street Police Station were by no means famous for their softness, and the cell block was even noisier than the street where Ned Knob lived, but Ned was not a man used to a thickly-padded mattress, silken sheets or silence. He slept tolerably well.

The establishment was not famous for its breakfasts, either, but Ned was quite satisfied by the hot sugared porridge he was brought at 6 a.m., and the tea that came with it was perfectly drinkable, even though it had only one spoonful of sugar in it–and not one that had been heaped by Gregory Temple.

Ned also made full use of the bowl of hot water and the brick of soap that the turnkey brought him–he was, after all, still *Gentleman* Ned Knob as well as Red Republican Ned, and he was determined not to conduct himself like any common jailbird.

He would have slept somewhat later than usual if he had been given the chance, having had an unusually exhausting Sunday, but his jailers had a routine to observe. When he had finished washing, however, he lay back down on the bed and dozed, fully expecting Gregory Temple to come to his rescue at any moment.

As things transpired, the moments dragged by while Bow Bells chimed seven, eight and nine, and Ned had almost begun to suspect that he had been cheated when the lock finally turned in his door and the great detective came in.

"Get up, Master Knob," the detective said. "We've no time to lose, and this is no time to be lazing in bed till mid-morning."

"I would have been glad to turn my hand and my head to more profitable occupations, Mr. Temple," Ned said, in an aggrieved manner, as he was hustled up the stone steps and out into the yard where the armored wagons waited to carry prisoners to the court, "had you only seen fit to make such provision. I've been on tenterhooks for hours, eager to be off."

The carriage into which they climbed was no court-ferry, nor did it bear any official insignia. Evidently, Gregory Temple's re-recruitment to the not-so-secret police did not inhibit him from traveling incognito. The bench inside was a good deal better upholstered than the bed on which Ned had been lying, and the cab was closed against the biting wind, so the journey promised to be a comfortable one.

"To Purfleet, I suppose?" Ned murmured, as they headed down Kin William Street towards London Bridge.

"Greenhithe," Temple told him.

"Not even Tilbury," Ned said, pensively. "I suspected that Mortdieu was lying about that. Strange, is it not, that one can sense a lie even in a man who has come back from the dead?"

"You're a veritable genius, Master Knob," Temple said, sarcastically. "Events have moved on, by the way, since we spoke last night. I sent men to investigate the house at Purfleet, but they arrived too late to prevent its destruction."

"Destruction!" Ned echoed. "John Devil survived the blast, then, and wasted no time in striking back at his ungrateful Lazarus?"

"Not so far as my men could tell. The sinking of the *Prometheus* sparked another reaction, it seems. The harbormaster at Purfleet had been unhappy for some time, it seems, and all the dock-workers too. Business had declined sharply since certain rumors began to run along the shore regarding the cargoes brought into port by the unlucky vessel, and considerable resentment had built up against her master. No one, of course, saw fit to involve higher authorities in their anxieties–these are men used to taking care of their own problems. The explosion in the harbor was the last straw. In the old days, mobs used to give notice of their intentions with a few hours of rough music, but we live in precipitate times. The house in Purfleet was visited by an armed gang whose only purpose was to burn the owners out, and they did so with remarkable precision. The house–all of it, at least, that stood above ground level at the front–is now a blackened shell."

Ned considered this for a few moments. "Well," he said, eventually, "if General Mortdieu had nothing against the living when he spoke to me, he has something against them now. Did he manage to get Germain Patou's equipment out of the cellars, and the dead-alive out of their rooms, before the fire took hold?"

"It seems so," Temple told him. "My men found nothing in the cellars but a few dead bodies that were by no means fresh, and there were no obvious skeletons among the rubble of the main body of the house."

"And you think they took their plunder to Greenhithe?"

"My agents were unable to determine where any material removed from the house might have been taken. Fortunately, my former colleagues had maintained their own surveillance at Sharper's."

"What was fortunate about that?" Ned asked. "Jenny's customers must have melted away like snow in June after your grand entrance. No one of interest to you could possibly have remained there."

"Indeed not," Temple agreed. "Even your friend Sam Hopkey and his doxy decided to go home, though their lodgings are even less salubrious than your own. They did not even get as far as the end of Low Lane. There was a carriage waiting at the corner, and they were persuaded to get in."

Thus far, the porridge he had eaten for breakfast had sat in Ned's stomach in a very satisfied manner, but now he felt suddenly queasy. "What do you mean, *persuaded*?" he demanded. "How? By whom? Why?"

"Don't alarm yourself unduly, Master Knob," Temple said. "By *persuaded*, I only meant to reassure you that they were not treated violently. They got into the carriage willingly, after a brief conversation with their former employer, Alexander Ross. How many people might have been waiting in the carriage the watcher could not tell–it was a capacious vehicle, and the curtains were drawn–but one other person got down: the large man who was with Germain Patou when he came to collect Ross on the previous night. Patou might have been inside, of course, but he was not seen. I had already been transferred, as you know, but the orders I had given before I was moved were still in force. The agent followed the carriage, which made slow enough progress to enable him to do so, until it was nearly to Deptford. He lost sight of it there, but found it again at Deptford Creek. There, for once in his life, he found witnesses ready and willing to talk–it's not only the inhabitants of Purfleet who have taken alarm these last few days. The grey men and their companions went aboard a launch; the steamship to which it belongs is moored at Greenhithe."

"A steamship! It wouldn't be the *Deliverance*, by any chance?"

"No, it wouldn't–but I'm not in a position to judge whether it might have borne that name in the past. Steamships are becoming a familiar sight on the Thames, but they still attract attention, especially if they are French. This one is called the *Outremort*. John Devil still has his sense of humor, you see."

Ned thought hard about that for more than a minute before saying: "No, Mr. Temple, it makes no sense. This carriage of which you speak arrived at Jenny's after you had taken me into custody. You say that it was a slow vehicle, but I had to wait at the coach-stop for more than an hour before I could even begin my homeward journey. I did not see Sawney or the giant while I was in the house at Purfleet, but Patou was there, and I do not believe that he would have sent them out without his guardianship after what had happened on the previous night.

"The carriage must have left the house *after* I spoke to Mortdieu–and it cannot have done so on John Devil's orders. I can believe that Patou might have made his escape when the house was besieged by Mortdieu's dead-alive, and that he would surely have taken Sawney and the giant with him if he could, but I cannot believe that he would have driven to Low Lane to see Sam Hopkey. Sawney might well have done that of his own accord, just as he had the previous eve, but if he acted under orders, those orders can only have come from..."

He stopped, suddenly confused. When he resumed, it was to say: "No, surely *that* makes no better sense. Perhaps you're right, after all, Mr. Temple, and the *Outremort* is John Devil's. He always has more depth to his plans than he permits others to see, and it must be the *Deliverance* renamed... although it is hard to imagine how he reclaimed the vessel from his widow without exciting her suspicions. No matter... the real issue is that if Sawney has taken Sam and Jeanie there, it's more like to be on John Devil's business than Mortdieu's. I wish I had a clearer idea of what each of them desires and intends to do with their secret, while it still remains secret."

"It had crossed my mind," Gregory Temple observed, "that your friends might have been taken in order to exert pressure on you, once it was known that you had been arrested–to inhibit you from telling what you knew."

"If so, I was far too much of a blabbermouth to be so easily dissuaded," Ned said. "I doubt it. Mortdieu intended me to speak, and the Comte was unworried by the knowledge that I would have to talk to you again. Had ether wished to silence me, he could have done so very easily. If Sawney came for Sam, it was likely for his own reasons–he came to Jenny's of his own accord the previous night, although he seemed very uncertain of what he wanted to say and do once he was there. I tried as hard as I could to jog his memory–I must have succeeded better than I thought."

"Perhaps it was as well that I arrested you," Temple observed, "or he'd have collected you too."

"Sam and Jeanie went with him voluntarily," Ned pointed out, "and I'd have done the same, even knowing that he really had been brought back from the dead. He's neither a vampire nor a ghoul, but a walking miracle of science. Whatever he wants Sam and Jeanie for, it's not to murder them."

"Are you certain about that, Master Knob?" Temple asked, with sudden intensity. "If he belongs to the ranks of the dead-alive now, he might be urgently desirous of sharing his condition with his old friends. He is no longer human, you must admit."

"I admit no such thing," Ned retorted, fiercely. "Though he has something other than blood in his veins, he is as human as you or I. This is the Age of Enlightenment, Mr. Temple; we should no longer fear demonic possession, and need no longer assume that anyone returned from the grave must be a thirsty vampire eager to suck the blood of those he once loved. We must put superstition behind us now that we live in an age of vital electricity and mutable species. If only we would open our eyes wider, and clear away the fog of ancient childish terrors, we would understand that every living creature is engaged in a ceaseless quest for improvement. I have been to the Jardin des Plantes, you see, as well as the Royal Institution. I have heard Monsieur Lamarck speak. Even though he is old and blind, he is more clear-sighted than any other man alive, for he knows that our humankind was a long time in the making, and is not yet complete. Sawney is not a monster, Mr. Temple–he is Sawney still, with a second lease of life. We must understand that, if we are to serve the ends of progress in this matter."

"And this Mortdieu?" Temple challenged him. "Is he too an angel of progress rather than a demon of destruction?"

"Yes," said Ned, firmly. *"He has nothing against the living,* he says, and he will be tolerant of their misunderstandings, at least for a little while."

"He is fortunate to have chosen such a willing messenger," Temple observed, "although he cannot understand the living very well if he thought that they might listen to a worm like you."

"I remind you once again that you should not call me that, Mr. Temple," Ned told him, flatly. "I am a man like you, though short of stature and born to poverty. I have committed crimes in the past, I admit–but I did so because I was not content to live as I was, and wanted to be better. And you should not insult worms either–in Monsieur Lamarck's great scheme, every worm is striving to evolve, just as every man and woman is striving, in opposition to every obstacle. Every insect and spider, every slug and snail, every scorpion and serpent is on the path of progress. A man as clever as you should know that, Mr. Temple, in spite of the fact that you have lately been employed to set such obstacles in the course of your own kind, exerting all your might to oppose a change that will prove irresistible in the end. Perhaps I think better of you than you think of yourself, but I cannot believe that a man like you would have fired on the crowd at Peterloo had you been on duty that day, or delivered a false verdict against Tom Wooler had you served on his jury. Or are we going to Greenhithe merely to raise a mob to burn out the grey men wherever they might be hiding, in houses or on steamships, lest they pollute our glorious lives by bringing us back from the dead when *our* need arises?"

"You do not have the right to criticize me, Master Knob," Temple said, flatly.

"I do," Ned informed him, stoutly. "Why should I not?"

"Sam Hopkey and Janie Bird gave false evidence in the trial of Richard Thompson," Temple said, spitting out the words as if they were venom. "Recruited by Alexander Ross and paid by you, on behalf of the real murderer. You all did your level best to hang a honest man, and were all so proud of what you did that the doxy even kept the name in which you baptized her for her court appearance."

"And you fed liquor to my pretty Molly in order to trick her into telling you what happened in Paris on the night that Noll Green and Lochaber Dick turned on one another," Ned retorted, "and were only too anxious to believe what she said, in spite of her maudlin condition. But Richard Thompson did not hang for the crime he did not commit, did he? Are you really bitter because he was convicted on false evidence, or because he had already been liberated when you arrived to save him? If you value him as a friend and a son-in-law, why have you not visited him for four years? Perhaps you're angry with me because I have–because I've sat your grandson on my knee, and laughed in delight with his mother and father."

Gregory Temple hammered on the partition with the head of his stick, and cried; "Stop the carriage! This ungrateful whelp is getting down here, in order to make his own way to Greenhithe, London or the Devil!"

The carriage stopped, but Temple did not throw the door open. Ned sat where he was, waiting–but he could not resist peeping out of the window to see where they were. He did not know the south shore of the Thames at all well, but he did not think that they could be any further away from the point opposite Tower Hill than the region across from Greenwich. They still had a long way to go to Greenhithe.

In the end, Temple rapped on the pane again, and told the driver to move on.

"You do not know what that man said to me that night," he murmured. "You do not know how he tried to drive me mad."

"I know how wholeheartedly he plays his roles," Ned said. "I know what he can do, when he sets his mind."

"Can you guess, then, how he intends to use the secret of resurrection, if he can retain control of it against opposition from his own creations?" Temple demanded. "Can you guess what kind of empire he dreams of building *this* time?"

"Not exactly," Ned admitted, "but I think he has had his fill of Napoleonic dreams. He did say that this was a more important matter than empire-building in India. I suspect that his plans are still ill-formed, because he does not know as yet what capabilities the dead-alive might have."

"And this Mortdieu?" Temple countered. "What sort of dreams do you suppose he entertains?"

"I don't know," Ned admitted, "but I suspect that his situation is exactly the same. He does not know, as yet, exactly what he is, or what he might make of himself. What he and his rival both desire, for the time being, is time. Each, in his unwisdom, wants to retain control of his research for himself–what each wants is to be the new Prometheus, the titan and the demigod. However young they may be, each of them is still bound to the assumptions of the old order. Patou might be different, given the chance, but he has been working thus far in their shadow. As I said before, it does not matter how hard they strive for selfish monopoly; they cannot keep it. What the scientific method produces once, it will produce again and again. Mr. Davy understands that, if they do not–I mean Humphry Davy, of course, not the false James Davy who cheated you."

"But what if either or them *does* harbor dreams of world domination, and of the enslavement of the living to the dead-alive?" Temple demanded. "You spoke in those terms yourself, while you were listing your points–indeed, you spoke as if the dead-alive are certain, in the end, to become the world's rulers. If that is their ambition, what should we humans do, little man? Should we stand aside, in the holy name of progress, and wish the *Outremort* and her master– whoever he might be–*bon voyage* and the best of luck?"

"I know that we should not act like superstitious fools," Ned said. "We are not children to panic at the idea of the bogey-man. We must use our heads, Mr. Temple, and calm our rough-hewn instincts. If humans have found the secret of resurrection, we should be ready and willing to employ it–just as Jesus was, and did, if the scriptures are to be believed. Jesus was selfish in the end, rising from the dead himself but leaving his fellow to wait in vain for a different redemption, but we might be better than that, Mr. Temple, if only we were prepared to try."

"That's blasphemy!" was Temple's response

"Indeed it is," was Ned Knob's calm reply. "Time has moved on, Mr. Temple–we are no longer living in the mythic past. Perhaps the dead-alive will be better fitted to rule the world than the living, if only they can recover the wisdom of their first lives to add to the wisdom of their second. Perhaps they will be kinder to my kind than your kind ever were. You fear enslavement, as fervently as any slavemaster must, but it is not such a bugbear to those whose servitude has ever been immiseration and degradation. I would rather hope for a Republic, even in a world ruled by the dead-alive–but no, Mr. Temple, I do not think we should stand aside. I think we should do exactly what we are doing now. We should try to find out the truth of the matter, so that we can make a reasoned decision as to how to act."

"I thought you might be useful to me," Temple said, "because I thought you would be anxious to rescue your friends. You are forcing me to doubt my judgment."

"I am anxious to discover whether my friends are in need of rescue," Ned replied. "If that turns out to be the case, I shall be glad to do what I can in that cause–but as for *being useful to you*, that I cannot and will not guarantee. I see no need for us to be enemies, but in matters political, we are not allies and I shall make no pretense that we are."

Ned remembered, as he concluded this speech, that the *ci-devant* Comte Henri de Belcamp had commented on the fact that he had changed. He complimented himself on the fact that the renegade aristocrat had spoken more truthfully than he knew.

"Be careful," Temple advised him gruffly. "You might easily end up in jail again."

"As poor Tom Wooler did, even though Shepherd could not pervert a second jury. I could doubtless end up in the pillory just as easily, like valiant Dan Eaton, or be cut down by a saber wielded from horseback like so many innocents in St. Peter's Fields. You cannot frighten us in that fashion any more, Mr. Temple. We are too many, and too fervent in the business of making progress. We are poorly armed as yet, but science, the new Prometheus, is stealing new fire even as we speak. You cannot hold back that tide."

Temple did not answer that. Instead, he lifted the curtain to look out. "Bexley," he said. "We'll be in Greenhithe in a matter of minutes. We'll need a plan of action, if the *Outremort* is still at her berth."

"Action would not be to our advantage," Ned pointed out, "given that we have no army far our back–or have you mustered one to follow us at the gallop?"

"I've summoned agents of two sorts," Temple admitted, "but I have not the authority to mobilize men by the dozen, let alone the hundred. The show of strength in Sharper's relied on local men whose commander had his own reasons for making his presence felt there. By noon, I should have nine or ten at hand– but if I can send the right message back to Scotland Yard and Whitehall, I can gather a much larger force by dusk."

"But you and your men will need to see with your own eyes what kind of crew the *Outremort* has, and gather firm proof that there are honest citizens in danger... although I dare say you'll settle for Sam and Jeanie if there's no one else, no matter how much resentment you've stored against them. If only Germain Patou were a Napoleonic spy... but fat George and Louis XVIII are better friends now, are they not, and their secret police forces are presumably hand-in-glove? The Brotherhood of the Deliverance is no more, and even the *Deliverance* may have become the *Outremort*...."

"A plan, Master Knob," Temple reminded him. "I had hoped simply to be able to tell you what I wanted you to do, but I see now that we cannot proceed on that basis. Would you care to tell me what *you* would like to do?"

"The first thing I would like to do," Ned told him, "is to find out who the master of the *Outremort* is. I should also like to know whether Sam and Jeanie are aboard–and, if so, under what terms. What I do not want to do is to instigate any violence of any kind, aimed at anyone. I think we should both be discreet, Mr. Temple, and learn what we can by stealth before we reveal our presence. So, for the time being, I am ready to stay discreetly by your side, and do my best to help you in any covert enterprise that will improve our understanding of the situation."

Temple shook his head slowly. "You're a true marvel, Master Knob," he said. "I apologize for calling you a worm."

"Thank you, Mr. Temple," Ned replied, judging that the time had come, at last, to be magnanimous.

Chapter Eight
Aboard the Outremort

The docks at Greenhithe were a good deal busier than those at Purfleet had been, and the *Outremort*'s mooring was a relatively quiet spot in a hive of activity–so much so, in fact, that the activity to either side had encroached somewhat upon working-space than ought to have been hers. The warehouses along the waterfront provided an abundance of coverts from which observers could keep watch, so Ned Knob and Gregory Temple had no trouble approaching a very convenient position at the entrance to a narrow alleyway running between two such storehouses. A cargo was in the process of being unloaded into one to their left, so the quay in front of it was strewn with tea-chests and various bales, but the traffic from the one to their right was in the other direction, casks of wine being loaded on to a series of carts to be hauled away.

There was no one visible on the deck of the steamship, but there was a carriage standing on the quayside with its horses still in harnessed, tether to a trough. The animals had been given feed-bags, but they seemed to have consumed the oats therein.

"Waiting for passengers," Temple opined. "Perhaps to return your friends to Covent Garden."

"Perhaps," Ned agreed.

Temple took a small naval telescope from his greatcoat and extended it to its full length. The steam ship was no more than 40 paces away, but he evidently wanted to magnify the portholes in the hope of being able to glimpse something within.

"I can make out a grey head in one of the spaces aft of the engines," he reported. "There's another–but it's impossible to tell whether either is Ross or the giant. A human head might be easier to identify. Judging by the conformation of the ship, there must be at least one cargo-hold in the stern, but whether the porthole where the head is visible is in a separate section or lighting the hold I can't tell."

"Her fire is burning low," Ned observed, studying the smoke drifting from the two funnels. "They'd be stoking her up by now if they intended a swift departure. They're lying very low, though–if they're not waiting to put anyone ashore, they must be waiting for others to come aboard."

"Her launch is missing," Temple said. "There's no way of knowing whether your friends really were brought here, although it's not unlikely that it set out on some other ferrying mission once it had deposited them."

Ned nodded his head. If this was Mortdieu's vessel rather than John Devil's, and the dead-alive had contrived to extract James Graham's magical baths from the cellars before the house in Purfleet was torched, along with their electric batteries, the salvagers would have had to ferry them across the river for want of a convenient bridge. That would have required several journeys in a launch. Greenhithe was a good deal closer to Purfleet than Tilbury, but it would not have been the work of a mere hour–even by night, when the traffic was far less heavy than it was now. On the other hand...

"Here's someone," Temple muttered, cutting into Ned's speculations. Two men had emerged from below the steamship's decks into the bow, where the gangplank was situated. They were not grey men, but perfectly ordinary sailors;

they were dark-skinned, but Ned could not identify their country of origin. They seemed to be arguing as they crossed the gangplank, but not angrily. They untethered the two horses from the trough, but did not bother to climb up into the driver's seat before leading the animals away along the quay.

"Not going far," Temple opined. "Probably collecting supplies. No need to leave the quayside, if they know where to go. It'll take time, though, if they've a complex shopping list."

"Here's more of them," Ned said, as a second cart drew up at the spot from which the first had departed. This one was laden with various goods packed in boxes, bales and barrels. The job of unloading it would have been completed very quickly had half a dozen men come out from the steamship, but it would not have been a diplomatic move for the grey heads Temple had glimpsed through the aft portholes to show themselves on such a busy quay in broad daylight. The only man who emerged from hiding was a ship's officer, obviously a European, who set about issuing instructions to the two sailors aboard the cart. They complained, but he ordered them to get on with the work.

Temple and Ned watched intently, hoping that someone else might come out, if only for a moment. They were watching far too intently, as it turned out, for they did not hear the man who crept up on them from the far end of the alleyway until he was close enough to put a pistol to Gregory Temple's head.

"Forgive me, Mr. Temple," the *ci-devant* Comte de Belcamp said. "I have no wish to harm you, but I feared your reaction to the sight of me."

Temple stared into the barrel of the weapon as though it were a cobra poised to strike.

Ned, by contrast, looked John Devil up and down, astonished to find him not in the least damp or bedraggled–although he was not wearing his Quaker hat. "You have a remarkable immunity to fire and flood, my friend," he said.

"I hope you *are* my friend, Ned," the blond man replied, "For I lost a fair few last night–more to desertion and kidnap than death, thank God–and can spare no more. I need to take my old ship back, and I need to rescue Germain Patou, who I believe to be a prisoner on board. You can imagine the insult I felt when I found out what vessel it was that Mortdieu had obtained in order to hunt me down. The ship is stolen, by the way, and illicitly renamed, so I have perfect right to reclaim it."

"Given that you are legally dead, Monsieur de Belcamp," Gregory Temple said, acidly, "even this radical scoundrel could not claim any such right on your behalf. According to Ned, your wife still thinks herself a widow, and you cannot pretend to be working on her behalf."

John Devil sighed. "You're as tiresome as ever, Mr. Temple," he said, holding the pistol very steady. "According to our mutual friend, *your* daughter still thinks herself no better than an orphan, but we have no time to trade insults of that sort. How many men does Mr. Temple have nearby, Ned?"

"He is hoping to have nine assembled by noon," Ned told him, "but he has not made contact with any as yet."

"And does he intend to try to seize the ship from Mortdieu?"

"His plan is not yet developed," Ned replied. "For the moment, we are simply gathering intelligence–but I doubt that he will let the vessel depart, if he can prevent it, and he probably has the authority and the means if he can get a message back to Westminster."

"Then it's as well I happened along, for I have more intelligence than the pair of you could gather in a fortnight, even with the aid of a trawler. Will you get down on your knees, Mr. Temple."

"No," said Gregory Temple. "Blow my brains out if you must, but I will never kneel to you."

"I'm not asking for worship," John Devil replied. "I'm asking for you to take up a position in which Ned can conveniently tie your wrists to your ankles, to keep you out of harm's way."

"I will not," Temple said, stubbornly. "Blow my brains out, if you so desire."

The *ci-devant* Comte shook his head wearily. "Tiresome as ever," he repeated. "Suit yourself." Then he put his fingers to his lips, and whistled the old signal, which Ned Knob had first heard in Jenny Paddock's in March 1817.

Had Ned had the chance, he would have demanded that John Devil hold off for a discussion, and he was sure that he could have convinced his former master not to do anything stupid–but John Devil really was laboring under the delusion that he was a man of fine intelligence, and was determined to act the idiot as only a vain man could.

Events unfolded in a tremendous hurry. The two men who had been unloading the cart in to the *Outremort*'s deck were both on the quay, each burdened by a bundle taken from the back of the cart. There were a dozen other men within five paces, stacking up goods that were being unshipped from the neighboring vessel–but eight of the dozen, it seemed, were John Devil's men, for two of them immediately leapt on the *Outremort*'s sailors, while two more went or the officer on the deck. The other four swarmed aboard, armed with billhooks and cudgels. More men were already converging on the gangplank from the other side, where the work of loading up carts at the second warehouse had also served as a cover for the infiltration of the *ci-devant* Comte's remaining followers.

"Who loves me, follow me," John Devil muttered, as he joined his crew. Ned opened his mouth to protest, but he could see that it would do no good, so he rocked back on his heels fully prepared to watch and wait. He realized too late that Gregory Temple was not so wisely hesitant. The detective brought a metal whistle from his own pocket, and blew the long shrill blast upon it that the policemen of London used to summon help. Now more men came running, from both ends of the quay–but only four of them that Ned could count.

Temple did not pause to shout out any orders before he hurled himself after his nemesis, avid to grab him from behind now that the pistol was no longer pointed at his head.

"Imbecile," Ned muttered. "You had only to do nothing for a little while, and you could have taken control of the situation once your men were fully gathered–but perhaps it will work out for the best."

The bandit was too quick for the policeman; by the time Gregory Temple had gained the deck, John Devil had disappeared below decks, into the narrower half of the vessel, where the crew-quarters were probably located. The noise of shots was immediately audible.

All along the dock, work stopped as honest laborers paused in honest wonderment. When the four policemen arrived at the end of the gangplank, though, they paused, having no idea who their appointed adversaries might be.

Gregory Temple was already embroiled in a brawl on the deck–although no one there seemed to know which side he might be on, and he was therefore not subject to any immediate or deadly attack. He tried to push the wrestling sailors out of the way in order to follow his quarry, but there simply was not room. He called to his subordinates for help, and they rushed to his aid, evidently forming the opinion that, since all the men on deck was in their commander's way, every one of them must be a heinous criminal. The policemen started laying about them with their truncheons, to the left and to the right, hitting anyone and everyone save for their master–with the inevitable result that anyone and everyone began hitting them *and* their master.

"Things will be much better ordered under the Republic," Ned observed, sadly. "If the dead-alive can conduct themselves more seriously than this, I shall be glad to cast my vote for their election to the National Assembly."

The combined efforts of the two sets of combatants and the policemen had already resulted in four men being knocked down, three more thrown overboard, and a small group of defenders retreating to the doorway that gave access to the bow of the ship. There was now a considerable quantity of empty space on the deck now, and the gangplank itself was clear.

Ned scurried forward, crossed the gangplank, and made his way aft to the part of the deck that had not yet seen any movement at all. There he searched or a second means of ingress to the spaces below deck–and having found a hatch, made his descent into a well flanked by two big doors. He tested one at random, found it to be unlocked, and opened it.

He stepped into a capacious cargo-hold–or, at least, into a space that had been designed as a cargo-hold, although it had evidently been pressed into service as passenger accommodation. By the yellow light of two oil-lamps, he saw 16 grey men and one man who had not yet died sitting meekly on the floor, all awake and somewhat agitated.

The man who had not yet died was Germain Patou. His hands were tied behind his back, and his ankles bound together. Ned whipped out his knife, and sawed through the bonds as quickly as he could.

"The deck's clear, at present, Monsieur Patou," he said. "You may make your escape in safety."

"I cannot leave them!" Patou retorted, indicating his companions with a brief turn of the head. "What is happening, Monsieur Knob? Is it Arthur?"

"I fear that Arthur Pevensey may have gone the way of all his other aliases," Ned said. "He is in a piratical mood, I fear. Do you know if my friends are aboard?"

"In the port hold, twin to this one," Patou said. "Please go—I need to calm these people."

The dead-alive had not menaced Ned in any way; their disturbance was fear and anxiety, not anger. He nodded, and closed the door behind him as he went to its mirror-image. The second door was similarly unlocked, and the second space was a duplicate of the first—except that there were two humans sheltered there as well as a similar company of grey men, and three people standing: Sam Hopkey, Jeanie Bird and Sawney. None of them was tied up, so Ned folded up his knife and put it away.

"Ned!" cried Sam. "Come in and shut the door—there's a battle royal raging beyond the engine-room, it seems. You might get hurt."

Ned did as he was bid. "I only came aboard because I feared that *you* might be hurt," he explained. "I think we might be able to get out if we made a run for it—but Sawney would have to stay behind, for there's a crowd on the dock, and I don't know how they'd react to the sight of a grey man."

He watched Sam and Jeanie turn inquisitive eyes to the man who had been their dearest friend and second father, and knew that there was no question here of any kidnap or evil seduction. In all of this confusion, one thing at least was perfectly plain. When Sawney had said that he had come to Jenny Paddock's because he wanted to see the people who had meant most to him in his previous life, he'd told the simple truth—and he'd come back for exactly the same reason, evidently with Mortdieu's permission, if not his actual encouragement. Sam and Jeanie must have come with Sawney to say goodbye, before he went away on a sea voyage from which he might not return for many years.

Sawney's grey lips twisted into a faint parody of a wry smile. "Best go, Sam," he said, softly. "Don't fear for me—I have my mind back now, and my feelings too. I have what I need, thanks to you, and what these others need in me. I can play the man, now, as the part deserves to be played."

"Sawney, old friend..." Ned began—but then the door that he had closed behind him burst open again, smashing into his back, and sent him tumbling upon the planks that formed the floor of the hold.

Ned twisted as he fell to look back over his shoulder, and saw that it was John Devil who had come tumbling after him—but he had to wait a second more

281

to see who had shoved John Devil, and was following closely behind, apparently intent on killing the man who seemed so very hard to kill.

It was neither Gregory Temple not Mortdieu; it was the giant named John, wielding a club in one hand and a machete in the other.

The giant had been meek when Ned had seen him last, but he was not meek now. The black dots in his strange eyes seemed unnaturally sharp, perhaps because the eyes were protruded slightly by wrath. His face was scored along one side where a bullet had ploughed through his exotic flesh, tearing a groove into which Jeanie Bird might have been able to insert a slender forefinger. The wound was leaking viscous fluid, which foamed as it bubbled out, as unlike blood as anything that could conceivably surge in any creature's veins, driven by a human heart.

John Devil's pistol was empty now, and it made a very feeble club. Even so, the *ci-devant* Comte de Belcamp was determined to come to his feet and face his pursuer–to die hard, if he had to die at all.

Sawney was the first to try to step between them, but the giant swatted him aside with a thrust of his left arm–the one that held the club. Sawney sprawled among his fellow grey men, whose alarm was increased by his flailing limbs. They began to rise to their feet.

Ned was slightly glad that he was flat on his back, in no position to intervene even had he wanted to–but his gladness vanished when he saw Jeanie Bird step between the two fighters, with her back to the *ci-devant* Comte. She looked up into the giant's crazed eyes.

"No, John," she said, speaking to him as a friend might. "That's not your way. Leave him be."

For one awful moment, Ned thought that the dead-alive giant might sweep Jeanie aside as dismissively as Sawney–but with the other hand, perhaps slicing her head in two if she should happen to catch her with the blade. Instead, the giant stopped, as if frozen by the sound of her voice. He looked down at the tiny woman–who did not seem as tiny as she was, now that she had struck a pose that Ned had seen a hundred times before, on the stage at Jenny Paddock's. She looked magnificent, even in the presence of such a colossal leading man.

The giant slowly relaxed his pose, and let his head nod forward, becoming as meek as any of his peers–any, that is, except the one who stepped through the open door behind him, who held a pistol in each hand.

These pistols, Ned had to suppose, were still loaded.

"She's right, John," said General Mortdieu. "In life, that was never your way, and no good can come of finding a new identity while you have not yet recovered the old. I, on the other hand, know exactly what I was when I was alive, and this *was* my way–far more than it was ever yours, Monsieur de Belcamp."

John Devil had recovered his balance and his poise now. "*I brought you back to life*," he said. "I made you what you are."

"So you did," said the grey man. "But you do not own me. I am my own man, and these are my people. We are not your slaves, nor the instruments of your future glory. Our destiny is for us to discover and choose, *mon ami*–and if I must shoot my redeemer in order to achieve that end, I shall not hesitate. You have five seconds to decide."

"You were a better man that that in your former life, Mortdieu," the *ci-devant* Comte replied, without letting a single second go by. "You were a man of pride and principle. Let us settle this like men of honor, up on deck. Single combat, with weapons of your choice. Let us settle it once and for all, each agreeing to accept the judgment of destiny."

"A generous offer, since I have two loaded guns and you have none." Mortdieu replied. "Exactly what I would have expected from a gentleman of your sort. Destiny has already judged; the matter is already settled. It only remains for you to accept that judgment–or die."

Ned Knob had clambered to his feet while this exchange was taking place, deciding that his turn had come to take center-stage and play *deus ex machina*. He stood beside John Devil, and said: "A few minutes ago, this man put a pistol to the head of Gregory Temple, who would not back down. Temple told Monsieur le Comte to shoot him dead. If you knew this man, you would know that he cannot possibly show more weakness than his arch-adversary, his other half. He will invite you to shoot him, just as Temple invited him–but I beg you not to do it, no matter what kind of man you were in your first life. If you're to be the founder of a new race, you must set a better example now than you were ever able to do as a mere man."

"Damn you, Ned!" John Devil murmured. "This is not your scene. How dare you try to steal it!"

"No," said a new voice, speaking from behind the emperor of the grey men and over his head. This scene is *mine*. Give me one of those pistols, sir, and I shall shoot him dead, if only to show that I can hate longer and harder than he."

Mortdieu had to change his position then, so that he could point the pistol in his left hand at Gregory Temple, and the one in his right at the *ci-devant* Comte Henri de Belcamp. Ned took note of the fact that the corridor through which all the new arrivals must have come seemed quiet now, and concluded that the fight for possession of the *Outremort* must have been suspended, if not concluded.

"Who the Devil are you?" Mortdieu asked Gregory Temple.

"I am English law and order," Gregory Temple informed him. "Intolerant of grave-robbers and of brawling... although Master Knob informs me that I might soon have to change my opinion as to the ethics of grave-robbing. My forces will increase as the day wears on, and my men can have an army here by dusk if the need arises. If you shoot me, the necessity will be obvious–we'll see then how the dead-alive will fare in the hangman's noose."

283

"It would certainly be best," Ned Knob observed, "if no one shot anyone, whatever our habits might formerly have been."

"Spoken like a true Republican, Ned," said the *ci-devant* Comte. "Alas, you are forgetting the lessons of history. There are deep differences of opinion here, and they cannot be settled without violence."

"I cannot believe that," Ned said, "any more than my darling Jeanie could believe that the giant would hurt her, wounded and wrathful as he was. Monsieur le Comte, you and your men must quit the *Outremort*, and retire with the only prizes that you really need, and which Monsieur Mortdieu cannot steal from you unless he shoots you–your knowledge and your intelligence. You must also give your word that any other persons you might raise from the dead in future will be free, not instruments of any of your schemes. Monsieur Mortdieu, you must allow Germain Patou to choose for himself where, and in whose company, he will pursue his own researches–and Sawney too. Mr. Temple, you must leave your army unsummoned and withdraw, allowing the *Outremort* to depart unhindered when she is fully provisioned. All this is obvious–no good can come of any other eventuality. Why should it require a fool like me to explain something so simple?"

"There is nothing obvious about it," said Gregory Temple and John Devil, speaking in unison, as if they really were two halves of the same paradoxical person.

"I have won the battle," General Mortdieu pointed out, "and I hold the loaded guns. It is for me to make the terms."

"We are not talking about a battle," Ned insisted, "or even a war. There should never have been a battle, and there is nothing to be gained by a war. We are talking about how best to make progress, how best to move into the future with intelligent purpose and good heart. That is surely the one cause and the one course to which we can all commit ourselves, and the only one that intelligent men need consider."

Mortdieu had already hesitated far longer than the five seconds he had originally conceded his adversary, and Ned no longer feared that he was about to blast anyone's face away, but he went on regardless. "What you must see," he said "is that things are different now. The future will unfold more rapidly if you do the sensible thing–which is to make a record of all your discoveries and experiments, sending copies to Humphry Davy and Michael Faraday in England, and to the heirs of Benjamin Franklin in America and Antoine Lavoisier in France, so that a thousand men might take up your work of raising and educating the recently-dead–but it will not matter in the long run how long, or how successfully, you try to hoard your secret away for your use alone. The thing can be done, and will be done, even if the thousand have to labor long and hard to figure out the first steps for themselves. I have no idea what each of you hopes or plans to do, but I do know that your achievements will be dissolved soon enough by the tide of history, and that if you desire to be remembered fondly for what you have achieved so far, you will *all* put away your weapons, now and forever, and return to your real work."

He was speaking to everyone, but Mortdieu was the one who had the guns, at present, and it was into his remarkable eyes that Ned had looked while he delivered his speech. There, despite their alien quality, he read the record of his success.

Mortdieu lowered his hands, and pointed both his pistols at the floor.

"If we ever have occasion to play this scene on the stage, Ned," Sam Hopkey put in, "I shall be proud to speak those lines."

Ned was still anxious lest anyone take advantage of Mortdieu's inaction to start the fight all over again, but no one did.

"It is a compromise I can accept," the grey general said, "for the sake of peace–provided that you will both agree to it."

"I will if Temple will," the *ci-devant* Comte was quick to say. "Ned's right–if a fool like him can see it, so should we all."

"There is a matter of my duty to the Crown..." Gregory Temple began–but then he stopped, perhaps remembering the head on which the Crown of England was resting just at present, and what he had suffered at the whim of the former Prince Regent. "And England, I suppose," he resumed, "will be grateful to me for helping to remove the grey men from its shores, at least for a little while. I'll give you 24 hours. Go, all of you, and good riddance–but woe betide any of you who are still here on Wednesday."

Ned observed, though, that Temple shot a venomous glance at the *ci-devant* Comte, which said as clearly as if the words had been spoken aloud: *especially you.* It was impossible to tell whether the policeman was more regretful of not having had a pistol to shoot his arch-adversary dead, or of being contemptuously spared by his arch-adversary when the pistol had been in the other hand.

Jeanie Bird took Ned's left hand in hers, and squeezed it gratefully. Ned looked around–not at her, but at the restless dead-alive who were as yet unknown to themselves. Their agitation had calmed somewhat while everyone was standing still. Their black-pointed eyes were very intent, and their ears were pricked. Ned felt free to be hopeful that they were all a little closer to finding the power of intelligence and motive for a second time.

Ned reached out to Sawney with his right hand, and Sawney clasped it. "Thank you for coming to see us, Sawney," he said. "I wish I had been there when you came back last night, so that we could all have made a proper farewell–but Sam and Jeanie have a performance tonight, and you always told us that the audience must not be disappointed." He remembered, as he said that, that Sawney had always told him something else–that if a playwright puts a gun into a scene, the gun must eventually go off–but he decided that it would be best to disregard that maxim at this particular juncture.

285

He made as if to go, taking his protégés with him–for his first duty was, after all, to them. Someone had to set an example. The others seemed grateful for his lead, and he was confident that they would follow him into the wings.

"We'll meet again, *mon ami*," said the *ci-devant* Comte, his posture suggesting that he was speaking to Ned, although his heavy-lidded eyes were fixed on Gregory Temple.

That was yet another thing that Sawney had always said, Ned remembered, in the days when he had played the puppet judge in the mock tribunal. On the stage, where everything is pretense and everything is possible, old friends and old enemies alike must always meet again, until their differences were settled for good and all.

END OF PART ONE
(To Be Continued in Volume 3)

Credits

Ex Calce Liberatus

Starring:

	Created by:
Charles Folenfant	Maurice Leblanc
Arsène Lupin	Maurice Leblanc
Philippe Guerande	Louis Feuillade
Oscar Mazamette	Louis Feuillade
Kogoro Akechi	Edogawa Rampo
The Vampires	Louis Feuillade
Lancelot (a.k.a. Père Dulac)	Chrétien de Troyes

Introducing:

Nora Fuset (a.k.a. the Black Lizard)	Edogawa Rampo

Also Starring:

The Correspondents:

Justin Ganimard	Maurice Leblanc
D.A. Kasamori	Edogawa Rampo

The Statues:

Cyrano de Bergerac	Edmond Rostand
Bussy d'Amboise	Alexandre Dumas
Comte d'Artagnan	Alexandre Dumas
Henri de Lagardère	Paul Féval
Agnes de Chastillon	Robert E. Howard
Jirel de Joiry	Catherine L. Moore
Zatoichi	Kan Shimozawa & Minoru Inuzuka
Prince Hugrakkur	Hal Foster
André-Louis Moreau	Rafael Sabatini

Written by:
Matthew BAUGH is a 43-year-old ordained minister who lives and works in Sedona, Arizona, with his wife Mary and two cats. He is a longtime fan of pulp fiction, cliffhanger serials, old time radio, and is the proud owner of the silent *Judex* serial on DVD. He has written a number of articles on lesser known pop-culture characters like Dr. Syn, Jules de Grandin and Sailor Steve Costigan for the Wold-Newton Universe Internet website. His article on Zorro was published in *Myths for the Modern Age*. This is his second contribution to *Tales of the Shadowmen*.

Trauma

Starring:	Created by:
The Boy (Britt Reid, a.k.a. The Green Hornet)	George W. Trendle
His Father (Dan Reid, Jr.)	George W. Trendle
Jules Maigret	Georges Simenon
Prince Vladimir	Marcel Allain & Pierre Souvestre
Fantômas	Marcel Allain & Pierre Souvestre

Written by:
Bill CUNNINGHAM is a pulp screenwriter-producer specializing in the DVD market and contributed the story *"Cadavres Exquis"* to the first volume in this series. A recognized authority and speaker on low budget filmmaking, his website, www.D2DVD.blogspot.com , offers screenwriters and filmmakers useful tips and insight into the DVD industry. His media empire, *The Lab*, launched from his Echo Park, CA kitchen table is preparing several pulp cinema and literary properties for release in 2006.

The Eye of Oran

Starring:	Created by:
Lieutenant Aristide	Vladimir Volkoff
SNIF	Vladimir Volkoff
Doctor Natas (a.k.a.	Guy d'Armen
Li Chang Yen,	Agatha Christie
Hanoi Shan,	H. Ashton Wolfe
Fu Manchu)	Sax Rohmer
Huan Tsung Chao	Sax Rohmer
Pao Tcheou	Edward Brooker
Fen-Chu	George Fronval
The Korean (a.k.a. OddJob)	Ian Fleming
Doctor Rieux	Albert Camus
The Diogenes Club	Arthur Conan Doyle
Raymond Rambert	Albert Camus, Marcel Allain & Pierre Souvestre
Magistrate Othon	Albert Camus
Inspector Fabre	Leo Malet
Inspector Fauchet	John Pearson

Doc Ardan	Guy d'Armen,
	Lester Dent
James Bond	Ian Fleming
Also Starring:	
Adelaïde Johnston	Win Scott Eckert
Violet Holmes	Matthew Baugh
	& Win Scott Eckert
And:	
The Silver Eye of Dagon	Roy Thomas
	based on Robert E. Howard
	& H.P. Lovecraft

Written by:
Win Scott ECKERT graduated with a B.A. in Anthropology and thereafter received his Juris Doctorate, enabling him to practice law. In 1997, he posted the first site on the Internet devoted to expanding Philip José Farmer's original premise of a Wold Newton Family to encompass a whole Wold Newton Universe. He is the editor of and a contributor to *Myths for the Modern Age: Philip José Farmer's Wold Newton Universe*. Win lives near Denver with his family and four felines, in a house crammed to the rafters with books, comics and *Star Trek* action figures. This is his second contribution to *Tales of the Shadowmen*.

The Werewolf of Rutherford Grange

Starring:	**Created by:**
Harry Dickson	Anonymous
The Westenras	Bram Stoker
The Rutherfords	Philip José Farmer
Sâr Dubnotal	Anonymous
John Roxton	Arthur Conan Doyle
Gianetti Annunciata	Anonymous

Written by:
G.L. GICK lives in Indiana and has been a pulp fan since he first picked up a Doc Savage paperback. His other interests include old-time radio, Golden and Silver Age comics, cryptozoology, classic animation, British SF TV and C.S. Lewis and G.K. Chesterton. He is, in other words, a nerd and damn proud of it. This is his second contribution to *Tales of the Shadowmen*.

Dr. Cerral's Patient

Starring:	Created by:
Dr. Cerral	Maurice Renard
Victor Chupin	Emile Gaboriau
Irene Chupin	Narciso Ibáñez-Serrador
	& Juan Tébar
Victoire	Maurice Leblanc
Raoul d'Andresy (a.k.a. Arsène Lupin)	Maurice Leblanc
Henriette d'Andresy	Maurice Leblanc
Théophraste Lupin	Maurice Leblanc
Mathilde Grévin	Narciso Ibáñez-Serrador
	& Juan Tébar
Teresa Grévin	Narciso Ibáñez-Serrador
	& Juan Tébar

Written by:
Rick LAI is a computer programmer living in Bethpage, New York. During the 1980s and 1990s, he wrote articles utilizing Philip José Farmer's Wold Newton Universe concepts for pulp magazine fanzines such as *Nemesis Inc*, *Echoes*, *Golden Perils*, *Pulp Vault* and *Pulp Collector*. Rick has also created chronologies of such heroes as Doc Savage and the Shadow.

A Suite of Shadowmen

Starring:	Created by:
Rouletabille	Gaston Leroux
Doctor Omega	Arnould Galopin
Hoppy Uniatz	Leslie Charteris
The Trafalmadorians	Kurt Vonnegut
Arsène Lupin	Maurice Leblanc
Erik	Gaston Leroux
Fantômas	Marcel Allain
	& Pierre Souvestre
Doc Ardan	Guy d'Armen
The Little Prince	Antoine de Saint-Exupery
The Nyctalope	Jean de La Hire
Jacques de Trémeuse (a.k.a. Judex & Vallières)	Arthur Bernède
	& Louis Feuillade
Favraux	Arthur Bernède
	& Louis Feuillade
Kaspar Gutman	Dashiell Hammett

Illustrations by:
Fernando CALVI was born in Cordoba, Argentina, in 1973. He has illustrated several graphic novels for the Spanish and Italian-language markets, including *Cybersix* (with Carlos Trillo), as well as writing and drawing his own comics, *Megaman!* (1996) and *Bruno Helmet* (2000). In his home country, Fernando is much in demand as a commercial artist and book illustrator, having contributed to a dozen children's books, including a prestigious edition of *Don Quixote*. Fernando lives in Buenos Aires with his younger sister (also a talented artist) and his collection of books and toys.

Written by:
Serge LEHMAN, born in 1964, is the best-known *nom-de-plume* of French writer Pascal Fréjean, who has also published under the names of "Corteval," "Don Herial" and "Karel Dekk." Pascal is one of France's most talented scienmce fiction writers, the author of the notorious *F.A.U.S.T.* trilogy (1996-97), *Wonderland* (1997), *Aucune Etoile Aussi Lointaine* (1998) and the editor of the ground-breaking anthology *Escales sur l'Horizon* (1998). More recently, he collaborated with graphic novelist Enki Bilal on *Immortal (Ad Vitam)* (2004), Bilal's own feature film adaptation of his *Nikopol* series of graphic novels.

Written by:
Jean-Marc & Randy LOFFICIER, the authors of the *Shadowmen* non-fiction series, have also collaborated on five screenplays, a dozen books and numerous comic books and translations, including *Arsène Lupin*, *Doc Ardan*, *Doctor Omega* and *The Phantom of the Opera*, all published by Black Coat Press. They have written a number of animation teleplays, including episodes of *Duck Tales* and *The Real Ghostbusters* and such popular comic book heroes as *Superman* and *Doctor Strange*. In 1999, in recognition of their distinguished career as comic book writers, editors and translators, they were presented with the Inkpot award for Outstanding Achievement in Comic Arts. Randy is a member of the Writers Guild of America, West and Mystery Writers of America.

Be Seeing You!

Starring:	Created by:
Sherlock Holmes	Arthur Conan Doyle
Denis Nayland Smith (a.k.a. No. 2)	Sax Rohmer
Von Bork	Arthur Conan Doyle
Azzef	Anonymous
Ned Hattison	Gustave Le Rouge
Arsène Lupin	Maurice Leblanc

Also Starring:
Sir Winston Churchill (a.k.a.
No. 1)
And:
The Village   Patrick McGoohan
                                   & George Markstein

Written by:
Xavier MAUMÉJEAN won the renowned Gerardmer Award in 2000 for his psychological thriller *The Memoirs of the Elephant Man*. His other works include *Gotham*, another thriller, *The League of Heroes*, which won the 2003 Imaginaire Award of the City of Brussels and was translated by Black Coat Press in 2005, and the recent *La Vénus Anatomique*, which won the 2005 Rosny Award. Xavier has a diploma in philosophy and the science of religions and works as a teacher in the North of France, where he resides, with his wife and his daughter, Zelda.

The Vanishing Diamonds

Starring:	Created by:
Joseph Jorkens	Lord Dunsany
Allan Quatermain	H. Rider Haggard
Captain Nemo	Jules Verne
Lord Baskerville	Arthur Conan Doyle
Hareton Ironcastle	J.H. Rosny Aîné
Griffin (a.k.a. The Invisible Man)	H.G. Wells
The Time Traveler	H.G. Wells
Comte d'Artagnan	Alexandre Dumas
Isaac Laquedem (a.k.a. The Wandering Jew)	Alexandre Dumas

Also Starring:
The Duke of Buckingham
King Louis XIII of France
Queen Anne of Austria
Cardinal Richelieu
Alexandre Dumas
And:
The Queen's diamonds   Alexandre Dumas

Written by:

Sylvie MILLER is one of France's best English and Spanish translators, having adapted works by Juan Miguel Aguilera, Brian Hopkins, Stanley Wiater, Peter Crowther, Nancy Collins and Colin Greenland. With Philippe Ward, she co-wrote *Le Chant de Montsegur* (2001), a thriller which explores the myths and legends of the Cathar country. Sylvie teaches economics and has also authored several textbooks. She lives outside of Paris.

Philippe WARD is the nom-de-plume of French writer Philippe Laguerre who has built a substantial reputation for tapping the darkest veins of French regional folklore. His first novel, *Artahe* (1997), translated by Black Coat Press in 2004, received considerable critical acclaim when it was initially released. Since then, Ward has authored *Irrintzina* (1999), a Basque thriller which has won several literary awards, *Le Chant de Montsegur* (co-written with Miller, 2001) and *La Fontaine de Jouvence* (2005), starring Gilles de Grandin, an homage to Seabury Quinn's legendary hero. Philippe is the editor of *Rivière Blanche*, Black Coat Press' French science fiction imprint.

A Jest, To Pass the Time

Starring:	Created by:
Bernard Sutton	Max Pemberton
Inspector Jordan	Jules de Gastyne
Inspector Tony	Gabriel Bernard
Flambeau	G.K. Chesterton
M. Dicky	Louis Boussenard
Zigomar	Leon Sazie
Baron Cesare Stromboli	Jose Moselli
Colonel Clay (a.k.a. Picardet)	Grant Allen
The Lone Wolf (a.k.a. Troyon)	Louis Vance
Horace Dorrington (a.k.a. de la Zeur)	Arthur Morrison
Belphegor (a.k.a. the Phantom of the Louvre)	Arthur Bernède
Sigono	Edward Brooker
Fantômas (a.k.a. *le génie*)	Marcel Allain & Pierre Souvestre
Zenith the Albino (a.k.a. the Romanian Prince)	Anthony Skene
Gaston Dupont (a.k.a. the veteran)	Frederick van Rensselaer Dey

Ténèbras	Arnould Galopin
Emil Lupin	Anonymous
Filip Colin (a.k.a. fake Emil Lupin, Professor Pelotard, the Breton)	Frank Heller
Ruder-Ox	Antonio Quattrini
Mademoiselle Miton (a.k.a. English tourist, female server, Elena Acevedo)	G.H. Teed
Simon Carne (a.k.a. Bertrand Charon, Prof. Bondonnat)	Guy Boothby
Vera Roudine	Charles Lucieto
Maxim de Winter	Daphne du Maurier
Lord Lister	Karl Matull & Theo Blankensee
Lord Stuart	Ernst Pinkert
Percy Stuart	Anonymous
Raffles	E.W. Hornung

And:

The Moonstone	Wilkie Collins

Written by:
Jess NEVINS is a reference librarian at Sam Houston State University in Huntsville, Texas. He is the author of two companion books on Alan Moore and Kevin O'Neill's *League of Extraordinary Gentlemen* and of *The Encyclopedia of Fantastic Victoriana*, a comprehensive guide to 19th century genre literature. Jess is currently working on *The Encyclopedia of Pulp Heroes*, an exhaustive list of series heroes, in numerous media, published around the world from 1902 to 1945. Jess lives outside of Houston with his wife Alicia and their menagerie of animals.

Angels of Music

Starring:	**Created by:**
Christine Daae	Gaston Leroux
Trilby O'Ferrall	George du Maurier
Irene Adler	Arthur Conan Doyle
Erik	Gaston Leroux
The Persian	Gaston Leroux
Etienne Gérard	Arthur Conan Doyle
Joséphine Balsamo	Maurice Leblanc

Count Ruboff	Raymond L. Schrock & Elliot Clawson
Baron Maupertuis	Arthur Conan Doyle
Michael Elphberg	Anthony Hope
Basil Hallward	Oscar Wilde
Spalanzani	Jules Barbier & E.T.A. Hoffmann
Cochenille	Jules Barbier & E.T.A. Hoffmann
Coppélius	Jules Barbier & E.T.A. Hoffmann
Duke of Omnium	Anthony Trollope
Chevalier del Gardo	F. Brooke Warren
Simon Cordier	Robert E. Kent & Guy de Maupassant
Cardinal Tosca	Arthur Conan Doyle
Walter Parkes Thatcher	Orson Welles & Herman J. Mankiewicz
Aristide Saccard	Emile Zola
Georges Duroy	Guy de Maupassant
Olympia	Jules Barbier & E.T.A. Hoffmann

Written by:

Kim NEWMAN's literary career began as a film reviewer and critic. His first stories were published in *Interzone*. In 1985, he wrote two non-fiction books, *Ghastly Beyond Belief* (with Neil Gaiman) and *Nightmare Movies*. His first novels were *The Night Mayor* (1989) and *Bad Dreams* (1990). The publication of *Anno Dracula* (1992) established him as a major name in horror fiction. That series continued with *The Bloody Red Baron* (1995) and *Judgment of Tears* (1998). Other novels by Kim include *Jago* (1991), *The Quorum* (1994) and *Life's Lottery* (1999). Kim's short story collections include *The Original Dr. Shade* (1994), *Famous Monsters* (1995), *Seven Stars* (2000), *Where the Bodies are Buried* (2000) and *Unforgivable Stories* (2000).

The Incomplete Assassin

Starring:	**Created by:**
Joseph Rouletabille	Gaston Leroux
Sainclair	Gaston Leroux
Michel Strogoff	Jules Verne
Dr. Génessier	Jean Redon

Written by:
John PEEL was born in Nottingham, England, and started writing stories at age 10. John moved to the U.S. in 1981 to marry his pen-pal, Nan Taylor. He, his wife ("Mrs. Peel") and their 13 dogs now live on Long Island, New York. John has written just over 100 books to date, mostly for young adults. He is the only author to have written novels based on both *Doctor Who* and *Star Trek*. His most popular work is *Diadem*, a fantasy series; he is currently writing the ninth volume.

Annus Mirabilis

Starring:	Created by:
Doctor Omega	Arnould Galopin
Denis Borel	Arnould Galopin
The Xipéhuz	J.H. Rosny Aîné
Also Starring:	
Albert Einstein	
The Phenomena:	
Prof. Wellingham's Panergon	Skelton Kupport
Prof. Mirzabeau's Violent Flame	Fred T. Jane
Henry R. Cortlandt	John Jacob Astor
Apergy	Percy Greg
Vril	Lord Bulwer-Lytton

Written by:
Chris ROBERSON's short fiction has appeared in the anthologies *Live Without A Net* (Roc, 2003), *The Many Faces of Van Helsing* (Ace, 2004), *Black October*, *Electric Velocipede* and *Asimov's*, with new stories forthcoming in *Asimov's*, *Postscripts* and *FutureShocks* (Roc, 2006). His first major release novel is *Here, There & Everywhere* (Pyr, 2005); forthcoming titles include *The Voyage of Night Shining White* (PS Publishing, 2006) and *Paragaea: A Planetary Romance* (Pyr, 2006). Roberson has been a finalist for the World Fantasy Award for Best Short Story, the John W. Campbell Award for Best New Writer, and twice for the Sidewise Award for Best Alternate History Short Story (winning in 2004 for the story "*O One*.") He lives in Austin, Texas with his wife, their daughter and his library.

Legacies

Starring:	Created by:
Arsène Lupin	Maurice Leblanc
Justin Ganimard	Maurice Leblanc
Joseph Joséphin (a.k.a. Rou-letabille)	Gaston Leroux
Baron Karl von Hessel	Lester Dent & Philip José Farmer
Lily Bugov, Countess Idivz-hopu	Philip José Farmer
Lady Diana Wyndham	Maurice Dekobra
Théodore Béchoux	Maurice Leblanc
Also Starring:	
Marcel Proust	

Written by:

Jean-Louis TRUDEL, born in Toronto in 1967, holds degrees in physics, astronomy and the history and philosophy of science. Since 1994, he has authored a couple of science fiction novels published in France, one collection of short stories and 24 young adult science fiction and fantasy novels, not counting two co-authored with fellow Canadian writer Yves Meynard. His short stories have appeared in French-language magazines like *imagine...* and *Solaris*. In English, his short fiction has been published in several Canadian and U.S. anthologies, such as *Northern Stars* (1994) and in magazines such as *On Spec*. When time allows, Jean-Louis also works on translations (such as Jean-Claude Dunyach's *The Night Orchid*, published by Black Coat Press) and science fiction criticism.

The Grey Men

Starring:	Created by:
Ned Knob	Paul Féval
Jenny Paddock	Paul Féval
Sam Hopkey	Paul Féval
Jeanie Bird	Paul Féval
Sawney (a.k.a. Alexander Ross)	Paul Féval
Germain Patou	Paul Féval
Gregory Temple	Paul Féval
John Devil (a.k.a. Henri de Belcamp, James Davy, Tom Brown, Arthur Pevensey)	Paul Féval

Written by:

Brian M. STABLEFORD has been a professional writer since 1965. He has published more than 50 novels and 200 short stories, as well as several non-fiction books, thousands of articles for periodicals and reference books and a number of anthologies. He is also a part-time Lecturer in Creative Writing at King Alfred's College Winchester. Brian's novels include *The Empire of Fear* (1988), *Young Blood* (1992), *The Wayward Muse* (2005) and his future history series comprising *Inherit the Earth* (1998), *Architects of Emortality* (1999), *The Fountains of Youth* (2000), *The Cassandra Complex* (2001), *Dark Ararat* (2002) and *The Omega Expedition* (2002). His non-fiction includes *Scientific Romance in Britain* (1985), *Teach Yourself Writing Fantasy and Science Fiction* (1997), *Yesterday's Bestsellers* (1998) and *Glorious Perversity: The Decline and Fall of Literary Decadence* (1998). Brian's translations for Black Coat Press include Paul Féval's *Knightshade, Vampire City, The Vampire Countess, John Devil, The Wandering Jew's Daughter, The Black Coats: 'Salem Street* and the forthcoming *The Black Coats: The Invisible Weapon.*

TALES OF THE
SHADOWMEN
COLLECTION

Volume 1: The Modern Babylon (2005)

**WATCH OUT FOR
VOLUME 3: DANSE MACABRE
TO BE RELEASED
EARLY 2007**

Printed in the United States
42853LVS00003B/49